HADES
AND
PERSEPHONE

CURSE OF THE GOLDEN ARROW

HEIDI HASTINGS
ERICA HASTINGS

ISBN: 978-1-7344762-0-0 (Paperback)

Library of Congress Control Number: 2020930315

Any references to historical events, real people, or real places are used fictitiously. Names, characters, and places are products of the author's imagination.

Front cover image by Heidi Hastings.
Book design by Heidi Hastings.

First printing edition 2019.
Heidi Hastings
New York, NY.
10065

www.heidihastingsart.com

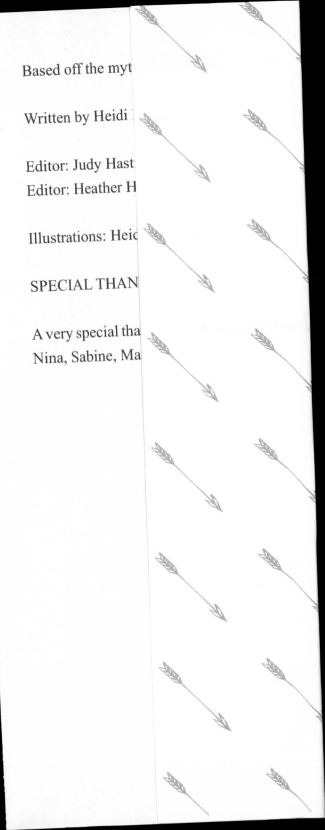

Based off the myt

Written by Heidi

Editor: Judy Hast
Editor: Heather H

Illustrations: Heid

SPECIAL THAN

A very special tha
Nina, Sabine, Ma

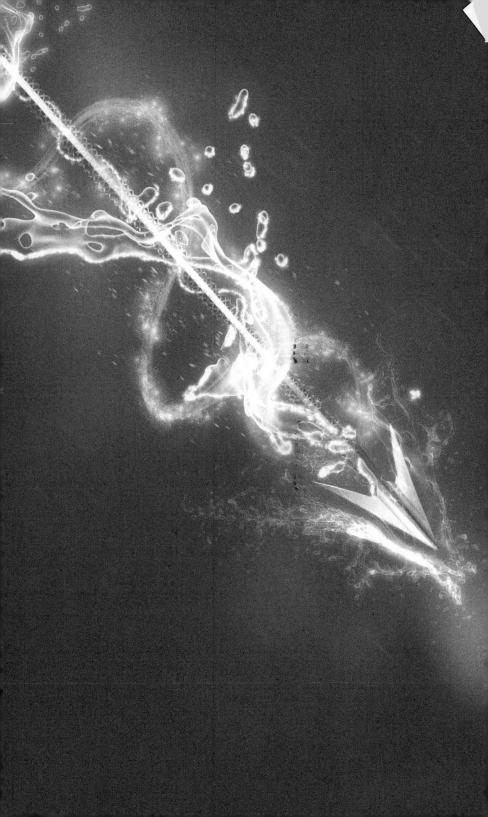

CHAPTER
I
ZEUS'S REVENGE

EARLIER THAT DAY

HIGH ON OLYMPUS, nestled by an inlet, sat Demeter's temple. It was cloaked in ivy, and the grounds on which the sanctuary lay was fertile with fig trees and flowers that perfumed its fields. It was a beautiful shrine, concealed from the other Gods, and that suited Demeter's needs perfectly. Ever since her daughter had come of age, Demeter had hidden her deep in the forest, away from the view of men. The Gods were fighting for her daughter's hand like dogs over a bit of meat, and Persephone was a Goddess, not some spare scrap to wrestle over. Hermes and Apollo had been the most recent rivals to attempt a claim at her daughter's hand, but Demeter was not ready for her child to be wed. And certainly not to any of the boorish brutes who had sought her. As of yet, there was no contender that was worthy of Persephone, and she needed to protect her from the game-playing Gods. It was no secret how manipulative the Olympians could be. Gods loved to play tricks, to woo and deceive, to coerce and destroy the innocent. Be it man or God, no one's life was safe from their game of chess, and the more twisted the game, the better. Her daughter was different from them. Persephone had a gentle heart and a pure spirit. She thought no evil of others. Demeter, however, was not so naive. She knew all too well how cruel the Gods could be.

Years ago, Demeter had loved a mortal man named Iasion. He was a Prince of Crete and Persephone was the result of the love between them. Her daughter had inherited her goodness and sweetness of temper from her father. The Gods knew she certainly did not get it from her mother, she thought with a wry smile. It was his gentle disposition that had drawn Demeter to him and now Persephone was all she had left of their love. She was not going to give her daughter up easily. Demeter closed her eyes, remembering Iasion. No one compared to his beauty, from his spirit to his perfect face and lithe young body, he had been all she had ever desired in a mate. And for a brief, very small moment in time, she had been desperately and blissfully happy. Until the King of the Gods had found them together one day, and in a jealous rage, Zeus struck down her lover with a thunderbolt, leaving his soul to roam the Earth for eternity. In just a flash he had destroyed her entire world on a jealous whim. Even now she felt her lips curl back as the bitter memories surfaced. It would have broken Demeter, but knowing her daughter grew inside of her gave her the will to go on. To deliver the final shattering blow, Zeus boasted to all the Gods that "he" was the father of her child and everyone had believed that the proud Demeter had spread her legs for that swine. He thought he would crush her with his lie, but she did not allow his treacherous words to touch her. She remained strong for her daughter and did not even attempt to correct the falsehood he spoke. To speak against Zeus would only bring pain and a long drawn out battle. It was a fight she was willing to forgo. She had her daughter - and that was enough. Only Demeter, Zeus, and Persephone knew the tragic truth.

Her eyes grew misty as she looked out at her daughter. Persephone lay on her back in the grass by the temple, playing idly with the flowers as they blew gently in the breeze. The sun flickered through the trees, making her dark hair glitter as it lay around her head like a halo. She was a beautiful forest goddess and it was no wonder the reprobate Gods sought her. She had the elegance of a deer, her limbs and neck were long and pale and when she moved it was with an unconscious grace that even the most sensual Goddesses could not emulate. Persephone's eyes reflected the green of the forest, and sometimes when Demeter looked at her daughter, she imagined she could see the eternal beauty of nature staring out through her wide and innocent gaze. Her lips were bee stung pink, and in repose may have had a slight pouting look, but Persephone's face was rarely relaxed and usually a smile curved the corners. All in all, her daughter possessed the kind of beauty that endangered her. This world was not kind to beautiful women, Goddesses or otherwise. Demeter watched as Persephone gave a delighted laugh as a group of butterflies passed her and fanned their wings happily against her toes, and an irrational fear twisted in her stomach.

She knew that though her daughter had the face of a sensual Goddess, she was a pure spirit of the forest and she could be broken as easily as a flower in the wrong hands -- too innocent, too trusting.

When it came time for her to choose a husband, it would be a good and strong man who would stand at her daughter's side, Zeus be damned. Her beloved Persephone would be protected from the Gods at any cost. They would not be allowed to destroy her. Demeter swore an oath to herself. "At whatever cost," she whispered.

Her mother's voice drifted down from above. "Persephone my love, do not leave the grounds today. I do not think we should venture from the temple. I fear that your suitors may seek you out."

Persephone looked up at her mother, a gentle smile on her lips and gave a swift nod of her head as she bit back a sigh of frustration. How much longer would she have to stay confined to their temple? She felt like a prisoner hiding from the outside world. Life had not always been like this, but ever since she had come of age she had been forced to hide behind the walls of the temple and she missed the freedom she had possessed as a child. She had been as wild as the wind then, and now her life was as stagnant as a shallow pond. Suddenly she felt restless and she sprang up from the ground and walked to the edge of the temple. She could feel her mother's eyes on her back and she tried to relax her stiff posture. She did not blame her mother for her worry, but she only wished that she could just be allowed a small amount of freedom. Surely there were not men always watching her? With a gentle wave of her wrist, she covered the trees in lush pink roses and the Earth in soft, green moss. She breathed in the stillness of the foliage, the soft perfume of the flowers and tried to calm the rising discontent in her soul. She longed to be free, to roam, to simply be. It was becoming more difficult every day to tolerate the confines of the temple. She took a stick and sketched a constellation into the dirt then looked up at the sky.

"Under the stars," she muttered aloud. Her freedom seemed

as far way as the constellations above and she felt tears well in her eyes even as she shook them away impatiently. "No more daydreams today, Persephone," she said sternly to herself. She felt a gentle tug on her gown and looked down to see a fox cub nipping at her with its pearly white teeth. "And what do we have here, little one?" She picked up the fox, its fur rubbing softly against her skin, and she buried her face in his softness to wipe away the last of her tears.

"Well my friend, what do you think of all the Gods who want to marry me?" She waited for the fox's reply but it merely cocked its head and watched her with clever black eyes. She laughed. "Well, can you keep a secret?" A white toothed yawn was her answer and she smiled. "I know one should not speak ill of the Gods, but I think they are mad! And if I may be honest, I do not want any of them. None of them can tempt me with their empty gifts. Hermes' caduceus does not tempt me, and neither does Apollo's Lyre. They watch me with hungry eyes and empty hearts."

She leaned closer to whisper in the ear of her friend the fox, "Do you know what I wish? That I could be like Athena and have never to wed." She brushed her hand over the fox's baby soft, tawny fur, then leaned back watching the sun dance through the leaves. "But sometimes, every now and then when I am alone, I am consumed with a wish that someone could love me fiercely, and the poets would sing about our devotion. That he would love me just as I am, and I would take him just as he is." She gave a small laugh, surprised at the bitter taste in her mouth. How ridiculous she sounded. When had she ever seen such a union between Gods? When had she ever seen anything other than hatred and deception and unfaithfulness. "I do not want a marriage like Zeus and Hera, or Aphrodite and Hephaestus. I want true, honest love." She felt her heart tug. "If it exists."

Her little forest friend was anxious to play though, and he gave her a long lick on her nose as if to express his sympathy at her dilemma, and then down he jumped making his way to the forest. He looked back at her and gave a little huff and a shake of his tail as if to say, "Don't you want to join me?" She hesitated, glancing back at the temple, but her mother had returned inside. A little extra time in the forest would do no harm, she thought. She gave the fox a mischievous smile, and then she lifted her skirts, and darted through the trees to give chase to the cub, running as fast as her feet would take her. She felt laughter bubbling up in her throat and thought she heard her mother's voice calling her in the wind, but for a moment, oh just for a blissful moment, she felt free chasing this little happy creature. Together, they tore through the forest, the fox's little paws making more noise than she did, as the sunlight danced through the trees. Suddenly the fox stopped and Persephone approached him as he made a whimper of fear, cowering against a nearby tree. "What is wrong, little friend?" she whispered, kneeling down to give a gentle rub to the cub. Persephone glanced around the darkened forest. The sun had disappeared behind a cloud and shadows obscured the interior. Something was amiss, she thought with a chill, the forest had gone quiet; no birdsong, or chattering of the animals.

She stood up filled with anger. Someone was trying to scare her. Someone who dared to trespass at her mother's sacred temple. She shivered in the shadowed forest then straightened her shoulders. Who dared to scare these precious creatures of her domain? Drawing herself to her full height, she cried "Who is there? Reveal yourself!" For a moment there was only silence, but then in the distance, this time, Persephone. Stay inside! Do not leave the house in case Ares sends the birds back or something worse. The temple will protect you, but outside these walls you have no protection. Do you understand this?"

Persephone nodded her head vigorously, locks of her dark hair whipping around her face. "Mother, tell Zeus I need more time before I marry and that I would like to choose my own husband."

For a moment Demeter looked at her daughter and there was a flicker of something in her eyes, and then she smiled. "Of course, daughter. I will tell him." As she turned to leave, she glanced back. "Persephone, do not go outside."

Demeter raced as fast as the wind would take her, high up Olympus to Zeus's temple. Pray the Gods it was not too late. It was a magnificent palace built of white marble and gold and it rose from the clouds like a beacon at the highest cliff of the mountain. What beauty without and what evil within, she thought. She had not known the evil that lurked around every corner, but she did now. She and Persephone had once attended lavish parties here until her daughter became the desire of every God on the mountain. As she looked around, she remembered the grand feasts. The memories of preparing for the opulent occasion filled her mind. Persephone had been so excited, picking olives of every shape and size, gathering honey from her bees, fresh honeysuckle, raspberries, freshly baked bread from her finest barley crops. What fools they had been! She landed on the front steps of the palace and straightened her back. She must show no weakness here. She held her head high as several Gods passed by giving her curious glances and she walked boldly into the throne room. She knew the way, too well. The room was enormous with massive chaises lining the walls, and the floors were covered in soft pillows. On one of the chaises, Aphrodite lay sprawled against Hermes' lap, her gown slipping further and further to her navel and baring more of her perfect bosom with every titling laugh that left her lovely pink mouth. Demeter rolled her eyes as Hermes spilled ambrosia across her round breasts, and glancing around, she saw Zeus on his throne speaking to Athena in low tones.

As Demeter approached the throne she was able to make out the words. "Athena, there have not been enough sacrifices. Perhaps a war would bring my subjects around? Nothing makes them cling to me more than a war," Zeus finished with a laugh.

He was vile, Demeter thought in disgust. Of course he wanted more blood spilt, after all, humans were so easily discarded. For a moment, rage blinded her vision but she pushed it carefully back down. Now was not the time. Someday she could avenge herself on him. Someday, but not now. Demeter crossed the room quickly to stand next to the Goddess, and Athena turned to Demeter with a brief but genuine smile.

"Greetings, Demeter. We have not seen you or your daughter at my temple recently. We miss her and I miss your sensible head at my table."

Demeter laughed and gave a careless shrug of her slender shoulders, "It has been difficult since she has come of age. I am training her to use her abilities, so she can take on more responsibilities in the forest. She is essential at my temple."

Athena smiled, "Let your daughter know that the temple is not half as radiant without her there. You both would be welcome at any time." With a nod of her head, Athena turned and left the room, likely guessing why the Goddess wanted to speak with Zeus.

Zeus merely stared at her from his high throne and she won-

dered if he would acknowledge her presence when he finally spoke. "And to what do I owe the pleasure of your company, Demeter?"

Demeter bowed down and then lifted her head, looking over at Hermes and Aphrodite. Hermes was lifting one perfect breast to his mouth, his toga unfastened, and if she was not mistaken, Aphrodite was now stroking a particularly erect portion of his anatomy. Demeter quickly averted her face. She should never have let Persephone come here, she thought with disgust. Turning back to Zeus she said firmly," I would like to speak with you -- alone."

Zeus glanced over at the lovers, taking time to eye Aphrodite's exposed breasts. "Much as I enjoy your display, continue your lasciviousness elsewhere, Hermes. We do not want to offend the virginal sensibilities of our guest. Do be sure to pay special attention to her nipples, I know how she enjoys that." With a small grin, Hermes ushered Aphrodite out of the room, neither making any effort to cover themselves, and Demeter stood alone at Zeus's feet.

She took a moment to gather her courage and then said, "Cancel this engagement to Ares."

Zeus played with the goblet in his hand, "No, not this time Demeter, it is time she married. She is of age. I have already withdrawn my consent from Hermes and Apollo, as you demanded. They would have made perfectly suitable husbands for a girl as illustrious as our Persephone." He looked at her with a sly look on his face. Oh how he enjoyed making her angry.

Demeter ground her fingernails into her palm, drawing blood. She must not give into her temper, she needed to keep a cool head right now. This was not about past wrongs, this was about her beloved daughter. She would keep calm for her sake. With a deep breath, she continued. "She does not want a husband at this time, she should not have to wed. You have not forced Athena to wed. She does not want Hermes, she does not want Apollo, she does not want Ares. I need her at my Temple, she has obligations to fulfill as my daughter."

The smile left Zeus's face and lightening twisted around his fingers as he dropped his goblet. It fell with a clang to her feet, spilling in a pool of red that flowed like blood, and she swallowed down bile as it soaked into her sandals. He leaned forward, his voice like ice, "Troublesome bitch. Who is good enough for your daughter?" He glared down at her from his throne and said with a sneer, "Perhaps she prefers the cocks of mortals, like her whore mother."

Demeter felt rage infuse her, "How dare you, you coward," her voice quivering with rage. Lifting her arms with a burst of wind, "My daughter will not marry your son."

He leaned back as if pleased by her anger and a smile spread across his mouth. "Beg."

She lowered her arms and drew back to stare up at him incredulously. "What?"

He snapped his fingers and a naked nymph appeared, placing a full goblet in his hands. "Get on your knees and beg me to grant you this request."

She stared at him and then dropped to her knees. "Oh, mighty Zeus, please grant me this desire. Please release my daughter, Persephone, from this engagement to your son." She bowed her head. After several moments of silence, she looked up to see Zeus fondling the breasts of the nymph while he was smiling down at her.

"How nice to see the mighty Demeter on her knees. I have waited a long time for this, though I must admit I imagined my cock in your mouth. This is almost equally as satisfying. But, I think not." He finished with a smile and Demeter leaped up in rage. "Our daughter will marry my son. Unless," he paused, "you can find another God who will consent to marry her before sunset. Which I think unlikely, since I can think of no God willing to cross the ire of my son," he said. "He is coming for her with, or without, your approval. And he is a man who does not like to share. I imagine you will not see her again."

"She will not marry any of them!" Demeter shrieked in rage. As she did so, a great clap of thunder burst forth and lightning clashed. The wind ripped at her clothes and her hair, painfully whipping it around her body, but Demeter was too incensed to be afraid. She shouted again, "Ares will not touch her!" Her screams echoed through the temple for all to hear and Zeus began laughing as she ran from the throne room.

His voice shouted, "Before sunset, Demeter, remember, before sunset." The words echoed in Demeter's ears as she raced through the halls like Hades himself was at her heels.

CHAPTER II
KIDNAPPED

PERSEPHONE SAT ON her bed, biting her thumb fretfully. What was taking her mother so long, she wondered, surely nothing had gone awry? With a frustrated sigh, she closed the book she had been attempting to study and stood up, beginning to pace. Why had her mother insisted on going alone when they both knew how dangerous Mount Olympus could be? Was it not the very reason Persephone was forced to hide like a coward behind the walls of her mother's temple? Her mother had not considered that Olympus could be as dangerous to her as it was to her daughter. They both knew Zeus had good reason to try to punish Demeter. Persephone could have gone with her, helped to ensure that they both left Zeus' palace safely but instead she had had to stay behind, hidden, and once again completely useless. She could go there, she considered, and demand that she be allowed to see her mother. But, now that she thought about it, she realized that did not even know how to find the palace on Mount Olympus. She had been there as a child, but it had been years since her mother had brought her there. No, she just had to wait and hope that her mother was simply taking her time in returning. "And in the meanwhile I am completely safe and completely unable to help anyone," she muttered angrily under breath.

Persephone paused before a large looking glass in her room to study her reflection. It was a pretty face, beautiful even, she thought dispassionately, her eyes luminous in the gathering darkness. And she hated it. Her face had cost her everything, her freedom, her very way of life had been taken from her because men had decided her body was appealing. She sometimes wondered if being hidden away had made the matter worse, had made her appear even more appealing. The harder won prize was always more desirous, she thought in bitter disgust as she turned away from the mirror. With a sigh, she lay back on the bed. After her mother had departed, she had brushed the tangled hair of the horses, carefully braiding each tail and mane, scrubbed her face and her body so thoroughly her skin still felt raw, helped organize seeds for the nymphs to distribute to the newly tilled lands, and finally, she had tried to study to pass the time. But she still felt restless. The thought of Ares asking for her hand made her stomach twist, and since she had seen the note, a wild rebellion had seemed to rise up in her. Desperation, her mind whispered. Desperation coupled with fear and vulnerability, all combined to make her in a particularly foul mood.

The thunder rumbled in the distance as if reflecting her dark emotions and there was a heaviness in the air. She watched from her bedroom window as the sky turned deep pink, and purple storm clouds rolled in. She could almost taste the rain. It had been as hot as Tartarus outside today, and it would be so nice to leave the temple, to smell the stormy air as it brought the fresh scent from the sea with it. She stood up then, only to sink back down with a frustrated sigh. She *had* promised her mother to stay inside and Demeter would be very upset with her if she didn't. But then again, if she did not leave her room soon she may well go insane. Persephone stood again slowly and went to the window, leaning out to let the wind blow through her room. It lifted the damp tendrils of hair from her sweaty face and she felt a beckoning, an almost irresistible pull to join the wilderness outside.

Persephone! a voice seemed to whisper on the wind...*Persephone!* She shook her head, how fanciful she had become lately. A reprieve from the temple was necessary for her sanity. She watched as golden pollen danced on the breeze, the eddy travelling away from the temple, and that shimmering golden powder helped to make up her mind. Without further thought, she quietly slipped out the door closing it firmly behind her. Her mother would never be the wiser.

As she stepped into the storm, she gasped at the first touch of the cool drops against her flushed body and closed her eyes, letting the rain soak into her skin, hoping it would wash her troubled contemplation away. The gold shimmer appeared again and she began to follow it, letting her feet take her without thought, further and further from the temple. The wind pulled at her hair and a part of her mind whispered to her that she was going too far, that it was unsafe, but she could not stop herself. The pull was too tantalizing and she had resisted the call of freedom for too long.

She walked, letting her bare feet sink into the cool, damp earth, always keeping the swirling gold dust in her sight. She passed the forests and the lakes and when she crossed the mountains that bordered the edge of the temple, she did not notice. Her eyes were fixated on the glimmering dust.

Finally, she paused as the wind shifted, momentarily altering the trail of gold from her gaze, and she blinked in surprise as she realized that she had reached a part of the forest that she had never seen before. Persephone had left the confines of the temple far behind and realized that she stood in the center of a large lavender field bordered by a cliff. It was breathtaking! The storm washed over the sea of purple and she breathed deeply. She thought about all that the storm had brought with it to the land: new seeds, scents, insects, precious water ... to refresh and replenish the forest. The wind would scatter the seeds and life would begin anew. The air tugged at her dress impatiently, pulling at her hair and body and it felt almost as sensual as a lover's hand, shaping her gown to her breasts and legs. She lifted her face and saw the stream of gold flowing towards the edge of the cliff and she edged closer to the precipice as the wind pulled with gentle insistence. In the back of her mind she heard her mother's warning, but she could not stop herself from following. The scent was intoxicating.

There was something hypnotic about this storm. Persephone felt that a little more time spent exploring would not hurt anything. The golden particles danced once more before her eyes and she turned to follow the path when she saw -- alone in a sea of lavender, a golden flower blooming, gleaming iridescently. She stopped to stare at it. A golden light emulated from it's center reflecting off the petals so it glowed as brilliantly as the sun, a beacon in the darkened sky.

Its petals waved in the wild wind and the path of gold encircled the flower, inviting her to touch it. Had that golden trail led her here intentionally? Apprehension flashed in her mind, but she stepped helplessly closer, mesmerized by its brilliant glow.

She bent to the flower and as she touched the golden petals, she felt a curious swooping inside her body, like her soul was being heated from the inside out. Suddenly the world was immersed in inky blackness. She let out a gasp of shock and then stood still, as she felt something else there in the darkness, something that reached out to touch her. It felt strong, powerful and ancient, and she was frightened of its nearness. It moved against her soul and she drew back, terrified at the unfamiliar touch. Her slightest movement seemed to act as a catalyst as the light returned as suddenly as it had gone, and a high-pitched noise split the wind sending chills down her back.

She covered her ears and fell to the ground as splintering screams filled the air and one loud cry rose to the forefront and echoed in her mind. Cries of the dying! Cries of the damned!

"No, no, no," she moaned.

The ground shook with a pulse and seemed to shake with her own heartbeat as she struggled to stand, desperate to flee when a large crack rent the air and the Earth split open, oozing red liquid from its center. It spilled towards her and she realized in horror that it was blood, the sickening metallic smell filling her nostrils as it soaked into her bare feet. She gave a cry of horror as the Earth rolled and swelled and she fell again into the red pool, unable to keep her purchase on the unstable ground. She raised her eyes to the golden flower and watched as it withered and turned to dust when the blood swirled at its stem, and like an omen of death, the entire lavender field wilted and died before her eyes.

One last, single golden petal danced in the wind towards the gaping abyss, and as it reached the edge, thunder shook the sky as the petal drifted over. One heartbeat. Two. A hoof appeared. Persephone drew back in horror as a second hoof emerged, until finally an enormous ebony stallion burst through the depths of the blackness. On its back sat a cloaked rider. The creature who sat astride the monstrous beast was covered in black, tattered robes and was headed straight towards her -- with deadly intent. She felt frozen, unable to move as the Earth pounded beneath her body. The horse's red, rolling eyes stared into her own, the steam rushing from its flared nostrils, and she could feel the seething rage of the rider, a powerful anger directed at her.

"Get up, Persephone!" she whispered to herself.

She jumped suddenly to her feet, but the ground was wet beneath her. She felt herself slipping as she tried to gain her footing; the pounding hooves were right behind her now. She gave a cry of terror as a powerful arm wrapped around her and she was lifted onto the giant mount. She fought wildly against the tight hold and her struggles increased as she saw that the horse had changed directions and was heading once more toward the gaping crack in the Earth. The body against her own was hard and muscular, and despite how much she struggled, the grip on her did not loosen. She opened her mouth to scream when with one, impossibly long leap, the horse entered the crevice. The air whooshed out of her lungs and Persephone felt a peculiar weightlessness as they went further and further downwards. Another shattering noise filled her ears and they were immersed in darkness as the Earth closed above them. She let out a helpless whimper of fear and the arm tightened around her.

"Do not let go, Persephone," a deep voice whispered in her ear and she tried to turn back to glance at her captor but his fingers kept her face tucked into his chest.

Screams echoed in the darkness as the Earth seemed to fall

apart around them, dust and rock hitting and tearing into her skin. The piercing cries intensified and suddenly she felt hands pulling at her. The smell of decay was overpowering and she could feel cold fingers reaching and grasping at her. She began to slip from the horse when a sudden burst of light blinded her and the fingers fell away. Down and down they fell, the horse galloping swiftly and savagely through the ground and air. The dust was covering her face and she could not seem to catch her breath. They seemed to be falling through darkness, and she feared she would suffocate when suddenly, she realized they were standing still.

She opened her eyes slowly and saw that they were in a stone courtyard that was dimly lit by torches on the walls. The arm loosened slightly from her waist and she pushed herself from the horse and staggered to the ground, landing in a crouch. The rider stared down at her, his face still hooded, and then he jumped down landing quietly on his feet. She stood quickly and staggered back, staring at him with wide fearful eyes as he threw back his hood. He was tall; the paleness of his skin was enhanced by the black hair that curled slightly around his face. There was a darkening beard around his firm jaw and his lips were full -- though curved currently in an unpleasant expression that hinted at cruelty. Her gaze darted up to his, and for a brief second a hint of purple flared around his irises, but then it was only black eyes that blazed into her own. She knew three things: He was a God. She had never seen him before. And he was furious.

"Who are you?" she whispered.

"You are a child indeed if you do not know who I am. Are you not able to recognize the King of Death when you see him?" he answered impatiently.

She gasped and took another step back. "You are...you are Hades?"

He gave her a slight bow. "At your service." He took a step closer to her, narrowing his eyes. "And now that we have completed introductions, I must ask you to remove this." He jerked his robe down baring his chest, and she gasped. A golden arrow was embedded directly over his heart, and the wound was seeping dark red blood that oozed slowly onto his pale skin. Her eyes grew wide as recognition flared in her mind. By the Gods, that was an arrow of love! Persephone looked at him wildly, her mouth gaping open at him as she processed his words.

"I-- what? You wish me for me to remove this arrow? That is why you brought me here?"

He studied her, anger flickering again in his gaze. "It was you who shot it at me, was it not?"

She gasped in outrage, the shock of his words momentarily abating her fear. "It was most certainly not! I have never seen you before and I can assure you I am not in the habit of entrapping any God with love arrows. I do not know who did this to you, but it was not me."

He regarded her for a moment as one dark brow arched, and then turned walking down the nearest dark tunnel. "Interesting," he murmured, his voice echoing behind him as the horse followed docility behind him.

Persephone blinked. He was mad, she thought, completely mad. Was she truly in the Underworld? Hades was little spoken of on Olympus and she had heard he was unstable, a God to be feared. What could he want with her? She was a Goddess of minor importance. He was obviously as mad as everyone said. Her mother would come looking for her sooner or later, and the less she moved from this spot the easier it would be for Demeter to find her. But would she know how to find her, she wondered with a prickle of fear? The scorched field would be a clue and if anyone was able to figure out where she was it would be Demeter. What did this God mean by all of this, she thought angrily, bringing her down here and now leaving her! And what reason could he possibly have to suspect it was *she* who had shot that arrow at him? She would stay right here and wait for Demeter to find her. Unfortunately, her resolve was weakened as a painful moan echoed loudly in one of the adjacent chambers and she felt compelled to hurry after Hades, as he was rapidly moving away.

She was panting by the time she caught up with him, his dark robes billowing behind him like he was an angelic demon, and she raced in front of him to halt his relentless progression. They seemed to be heading down deeper into the Underworld and that was not the direction she wanted to go. She must resolve this, try to reason with this unreasonable God, and have him release her. She pushed her hair out of her face and regarded him.

"Why do you think it is I that shot this arrow at you? I can promise you it was not."

He looked at her with fathomless black eyes and a slight curve of his mouth as he considered her, his head cocked to one side as though he found *her* a curiosity. "Every love arrow is inscribed with a name, did you know that?" She nodded. Her mother had told her this when she was but a babe, when she had still believed in love. "Why don't you read the name that is written on this one?"

"Oh, very well," she muttered. She furrowed her brows leaning forward, getting close enough she could feel the heat radiating off of his skin.

Strange, she thought he would be cold, like marble or like death. Instead he felt... hot. She shook her head slightly and looking at the hilt of the arrow buried deep in his flesh she read: *-ersephone*.

"No," she silently gasped.

"I assure you -- yes. The P is currently embedded in my person. As I am sure you are aware, only the name of the person inscribed on the arrow can remove it. Hence, why your presence is required."

Persephone stood rooted to the ground, horror in every rigid line of her body. "This cannot be. There must be some mistake. Who would do this?"

"Cui bono. Who indeed?" It took her a moment to realize he had set off once again at a leisurely pace. She ran after him. Glancing around she realized the horse was gone. Where on Earth had it disappeared to so quickly? Her footsteps echoed eerily down the long hallways while his feet moved noiselessly over the ground.

"You - you must believe it was not I who did this. Why would I do such a thing to you? I have many suitors, I have no need to use a love arrow. You may ask my Mother if you like--"

"Why would I ask your mother when I can ask you?" He stopped and regarded her with cold black eyes. "You will not remove this arrow?"

"No! I will not!" To remove the arrow would be as good as to admit guilt to him and she crossed her arms firmly over her chest to emphasize her resolve.

"Very well," he said and raising both hands he began to pull on the arrow. The muscles in his arms bulged as he attempted to try to pull it out of his flesh, and though his face remained stoic, fresh blood began to pour from the wound. The arrow remained firmly in place. She felt her own her heart contract in agony for him. She would not let a creature in the forest suffer like this, how could she treat this God as any less?

"Stop!" She laid her hands over his and she felt his hands tense under hers. "Stop," she commanded softly again, wrapping both of her hands around his, around the arrow. "If it is indeed somehow my name on this arrow, I will help you. And then you will release me."

He looked down at her, his blood dripping down both of their hands. "Then pull, Persephone, pull and do not stop until it is free."

He placed his hands over her own, and as their eyes locked she thought she saw pleasure reflected in the dark depths of his gaze. She hesitated and then began to pull, looking only at the arrow and not the God who seemed to watch her with some strange triumph. For a moment nothing happened, and she felt hope soar in her heart that perhaps it had not been her name on this arrow. Then slowly, she felt the arrow begin to slip from his flesh. Fresh blood flooded over their hands and she loosened her grip.

"I'm hurting you!" she cried.

"No do not stop, pull harder. Do not stop until it is out." His lips were close to her ears and she gave a shudder of revulsion at his nearness.

Furrowing her brows, she braced her feet against the ground and began to pull, ignoring the tearing of his skin, the ripping of muscle, the pounding of the heart which it had pierced, until the *P* appeared, until the very tip left his torn flesh and the arrow fell to the

ground clanging at their feet. His hands tightened almost painfully over her own and a slow quiet laugh escaped from his lips.

She looked up in surprise, and it was as though a mask had been removed from his face. Small lights danced in his eyes as he stared at her, and the wild look in his gaze caused the fine hairs on her neck to rise. He looked untamed and dangerous. He looked like the King of Death and there was possession in his eyes as he stared at her. Panic filled her mind and she tried to step away from him. For a moment she was afraid he would not release her, but suddenly he allowed her hands to drop from his bare chest -- hands that were covered with his blood. She snuck a look at him again, but his face was free from any expression and she wondered if she had imagined the madness in his eyes. She hesitated and then lifted her gown, still damp with the blood from the scorched field, and pressed it tightly to his wound, new blood darkening the fabric. He pushed her away gently, his face paler than before if possible, his breath coming in quick gasps.

"That is unnecessary." He bent down to retrieve the arrow as blood continued to seep from the gaping hole in his chest, and then inexplicably continued his downward descent. She watched as the trail of blood from his chest left small, dark pools on the stones below them and then she hurried after him.

"Wait!" she desperately cried. "I did what you asked. Now, let me return to my Mother. She will be missing me!" She strained her ears-- was that water she heard ahead?

"Oh no, Persephone, that was never part of the bargain," he replied, not breaking his stride, not even doing the courtesy to glance at her.

"We made a bargain," she appealed to him, outraged. "I

helped you and now I demand that you return me to my temple!"

He suddenly stopped and quickly turned to her. "You do not know all there is to know about a love arrow if you do not understand why you cannot leave this place. Why you will never leave this place." When she shook her head, he grasped her by the arms. "Love is a poison that drives even Gods mad. If you leave, I will find you, and I will bring you back. Even now the poison from the arrow is spreading through my veins and will slowly drive me to madness. In time, without your love, I will become deranged. I, the God of Death will wreak havoc upon the land. I want this no more than you! But someone took away my choice."

Persephone's hands trembled. "I will not stay here."

"I tire of this. Come," he demanded. Keeping a firm grasp on her arm, he dragged her forward down the dark chamber and bellowed, "Charon!" They came suddenly to an opening and a dark river moved swiftly ahead. A small boat sat near the shore with a man huddled at one end, a staff leaning against him. "Is it ready?" Hades asked. The old man nodded and Hades walked over to him handing him the arrow. "Here, keep this for now." Charon reached out to claim it, and then before she could blink, he had resumed his previous position, huddled over in his seat as the boat rocked gently in the murky water below.

Hades caught her watching the river guide. "Do not mind Charon," he said, "he is no longer used to the living." While he spoke, he began to gently tug her towards a darkened anteroom. The room was lit with only a few candles, there was a marble white altar, plush rugs lined the walls and the rich scent of frankincense perfumed the air. As her eyes began to adjust to the darkness, she made out a lone figure standing at the head of an altar, a glow emanating from his skin. A God, she thought with trepidation. Another God, she corrected herself. Maybe she could ask for his help.

"What is this?" she asked, noticing the cups he held in both hands. She dragged her feet against the ground as fear settled into her heart. "Who is that person?" Hades watched her silently, his dark eyes burning with hellfire as he met her gaze.

"Hymenaeus, son of Apollo, has kindly agreed to facilitate the wedding vows." The God stared back at them with a nod of his pale, silvery head.

"I owe Hades a debt. It is a pleasure to finally meet the lovely Persephone."

Persephone looked wordlessly at him and then shook her head. "What are you talking about? What wedding?"

Hades moved them closer to the altar. "I understand that Ares was asking Zeus for your hand in marriage. You will trade one husband for another, I can assure you I will be no worse a husband than he, and probably a great deal easier to live with."

Persephone glanced wildly around the room and noticed Charon had moved from his ghostly boat to accompany them, to bear witness to this farce. Her whole body began to shake with violent denial and her mouth twisted with rage.

"You must be mad if you think I would consent to be your bride! I will not live my life in such a tomb! I will not marry you, I will not!" She ran quickly to the door and Hades lifted his arm, drawing her to him as if an invisible chain had pulled her backward. His face hardened as he looked down at her.

"No," he said, "you are not leaving." He firmly grabbed her arm. "Ares will not be the one calling you his wife tonight. Hymenaeus, bring forth the goblets."

Persephone watched as Hymenaeus reluctantly stepped forward and she released a violent cry. She fought and clawed like a wild beast, drawing blood from both the Gods as they tried to approach her. Fear wrapped around her heart as tightly as vines. Hades swore a savage curse and wrapped his arms around her even as she clawed him, his hands holding her face up towards the God of Matrimony.

"You make this needlessly difficult, Persephone," he whispered in her ear. "There is no escape for you. Stop this now!" She could feel the tears coursing down her face as she panted in helpless rage and Hymenaeus eyed her warily as he tried to approach her again.

"Perhaps if she is not willing, Hades," Hymenaeus began, "you could delay your nuptials."

"Continue," Hades snarled at him. As Hymenaeus lifted the cup, Hades made a vow, "This is the water of the Styx, the river of unbreakable oath. By drinking from this cup, you vow that you will be my wife." She began to thrash her head back and forth, biting her lips closed and Hades held her more firmly. He pinched her nose and she held her breath as long as possible, but eventually was forced to gasp open to breathe and Hymenaeus poured the contents of the goblet down her throat. The black putrid water burned her throat and she spit the drink out into Hades' face. Without expression, he bent forward and sipped the remaining water from her lips. She bit his mouth hard and watched with satisfaction as dark blood oozed against his pale skin. With a cruel smile, he grabbed the cup from Hymenaeus and gripped her arm like a vice, forcing the evil draught once more down her throat. He held her jaws firmly shut until she choked the dark murky water down, gagging like the most wretched of animals. There was no option to refuse the marriage. Sobs of anguish rang from her lips through the chamber of the secret ceremony as she collapsed to her knees in defeat.

Hades refilled the goblet and drank from it deeply as Hymenaeus began to recite the unbreakable vows. He picked up her limp body, forcing her to stand, and she kept her eyes tightly closed. She imagined the softest touch against her mouth and a whisper so quietly in her ear she was not sure if was real.

"I'm sorry little flower. In time you will come to realize why this has to be."

When she opened her eyes, he was placing a golden ring on her finger, "Say you will be my wife. She shook her head back and forth, her long chestnut hair whipping her in the face. Grabbing tightly to her arms, he pulled her fully to her feet.

"Say it!" he bellowed.

Persephone looked into his furious face and an icy calmness settled into her bones, a sense of finality. Her face was pale and ravaged by her tears, but she stared back at him boldly with hatred filling her beautiful eyes. Had she been paying closer attention she would have noticed his slight flinch. However, she only saw his fingers digging tightly into her arms and the ring he had forced onto her slim finger. She stepped back from his embrace and he let his arms fall. "I am--."

Merciless eyes burned back at her, his low, dead voice echoing once more, "Say it."

"Your wife," she whispered.

Hades swung his dark cape around her and pulled the hood over her face.

"We must cover your sweet face lest someone mistake your tears for anything other than joy," he murmured as he pulled the cloak tighter around her. With that, he lifted her up and quickly carried her through a long hall and into a private section of the castle. Too tired to fight at the moment, Persephone watched listlessly as he took her down another long hallway, kicking open two large doors that led into a bedroom. She looked around briefly to take in the large four post bed made of emerald, a tree barren of leaves hung upside down from the ceiling. Crystals were dangling from each tree branch, swaying two and fro, creating a sound similar to that of wind chimes. The light of the fireplace bounced off each stone, scattering tiny fragments of light onto the ceiling and floor. The room was opulent, mystifying and strange. Hades suddenly bent and laid her on the satin bed. She scurried off quickly and pressed herself to the far side of the wall staring back at him with a searching, frightened gaze. A faint smile curled his lips as he went deliberately to the bed and sat, sprawling out his long legs.

"A comfortable bed, is it not?" He ran his hand over the green stone and a wicked smile crossed his face, "Emerald encourages romantic bliss." He gave a small sigh as he looked at her huddled in the corner. "This is *your* room my Queen. Mine is across the hall."

Relief washed over her. "You...you do not want a wedding night?"

Embers burned in his black eyes, "I do." His gaze swept over her body with frankly sexual appraisal and she stiffened, pulling his cape tighter around her, preparing to do whatever necessary to keep him from touching her. She shivered, her dress cold from the blood that had stained it. "I forced you onto my horse and into the Underworld, I forced you to stand and drink from the wedding cup, and to put the ring on your finger and say yes at the ceremony." He stood from the bed and approached her lazily, reaching one hand to play with a lock of her hair that curled against her neck. He watched her expression carefully. His other hand moved to the strap of her dress which had slipped off her pale, sloping shoulder. He felt her gasp as he took the strap in his hand, fondling it. "And you are a beautiful Queen, any man would want you." He took the strap and snapped it back onto her shoulder. "But I think I have forced you enough for one day, my unwilling bride. "Besides," he said turning away from her, "I throw men into Tartarus for what you suspect I would do next."

Oh what a wicked man he was, she thought. As she stared at his broad back she felt her impotence and how much she hated him!

"Let me go home then," she said in a low voice.

He looked at his bride who was the most beautiful woman he had ever beheld. The wild dark hair framing her face like a halo. Her delicate hands clung tightly to his cape as she pulled it closely around her body, framing her delicious curves. She would not cling so tightly if she knew, he thought with a smile. And her eyes, green as only springtime could be, stared into his, as though she was trying to appeal to his very soul. Foolish girl, she did not know that there was nothing left of his soul. He could see her dress from that day under the cape. The simple toga she'd worn in the fields would forever be imprinted in his mind, her wedding dress, a reminder of the cursed day she forever became tied to him. The dress was stained copper with blood, his blood and the blood of others. Stained like his soul.

He breathed deeply trying to calm his rapidly beating heart and inhaled her scent. She smelt like flowers and sunshine, like freshness and hope, and it was intoxicating to him. He was drawn to her as surely as a flower wept for the warmth of the sun, and he felt desire fill his body. He turned away quickly and closed his eyes for a moment; she would never be allowed to go home. Never be free in her forest. This was his gift to this precious creature, that she was doomed to spend eternity in Hell.

With his back to her he replied, "What poor choices you were given, little one. A God who sends men to their grave, or the God of Death himself." He turned to face her, the bed between them. "Goodnight, my beautiful wife. Try to sleep. Stay in your room to-night. I mean it, Persephone." She blinked at his words, which iron-ically echoed her mother's from this very morning. "There is no reason we must see each other more than we have to, and if you abide by my rules you will have a comfortable life. It would not do to wander far in the land of the dead. For your own sake, do not defy me." With a bow, he swept from the room and she was left alone.

CHAPTER III
LIFELESS KINGDOM

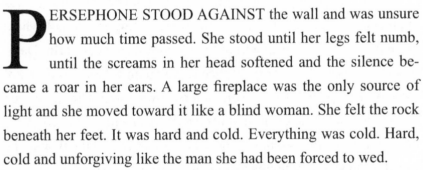

PERSEPHONE STOOD AGAINST the wall and was unsure how much time passed. She stood until her legs felt numb, until the screams in her head softened and the silence became a roar in her ears. A large fireplace was the only source of light and she moved toward it like a blind woman. She felt the rock beneath her feet. It was hard and cold. Everything was cold. Hard, cold and unforgiving like the man she had been forced to wed.

Removing the satin bedspread, she laid it in front of the fire to get warm. Tears were welling up in her eyes. "Gaia...Mother... someone... help me. Please hear my prayers." Her body crumbled on the ground as she sobbed at her fate.

Hades stood in his room, his hand outstretched onto the fireplace mantel, the flames blue and high, throwing shades of light against the dark walls. The shadows embraced him lovingly and seemed to seep inside of him and he welcomed the coldness it offered. He had long ago accepted that he was a creature of darkness, never meant to touch the light. Whatever good had been inside of him was long gone, squashed out so casually by those who had once held power over him. And what was Persephone if not the light of the Earth.

By the Gods he should never have even looked upon her. She awakened something dangerous in him, something he had long ago suppressed. The flames danced in his eyes as he clenched his fists, breaking off a piece of the marble. He let the dust fall to the ground from his hand and stepped further into his room, opening his robes to inspect the wound in his chest. It was still raw and bleeding and with every pump of his heart, more fresh blood dripped down his chest. Walking out to the balcony he looked into the swirling waters of the river Styx below, and exhaled deeply.

The wind rippled off the dark water and he knew a storm was approaching. Persephone would be alone during the squall which often turned violent deep within the vault of the Underworld. Damnation, it was not the way he wished to welcome her into his domain! He took a step back towards the doors, towards his wife, and then shook his head as he glanced at his hands fresh with blood. No wonder she was terrified of him. These hands had forced the woman he loved to do so many things against her will today. Hades closed his eyes, remembering her face as she repeated her vows, how she had looked at him. Like he was a monster. But he had no other choice, though that was little comfort to the Goddess. She would never forgive him, and he would always represent the one who had stolen her precious freedom. His hand had been forced, and now she had to stay with him. He went to a table and poured a glass of wine, his hand unsteady as he gripped the bottle. God's damn, who had done this? Who had dared to shoot an arrow into the chest of the God of the Underworld? He knew there was something more to this game, but he did not know who his opponent was. The fact that Persephone had somehow become part of this vendetta against him made the stakes even higher. He would never let harm come to her.

Wind rippled across the river as the storm grew in intensity. The sounds of thunder and screams echoed through the caverns as the wails of dying men filled his ears, their very souls being ripped prematurely from their bodies - stuck somewhere between earth and the Underworld.

As their wails escalated, Hades clenched his fists, "Ares." Setting his glass down, he pulled his robes closed and strode into the throne room.

Charon the river bearer was waiting for him and whispered in his reedy voice, "I cleared your throne room, my Lord, I thought you would not wish for company tonight. It is a war. The river is flooded with blood and dying men."

Hades flung himself into his chair as his vision blurred for a moment. He had lost too much blood. He grabbed the side of his throne tightly and looked at Charon with a steady gaze. "It begins. We knew Ares would act. Charon, lead them across the river after they pass. Their souls will be stuck in between for some time. They are being tortured for Ares' pleasure."

Charon bowed his hooded head, always the faithful servant. They both knew what was happening. Ares would not let him have a peaceful wedding night. Like a petulant child mourning the loss of their favorite toy, Ares would not rest until the Underworld wept with blood.

"Hot-headed ass," Hades muttered, "Sending men to their

death and laughing about it. Life is not precious to him. He is just like his father. Tonight, will not be a quiet one. Charon, I leave this to you."

He stood and blinked as black dots momentarily blocked his vision. He must rest, the pain in his chest was growing and even now he could feel the hot blood running down his robes. Nodding once more to Charon, he made his way back to his room, and as he passed Persephone's door, he stopped to lay one hand against the darkened wood. He could hear her muted sobs from the room within. If only he could comfort her, but no, she would not want that. She would never want that. His beautiful Goddess despised him. He felt her despair as if it were his own, and for a moment the pain was so acute he could not breathe. He had long ago learned to push down the grief of the souls he met on their journey to the Underworld, their suffering, regrets, the sorrow of leaving those they loved behind. Sometimes it seemed he died a small death with each soul he encountered, until there was nothing left of his own, until he was empty inside. He turned away impatiently from the door. It would be a long night for both of them. He smiled ironically as he returned to his room; at least they were united in their misery.

Demeter sat in her temple, her hair wild and tangled. Her eyes felt swollen and were mere slits in her face. She sat on her daughter's bed crying, letting her tears soak into the blanket. A tall blonde God entered her temple and she could see by the golden halo above his head who it was. -- Helios, the God of Light. He bowed down to Demeter and placed his hands on her shoulders as he knelt beside her.

"Demeter," he whispered softly, stroking her hair away from her face. "I come with news. I watched your daughter be spirited away by 'The Unseen'."

A sob escaped her lips as Demeter turned her face back into the blanket. "She is in that dead kingdom. She must be terrified," she cried in anguish.

She glanced at Helios and she saw a frown cross his face. "Demeter, I know your daughter harbors secrets. I have seen *all* that the light touches. Hades will uncover everything, and he always gets to the truth. It will not be easy for her."

Demeter shuddered at his words. She knew the secrets Persephone carried.

"What can I do?" she whispered.

"Two men want your daughter, one is brash and brazen and the other is… insidious. There is darkness in Hades that he will never be able to obliterate." He paused for a second, "If his love is superficial, he will coerce her. But... If his love is true, he would die for her."

Demeter grasped Helios' arm. "Does he love her Helios? I need to know, does he love her or is it only lust? Is he like all the others?"

Helios shrugged his bronzed shoulders, "There is no way of knowing what harbors inside his mind. His secrets are his and his alone."

"Zeus -- you bastard," she whispered bitterly, "this is all his fault." Demeter put her face in her hands and sobbed as tiny flakes of ice fell from the sky.

Persephone woke by the embers of the burnt-out fire. For

a moment she was disoriented, wondering why she was not in her bed at home. She arched her stiff neck and huddled closer in the blanket as shivers wracked her body -- and she remembered. She shuddered as the thoughts invaded her mind, the golden flower, and the gaping Earth, and wretched, *wretched* Hades! For a blissful moment she had thought everything had been a bad dream, but she felt dragged back into a nightmare when she realized where she was. Was it morning or night? Her room was too dark to tell. She stood and threw his robe to the ground. Damn him and damn his robe. She quickly lifted her hands and weaved herself a shawl of moss, taking a moment to appreciate its dark softness, grateful for the touch of this soft living thing in this dead palace before she slung it over her shoulders. At least the moss did well in the darkness.

"I am leaving this place," she whispered to herself. "He cannot hold me here." She opened the door as slowly as possible and glanced carefully up and down the hall. Glancing down she saw that his blood still stained her hands. She refocused her thoughts, straining her ears for any sound. It was silent. She shuddered as she considered the horrors that could lurk in the darkness here, but every moment counted and so she quietly slipped from the room. She tiptoed down the hallway as quietly as possible, trying to remember the way back to the anteroom where they had recited their vows. Perhaps a trail of Hades blood remained that she could follow, like breadcrumbs. She giggled rather wildly and lifted her hand to cover her mouth as it echoed loudly against the high stone walls. "Oh, do not lose your mind down here, Persephone," she said sternly to herself. Taking a deep breath, she considered what her mother would advise her to do. Demeter was always calm in the face of adversity. She reasoned that if she could return to the river, she could follow

it to the horrible room where she had been forced into a loveless marriage. Once there, she may be able to find the pathway they had originally taken. If she ever saw Hymenaeus again, she would rip every lovely strand of blond hair from his head. She listened carefully for any signs of the river being nearby, but heard nothing except her own heartbeat.

Wandering through an endless maze of stone halls, she began to feel desperate. The castle was like a labyrinth and she had not heard any signs of Charon's river, and not even the faintest drop of Hades' blood remained. Nothing looked familiar. In fact, she was quite sure she had never passed this way before. She entered another hall and paused as she stared at a window ahead of her. It was filled with crystallized glass giving off dull shades of red and yellow and something about it caused the fine hairs on her neck to raise. She considered it and blinked as she saw faint shadows moving on the other side. And the strange thing was, as she stood there, she began to imagine she could hear whispers behind the glass, insidious whispers so quiet she could not make out the words but they caused her to shudder in revulsion all the same. Still, the window must lead somewhere, she reasoned. She shook her head, she had no choice. She must try. Going back to that prison of a room was simply not an option. She took a steadying breath and then grabbed the ledge and began pulling herself up.

A deep voice echoed in the darkness, "How tiresomely predictable," shocking her so completely that she fell from the ledge. She gave a little scream as she felt rough hands catch her before she hit the ground. She was turned around and suddenly faced with Hades' dark face close to her own. She looked up into his black gaze. "Leaving so soon? How rude -- and on our wedding night, too. Tsk,

tsk what an undutiful wife."

"I am not staying here!" she cried, kicking out at him viciously. "You cannot make me. I am going home." She reached out desperately once again for the ledge and he yanked her leg back.

"Do not touch that window! I told you not to wander in this darkness. What is beyond that window is certain doom, even to a God. There are things here you do not understand, Persephone."

Her emerald eyes glared at him defiantly. "I do not want to understand this place! I want to go home! If you think my mother will allow me to stay down here you are mistaken. She will come for me, wage war against you to get me."

Hades put a hand to his throbbing head. Despite his increasing weakness he could not rest, and he had watched her in the darkness, knowing she would not resist the urge to try and escape from him tonight. "How long must I keep hearing that you want to go home. I have explained to you, you cannot leave the Underworld now."

Persephone felt her anger flare and she pushed hard on his chest, too incensed to notice as he gave a grunt of pain. He released her suddenly. "My home is not here," she raged, "you kidnapped me and put me in that dark cold prison. I am not meant for your world. I will go mad here! Why can you not understand this?"

His eyes narrowed at her. "I tire of this song and dance. You placed yourself needlessly in danger and ignored my warning. Perhaps," he said, stepping closer to her, "you would feel warmer in my room."

She flung out a hand. "Stay away from me! I do not want to be in your room or anywhere around you."

With a smile and an arch of one dark brow he moved closer.

"And what will you do to stop me, my gentle Goddess."

She hesitated and then whisked her hands quickly causing thick, green vines to burst from the ground and wrap around his legs, tightening as they wound up his body.

Hades laughed, and with a touch of his hand the plants withered and died. Persephone gasped. "You think living things can hold me down? Do you not know who I am? What I do? I am the God of Death."

They faced each other like adversaries on Ares' battlefield, her with a rage that caused her hair to crackle and he with a cold, calculating resolve, arms crossed over his powerful chest. She suddenly sprang from the window and began running. He paused to admire her form for a moment as she flew over the rocky terrain like a deer, her skirts flying behind her like the wings of an angel. She was magnificent, he thought with a smile, uncrossing his arms.

She felt a thrill of victory, she knew she was fast, no nymph could outrun her, and she heard no noise behind her. Perhaps she had a large enough of a lead that she could reach the gates before him, perhaps he was bleeding so much he could not give chase. Perhaps he would die. No, not that her mind countered swiftly, she did not want him to die. But she hoped that he was too weak to catch her. She shrieked when a hand grabbed her suddenly by the shoulder, and they tumbled to the ground. Hades' large body covered her own, breathing easily while she panted up at him. He pressed a large thigh between her own.

"It seems I will lay with you tonight after all, wife," he whispered into her ear.

"Get away from me," she spat. "If you touch me, I will claw your eyes out!"

Hades pinned her more tightly to the ground. He said with a scowl, "You do not seem to grasp the situation. Your free will is gone -- as is mine. If you leave me, it is certain madness for both of us. Save your wrath for the person who cursed us both with that damned, forsaken, golden arrow! Because of that arrow, I will go insane if you are not near me."

"You are already insane!" she roared into his face. Charming, he thought, as he watched her nostrils flare and her sweet lip curl with anger. She looked as ferocious as a baby fox with her dark hair spilling behind her.

"True, my heart, true. But I am afraid I will become madder still if you do not help me resolve this situation. I am no more at fault than you. You could try to work with me."

She snorted now. Her snort was more reminiscent of a wild piglet, he thought. But a very adorable piglet. He fought back a smile as she glared at him. "Your idea of working together is for me to blindly follow everything you say, to be as obliging as a sweet little nymph. I am a Goddess, I am at the mercy of no one! Now get off of me you great brute!"

He lifted her off the ground "You worry needlessly. I am not in the habit of forcing women." He extended a hand to her.

She stiffened at his words then bit down hard on his hand and took off towards the gates ahead, beginning to climb up the entrance. He jerked her down catching her in his arms.

"Put me down! I do not care about your stupid curse!" she screamed.

His cool demeanor dissipated as he shook her, "Stop yelling, you little fool!" he said through clenched teeth, "You jeopardize the entire Underworld!"

"Hades is cursed!" She yelled out loud. "Hades is--."

"Stop it," he snapped covering her mouth with his hand, "If you scream that again -- I will kiss you."

Falling silent she looked at him, green eyes glaring into black ones, a declaration of war finally issued. He removed his hand. "You would not dare," she countered through clenched teeth.

She struggled against his grasp and he tightened his arms almost painfully around her. "You think to dare me, my Queen?" She only had a moment to quicken her breath, when he descended swiftly towards her. At the first touch his lips were rough, but after a moment they gentled over her own and his full lips moved soft-ly against hers, coaxing and pulling at her mouth. He brought her more fully into his arms and she felt the long length of his body pressed so tightly against her own and she shivered. As he angled his head and ran his tongue against the seam of her lips, she let out a small sound and without conscious thought, her mouth begin to open when he suddenly lifted his head and looked down at her with cold and gleaming eyes. He had merely been playing with her, she thought angrily. She pushed him away with all her strength and gave him a withering glance. Please to the Gods he had not noticed. She opened her mouth to yell again, and he looked without expression.

"If... you... shout... I will do it again, and this time I will take my husbandly compensation, as well."

"You said you did not force women," she whispered with wary eyes.

"Who said I would be forcing you, my sweet?" he infuriat-ingly responded.

She took a step back from him. She knew he would. Shaken, she shook her head. "I will not shout again," she held out a hand as

he moved towards her, "but please do not touch me, you promised you would not force me. Take me back to my room."

His dark eyes watched her, and he inclined his head, "As you wish, my Queen. Come."

CHAPTER
IV
THE PARADE

AFTER HADES DEPOSITED her in her room with the threat of chains if she left it again, she had fallen into a dreamless sleep before the burning embers of the fire. She awoke, jolting off the floor as someone pounded insistently on the door. Her heart leaped in her throat as the door rattled again. So far no one aside from Hades had come to her room and he certainly would not bother with the politeness of knocking. "Who is it," her voice coming out in a strangled cough, suspiciously high even to her own ears. She cleared her throat and summoned the best imperious voice she could muster. She had heard Athena use it several times with great aplomb. "Who is it!" There, she thought with satisfaction.

"Good morning, your Majesty," a woman's voice called, "we are here to break your fast and dress you."

It was morning then, Persephone thought, feeling her hopes dashed as she glanced about the room and saw it was as grey and lifeless as it had been the night before. She had spent the whole evening in this wretched place. How her mother must be worried!

She considered denying the woman entry, if she worked for Hades, she should not accept her help. And she certainly did not trust any servant that did his bidding. However, she was hungry and there was no reason to be rude to the poor woman, perhaps she was a prisoner, too. All here to serve the mighty Hades' will, she thought angrily. And perhaps this morning there may be more light to see by than there had been last night, her heart beginning to quicken at the thought of freedom. She placed her hand on the large handle and twisted quickly, darting out of the room when an overly tall, enormously muscled guard pulled her back inside. Good Gods! He must be a giant, she thought as she stared at his tree like form. "We were warned you might do that. I have strict orders you are not to leave yer room, yer Majesty," he grunted at her in a very giant like manner. She glared up at him as three women dressed as servants laughed and carried in trays laden with food, a large bundle of dresses and bottles of fragrant oils. They closed the door firmly behind them and her chance of freedom vanished with a soft thud. For now, she promised herself grimly, as she turned to watch her captors.

They seemed like ordinary women, humming happily as they went about their duties. In fact, she considered with narrowed eyes, watching as they laughed and smiled at one another, they seemed perfectly content, more content even than the servants she had known in her mother's temple. Perhaps they were under a spell, she reasoned. It would be just like Hades to have a mindless palace of servants at his disposal. Persephone went closer, curiosity getting the best of her as they laid out breakfast on shining silver platters and steaming drinks filled with spices. Her mouth actually watered as fresh fruits were laid out, fruits from above ground! Her eyes greedily soaked up their vibrant colors, reds and purples and yellows and she could not help herself as she grabbed an apple and hungrily devoured it. Hades need not know how much she had enjoyed her breakfast. The elder servant watched with satisfaction and then tutted around the other women as they began to lay out items on her bed. Nibbling on the remnants of a particularly juicy grape, she stood to see what they were doing, when one of the women turned to her and deftly pulled off her tattered tunic. She let out a squeal and quickly covered her breasts, flushing. "Wh-What do you think you are doing?" She gasped outraged, grabbing desperately for her gown as it soared over her head and into the fire they had revived. "That is my only gown!"

The elder servant spoke again, sniffing her nose. "Your Highness is riding in the wedding parade today and that old cloth was not suitable to clothe a beggar, if you pardon. The whole Underworld will be there to see Hades' Queen and he gave the strictest orders that you would require traditional clothing for the Chariot ride."

"A parade," Persephone said through clenched teeth, as one of the servants happily stoked the fire with the remnants of her gown. "Hades said nothing of this to me. You may tell him I am not interested in attending."

"Oh, but you must," the head servant replied with genuine distress. "The master made that very clear and the whole of the Underworld is expecting you. It is the event of the season. I expect you are overtired," she said, nodding her head as though that settled the matter and with a snap of her fingers directed the two younger servants to the back of the room as she took a key from her waist to unlock an adjacent door, opening up into a smaller anteroom.

Persephone scowled at her, following behind, eyeing the belt of keys at the waist of the servant. Perhaps if she got close enough, she could snatch her belt. The servant placed her arms firmly at her hips and Persephone let out a huff of annoyance. "No, I am not over-tired," Persephone replied stiffly, "that is, I am tired but I --." They were filling a small pond in the back of the room with fragrances turning the water a variety of colors, while steam rolled merrily off the top of the hot, bubbling water. It looked better than Olympus itself, she thought longingly. She lifted a hand to her hair and felt the mud and dirt caking it. What would be the harm of a bath? It did not do any good to be filthy and she did not have to tell Hades she savored it. It would be so nice to be clean again.

"There, there dear, nothing that a hot bath will not set right. In you go, your Highness." And before she could hesitate further, three pairs of helpful arms slid her into the bubbling pool.

For a moment Persephone was submerged under the hot water and she felt a wild freedom in the quiet solitude as she looked up into the hazy world above. Down here no one could tell her what to do or what she should think. If only she were a bird or a fish, she thought longingly, far away from the will of Gods and the desires of men. Only once her lungs began to seize did she move her legs and shoot to the top of the pool. Ready hands waited and began to cover her hair with oils while another gently pulled her arms from the pool to smear creams on her person. They chatted happily, their voices drifting around her, and Persephone closed her eyes, slipping into a relaxed state. What bliss this was, she breathed with a sigh, feeling the hot water release the tension from her muscles. No different really than a bath at her home. She cracked one eye at the sudden mention of Hades' name from one of the maids. Hmph, she thought sulkily, must he even intrude here in her bath.

"You seem quite content to serve my husband?" she inquired, addressing the older woman.

"Oh yes, my Queen," as she began to work a comb into Persephone's matted hair. He is a fair and honest master. I would not trade my services for any God above ground."

"And how long have you served Hades," Persephone questioned sulkily.

"Since my death, your Majesty. My family has served him for generations. These are my nieces you see here, Phoebe and Cleo. It is our privilege to serve him. Upon each of our deaths we enter into his service."

She smiled at them and they smiled shyly at her. "And what is your name?"

"Jocasta if you please, my lady."

"Jocasta is a lovely name. If it is suitable to you, while I am here, would you mind helping me?"

Her brows drew over her eyes at her phrasing, but she was too good a servant to question her Queen. "Oh yes, your majesty. And it was what my lord asked of me as well. He said I was to attend to your needs."

Persephone felt annoyed at the mention of her husband's name, but she could hardly find fault with Jocasta for that. "Well then, for once my husband and I are in agreement. It would be an immense help for me."

Jocasta smiled her pleasure. "Just wait, my Queen, until you see the finery that you may wear today," she began to wring the water from Persephone's long dark hair, wrapping it tightly in a hot white cloth.

"I am not going to the parade, I am afraid I cannot--"

"Oh, the children will be so disappointed," Jocasta said sadly, shaking her head, her grey curls bouncing. "They have little to look forward to down here."

She felt her heart twist as one of the nieces extended their hands to help her from the pool. "Children?" she asked as she stood from the pool and a white towel was quickly wrapped around her.

"Oh yes, my lady. And they have been so looking forward to seeing you. They are orphans who await their parents to join them."

"I did not think of children down here," Persephone murmured quietly, feeling foolish at her lack of knowledge of this dark world. How selfish had she been that she had never given a thought to what may happen when a child enters Charon's boat alone. Her entire life she had gone without any thought of the Underworld, content with the sunshine and peace of the meadows above. There were children alone here in this darkness. How could she deny them this pleasure when it was something so small for her to do -- just to be spiteful to Hades. "Very well, I will go to the parade. However, I do not wish to wear something too ostentatious. A simple gown will suit my needs."

"Well, we'll see about that," Jocasta said with a smile. They began to dry her naked body vigorously. They moved her quickly back to her bedroom, a warm cloth wrapped around her. She surveyed the selections on her bed with horror. Several of the gowns were almost entirely diaphanous with only a few choice portions of fabric leaving any modesty at all. All of them had low cut necklines, some dipping as low as the navel! She threw each to the ground in growing dismay.

"No! No!" She repeated adamantly seeing the expression on

Jocasta's face. "I dressed simply at home and these are extravagant enough for Aphrodite to wear. I do not wish to dress in such an unclothed state. My bosoms may fall out of those gowns!"

"But your majesty there is no time, not if you will arrive at the parade on time."

"I do not know what sort of women Hades typically parades about the Underworld," Persephone stated with scorn.

"But your majesty," Jocasta interrupted. "Hades does not parade any women. You are the first that has been in this palace."

Persephone closed her mouth in surprise. "Never?" she asked in amazement.

"Never," Jocasta emphasized with a firm nod of her head.

"Still, these dresses are not suitable."

"I could I suppose manage to make a new dress but it would take several days. If you wish, of course we can arrange it, if you do not mind to make the people and the children wait who have been gathering since last night…"

"Oh very well then!" Persephone said reluctantly, feeling that she had been very adeptly and expertly managed when a contented smile creased Jocasta's face. They debated which gown she should wear and finally Jocasta gave in letting her select the most demure of the gowns, which was not saying much.

They dressed her in a sheer gown that shone like sunlight and was embellished with flattened gold fragments and sparkling gemstones. As she stared at the bright beauty of the dress, she felt a painful longing to see the sun again, to feel its warmth on her skin. The neckline plunged low in the front and her small breasts were on full display, but it had been the most modest of the choices. The train of the dress drug behind her, trailing like the plume of a peacock's feathers. The maidens kohl-rimmed her eyes, carefully curled her dark hair with hot irons, and finally placed a jeweled tiara of gold and diamonds on her head. After they surveyed their handywork, congratulating one another on her beauty, Jocasta knocked on the door lightly and the giant appeared again.

Persephone felt her heart quicken as she was led down the dark hall. She had been preparing herself to come face to face with her captor again and she needed to make it clear to him that the only reason she agreed to this parade was to please the children. It was certainly not to make a show of their mockery of a marriage. The gown she had borrowed was a necessary evil since her own was now merely ash in the hearth. She tugged uncomfortably at the neckline feeling a cold draft blow against her chest. Her breath caught when the giant led her through two large doors to a gleaming golden chariot that was just beyond them. Four enormous black stallions were at the front, pawing the ground with their large hooves. Their manes were intricately braided, and each was gilded with golden bridles. Her eyes, though, were not on the carriage, but rather on the man standing at the head. His broad back was to her and she watched as he fastened a blood red cape onto his black tunic, turning slightly so that he was in profile to her. Many of his servants were running frantically to and fro and one approached to consult with Hades, who bent his head to listen. His dark hair slid over his forehead hiding his black eyes. In repose his lips looked soft and full and her stomach did a curious swoop as he bit down on his lower lip, and she remembered their kiss. How hot his mouth had been and how she had wanted to... she felt her cheeks redden when he suddenly turned to face her. His mouth had partially opened, but as he stared at her, an arrested look came over him and he lifted a hand to his wound as if it pained him. His chest was entirely covered by his tunic, but surely it had begun to heal? He was a God after all. Perhaps he was unsatisfied with her appearance, she thought with a frown.

She tried to pull discreetly at the neckline of the dress. "I picked the least offensive one."

He blinked down at her, taking a moment to respond. "What?"

"You are displeased with my choice, but the others were un-acceptable--."

"No," he shook his head, stepping from the chariot, "no, you look beautiful." For some reason his simple statement made her blush again which displeased her immensely. He handed the reins over to a servant, and as he approached, she saw small beads of sweat dotting his forehead. Was he still ill? Gods healed quickly from any injury, she knew that well. She remembered disobeying her mother as a child and playing on the rocks of a river. She had fallen down a treacherous ravine and her blood had made the river red. By sunset though she had completely healed and her mother had never been the wiser. But Hades seemed to be too pale still and there were faint lines around his mouth. His injury was deep, but he was a powerful, ancient God and he should be entirely healed by now. Perhaps she should look at his wound.

"Hades," she said slowly, "this parade does not have to be today."

His mouth curved as he looked down at her and he lifted his hand to her. She hesitated a moment before placing her smaller hand in his and felt his long fingers curl around her own.

"And disappoint the whole Underworld? Everyone is long-ing to see the beautiful Goddess of the Forest." He led her back to the chariot, helping her up. He joined her in the small space and leaned closer to her. "Hold on tightly. All that is required of you is to smile and wave. They only want to see you. As I do."

Feeling uncomfortable with his gaze and confused by his words, Persephone leaned forward to stroke the flank of one of the horses. She could sense their anxiety of the large crowd which must be gathered outside the gates, and she sympathized. She knew the feeling all too well. Persephone stiffened as she felt him press closer behind her. He grabbed her arm and opened her palm, wrapping her fingers around an apple.

"Orphnaeus loves apples," he whispered in her ear as though telling her a great secret, nodding his head towards the horse. She leaned closer and let Orphnaeus gently eat the apple from her hand, smiling at his enthusiasm. She glanced over her shoulder and saw that Hades, too, was smiling at him and her heart seemed to stutter.

"And how long will this parade take?" she asked coldly.

He stepped away and took his place at her side and she felt a moment's disappointment at the absence of his warmth. Warmth, she scoffed at herself, he was the God of the Dead, not Apollo. Perhaps she truly was losing her mind. Perhaps Jocasta had poisoned her.

"Just several hours, I presume. And afterwards there will be the dance, of course, and then you may retire for the evening."

Persephone had been concentrating on watching his strong pale hands grasp the gleaming reins, but her head jerked up at his words. "A dance!" her voice high pitched. "I was never told anything about a dance! I do not wish to attend."

"You will attend, my Queen," he demanded. "This is not a request."

"Then do me the courtesy of delaying it, I am not prepared!"

He calmly looked down at her "No." They stared at each other as Persephone felt her body tighten with anger. Just when she thought there was an ounce of kindness in him, he proved again his cruelty. Was nothing to be allowed to her? He smiled as though reading her thoughts, her quiet rage seeming to please him.

"Does my anger amuse you?" she bit out coolly between her teeth.

"I must own it is rather refreshing. Few have the courage to express their dislike for me so outright. I find your obvious hatred rather charming," he said contentedly.

She turned to face forward, staring at the iron doors ahead. "I am glad I amuse you," she said indifferently. If she had to look at him, she might attack him, and the price for attacking a God was Tartarus. Charon would toss her in the hell fire and throw away the key, probably with a grin on his macabre face.

Feeling his eyes on her, she heard Hades ask, "Is everything ready Alessandro?"

"Yes, your highness!" cried a curly headed young man.

"Very well, let us proceed." With a shake of his hand the horses stepped forward suddenly.

The carriage jolted and Persephone reached out, grabbing Hades' arm to keep from falling, feeling the solid muscles beneath her grasp. She let go as quickly as possible and grasped tightly to the chariot, her knuckles turning white over the edges. She was unused to standing in chariots, she and her mother had never had cause to be the focus of these lavish parades. The humans that sought them bowed to the land for tribute, not to them.

"Be careful, my sweet one." He wrapped her hands more

tightly around the handles of the chariot. "Oh, and Persephone?" The stiffening of her back was her only acknowledgement to his inquiry. "There can be no misbehavior today. My subjects cannot know their God is cursed."

Her only response was stony silence. As the chariot stopped behind the iron gates, she could feel the tension building on the other side of the doors like a cork that was ready to burst out of a bottle. The horses were becoming uneasy and they shook their manes anxiously.

Hades looked at her with a wicked smile and said, "Get ready." She furrowed her brows at his words, the Underworld could surely be nothing compared to the opulent decadence of Olympus. Did he think her completely oblivious to the ways of the Gods? He lifted his hand and whispered "Elysium," and as the iron doors unlocked and opened, a blinding light poured through the dark, heavy gates.

Persephone's heart beat uncontrollably as she lost her grip on the rapidly moving chariot, her eyes temporarily blinded by the sudden flash of light. Thunderous booms of applause and cheers from the crowd were so loud they sent a wave of sound that pushed her back, and panic overtook her as she felt herself stumble blindly. A strong arm at her back steadied her and she felt his mouth at her ear, "It will pass soon, the light blinds everyone at first. Hold tight." And once again she felt his hands placing her own firmly on the chariot. As her vision began to clear, Persephone was not prepared for what she saw. It was a sea of thousands upon thousands of people, so many that she could not make out their blurred faces as they raced by. Golden confetti and rose petals rained down on them and Persephone felt her feet slip as the floor of the chariot began to fill.

Everything seemed to be in slow motion as the scenes passed swiftly by her. She was unaccustomed to such a massive gathering, she was a creature of the forest; the swarm of people caused panic to rise up in her chest. Black dots began to dance across her vision as her breath came rapidly.-

"Persephone," she heard Hades voice distantly. "Persephone," he said more firmly. He glanced at her. "Look at me." She looked at him with wide eyes, her dilated pupils making them appear black. His hands were relaxed on the reins as he extended one hand to her hair and tugged gently. "Breathe. I will not let you fall." He gave her a sideways grin, "Smile and wave. This will be over soon." She nodded at him, calmed somehow by his composure, and she discreetly wiped at the sweat on her forehead as she pasted a smile on her face. She began to wave to the crowds as they passed, and they exploded with a thrill of excitement at the acknowledgement by their queen. Persephone was astounded as the crowd began to chant Hades' name, and when he raised his hand the chanting intensified to deafening levels. She would never have believed it, but the people of the Underworld seemed enchanted by their surly God. Persephone glanced over at Hades to see his reaction and caught her breath. Standing next to her was not the cold King of Death she had met the night before, but in his place was a smiling, devastatingly beautiful God looking benignly, even lovingly, on his people. She felt her treacherous heart soften at his smile and when their eyes met, she could not help but return a shy smile of her own. She looked away quickly and noticed a large group of children cheering wildly to her right.

"Oh, stop the chariot, please!" she cried.

Hades drew back on the reins. "These are the Orphans of the

Underworld - they are still waiting for their parents to join them. You wish to meet them?"

She nodded eagerly. "Yes, I would very much like that."

He laid a hand on her arm preventing her from exiting before him, and he jumped down to assist her. Hades took her hand and led her to the large group of children. The crowd parted before them, his subjects bowing as they passed. The children bowed too as they saw the royal couple stand before them and Hades quickly went to his knees. Persephone tried to hide her surprised gasp; she had never seen a God take a knee to a mortal before, certainly not to human children. She would have thought a group of orphans would be below the notice of a God such as he. She could not imagine Zeus showing such compassion. Persephone watched in astonishment as he gently took the hand of a little girl and brought her back to her feet. "You have no need to bow to me, little one. What is your name?"

"Agnete," she replied in a quiet, shy voice, a blush infusing her cherubic face.

"Sacred one. A perfect name for you. You are new here." The little girl nodded. He stood up, lifting the child in his arms. "I would like for all of you to meet my Queen, Persephone. She especially wanted to meet all of you. Can you tell her hello?"

A chorus of cheerful greetings rang in her ears and the crowd around them cheered wildly as some of the children broke into animated dances. She caught the eye of several smaller girls staring up at her with awed faces.

"Hello," she replied with a smile. "I would very much like for you all to call me Persephone."

A girl with small blond ringlets ran to her, hugging her legs tightly and Persephone sunk to her knees returning her hug. Encouraged by the reception of their friend, the children rushed towards Persephone gently touching her dress and hair and taking their turn for hugs.

"You're pretty," a dark-haired girl giggled at her.

"Thank you," Persephone smiled back at her. "I had a lot of help today."

The little girl placed her hands on Persephone's knees and stared earnestly into her face. "Is Kýrios Hades your husband?" At Persephone's nod they looked at her with wonder. "We think Kýrios Hades is very handsome. Don't you?" Many small faces looked at her expectantly and she felt her face grow hot as she risked a glance at Hades. Of course, he was listening, a smug smile on his face as he tossed a ball back and forth with Agnete and several little boys.

"Yes, his majesty is very handsome. But handsome is as handsome does I'm afraid." She shot him a quick look under her brows, and to her annoyance saw he merely continued to look amused.

"Oh no, Queen Persepine!" the child exclaimed loudly.

Persephone hid a smile at the pronunciation of her name, she rather liked it actually. The little girl crawled into Persephone's lap and gazed up at her with a frown on her little face.

"Kýrios Hades is the kindest master. We have many visitors and toys and we never want for anything. He told us that we would never be lonely here. We are happy that he has you, and so neither of you will be lonely now!"

Persephone shifted her eyes from the sweet gaze of the child, turning her head away. If it were only as simple as that, she thought sadly.

They sat and talked for a while longer until Persephone felt Hades' hand at her shoulder.

"We must go, Persepine." She tilted her head back and looked into the laughing black eyes of her husband and could not help her reluctant smile.

When she glanced at the sad little faces, she felt her heart contract. "Can we not stay a bit longer?"

Hades shook his head. "There are many others anxious to meet you. We can return to visit your new friends again soon and better yet, next time we will bring presents!" At that news, the orphans let out several hearty cheers and rushed toward Hades, and Persephone actually giggled as she saw him stumble slightly at the combined weight of all the children.

Hades finally broke free and strode towards Persephone, gently lifting the little girl off her lap. With a movement of his hand he produced a perfect miniature replica of Orphnaeus, golden bridle and all. The little girl squealed with delight and hugged the toy tightly to her chest.

"We will see you again soon, Cora."

Persephone watched with wonder. Did he truly know all these children?

"Come again soon, Persepine," her new friend cried as Hades set her carefully on the ground and took Persephone's hand in his own while Cora took her other one. The little girl accompanied them all the way to the carriage, and Persephone continued to wave until, looking back, Cora became a small dot in the sea of humans.

They pressed on and the crowd seemed endless. Persephone focused on smiling at the blurred faces as they passed instead of the tall God standing so closely next to her. She felt hot and flushed and exhausted. Hades confused her, and every moment she spent in his company seemed to contradict everything she had thought about him. Who was he underneath his dark mask? She had heard him mentioned only rarely by the other Gods and always in hushed tones. She had heard whispers of his wickedness, but it was hard to recall the details. If only she had paid more attention to the lurid gossip of Olympus. She had not imagined the trace of fear his name seemed to inspire even amongst the Gods. He had never attended any of the lavish parties at Mount Olympus. Was he unwelcome? Or did he simply hold such contempt for his heavenly counterparts that he could not bear their company. Her mother had certainly never mentioned him. He said he was cursed now, but what did that really mean? The fact remained that he had forced her into a marriage she did not want, but still... she could not continue to believe that there was not a small trace of good within him. But perhaps, the most surprising thing was, he did not seem to know it himself. She broke from her reverie as she noticed little green leaves that were now mixed in with the confetti. Persephone bent to pick up one of the glossy, green leaves and examined it. She was unfamiliar with this type of plant. Hades looked over as she studied the leaf closely. Did she imagine it or did his mouth tighten as she fondled the little leaf in her fingers?

"What are these leaves?" she asked. "I do not recognize them."

"Those are the leaves from the pomegranate tree. It is the tree of the Underworld."

"How curious that a plant should only grow here in the Underworld!"

She watched as Hades shrugged and if she did not know better, would have thought he was anxious to change the subject. "We draw to the end of the parade, now we enter the celebration," he continued. "Your night of misery will soon be at an end and you can then return to your room to hide from the world."

Persephone pinched her lips together. And just like that she was reminded of why it was so easy to dislike him.

Hades led the horses into a large courtyard and the shouting voices seemed to dim suddenly. Persephone gave a gasp of pleasure as she looked up. The courtyard sky shone brighter than starlight and the lights above twinkled and blinked merrily back at her. How were stars possible in the Underworld? She longed to ask Hades, but after his short dismal of her before, she did not want to give him the satisfaction. She could ask Jocasta later. The chariot drew to a halt and once again Hades leapt down and extended his hand to her, gazing steadily at her. Despite the light all around them, his eyes somehow remained inky black, as though no part of him would ever consent to allow lightness to reach him. A small smile lit his mouth as though reading her thoughts.

Taking a step closer, he murmured, "Are you ready my queen, to dance with the damned?"

Taking a deep breath, she placed her hand in his. Hades felt his heart swell as he looked at his beautiful wife and he resisted putting a hand to his aching chest. Looking at her seemed to make the blood from his wound run more freely, and her perceptive eyes saw far too much. As she placed her delicate hand in his own, he felt a thrill of pleasure all the way to his groin at that small, innocent touch and though his heart soared, his mind was deeply troubled. He needed no more reason to long for his queen, but this arrow seemed to have driven an obsession into his very soul that he could not fight.

He felt it growing with every breath he took. With every pump of his heart the infatuation grew and it flowed through his veins like a sickness -- until he could think of nothing but her, consumed with the very thought of her. If she knew what he was thinking she would throw herself into Tartarus and never look back, he mused with a grim smile.

As he led her closer to the large dancing chamber the sound of voices increased, and he felt her hand clasp tightly on his own. His wife did not enjoy crowds. She was not acknowledging him at the moment which was a blessed relief. When she smiled at him, he thought his heart might burst through his chest all together. She was foolish to let her guard down so quickly. Far too trusting, even of him, who had just forced her into marriage. Her mother had done her no good by sheltering her so fiercely. He needed to try to keep her at a distance until he found a way to get some control over his urges. There must be some way to delay the curse of that damned arrow! But right now, all he could think about was ripping that golden gown off of her pale skin and devouring her, crowded ballroom or not. The thought of what lay beneath that thin fabric made him painfully hard and Hades let out a dark curse letting her hand fall. He felt her gaze on him and he determinedly looked away from her.

"You may proceed me into the chamber. They are waiting for you after all," he stated coldly.

He glanced at her and saw a look of trepidation cross her face, her large eyes luminous in the lighted garden. She thought he was cruel. So be it -- that was better than her seeing the crazed, lust-filled beast that seemed to lurk too close to the surface, shouting at him to take what was his. He quickly looked away from her lovely, innocent face.

"Very well," she replied, failing to hide the slight tremor in her voice.

Head held high, she turned on her heel and headed for the lighted doorway, her long dress trailing after her, leaving him alone with his unwanted carnal thoughts. He watched her rigid back for a moment and then hurried after her like a lovesick youth.

"They will adore you," he leaned to whisper close to her and she gave a small jump.

"Stop doing that!" she hissed at him.

He gave a small smile at her scowl, pleased to see the fear on her face replaced with annoyance. He never wanted her to be afraid. As they approached the door, two servants opened it wide and the music poured from the room. Hades pressed his hand to her narrow back, his hand tingling at the touch of her skin.

"In you go," he murmured and gave her a gentle push.

The large dancing chamber was filled with more of his citizens and as a servant announced their arrival, Hades grasped Persephone's hand and brought her swiftly to the center of the floor. She looked around, distracted by the cheers that echoed too loudly in her ears. She hated this. She hated the noise and the press of bodies too tightly against one another. It reminded her too much of Olympus. But no, that was not right, she thought as she glanced around more carefully. The people here smiled with genuine pleasure, and as far as she could see, there were no orgies ongoing in the crowds. Just smiling happy faces -- pleased to see their King. So, maybe not like Olympus after all. She just missed the solitude of her forests, she thought sadly.

Hades gave a nod of his head to one of his servants and it must have been a signal because the guests quickly began to organize and form a line of procession. The line seemed to stretch end-lessly and one of the servants announced each citizen's name loudly as they took their turns bowing to their King and Queen. A maiden, a soldier, a fisherman, a craftsman, so many she could not remember them all, but Persephone watched them closely as they greeted her and saw no trace of fear or misery in their faces. Why were they so content here, she wondered? As they offered their wishes for their jubilant union she nodded and made polite remarks, a smile firmly on her face even as her head began to ache fiercely. Finally, the last of the crowd approached them, and as they stepped away the lights dimmed, and Hades and Persephone were left alone on the center floor.

"Just follow my lead," he said quietly watching her. "This will be over soon."

Hades whirled her around the ballroom, and he was surpris-ingly light on his feet. Persephone had always loved to dance, albeit in the meadows with a badger often as her partner. She had to ad-mit he was a much better partner than the poor badger that she had forced to join her. Soon the noise in the background faded away as she let her feet follow his. They did not speak to each other, but Ha-des eyes never left her own and she let the rhythm of the dance take over. As he spun her around the room his feet faltered for a moment, and pain flashed in his eyes.

"Is something wrong?" she asked with concern.

He shook his head, looking into the crowd now, avoiding her gaze once again.

"Keep dancing," was his only response.

With a nod of his head the lights dimmed, and other couples took their cue joining them on the floor. The room moved as one as they took the same steps as their King and Queen. The dance of the dead she thought, suppressing a giggle. It was a moment before she noticed her hand was wet. She tried to take her hand from his, but he tightened his grasp almost painfully. She glanced down and gave a small gasp. Blood had covered both of their hands and dripped steadily onto the floor below them.

"You are bleeding still!" she asked, aghast at the amount of blood he was losing.

"Hush," he said with a tinge of anger in his own voice. "Now is not the time to discuss this."

"Have you been bleeding all day?" she queried, returning his tone.

"It is not your concern, Persephone," he replied coldly, not doing her the courtesy of meeting her gaze.

She opened her mouth to reply that she was his wife and then shut it abruptly. Did she want him to think she accepted their vows? She must tread carefully. He was right, he was not her concern. If he bled out all of his immortal blood, it was none of her business. But why did that thought cause her heart to tighten painfully? She closed her eyes as she felt the blood trickle down her arm. How much blood could a God lose? Finally, the dance ended, and the crowd gave a thunderous applause as Hades and Persephone bowed to them.

A chant began to echo through the hall and Persephone felt her body stiffen as she understood their words, "Kiss! Kiss! Kiss!"

Finally he met her gaze and he did not bother to hide his smile.

"An old custom, I am afraid," he whispered to her. She felt her heart quicken as he leaned closer to her and she closed her eyes inhaling his alluring scent. "And one I think we can dispense with

today." She felt his chaste kiss on her forehead and if she was disappointed, she kept any expression of it from her face. The crowd seemed pleased and with another bow, Hades took her arm and led her from the room back into the coolness of the night.

Persephone watched Hades furtively as the chariot moved through the gathering darkness. The crowds had dispersed, and no sound broke the silence save the wheels of the chariot moving swiftly over the land. The shadows moved lovingly over the angles of his dark face and he seemed to become one with the darkness. Was he playing games with her? Sometimes it seemed as though he could not even stand the sight of her, while at other times he seemed to constantly be touching her, watching her with his dark eyes. What was the truth? Perhaps he truly hated this curse as much as she did, and she was a burden. She always seemed to cause trouble wherever she went. Her poor mother could attest to that. He certainly did not seem anxious to touch her now, he stood as far away from her as the space of the chariot would allow. Persephone watched as the wheels ran over the rose petals and confetti, carelessly crushing the lovely colors to dust. For some silly reason the sight of it caused her eyes to fill with tears and she averted her face. She felt his hand on her shoulder and she shook it off angrily. Why was he so attuned to her slightest moods when she could never tell what he was thinking?

"You must be pleased with my compliance today," she said bitterly.

He said nothing and she huddled against the edge of the chariot. She glanced again at him and felt a sudden wild compulsion to attack him, to rake her fingernails down his handsome face until... until what? Her head pounded relentlessly, and she gripped the edges of the chariot to keep herself from moving as she stared sightlessly ahead of her.

The horses rode through the massive gates and she watched as the sun was eclipsed by the darkness of the Underworld. Wanting to cry out for the sun's warmth, she turned to see the doors shut behind her. It was as painful as seeing an animal in the forest close its eyes with the wretched exhale of death. She wanted to beg her husband to leave her behind, but she knew that pleading was useless. Charon was waiting at the doors and Hades stepped down from the chariot to speak with him in quiet tones she could not hear. He turned to his wife with expressionless eyes and helped her from the chariot. She ignored the blood that covered her hand. "Meet me in my study" was all he said and after that, left with the river bearer. And she was once again left alone in the darkness.

Jocasta appeared and swept Persephone into the palace. She tutted at the state of her dress and she was allowed to wash her face while Jocasta repinned her hair. She was then taken to Hades' study, accompanied once again by her giant friend. As the door closed firmly behind her, she surveyed Hades' private room. It was intimate and lavishly furnished. Persephone moved to the open windows and saw that the view looked out over three rivers. She watched the gently churning water for a moment before she turned and gave a sigh of pleasure at the many books she saw tucked away in black marble shelves. Did he pass his nights reading? The thought surprised her but many of the books looked well worn. The fireplace carved from ruby emitted a dancing blue flame that warmed the chill she had felt since the end of the parade. Various forms of weapons hung on the walls and she touched the hilt of a long sword and wondered if Hades ever had cause to use them. She could imagine him coldly cutting down a man, she thought with a shudder. A golden helmet sat on a large ruby desk and she went over to inspect it when a glittering scroll caught her eye. She lifted the parchment and saw it was filled with names, it was a list of souls to be judged and the paper unfolded past her feet. How horrible to have to pass judgement over so many people. She imagined it would weigh heavy on one's heart, even a cold one like Hades, to have to determine how a soul would spend eternity. The good and evil in a person were often separated only by thin lines and sometimes the Gods dealt unfair hands. Rolling the paper up, she studied the rods which were adorned with gold and precious gems which shone brightly in the firelight. She sat the scrolls down next to a vase covered with jeweled flowers, and as she ran her fingers over the sharp stone petals, she felt a deep sorrow. His palace was adorned with riches, but it was hard, cold and lifeless. A chill from the window blew through the room and she shivered, walking to the fire to warm herself. Her head throbbed fiercely and the muscles in her face were tired from the smile she had worn all day. Her chest had a dull ache in it, and she rubbed at the pain absently. What a pleasure the quiet was after the continual noise of today. She wrapped one arm against a nearby column and leaned against it, closing her eyes.

"You must be tired," a deep voice said behind her. She straightened immediately but kept her back to him. She gave her best attempt at a careless shrug and kept her eyes on the flames, resisting the urge to look back at him.

"Oh, are you not talking to me again?" She heard him step closer to her and she watched furtively from the corner of her eye as he poured them both a glass of wine. He approached her carefully, like one would a wild animal in the forest, not coming too close.

"Perhaps we can have a temporary ceasefire for now?" he asked, extending her a glass. "I find that, I too, am tired for the moment. I have things I wish to say to you."

She hesitated and then took the glass from him, sipping it as she watched him over the rim. "What things?" she asked reluctantly. Her curiosity had always been one of her worst qualities. Her mother had warned her about it many times.

Hades smiled and motioned to a nearby daybed and she walked over, making herself as small as possible in the corner. She suppressed a small shiver, and with a stern glance, he unfastened his cape draping it over her. Of course, he had noticed, he noticed everything in his domain. And she was just another sparkly trinket to add to his collection, she thought bitterly. She considered throwing his cape into the fire, but it just seemed wasteful since she was still rather cold. He sprawled on the far end of the settee, extending his long legs with a sigh. She averted her eyes from his tall form and rubbed her chest again and he followed the movement with narrowed eyes.

"Are you in pain?"

She immediately dropped her hand and gave him a withering gaze. "I am not the one with a hole in my chest."

He smiled at her, "True," he said. "And for that I am grateful." He raised his glass to her and sipped from his goblet, staring deeply into the flames of the fire.

She drank from her glass, studying him carefully, mesmerized by the way his throat moved as he drank deeply from his cup and the grasp of his long fingers as they wrapped around the stem of the goblet. He lowered his glass slowly and licked a small drop of wine that trailed down his lower lip and she felt a slow warmth in her belly as she followed the movement with her eyes. His gaze suddenly bore into hers, and he smiled knowingly. Flushing, she quickly looked away and pretended to be fascinated with a loose thread on the chaise -- but it was too late. He knew. Damn him, he knew. She felt her cheeks flame, ashamed at the turn of her thoughts for a man she did not even like.

"We are ill suited," she said with aplomb.

"And why is that?" he asked casually, standing up to pour another glass of wine.

With his back to her she found it easier to speak. "Well, aside from that small fact that I was forced to marry you, I was trying to remember anything I had heard about you. And I was able to recall a few stories."

"Ah, stories," he drawled as he resumed his seat. "I do love a good story." He leaned towards her and she resisted the urge to scoot further away. He clinked their glasses together and then leaned back again. She took a small sip. "And tell me, my sweet wife, what do the other Gods whisper about me when they are high on the mountains of Olympus?"

When she found that she was able to look at him coolly, she saw that shadows danced angrily in his eyes, those black eyes that held such secrets. She hesitated.

He prodded, "Come now, are you such a coward that you cannot finish your tale?"

She sat up bristling and looked him directly in the eye. "They say you are cruel. That you are depraved. That you sought your position in the Underworld for riches and unyielding power over the souls trapped for eternity."

"And what else do they say?" he asked casually, turning his goblet in his hand.

"That you are treacherous, manipulative and unlovable." As soon as the words left her mouth, she regretted them.

She felt a sinking feeling in her chest, but she could not take the words back. For a moment she imagined a flash of emotion other than anger in his dark eyes, but it was gone before she could interpret it. He drank silently from his glass and she sat uncomfortable in the silence. Those words were the malicious whispers of the most depraved Gods she had known. Who were they to pass judgement over anyone? And she was no better for having repeated their gossip. She felt shame at her carelessness.

"Hades," she began, but as she spoke he stood up, moving towards the fire. She watched as he stoked it, causing a log to crash into the embers below where it was consumed quickly by an inferno of blue flame. Hades turned around suddenly and leaned against the hearth, the light placing his face in shadow.

"And does my wife believe everything she hears on the great Zeus' mountain?"

"Your wife," she replied hotly, "believes that sometimes there is a grain of truth in gossip. But she makes up her own mind."

He did not reply and instead watched her from the shadows, the blue flame dancing behind him. She could feel his eyes on her and she wondered what he was thinking.

"I said I had things to tell you."

"About the curse?" she asked.

"In a way," he replied slowly. "But it starts before that." Persephone sensed his hesitation.

"But it all comes back to the curse," she replied angrily, "It is the only reason I am here and the only reason we are having this senseless argument." She stood up and began frantically pacing. "You do not even love me. It is only a spell that makes you believe that you do." She put a hand to her chest, the throbbing driving her mad, but she was too incensed to notice that Hades grasped at his own heart simultaneously.

"Is that what you think, Persephone?" he asked quietly.

She stopped and looked down at the cold metal ring on her finger and said coolly, "That is what I know."

His eyes grew soft as he took a step towards her, "Persephone, I…"

There was a knock on the door, and Charon entered the room and uttered in a strangled voice, "Ares wishes to speak with you."

Hades watched as his wife's face turned pale, "It seems we have a visitor," he stated, "We will continue our conversation at some later point. Charon, take Persephone to her room." He looked back at his wife, her lips bloodless as she stared back at him. "Lock her door. And this time, bring me the key." He waited a moment expecting her to protest, but she merely stared at him with large, frightened eyes. He had asked too much of her today and of course Ares would choose this day to try and threaten him. He stepped closer to her but did not touch her. "Go to bed, Persephone. Tomorrow we can argue."

Persephone watched as Hades left the room. She found that fear seemed to have driven the power of speech from her. She went to the sofa, her fingers trembling as she bent to retrieve his cape, and on a whim, placed her hand where he had been sitting. She felt her heart sink as it came back red with his blood.

Hades walked towards the throne room feeling his blood pump angrily through his veins. Ares thought to come to his kingdom and to scare his wife? He had not missed Persephone's terrified look and it was time someone taught Zeus' spoiled son a lesson. He threw open the doors to his throne room and Ares, the God of War, sat on Hades' throne polishing a dark stain from the edge of his sword. He stayed seated as Hades entered, his blond hair comely against his dark military garb. He shone like a beacon of light in the greyness of the Underworld, but one merely had to stand a little closer to smell the blood that could never be washed away fully from Ares' flesh. Hades may be the God of Death, but it was Ares that laughed gleefully when their souls were ripped mercilessly from their human forms. He gloried in the misery of humans.

"Get up," Hades said silky.

Ares paused a moment and then stood stretching his tall muscular form. "I have been seated too long waiting for you to return from your corpses." He turned suddenly and pointed his sword at Hades, flinging back his golden hair as he assumed what he clearly considered an heroic pose. Hades thought he looked like a pompous ass. "Where is she?" Ares cried.

"She is not your concern."

Ares' perfect face twisted with rage. "You take my soldiers' lives, deplete my armies - and now you take that which is mine. Persephone was promised to me! She is mine!" Ares began to circle him. "Mine to fuck, mine to use, to bear my sons. You sit down here, alone amongst the corpses I send you. You are no God. You probably cannot even get a stiff cock from anything with a pulse."

Hades smiled slowly into the God's enraged face. "You have always been a spoiled boy, Ares. Your father and mother set no boundaries and so you think the whole world exists to serve only your whims. You find pleasure in cruelty and the pain you inflict on others. You play with mortals who have no choice but to obey your perverted demands. Persephone was never yours. She belongs only to herself."

Ares spat on the floor. He snapped his fingers and a flame lit on his palm forming the shape of a naked woman with long chestnut hair. The light cast a shadow about the room of a monster devouring its prey, "How was your wedding night?" he sneered, "Or is she still just your wife in name only? A beautiful Goddess like Persephone would never be satisfied with one such as you. She needs a God like me to keep her satisfied." He grasped the front of his pants crudely as he spoke.

Hades walked close to his nephew and placed his hand over the dancing light, extinguishing the fire. He grasped Ares' hand tightly, knowing he was able to crush the younger God's bones if he had the inclination to. He saw the spark of fear in Ares' blue eyes. It was easy to be brave when you were never challenged by an equal, and the cruelest were always the most cowardly, Hades though with disgust. How many lives had this God destroyed simply for the swiftly fleeting pleasure of killing?

"Hear me well Ares," Hades said in a low voice. "Persephone will never be yours." He removed his hand and ash fell to the floor at their feet. Hades dusted his hands, pleased as some of it settled onto Ares' eyebrows. "See your own way out. My wife waits for me to join her."

Ares' face turned red with rage, blood vessels bulging in his angelic eyes. There was the volatile God Hades knew, the God with the famous short temper that had led to the most gruesome wars the world had ever seen.

"You cannot keep her safe down here forever, Hades," Ares shouted, spittle flying from his lips. Hades turned his back and strode toward the doors. "One way or another, she will be mine." With a wave of Hades' hand, the door closed behind him, shutting out Ares and his demented curses. Charon was waiting for him.

"See that Ares does not make any stops on his way out, Charon. I am going to bed."

Hades entered his chambers and closed the door quietly. Leaning against the wooden frame, he opened his robes and looked down at his chest.The cursed wound pulsed with his heartbeat, still dripping dark fresh blood. It had not healed at all, and if anything, looked worse today. He hit his head several times hard against the wall. It was not just his life at risk, it was his kingdom. His sanity. And Persephone. He had to find a way to undo this. He made his way to his vanity and poured water into a bowl. Taking a rag, he took a deep breath, and then pressed it tightly to the wound. Pain shot through him and he grabbed at the wall for support as black dots danced across his vision. He continued to clean the dried and fresh blood from his chest and arm and then wrapped a fresh cloth around the wound. His hair was damp with sweat by the time he finished tending his injury. He felt as if he had just battled the chimera! Hades walked to the windows, opening them wide, and he looked out seeing nothing.

"Persephone," he murmured, "It was never the arrow that made me love you." The wound suddenly pulsed violently in his chest and he fell to his knees in agony as images of Persephone writhing naked in his bed filled his mind. His head pounded relentlessly as erotic images flashed through his thoughts, tormenting him,

arousing him. Her voice whispered wicked things to him, how she longed for him, wanted him to touch her. His hand travelled down to his painfully engorged shaft that pulsed in rhythm to his throbbing chest, and he grasped it tightly in his hand, imagining it was her that touched him. Debauched thoughts crawled out of the dark matter of his brain, go to her room like an incubus. He stumbled like a blindman to his door, his footsteps carrying him to her, to give her what she had asked for. But she had not asked for it, his rational mind whispered, she had not asked for any of it.

He walked like a man who had too much wine, back to his bed and pulled a white gown from it. Her wedding dress; it had been simple enough to restore it from the fire. He lifted it to his face and smelled her fragrance on it, the fresh scent of the forest. His cock pulsed angrily, wept at him for his impotence. He pulled apart his robes and began to rub her dress against himself, rubbing her essence over his body so it mingled with the masculine scent of his own arousal. He imagined it was her silken mouth between his legs, her soft hands on his cock, and it was only moments later when he shuddered with a blinding climax. As he emerged from the blackness, a small voice at the back of his mind whispered back, madness. He jerked himself awake. Madness, this was madness. His hands shaking, he threw down the wet gown and bolted his door. He threw himself down on his bed breathing heavily. The curse was beginning to take control of him. How long could he fight against this powerful force?

He closed his eyes and breathed painfully, pushing the mania deep down inside of himself, as deep as it could go. This was not love; it was a dangerous obsession -- how long before it would consume him completely? He brought his fist to his face and kissed it.

A pale light glowed between his clenched fingers and he reverently opened his hand. A golden thread lay on his palm. He held it tenderly in his hand gazing down at it. Along the fibers was a dark brassy indention that faded to a deep black. Hades ran his fingers over the mark inspecting it intently. "What have we here?"

CHAPTER
V
EXPLORING

PERSEPHONE LAY ON the grass, her eyes closed as the sun overhead warmed her body. The gentle buzz of insects filled her ears and she hummed along quietly to their sweet melody. It was a perfect day and Persephone felt peace in her heart. A shadow suddenly passed overhead, and she opened her eyes to see a dark figure towering over her, blocking the light. Strong arms grasped her painfully and she struggled in vain against their strength. A voice whispered into her ear, "You are mine." And she felt the darkness overtake her.

She woke up mid scream, her clothes damp with sweat. Panting wildly, she flung herself from the bed and took deep gulping breaths. It took her a moment before she realized she was still in her dimly lit room in Hades' palace. "It was only just a dream," she reminded herself, wrapping her arms tightly around her body, "just a dream." She walked over to the fire and leaned against the hearth, hoping the warmth would take away the chill that seemed to have settled into her soul. She had had bad dreams before, but now her waking hours were also a nightmare. She wondered what Hades had said to Ares. Had he come looking for her to demand she fulfill their engagement? Or perhaps there was some other score to settle between these two Gods who seemed determined to control her. She stretched out her arms and tilted her head to look at the ceiling, noting that it was entirely made of jade. He may be God of the Dead but he certainly enjoys having precious jewels around every corner of his castle, she thought with a grim smile. Constellations and stars crafted from gold stretched over the entire high vaulted ceiling, almost reminding her of her nights on the meadows. Almost. But it was just an illusion, nothing more. Her room, like everything else she had seen in this palace, was opulent. Her bed, fireplace and vanity were carved out of precious stones and seemed to emanate a gentle glow in the darkness that reflected off the white marble on the floor.

The quartz fireplace featured lavish engravings of Eros and Psyche. Running her hands over the coldness of the stone she thought of how passionate their love was. How Eros hid his identity from her when she believed him to be a monster. It was too late by the time she had discovered the truth of his goodness - for they were parted again. How tragic their tale of passion. Oh, how they were punished for their love. Tracing over the contours of the figures, she felt a flutter in her heart. How gentle Eros had been in his devotion. It was one of her favorite tales. And how very different he was from her husband who found such pleasure in pain.

There was a knock at the door breaking her from her reverie. It must be morning she thought dully, and she would have liked nothing better than to bury herself back under the blankets. Why did they even bother to knock when the door was locked from the outside, Persephone thought grumpily. The heavy door was unbolted and the eager, smiling faces of Phoebe and Cleo appeared wishing her a good morning as they carried a platter of fresh fruit and a flagon of hot malted wine. They laid their trays across the table and Jocasta appeared with an equally cheerful smile holding a new gown, long, white and flowing with what appeared to have another scandalous neckline. Was there no end to his depraved wardrobe choices, she wondered, feeling her mood turn more sour.

"And what has my husband planned for me today?" she asked. "Perhaps he wants me to take a swim down the River Styx so I can admire more of his Kingdom." She was still standing by the fire and she bit her lip to stop herself from continuing. She had no right to take out her frustration on these poor women, but she felt almost helpless against the spiteful words that seemed to spill from her lips. Feeling like a caged cat with its fur set on end, she dug her fingers into her hands as she pictured her husband's cold arrogant face. Nothing seemed to touch him. Persephone jerked herself away from the hearth as a sudden irritating itch moved under her skin and for a moment it seemed to center painfully on her chest. Catching her breath, she pressed her hand to her heart.

"By no means, your majesty," Jocasta replied, her voice seeming to come from a distance. "His highness must attend to his subjects and today you are to do naught but rest. I expect you are very tired indeed."

Persephone placed one hand on the mantle, breathing deeply as the painful sensation passed. Her chest had seemed to ache exactly where the arrow had pierced Hades' flesh. She hated to admit, even to herself, that this wretched curse was affecting both of them. The anger she felt was replaced with weariness and she sunk down heavily in the nearby chair.

Jocasta glanced back at her, a look of concern crossing her kindly face as she hurried towards her. "My lady, are you ill?"

"No, Jocasta," Persephone replied shaking her head. "I am fine. A little tired is all. You are right, I shall rest today, I think."

"Think nothing of it your majesty. We will help you dress and then leave you." With a snap of her fingers they quickly helped Persephone into the long flowing gown, that she had guessed correctly, plunged deeply down the front. A thin golden necklace was fastened around her neck dangling between her breasts, and a golden belt was buckled around her waist. Her hair was loose around her shoulders, slightly curled, and a golden band was placed around her head.

"There," Jocasta said, stepping back to look. "You look lovely, my Queen."

"Thank you for your help," she said with a wan smile, lying back on the chaise and closing her eyes. "I will rest now."

The servant inclined her head and gathered the discarded clothes in her arms before heading towards the door, the two younger servants following behind like loyal ducklings. Jocasta turned around suddenly, causing Cleo to bump into her. "Oh, your highness, I almost forgot."

She opened one bleary eye, "Yes Jocasta?"

"Hades has given you permission to leave your room. You are free to roam anywhere there is not a locked door."

Persephone sat up instantly, all traces of fatigue leaving her body.

Jocasta smiled as she turned to leave. "I will leave this open behind me then, shall I?"

The thought of exploring was too tempting. What did Hades do during the day anyway? She stood up and went to the door. Besides, now was the perfect opportunity to find a way out of here. With that cheerful thought she slipped from the door as quietly as a shadow.

She moved stealthily through the halls, still fearful someone would catch her and make her return to her room. Even the giant who had guarded her door was gone, but she did not want to take any chances. It would be just like Hades to tell her she could explore only to lock her away again. Why had he decided to trust her now, she pondered suspiciously? More of his games most likely. Her feet were quiet as she made her way down the dark corridors. So far, each door she tried was unlocked and every room was adorned in different gemstones or precious metals. One was made entirely of gold, the next, a ballroom of silver and sapphire. There was no end to the opulence of this palace, she thought, as she exited a room that was composed of glistening emeralds. But the palace appeared to be almost entirely devoid of any inhabitants.

She heard raised voices and quietly crept towards the sound. It led to a huge black door with a metal handle. Raising a hand, she jerked as hard as she could on the handle, but it did not budge. She waited a moment to see if anyone inside had noticed her attempt to enter, but when all was quiet, she began to assess the door. Hades had said she could only go into the unlocked rooms, but no one had said anything about listening, she thought reasonably. There was a small crack a little lower than eye level, so she bent and put her eye to it. It was the throne room and a man was kneeling before Hades.

She let out a gasp as she looked at her husband. If she had thought Hades had been unfeeling towards her, it was nothing to how he looked now. As he gazed down at his prisoner with eyes blazing furiously in his dark face, she saw him for the first time as he was -- the God of Death. He was terrifying in his coldness and she felt a shiver run through her. She wondered if the prisoner could see as she did, the doom written plainly in Hades' eyes. She heard voices but could not make out what was being said. Hades stood up suddenly, moving swiftly to the bowed man, a black chalice in his hand. He wrapped his pale hands around the man's throat and began to force a glistening red liquid into his mouth. Persephone gagged and averted her eyes, remembering her wedding day when he had done the same with her.

She slowly turned her eyes back to the scene and saw the man try to stand. He was off balance though and he fell several times, finally trying to crawl away, but Hades jerked him up and whispered something in his ear. The man replied, spit frothing from his purple lips as Hades threw him back to the floor and the prisoner lay motionless. For a moment, her husband disappeared from her view and she hoped it was over, but when he returned, he held a glowing hot iron in his hand. She let out a cry at the same time as the wretched man when Hades pressed it firmly into his flesh. For a second, her husband seemed to glance towards the door, but he quickly turned his gaze back to the man's searing flesh.

She felt tears well in her eyes when Hades leaned down and pounded his fist into the man's chest ripping his heart out. The yells of agony turned into brutal wailing that hid her own terrified screams. Blood dripped down Hades hand and arm as the heart beat frantically in his grasp. She saw him squeeze the beating heart until

it almost burst, then shove it back into the prisoner's chest. "Send this animal to Tartarus," Hades bellowed. The guards drug him away as he howled with rage and madness.

Persephone fell backwards landing awkwardly on her wrist as she dry heaved on the floor. She lay for a moment, willing her stomach to calm down, but she heard movement behind the door and got up quickly, holding her aching wrist to her chest. She could not stay here--she must leave! She hurried quickly down the hall-ways. There must be a way out of here, she thought desperately. Dear Gods, not only had she married a God she did not love, but he was deranged! He had shown no remorse as he had torn that poor man's heart from his chest. Why would he commit such an atroci-ty? He was the epitome of ruthlessness! Her hands trembled as she pushed open door after door, searching desperately for the means to return to the Gates of the Underworld. At one point she heard a chattering of voices and swiftly swerved to her left going through a darkened tunnel. She felt hopeless and she was beginning to think she was terribly lost rather than on her way to escape. She had no idea where she was now, and it seemed impossible to navigate the maze of Hades' palace.

She heard a shuffling noise and as she turned carefully around a corner, she froze in her tracks. Barring her path was a large black dog that emitted a low growl at her approach, the hair raised on his shackles. The growl however was not what had caused her pause, but rather the three heads with three pairs of golden eyes and three sets of very sharp teeth. She held her breath uncertain whether to try to run or to stay where she was. Would Hades allow a three-headed man-eating dog to roam freely around his castle? After what she had just witnessed, she was certain the answer was -- yes. One of the heads suddenly winked at her and a large pink tongue rolled from his mouth. She had a great affection for dogs and perhaps, despite his unusual head count, he did not intend to maul her. He was, after all, still a canine regardless of how many heads he possessed. She extended her uninjured hand carefully, and after a pause, all three heads approached her with cautious interest. Persephone held her breath for several moments as her hand was carefully inspected and then licked solemnly. Smiling, she extended a pat to the wet nose of the closest head and he suddenly rolled onto his back to reveal his soft belly.

"What a good boy," Persephone crooned to him, scratching his wiry fur. She noticed a collar around his neck with an inscription. Cerberus. "Cerberus," she repeated. "Why that is a lovely name." The six eyes looked at her adoringly. "Cerberus, can you show me how to get home?"

The dog bounded swiftly to his four large paws and trotted happily ahead of her, his tail wagging like a pendulum behind him. He took her a different way than she had come and every now and then one of the heads looked back to make sure she was still following. Finally, he approached two large black doors and her heart sank as she realized they had gone in a complete circle and Cerberus had led her to an alcove that connected directly to Hades' private rooms.

"Oh Cerberus, this is not home," she said with disappointment. He merely looked at her, clearly pleased with his cleverness, and pawed open the door to squeeze into the room. She felt saddened at the loss of her companion, it was a pleasure to be in the company of a creature who seemed to like her. At least she could find her way back to her room now instead of being lost in the maze of the Underworld, whatever small comfort that was. She turned to leave when a beam of light caught her eye. She hesitated as she saw it was coming from a crack in the rock directly adjacent to Hades' rooms. Just moments ago, she had seen the horrors that lurked within this castle. Did she really want to witness more of the monstrosities that took place here? She hesitated as a thought occurred to her. In his private chambers he might reveal the means to escape or some other vital piece of information she could use to make him release her. It may be worth a glimpse to acquire information she could use against him. Decided, she leaned closer to the narrow opening.

She watched as Cerberus jumped onto the large bed, turning in three small circles, before settling down with a contented sigh. Every eye was tuned to his master and his tail wagged fiercely each time Hades came close to the bed. The bed, of course, was ornate and grandiose, draped in fine dark red furnishings. Hades footsteps were muffled by the plush Persian rug beneath his feet, and she caught her breath as he paused suddenly and began to remove his robes. Persephone looked away feeling her face flush hotly. This was so wrong to watch him when he did not know. She knew she would be furious if the situation were reversed, and whatever crimes he had committed it did not excuse her behavior. But a wicked voice chanted in her mind, he would never need to know. Feeling terribly immoral, Persephone placed her eyes once more at the opening. She gave a quiet gasp. His wound was exposed now and it was still raw and bleeding with thin dark veins travelling out from the original injury. It looked horribly infected and she wondered how he could so stoically endure the pain of such a horrific injury. He wet a cloth and began to gently wash away the dried blood. When his chest was once more clean, he wrapped a fresh cloth around his wound and then began to remove the remainder of his clothing. She felt

her heart pound as she took in his muscular arms and broad chest that tapered into a narrow torso. He was beautiful! Could this God truly be the brother of Zeus and Poseidon? He was so...different. As he turned to wet the cloth once again, his now exposed back was revealed, and she saw the crisscross of scars that covered it. Had he been tortured at some point, she wondered with horror? And what kind of weapon could scar a God?

She let out a quickly suppressed sound as his robes suddenly dropped all together, and she covered her mouth aghast. Had she really just moaned? He was large and erect and perfect, and she had no business looking. Determinedly keeping her eyes above his waist, she watched as he once more began to cleanse himself. His gaze turned to the wall that she was hiding behind and a knowing smile curled his lips. She jerked her head back quickly. Did he know she was there? Oh, surely, he could not know, she thought desperately, she had been hidden from his view. What had she come to, watching the God of the Underworld undress, and worse yet, enjoying it. She was a voyeur! Her face now hopelessly red, she raced to her room and this time it was she who locked the door.

CHAPTER
VI
DINNER

PERSEPHONE HEARD THE pounding on the door and she ignored it as she had since her return to her room, and she pulled the blankets more tightly over her head. She did not want to see the smiling faces of his deluded servants. She had no more desire to explore a castle that was filled with torn out hearts, and she most certainly did not want to see her husband who seemed to both despise and desire her. Hades was truly the embodiment of callousness, and yet inexplicably she could not seem to stop remembering his body as he had undressed. She was clearly sick and there was no cure. Damn this curse! And, no matter how long she pleaded and no matter how hard she looked, she could not find the means to leave this place. So, there was no reason to leave her bed, no reason to answer the door. She would stay here until her mother came to collect whatever remained of her. Demeter would find her in due course.

The pounding eventually stopped, and Persephone closed her eyes. The silence seemed to reverberate in her ears. A moment stretched into hours and she stared upward, watching the stars move across the ceiling. She wanted to pretend it was the night sky, but it was a lie just like everything else in her life. She raised her head as she heard a quiet scratch on the door. It sounded like claws against the wood and she hurried out of bed to crack the door as two black muzzles pushed their way in.

"Come Cerberus," she said eyeing the deserted hallway. The dog padded into the room and she quickly locked the door. Turning back to greet her friend, she studied him carefully. Did she imagine it, or was Cerberus substantially smaller than he had been this morning? He almost appeared puppy-size right now. Maybe fear had increased his size in her mind, or perhaps it was just more evidence of her newly compromised state. With that encouraging thought she threw herself back down on the bed and felt it sink as Cerberus jumped up to join her, pressing his warm little body into her own.

Laying her head next to one of his, she whispered, "Cerberus, how can you stand it here?" His only reply was a soft lick on her nose. "I expect you are as loyal to him as everyone else here."

She dozed for a little while and when she awoke again it was to golden eyes staring into her own. How comforting it was to have a friend here. Feeling slightly more cheerful, she sat up and stretched as Cerberus watched, his tail thumping on the blankets.

"Oh, I know what you would like," she said with a smile. Waving her hands in an intricate pattern a lovely branch fell into her lap. "Would you like to fetch?"

The three heads barked madly, and Persephone shushed him with a laugh. "I presume Hades does not know you are here, so let

us not alert him to that fact." Throwing the stick across the room, Cerberus ran after it, his feet clattering loudly on the floor as the heads growled at each other for the right to the stick. They played an uninterrupted game of fetch for some period of time when the pounding came back.

"My lady, please open the door!"

It was Jocasta's voice. Persephone and Cerberus exchanged a glance, and she did him the courtesy of looking each head in the eye. They seemed to share an understanding.

"I agree, Cerberus, we will not open the door."

Persephone went closer, "Jocasta?"

Relief was evident in the servant's voice. "Your majesty, I have been instructed to ready you for dinner with my Lord Hades."

Persephone shook her head, forgetting that no one could see her. "No, I am sorry, but I will not attend. You may tell him I do not wish to join him for dinner."

There was a moment of silence and then Jocasta's voice slowly replied, "You mean you will *not* join him?"

Crossing her arms Persephone nodded firmly. "Yes, that is exactly what I mean."

There was no further response and it seemed Jocasta had left her to her solitude. She went to the fire and sat close to the flame that somehow still burned brightly. Cerberus curled into a small ball in her lap and she stroked his ears gently. Her stomach gave a loud growl and she pressed her hands against it tightly. One night without food would not kill her, but she regretted not eating some of her breakfast this morning. Poor Cerberus would need his dinner though. When she was certain no one lurked outside her door, she would release him back into the hall and then she would be alone again. She touched the branch gently that was now wet with Cerberus' slobber, studying the small green leaves at the edges of it. Could anything survive in this dark, cold palace?

Waving her hands again, a small leafy plant fell at her feet. Cerberus gave it a dismissive sniff. She picked it up gently stroking its smooth green leaves. Perhaps if she nurtured it and found a way to take it outside the gates and let the light touch it, then it may survive.

She gave a terrified shriek as a voice said menacingly behind her, "Good evening, wife."

Persephone turned her head to look behind her and a thrill of fear went through her as she saw a dark shadow towering over her. Her heart pounded against her chest and she willed it to slow. She remembered how the man had pleaded with Hades in the throne room and his heart had been casually crushed in her husband's grasp. Pleading would not work with the God of the Dead. Setting her plant down gently before the warmth of the fire, she picked up Cerberus and turned to face him. He need not know that she held her trembling hands beneath the dog's body.

"Get out of my room," she said haughtily, pleased by the steadiness of her voice.

His eyes darted to his dog held so complacently in her arms, and then he narrowed his gaze on her face. "Your room, my Queen? Everything in this palace belongs to me. Your clothes. That dog. Your bed." *Her,* she thought. It hung in the air unspoken between them. "Your use of this room is by my pleasure."

Persephone angrily replied, "You think to keep me a prisoner here and not do me the courtesy of having a room? Would you throw your wife into the fiery pits of Tartarus then?"

A muscle ticked in his jaw as he stepped closer to her. "There is much I have allowed my wife. Tread carefully, Persephone, lest you find what a prison is really like. You will join me for dinner."

"I will not!" she said fiercely. "I would rather starve."

"Would you? But I find I am hungry," he said silkily, "and if we do not dine in the hall I will have to dine here. Is that what you want?" His eyes blazed at her, almost feverish in their intensity.

She backed away warily, clutching Cerberus to her chest. "But I--I am not hungry."

He followed her retreat and she felt the wall at her back. "Oh, I think you are, Persephone. I think you are as hungry as I am." She buried her face in Cerberus' fur knowing he was right in front of her, afraid he might see the flare of desire in her eyes if she looked at him. She remembered the long hot length of him, and she felt her body pulse with need even as she willed it to still. His hand was on her jaw, and as he began to press her face towards him, her traitorous stomach gave a singularly loud growl.

Hades laughed. "Enough of this nonsense." Taking Cerberus from her arms he set the dog gently on the floor and grabbed so suddenly for Persephone that she did not even realize it until she was over his shoulder staring at his firm backside.

Persephone was fuming by the time he sat her firmly in the chair at the dining table. She crossed her arms tightly over her beautiful breasts and glared at him as he took his seat across from her. He motioned for a servant to begin to bring in the trays, hiding a smile as she hungrily eyed the plates piled high with exotic meats, fruits, cheeses and nuts. He indicated with a nod that his wife should be served first.

Hades sipped from his glass, "Tell me about your day."

She reluctantly drew her eyes from the plate in front of her that was now overflowing with food.

"It was most illuminating," she said coldly.

"That sounds... enticing. Tell me wife, what did you see?"

She fought a blush remembering his pulsing manhood. "I saw your many jeweled rooms and got lost repeatedly. But you saw the most interesting acquaintance I met today," she nodded her head towards Cerberus, where one black paw was just visible beneath the table.

"Ah yes, Cerberus, my guard dog."

"Guard dog? Is he not much too small for that, some harm could come to him!"

His own plate filled, he picked up a piece of juicy meat and was chewing it slowly, when he choked suddenly at her words. Coughing slightly he replied, "Cerberus can change size at will. He wanted you to pet and coddle him, so he made himself a smaller version of his true form, but when enraged, I assure you, he can grow large enough to fill this room."

He saw her study the small paw again with surprise this time.

"I knew he had seemed larger when I met him this morning. What a clever boy he is."

Hades snorted. "Yes, he is clever. He is not in general a fan of the living, or of the dead for that matter, but it seems you have bewitched him. He protects the gate so no one can enter or exit the Underworld without my consent. He can rip apart a man with his bare teeth if necessary - He is the offspring of Typhon."

Persephone gasped. Typhon was one of the deadliest creatures in existence, a creature who had fought against the Olympians in the Titanic Wars. She knew through her history that it had been long before her time.

"Is Cerberus safe then?"

"On my life. The sins of the father should not pass to the son. I have had him since he was a pup. Cerberus is innocent of any crime." They sat in silence for a moment as she stared down hungrily at her plate. She would not eat in front of him, he thought with a sigh.

"Excuse me," Hades muttered striding to the door, feeling her eyes on his back. He stood in the shadows of the doorway letting the darkness absorb him. When she thought he was gone she quickly devoured her food, glancing now and then at the door. What a stubborn creature she was. Giving her a few moments of privacy, he returned with a sifter of wine and refilled both their glasses, noticing how she stiffened as he leaned closer towards her. He politely ignored her empty plate.

Settling back into his seat he said pleasantly, "I saw you watching me today."

Her cup clattered loudly to the table as wine sloshed over the edge and a lovely blush infused her pale face. "Wh--what? You saw me--?"

"In the throne room," he finished her question with a quirk of his brow, seeing the obvious relief in her wide eyes. "There is no need to be embarrassed, though I distinctly remember conveying to Jocasta that you were only to explore those areas that did not possess locked doors. I assume she did not deliver my message sufficiently."

"No!" she replied quickly. "She did, I just did not listen. But I am not the one who should be ashamed."

"And who should be ashamed then?" Hades questioned.

"You!" she cried with blazing eyes. "I saw what you did to that poor man, you showed no mercy. You were barbaric! No creature deserves that kind of cruelty."

He picked up an orange and rolled it thoughtfully in his hands. "You are a child if you believe that. You have been sheltered in your mother's temple your whole life, you have yet to see the true depravity of man. That "poor man" committed such atrocities in his life that he deserved no kindness in his death. I do not regret my treatment of him. There is no shame in justice being served to those who deserve it. Can you think of no one, wife, who you would like to punish?" he asked with a sly smile.

"No one I would wish to be subjected to that treatment, not even you *husband,*" she quickly retorted.

"Ah, you are too generous, my love." She stiffened at his endearment. "Do you have any questions for me? You saw a soul subjected to the worst treatment a human soul can undergo. Do you wonder where he went? Where the others go?"

She stared stonily at him.

"But of course you do, my curious wife, otherwise why would you watch furtively from peepholes." A blush crept up her face again at his words. She wore her emotions too plainly on her face, no wonder Demeter had guarded her so fiercely. "The ordinary souls," he continued, "go to the Asphodel Meadows. These are souls whose touch on the world will be forgotten soon after their death. The souls who have remarkably changed the world go to Elysium, souls whose names will live on despite the rise and fall of empires. And only the most wicked and depraved, as you know, go to Tartarus, so that they might live out eternity in perpetual torment."

"The parade was in Elysium?" she asked reluctantly.

"Yes. The souls from Asphodel got to spend the day there to celebrate our wedding. Today they are back in the meadows."

"What are the meadows like?" she asked with curiosity.

"Blue skies, lush green grass that stretches on and on forever and flowers everywhere. You would like it. I will take you one day."

She longed to see blue skies again, just not with her husband. "Why is your castle not located in the Meadows or Elysium? Why live in this dark, cold palace?"

"My palace is the gateway to these realms. We do not belong with the dead. My job is to wait for the souls to be judged, separate the wheat from the chaff, and deal out their punishments."

"And you are happy with this day after day? Never being in the light?"

"Happy enough," he replied. "Some are not meant to touch the light."

Persephone considered his enigmatic statement, but then determinedly dismissed it from her mind. His happiness was not her concern, so she turned the conversation to a point more critical to both of them. "Are you any closer to discovering who shot the arrow at you?"

"I am afraid for the moment that still remains a mystery," he replied, his face partially hidden by the shadows of the room.

"Can't you think of any one who hates you enough to curse you?" she asked, disbelief dripping from her voice.

He smiled at her, a dimple appearing on one side of his mouth. "On the contrary, I can think of too many. But have no fear, I am considering each of them. Some have been dismissed as potential subjects, others are still being investigated. Perhaps I should, in turn, ask if *you* have any enemies who may wish to punish you? We may be wrong to assume it was I who someone wanted to harm."

Her face was pale, and she avoided his eyes, "No one comes to mind."

"Have no fear, we will eventually find the culprit," he promised.

"But perhaps when we can discover who it was, we may be able to remove the curse--," she stopped as she saw him shaking his head.

"No, Persephone, it is not possible to remove this curse," he said firmly. He needed her to understand the gravity of the situation. Neither of them would ever be free now, each was irrevocably tied to the other. "The only reason I seek to know the face behind the arrow is so we can prevent them from doing further harm. This damage has already been done."

He watched as her face fell and wished he could tell her otherwise, but this curse was not only permanent, it was fast acting. He felt like a man possessed, like the most wretched of lovesick fools, and he feared nothing would ever be enough to satisfy his need for her. He sipped his wine slowly in an effort to steady his breathing.

The silence once more became heavy between them and he could not keep his eyes from hungrily drinking her in. Her forest green eyes returned his gaze with uncertainty. Did she not realize how much he wanted her?

He stared at her mouth and bit back a groan as her small white teeth dug into her lush lower lip. Almost desperately she blurted out, "I saw the engravings of Eros in my room. I found their story very sad. If only he had been honest with Psyche, she would never have believed he was a monster. Much harm was done by his lies."

"On the contrary, wife," Hades interjected. "Psyche was a

silly woman indeed to allow herself to be swayed so easily from her love. Such cheaply lost affection is not worth any tears. What does a name matter if you have found the soul that calls to yours?"

"A little sweetness to balance your acidity, husband?" she asked with a smile, passing him a honeyed cake. He accepted with a smile of his own. "Had Eros simply trusted Psyche she would not have listened to the malicious words of others. What was she to think when she was met night after night by a faceless being? She believed he would kill her child."

"She let fear control her," he responded. "Her heart knew the truth, but her mind was poisoned by lies. She should have trusted him instead of listening to the malicious gossip from her family. She did not deserve him in the light if she could not love him in the dark." He felt his cock jerk in response to the ferocious look she gave him.

"I think she did what any woman would do in that situation, if she thought her child was threatened. I only wish he could have trusted her, and then in turn, she would have trusted him."

He pressed a juicy melon to his mouth feeling a thrill of satisfaction as her eyes followed the movement. "My Goddess of the Forest, you know better than anyone what happens when a planted seed sprouts and takes root. This is what happened with Psyche and her sisters. They planted a seed of doubt, but it was Psyche alone who nurtured it and allowed it to grow until it consumed her love. The only wisdom gained from this story is how little value you should place in the words of others."

Persephone blushed as she remembered how she had repeated the malicious gossip of Olympus. "I only hope they will find a way back to one another," she said softly.

"Their story has not played out yet." Looking into her sad green eyes he continued gently, "Perhaps they will."

Persephone averted her gaze from his, it felt too intimate to meet his black eyes in the dim light of the dining hall. A large red fruit caught her eye and she reached for it curiously. She had never seen this variety before and she cracked it open, watching in delight as many soft ruby colored seeds poured out. It was lovely. Picking up a seed, she placed it to her lips when suddenly Hades was before her, ripping it from her grasp. He took a cloth and wiped her lips and hands roughly.

"Wh-what are you doing?" she asked, and when she looked up at him, his face was filled with hot rage. She had only seen him this angry once before, in his throne room right before he had ripped out the heart of a man. She shrunk back in her chair watching him with wide, terrified eyes.

He snapped his fingers and one of the servers appeared. He placed the fruit and all its seeds into the hands of the servant.

"Find out who placed these here and bring them to my throne room." His back was to her and it was several moments before he turned around. When he did, his black eyes still blazed. "That is the fruit of the pomegranate tree. I told you it was the tree of the Under-world. If you consume its flesh, you can never leave."

Persephone sucked in a breath feeling fear clamp down on her heart. She had been only moments away from putting the seed in her mouth. She opened her mouth to offer her profuse gratitude when a thought occurred to her and she narrowed her eyes at him. "I thought I was already trapped down here! You said I could not leave, that the curse would not let me leave."

The anger in his face had been replaced by the distant look

that she had come to associate with him. "Ah, my discerning wife, your suspicious nature surprises me. I never said you were bound to the Underworld, I said you were bound to me. *I* will not let you leave, I *cannot* let you leave. It is our fates that are linked, and only by association are you required to reside here."

"It does not sound that different to me," she retorted.

"Then allow me to be clearer," he replied. "If you consume those seeds, by the Law of the Gods, you can never set one foot outside the Underworld. You would no longer be a guest, but an eternal prisoner here."

"Then I suppose I should thank you for keeping me an imprisoned guest," she said bitterly.

"Yes," he said quietly, "perhaps you should. How would you like to start?"

She blinked at him blankly for a moment. "What?"

He walked slowly towards her, "You made the offer, tell me, how do you wish to thank me? There are so many ways you can show me your gratitude."

He stood over her chair now and she held out a hand. "Do not come any closer," she said, her voice trembling.

"You claim you do not desire me?" he questioned.

"I do not! I do not want you to touch me!" she spat out.

He smiled at her slyly, "I think you lie to me, or maybe you lie to yourself. I saw you by my room today. I felt your desire. What a shocking turn of events that was -- my privacy being violated."

She tried to rise from her chair, but he pushed her back down, keeping his hand on her shoulder. She tried desperately to shrug him off, but he remained firmly in place. She stared at the table, feeling her face turn painfully hot. "I--I only watched you because I was concerned about your wound. If you succumb to that injury no one else here would have the means to return me above ground." The explanation sounded ridiculously feeble even to her own ears.

"Oh, Persephone," he replied softly. "What lies you tell; I am surprised Aletheia does not strike you down. I saw you stay long after you saw my wound, I saw you watch as my cock pulsed with need for you, and still you stayed."

"No," she said, but her voice was a fragmented. "I do - do not wish to discuss this. I do not trust you. For all I know you could have shot yourself with that arrow to get a wife to join you here, to make her a prisoner! Let me retire to my chambers."

His grasp tightened on her shoulder, "No, not this time, Persephone. You will stay until we have an honest discussion."

"An honest discussion!" she angrily retorted, her green eyes snapping to his. "You treat me like a pawn in your game of chess against some unknown enemy you either cannot or will not name. You do not trust me, and I will never trust you."

He swept the goblets from the table and they shattered to the floor. His right hand was filled with shards of glass as he went to his knees before her chair. "Persephone," he whispered, his eyes tortured, grabbing her hand with his uninjured one. "I do not use you, I, I..."

But she was too angry to allow him to speak, not noticing that his black eyes were alight with an emotion she had never seen in them. She pushed at his hand and stood, the chair toppling behind her to the floor. Her hands were fisted at her sides. "Today I saw you rip a man's heart from his chest and you express no regret about it and offer no excuses."

He ran his hands through his thick hair holding his head

tightly as though it pained him. When he looked at her again, his eyes were cold and dead, all the spark extinguished. Hades watched her a moment, still on his knees, and then stood slowly. "I told you, he committed unpardonable crimes."

"And you feel no remorse?" she countered.

His black eyes glared into hers. "None whatsoever! I would do it again a thousand times over."

"You are depraved!" she cried.

"You do not know the half of it. And moreover, while we are being frank" he replied, thrusting his face into hers, "I enjoyed it. I relished removing this piece of vermin from the world."

She jerked her head back. "You disgust me, I cannot stay in this sadistic place!" She whirled quickly and ran from the hall hearing a thunderous roar behind her, fear clogging her throat. When she reached her room, she bolted the door behind her and slid to the floor. Rough hands pulled her to her feet, and she let out a gasp of shock as she was pushed against the door.

Hades laughed at her startled expression and dug his fingers into her arms. "You think a locked door can keep me out? We were not finished with our conversation. You...," he hissed, "You and your little seeds of doubt. Your preconceived notions that I am the monster. I find it interesting that my beloved should assume the best of all others and the worst of her own husband. Let me tell you of that man you defend so nobly. He murdered women and children by cutting their hearts out. He reveled in it, bathed in their blood and desecrated their bodies. The little girl from the parade, Cora, ask her how she died, what he did to her. His soul is blacker than the deepest pits in hell. Now he will be forced to feel the crimes he committed every day in Tartarus. He is the monster, he is the sadist."

"Stop," she cried, "I do not want to hear anymore!"

"But you wanted the truth from me, Goddess. While we are being honest," he grasped her hand and pressed it against his bloody wound, letting out a moan. "I would be lying to say I did not want your hands on me." He brought her hand down over his stomach, all the way to his aching cock, his black eyes blazing wildly. "The truth… is often… wicked," he whispered against her ear. She could feel his long length beneath her palm and the intelligent thing would have been to remove her hand, to have given him a strong tongue lashing and send him on his way. She should not be touching him, she had no right to touch him. All that was between them was a curse and anger. But almost against her will, her fingers tightened just slightly around him and a flicker of surprise crossed his face. She felt him swell in her grasp as he pushed himself more tightly into her palm, while there was an answering dampness between her thighs. And she hated it, hated the depravity of it, the slip on her own control. But, a small part of her, the dark part she hid inside of herself, lifted its head and burst free and relished it, rejoicing in the loss of her restraint. She felt his hot mouth at her neck and closed her eyes against the sensation, even while she sought it. He wedged his thigh between her legs, and he seemed to rub at some sensitive part of her that caused her to gasp as little white lights danced behind her eyes. He pushed her more tightly against the door and it shuddered loudly at the combined force of their bodies. The rational part of her brain blushed at the noise, but then his mouth moved to the wide expanse of her exposed chest and all thoughts fled. He bit down with enough force that she felt a delicious tingle begin at the center of her body and she pushed the aching part of herself against his hard thigh. His hands tugged at her skirts and she felt one hand inch slowly up her leg. As his mouth moved up against her neck again, he grasped her wrist tightly and fear uncurled like a sleeping beast in her mind.

Panic welled in her throat and she pushed at him wildly, but it was not until she let out a whimper of fear that he finally drew his head back to look at her. He still held her one wrist in his hand, the other up her skirts, and he slowly released her even as she felt his bulging erection pressed tightly against her stomach. He studied her for a moment and finally stepped away, turning his back to her, his fists clenched tightly at his sides. Was he angry, she wondered? She opened her mouth and then closed it abruptly. There was nothing she could say to make this situation better and it just so happened that she was beyond the power of speech at the moment. She closed her eyes tightly, nauseated by the conflicting emotions tearing at her, the lust and fear warring with each other until she wanted to scream her frustration.

"I would tell you to lock the door behind me," she heard him say, "but we both know that would not keep me out. Goodnight, Persephone."

She felt the softest caress against her cheek and when she opened her eyes, she was alone. She looked down and gave a gasp. Going to her knees, she gently touched the withered brown leaves of her plant, feeling a tear run slowly down her cheek. It had died while she had filled her stomach at Hades' table. She pulled her knees to her chest, letting out a desperate sob for the life she had left behind and the future she would never have.

Hades strode back to his chamber in the blackest mood he could recall having in a very long time. She had been terrified and he had been so overcome with desire he almost had not noticed. He had been preparing to take her against the wall when he finally heard her whimper and had seen the fear in her eyes. The curse, the damned curse! He turned suddenly and punched the wall, feeling satisfaction as the marble made contact against his fist. He needed answers post-haste and he could only think of one immortal who might be able to provide them. Brushing at the blood dripping from his hand, he ignored the startled gasp of a passing maid. One way or another, he would find the culprit.

CHAPTER
VII
ESCAPE

W hen Persephone awoke, she was somehow laying in her bed. She had finally fallen into an exhausted sleep before the fire, but must have crawled into her bed and not remembered. She needed to look reality in the face. Hades was ruthless and he showed no remorse for the cruelty he dealt out. He was cold and callous and unforgiving. But in spite of all the horrific things she knew about him, things she had seen firsthand, she desired him and had been a willing participant in his carnal desires. She had felt her unwelcome but heady response between her legs, and even now her womb clenched with need at the memory. If she remained here, what would she become? If she gave into the dark desires that pulled at her, he would rule her, consume her, and she would lose herself in his darkness. She had felt the answering call in her soul, but she was the Goddess of the Forest, a creature of the light. It was time to leave this place once and for all, or there would be nothing left of herself to save. Turning the doorknob, she let out an exasperated breath--it was locked, and the key had been removed. It seemed Hades trust had been temporary. Placing her hand over the keyhole, she pressed small vines into the chamber, twisting and turning them until she felt the lock give way beneath their force. She could not make a mistake this time. Hades seemed to discount her powers and that had suited her needs. Her powers may not be suitable for combat, but they could serve her in other ways. True, she did not have the strength that she had above ground, but she was still a powerful Goddess and the Earth would assist her in escape. He would know she had used her magic to flee and she would not get a second chance to best him. He would not underestimate her twice.

Glancing down the hall she saw it was once again deserted and she picked up her skirts and ran. This time she let her feet guide her, and saying a prayer to her mother, kept her mind quiet. Fear had made her memory hazy, but if she just let herself be, she knew she would remember the way to the river. She recited the incantations of her mother's temple, not letting doubt cross her thoughts. She remembered the feeling of sunshine on her face, the smell after a gentle summer rain, and the sweet cries of a fox cub. Peace settled in her heart and she walked on and on. When she grew tired, she recalled the spells she had learned before she had come here. She recited them over and over again until her fingers sizzled with magic and still, she walked. Triumph filled her when she finally heard the rumbling of water ahead. The river Styx, she thought with elation, staring at its rapidly flowing waters. She knew that Cerberus guarded the gate at the end of the river, but if she travelled against the current, she would avoid her furry friend. She had no doubt Cerberus would return her to his master.

She must be swift now. Luck was on her side for the moment, but she could not trust it to endure. So, she ran and ran until her lungs ached, until the skin began to tear from her feet and blood trailed behind her like a stream of tiny rubies. She only hoped she would not accidentally plunge to her death in this darkness. Exhaustion began to pull at her, but she could feel she was heading up an incline and that surely was promising. She stopped suddenly, gasping for air as she saw a light behind a waterfall opposite the river -- a cave perhaps? Did it lead to an exit outside of the Underworld? She looked at the path ahead and still saw only darkness. It was worth a moment of her time to see if this was a shortcut out. She had been afraid of the shadows of the Underworld, but that was, after all, how she had met Cerberus and she could not keep up this furious pace, she had to rest. Hesitating only a moment, she stepped determinedly from the trail next to the river and approached the small opening.

The sound of the waterfall diminished behind the thick walls of the cave, and only the gentle drip of water broke the silence. The sudden stillness made Persephone take a step back towards the doorway, but then she stopped herself. This could be the exit she had been seeking, she could not be a coward now, not when she felt the sweet taste of freedom in the air. Stepping further inside, she glanced around. Stalactites hung like ice crystals from the ceiling, their tips razor sharp. They could easily impale a man, or even a Goddess, she considered as an afterthought. Suppressing a small shiver, she quietly advanced deeper into the cave, and as the light became brighter, so did the heat. Sweat began to pool on her skin and once again she seemed to be climbing steadily upward. So engrossed was she in her hike that she almost gave a shout of fear when she suddenly came upon an enormous sleeping lion. She held her hands tightly over her mouth, afraid that even her ragged breathing might awaken the beast. Small flames blew from his mouth with each gentle snore and a stream of smoke blew steadily from his nostrils. Thank the Gods it was asleep. A friendly Cerberus was one thing, but she doubted that she would receive the same friendly reception from this creature. She began to back away slowly, when a second head shot up abruptly in the shape of a goat, it's horns mangled against the back of his black head. Did every animal down here have at least two heads, she wondered desperately. Persephone gasped as the head twisted in a complete circle to look at her with gleaming yellow eyes, the dark vertical pupils staring into her own. It would have been almost comical, if it had not been so… terrifying. For a moment, the only sound was the goat's thick lashes fluttering in the silence, like the wings of a dying moth, and the noise sickened her. A dark red stain covered its mouth and she looked down at the lion to see dried blood matting its fur. No, not like Cerberus at all, she thought, feeling bile rise in her throat. She took one step back, then another. Inching slowly away, she kept her eyes on the goat and he seemed mesmerized by her gaze. Her eyes began to water because she knew instinctively that if she blinked, if she looked away for a second, the goat would attack. She began to feel relief as she had almost passed the doorway, when she felt her foot slide on the wet ground beneath. The sound echoed loudly in the chamber as rocks scattered noisily. Her eyes leapt to the lion and she let out a breath of relief to see his eyes remained closed. Her joy was short lived, however, as the damned goat emitted one very loud, very angry bleat. The lion's black eyes shot open with a deafening roar and this time she broke into an all-out run.

The way down was treacherous as the rocks slipped underneath her feet and she could feel the thundering on the ground behind her. Desperately she waved her hands and a wall of thorns grew between her and the beast. The lion gave a cry of rage, but the thorns would not keep him long. She glanced back to see fire flaming from the lion's mouth, and she turned to face her foe, thrusting her hand palm out towards him. Simultaneously, vines wrapped tightly around its mouth and gnarled trees spread up, blocking the path of the beast. The lion gave an impotent roar and one giant paw escaped from its prison and it ripped the flesh of her arm down to the bone. She gave a cry of pain as blood arced across the room landing on the wall of the cave. The goat had watched her silently, its eyes moved to study the bright red blood dripping slowly down the wall and she shuddered as he licked his blood-stained teeth. She turned her back on the lethal pair, one hand clutching her ravaged arm and she continued her descent. She drew an aloe plant from her hand and squeezed its precious juice into the gaping hole, pressing a healing warmth into it. The bleeding abated but the pain continued to pound at her. No matter, she thought with false bravado, she could deal with the wound, but she must not stop. She needed to find the river and continue her path along it. It had been a mistake to leave its safety and venture into the treacherous shadows of this desolate and dangerous world.

She kept her heart steady as she went downhill, desperately trying to relax her mind, but she could not seem to recapture her earlier tranquil state. Her hands shook as she brushed her hair back from her face, and the pain in her arm jolted her with each step she took. Why could she not heal it, she wondered? Was there some type of poison in the lion's paw? But she did not pause to allow herself to examine her wound. She did not have the luxury of time. How soon before Hades discovered she was gone? Perhaps he already had. She did not have nearly enough of a head start. She pressed on, firm in her resolve. Not even when she passed several unfamiliar landmarks did she allow herself to panic. But when the ground began to rise again beneath her feet and there was no sight or sound of the river, she had to admit the truth to herself. She was hopelessly and irrevocably lost in the caverns of the Underworld.

Persephone licked her dry, cracked lips as she paused to lean against a nearby rock. Though this new area was dreadfully cold, her hair was matted to her head with sweat. She cradled her injured arm to her chest and considered her options. No matter how she looked at it, she had never been worse off. She had tried to retrace her steps back but had somehow only ended up more lost. But all was not hopeless, she considered with a grim smile, she had succeeded in one thing -- even Hades would not find her here. She had finally bested her husband. Now she was wandering along a musty corridor and, likely as not, this place would be her tomb. Pushing against the rock, she brought herself back to her feet and found she had to blink rapidly several times to bring the path back into focus. It seemed highly probable now that the beast's claws did indeed have some type of poison in their tips. Could it kill a God? In these caverns, she suddenly felt that anything grotesque or gruesome was likely possible. Keeping a hand along the wall to steady herself, she continued her slow trek to who knows where. She may have walked for minutes or possibly for hours when she suddenly felt a gentle breeze from a tunnel further ahead. She gave a sigh of pleasure as it brushed the damp hair from her face. Perhaps wind meant a way out! She stumbled towards the entrance and paused as she saw it was covered in misty webs that frayed two and fro in the gentle puffs of air. What could spin webs this large? Her mind conjured a man-sized spider and she shuddered at the image. She put a hand to her hot head trying to gather her scattered thoughts and then made up her mind. There was no way back, she had already tried that. She had no choice but to go forward. Was there some type of sleeping monster beyond the web, more than likely, but the fearsomest monster of all was probably stalking her right now. Her husband's handsome face rose into her mind and it was the driving force her feet needed to start moving forward. Besides, she considered ruefully, perhaps the spider would not want poisoned meat. She pulled the finely spun threads down and proceeded into the darkened tunnel. She was blind in the inky blackness, but she stepped as softly as she could. If she was lucky, she could pass through without alerting her presence to whatever creature lived here. The snapping of what sounded like a tree branch startled her, and out of the darkness a head appeared two globelike eyes. A red ring seemed to encircle the pupils, but then they blinked and she saw that they were a guileless blue. She should have known she would have no luck in this cursed place. For a moment they merely watched one another, each waiting for the other to make the first move.

Finally Persephone spoke. Though her voice was quiet, it sounded like a shot in the dark. "Who are you?"

The creature's eyes rolled in ecstasy and as though granted permission to speak, a sweet melodic voice filled the tunnel. "I am Eurynomos." The streak of red flickered once more, and the eyes disappeared momentarily behind a large rock. She heard a wet smacking noise and then the protuberant eyes appeared again. "Oh, dear girl, I can see that you are hurt. Why not ... let me help you? Let me take the pain from your sweet flesh. Come. Oh, commmmmeee closer."

Her tired mind felt compelled to trust the beautiful voice of the creature. She watched him, and as she watched, his flickering gaze danced in the darkness, never seeming to stay in one place. Her eyes grew heavier and she took a step closer to the creature, missing the flare of triumph in its calculating eyes. Suddenly, a voice echoed firmly in her mind, Stop! She hesitated, and when she opened her eyes, she was surprised to see she was now only a few feet away from the creature. A flash of annoyance flared in the deceitful blue gaze.

She shook her head, trying to clear her feverish thoughts. "Do you wish to help me Eurynomos? I am looking for a way out."

"Oh yessss. Yes, I do. But you will not make it far with the scent of blood trailing behind you. Come over here... and let me... Fix. Your. Arm."

A drop of blood dripped to the ground and she saw its eyes follow it hungrily to the floor. She took a step back. Oh no, not again she thought desperately. How many times would something try to eat her today?

"I think-- I think I will go now. I do not wish to trouble you." She backed away slowly, hearing the crunch of branches beneath her feet. The eyes seemed to move with her.

"You do not trouble me; I only wish to help you." Were the eyes closer now? Her own eyes burned with fever and she longed to close them for a moment. But she dare not look away. This creature, her mind warned her, was more deadly than the fire breathing lion.

"But my husband will be looking for me. I have been away too long; Hades will expect me soon."

The eyes bulged even more and then closed as a nauseating groan filled the cave. "Hades! Hades has taken a wife? Oh how... delicious. Mmmmm, it makes me ache with pleasure." They flashed open suddenly and the red had entirely replaced the blue. "Did you stray from the fold, little lamb?"

"Wha-what do you mean? I only wished to explore my husband's kingdom. After all, he rules the entire Underworld, does he not?"

Each step she took, the eyes followed, like a macabre dance.

"Oh, not the whole Underworld. There are some places that even he cannot drive the evil from. Oh ho, oh no, oh how naughty to run away from the King. I am afraid you have traveled too far from his domain now, Goddess. There are such wicked things that lurk in the darkness here."

The eyes were less than an arm's length away from her now, and she imagined a hand reaching toward her in the blackness, grasping for a piece of her flesh. She gave a cry of fear and turned to run when her foot caught in the bramble beneath her. Her leg ripped open against the sharp stone below her and she felt tears fill her eyes as hot blood poured from her calf. She pulled the rock from her leg and gave a gasping shriek as she saw it was the ragged edge of a femur. She ran her hands swiftly over the ground and felt them then: skulls, ribs, fingers... the entire floor was a graveyard of bones. When she raised her eyes again, she looked directly into the round eyes of the beast and with a sickening, brittle sound he stood and finally revealed himself. A large heavy thud hit the floor. It was no boulder Eurynomos had been hiding behind. It was a body, hunched, contorted and lifeless. Hot, putrid breath hit her cheek and she turned her head choking at the foul smell. Those large goblin orbs stared back at her and its features were horrid; large blood red eyes, needle-like teeth, and a beak that had been partially ripped off. Its bluish black skin was that of a vulture; naked and pimpled, as if each feather had been plucked out. Enormous bird-like wings spread up and over its bony spine. She screamed in horror as a long string of drool dripped onto her calf and black smoke burned from her wound as the creature bent down and licked the blood from her leg with its long sticky tongue. It looked back up at her, with those horrid round eyes and three voices of different octaves escaped its mouth, "We are tired of rotten corpses and would love to keep a tasty little living goddess we could feast on for eternity. Eyes, heart, pancreas; we can eat off you forever and you'll regenerate for us to continue feasting. We just have to make sure we eat your legs off every day so you cannot run away like the last one did."

Persephone sat up suddenly and blasted the horrible creature with a burst of wind and it flew against the wall with a sickening but satisfying thud. She rose to her feet, but her vision was blurred and she was disoriented in the darkness. Her feet were wet with blood and sweat, and she felt herself slipping again to the floor. She heard the flapping of enormous wings close behind her and she gave a shriek when its claw like hands wrapped around her leg. She screamed in agony as its sharp teeth dug into her flesh. Over her already bleeding wound, the saliva burning her like acid. It moaned in delight, its mouth filled with her blood and flesh and Persephone vomited on the floor. The eyes rose over her, gleaming with gluttonous lust, and she felt around the ground desperately until she found the edge of a bone. Using all the strength she had left, she stabbed the bone deep into that round, horrible eye and it shrieked in rage. She began to crawl against the floor. "Please," She muttered into the darkness, "please help me." Her heart contracted painfully against her chest and she seemed to float weightlessly in a white light. One heartbeat. Two. "Hades," she whispered.

"Nobody can hear you down here," the demon snarled as its ruined eye dripped black blood. It flew up next to her and dug its claws into her thigh, and the blood splattered from her leg. She clawed at the beast with her hands. "Oh, it fights us, oh it hates us. We do like it when the food fights back." It took her leg in its mouth dragging her further into the darkness. "We will eat your liver first."

Persephone lay limply as the creature drug her roughly through the graveyard of bones. She opened her swollen eyes and saw something on the horizon. She tried to focus. Had she imagined that distant spark in the darkness? Raising a hand, she opened her mouth, but she could not seem to make a sound, the poison had taken root and she was so tired. Her gown was sticky on her skin and she knew it was clotted with her blood, her life force pooling to join the other corpses that littered the ground. She felt the cold darkness pulling at her and her lashes fluttered over her eyes. And then she saw it again. The small light. It was growing stronger until a purple aura appeared high on the rocks and she wondered if it was the dawn. The light began to travel towards them, hurtling at a great speed, and she risked a glance at the demon, but its ruined eye was facing the beacon. She felt it whoosh, the light rushing over her to hit the demon, throwing him far from his prey. But the demon could not keep her feverish attention. Persephone watched with astonished interest as her husband jumped off the highest peak and began to prance down the rocks like a stag. He lifted a staff in his hand and blasted Eurynomos with another bolt of light.

The creature howled its rage as it stood on powerful hind

legs and Persephone cowered back pressing herself into a small ball, but it seemed to have temporarily forgotten its dinner. It began its undulating motion again, the one good eye bulging madly at Hades and a guttural laugh exuded from deep within its throat. The smell of sulfur became overpowering as black, putrid smoke billowed from its mouth, clogging her throat. She wanted to dry heave at the sickening smell, but she pushed the nausea down, afraid to draw attention to herself. The smoke seemed to surround Eurynomos, wrapping around its pimpled, rotting flesh like a lover's embrace while Hades watched with a vague expression, seemingly unbothered by the smoke that reached out tiny fingers towards him. When the fumes finally settled, Eurynomos had transformed into an enormous decaying vulture. How horrifying, Persephone thought weakly, eyeing her husband to see his reaction. He looked entirely unimpressed. Jumping as lithely as a nymph, Hades inserted himself between her and the giant bird, and even in her weakened state, she felt annoyed that he had not yet acknowledged her. But perhaps he thought she was dead, she reasoned, feeling her limp hand dip into the pooled blood at her waist. It was a fair assumption.

"Are you finished with your theatrics, Eurynomos?" Hades voice rang out coldly in the tomb.

The demon spread its wings and rose high in the air screeching at him, "Your wife is delicious, Hades. She has filled my belly this night. I thank you for sharing her. She is almost as tasty as her husband."

Persephone furrowed her brow at the demon's words, but she could not make out the logic. She watched as Hades' eyes grew blacker, but his voice was serene. "Oh, I never share what is mine, Eurynomos. You made a grave error in touching my wife." He lifted

his staff into the air and blasted the beast with a hot flame. "Let's see how she tastes coming up your throat." He twisted his opposite hand and the animal began gagging, vomiting up the flesh it had just devoured. The beast tried to gobble up the black bloody vomit, but Hades twisted his opposite hand and a sudden snap caused the demon to writhe in pain, its left wing dangling loosely from its flesh. A sickening cry rang out and it half flew, half crawled towards Hades, raking deep furrows into his arm and chest. Hades shrugged off the demon, blasting it against the wall.

The flap of the devil's wings tossed the king's black hair across his face. "I should have fed you to Cerberus years ago! I warned you then to stay hidden in the shadows." He blasted the beast again, burning it with his hands. The smell was revolting; like burnt hair, flesh and defecation. The demon cried, shrinking back to it's pathetic shriveled form, like a baby bird newly hatched.

Its sickening screams tore at Persephone's ears and she shook her head, the movement drawing Hades' gaze. He would kill this vile beast, this hellish demon, he would do it for her gladly. But, his wife seemed unhappy with his decision to use deadly force on the beast.

"You wish me to stop wife? This creature would have eaten you, torn your flesh from you each night, over and over again until you went mad. And still he would not stop. You would beg for mercy and he would return your pleas with a knife to your heart. You wish me to spare him?" She saw the anger burning in his eyes, and she should have been afraid. But she was not.

She licked her dry lips, staring at him from the floor, her eyes blurring as she looked at him. "Not for him," she whispered. "Do not give up a piece of yourself for him."

He lowered his hand and stared at her. Hades knew it was foolish to let the demon go, knew its evil would come back to haunt him. The beast, sensing his weakness, began to slither further into the darkness, its ruined flesh charred and smoking. Hades turned his head and seemed to hesitate, and she breathed a sigh of relief as he stepped towards her, towering over her prostate form. As he bent to pick her up, she closed her eyes, relishing the strength of his arms. "Foolish Persephone. 'Give up a piece of myself' -- You cannot give up what you have already lost." And as she stared into his beautiful face, she did the one thing she had felt like doing since she had first come into the Underworld -- she promptly passed out.

CHAPTER
VIII
HEALING TOUCH

W HEN PERSEPHONE AWOKE, she was in her room. She was back in her prison. How much time had passed was hard to say, as the continual darkness offered her no clue. But as she lay in her bed, in the room she once despised, she could only feel one emotion: elation. Gods! She was happy to be back, and she could almost kiss the floor in relief. She was safe from those murderous, nightmarish creatures that lurked within the depths of this world. Oh, it was so horrible, and they had hurt her so badly. The wounds, she remembered suddenly, had her body flinching at the memory. She struggled to sit up when large hands pushed her gently back down. "Shh, lie still Persephone."

She looked up and Hades was staring down at her. He held a bloodied rag in one strong hand, and she watched as he wrung it out into fresh hot water. Looking up into his stony face, she felt guilt prick at her conscience as her eyes followed the deep bloody furrows that peeked up at the corner of his collar.

"Are you angry?" she asked in a small voice.

"Angry?" he repeated. "Oh, angry does not begin to explain the emotion I am feeling at the moment! That my wife willingly put her life in the hands of depraved, flesh eating monsters rather than finish dinner with her husband is beyond my comprehension. That she ignored my warnings concerning the dangers of other monsters, besides me, is also, beyond my comprehension. But, I think we can table that discussion for another day."

"At least you have never tried to eat me," she said helpfully.

"I would not count on that," he replied darkly.

She regarded him warily, confused by his words. She ought to continue their argument, just for the principle, but she was too tired, the fight had been drained out of her, quite literally.

"It seems you found your powers useful after all," he murmured as he poured several drops of oil into the steaming bowl.

"Perhaps you should not have underestimated the power of a Goddess," she replied sweetly.

"Do not worry wife, next time I will not."

She opened her mouth to deliver a fitting reply when he laid the soaked cloth tightly against the wound on her arm. She shot up again gasping in pain, causing the blanket to pool at her waist. Cool air pricked her skin and she let out a strangled cry as she realized her breasts were exposed, her nipples tight in the cold. She saw his gaze lower while she yanked the blanket back up again and he gave her a serene smile.

"Wh-where are my clothes?"

His eyes stared innocently back into her own. "We had to remove them, I am afraid, to see the damage that was done to you.

Believe me, it was purely for holistic purposes."

She snorted. "We?" she asked giving him an angry glare.

"Jocasta and me. If it makes you feel any better, she attended to the bottom while I did the top."

"It does not make me feel better!" she cried.

"Regardless," he replied, his large hands on her shoulders again, her naked shoulders, right above her naked breasts. She felt a tingle that shot through her core and her nipples tightened for a reason completely unrelated to temperature. "We are not finished yet. You woke, unfortunately, before the healing was finished."

She cleared her throat, trying to ignore her treacherous body. "There was poison?"

"Ah yes, Chimera. Do you feel better?" She nodded, the blanket pulled high to her chin. "I took care of that first, it has to be drawn out slowly. It is a particularly nasty poison. Tell me, what shape did this one appear in?"

"A lion and a goat," she replied with a shudder, remembering the hungry eyes of the goat.

He made a murmur as he wet the cloth again and she let out a gasp as he pulled the blanket suddenly off her right thigh, exposing a pale leg. She fought him for the edge of the cover, but let go with a horrified gasp when she saw the chunks of flesh and muscle missing from her thigh. Hades continued undeterred and began to rub at the wound centered high on her leg, and her pulse quickened as the cloth seemed to graze close to the apex of her thighs. Her gaze shot to his face, but he seemed oblivious to the effect he was having on her. She suddenly remembered the words of the demon -- Almost as sweet as you. The scars that covered his back, had that demon gifted him those?

"Hades," she began slowly, "did you know that creature?" His hand paused above her leg for a moment and then he merely began to clean the blood from her lower leg. Would he not answer her, she wondered?

"Eurynomos and I are acquainted," he replied slowly, as though considering his words carefully. "He found me once long ago, when I too was wandering in the darkness. He has a way of finding lost souls." She was silent for a moment, keeping in mind his words. When had he been lost? He seemed so invincible. His fingers ran down her leg, touching her wound carefully, and she gave a shiver. He smiled at her and moved to her other side to begin the careful administrations there. Gods, she did not know if she could stand it, she thought, biting her lip. The pain and the pleasure were a dizzying combination.

"Why were you lost?" she bit out. She wanted to know -- needed to know.

"I had… suffered a defeat and sacrificed more than I could afford to lose."

She longed to ask more but she knew he would not explain beyond his enigmatic answer. "How did you escape? Did you fight him? It must have been terrible," she finished with a shiver, her wide eyes staring into his. "The pain from it - I can only imagine."

He looked at her now, his face close, a dark lock of hair almost obscuring his eyes. "Yes, the pain was unendurable. He tore at my flesh, devoured my organs day after day, night after night. It was agony and he ate my eyes last so I could always watch him." He paused, his eyes flashing with anger. "And I rejoiced in it. Every bite, every rip of my tissue was succor to my soul. I thanked the Fates that they allowed me to be torn apart, again and again, so that I would never be whole again. I deserved that and more for the things I had done." She sucked in her breath at his words, her hand partially raised of its own accord to comfort him. She jerked it back down to her side. His gaze followed the motion and his expression became bland again as he continued. "Eventually, Cerberus found me and has been with me ever since."

"Cerberus, no wonder he is so loyal to you. And then you punished Eurynomos for eating your insides?"

"No, I punished him for touching my dog. Nobody touches my things."

Placing his hand high on her upper leg, he said "Hold still, so I don't leave a scar." He pushed his hands into the bite, and she felt a warmth infuse her flesh as hot white heat poured forth from his hands, tinged with the purple she had seen in the cavern. When she looked down, she gasped. The wound had completely vanished, not even a small scar marred the whiteness of her flesh. Even her mother was not such a skilled healer.

She bent her leg to study it closer and then she turned to him, smiling. "You truly have a talent! How did you perfect such amazing healing arts?"

His mouth lifted at her enthusiasm. "When you live among the dead you learn quickly to heal yourself." He rubbed her inner arm gently, his calloused fingers trailing over her soft flesh, and she resisted the urge to close her eyes. "What are these," he murmured.

She looked down to where he touched her and saw the scars on her arm from when the Stymphalian had attacked her in her mother's temple. It seemed like so long ago now.

"It was a Stymphalian, he grabbed me too roughly I am afraid. The scars do not bother me."

His fingers grasped her more firmly and once again heat infused her arm. When he removed his hand, only supple flesh remained.

"Why was a Stymphalian hunting you?"

She had been so mesmerized by his touch that it took her a moment to consider what he asked. "I do not know," she began finally, frowning. "It was rather odd. My mother thought Ares had sent them."

His thumb absently traced a pattern over the smooth skin of her arm. And she felt it again, that desperate pull towards him, heat seemed to creep up her neck with every stroke of his hand.

"Interesting," he replied.

Without further discussion, he proceeded to heal each of her wounds, placing his hands over even the smallest mark, and when he was finished her skin seemed to gleam. She studied her arm and looked up at him with a shy expression.

"Could you teach me some time, to heal like you?"

"If you wish."

They looked at one another, and she felt peaceful for a moment, until a thought popped into her head. "But you are so skilled, why can you not heal the wound on your chest? Have you tried to -?"

He gave an impatient sigh, the brooding expression returning to his face. "I told you, Persephone, nothing can help this injury. That arrow was forged by a God and cursed -- by a God. There is only one cure for this wound and I doubt you want to discuss it right now." He turned away from her and she grabbed his forearm and his body tightened at her touch. It was the first time she had even initiated touching him and she did not know which of them was more shocked. He slowly turned to face her.

"I should thank you," she said quietly. "For coming to me when you did. You saved me from a wretched fate."

"I will always come when you call, Persephone."

She gasped. "You heard me, in the darkness?" Her hand was still wrapped around his muscular arm and she knew she should release him, but he felt so warm and she was tired of being cold. She regarded her mysterious husband and said in a whisper, "What was the thing that happened, the thing that made your soul ache?"

"Perhaps," he said, "it was just knowing that I was eternally alone in the darkness." He picked up her hand and pressed it to his face. "This is a place where nightmares seem to come alive. Evil things lurk in the dark, Persephone, and goodness, the smallest flicker of hope draws them out. And you are light itself. Evil will always find you."

She shuddered at his words. "But I am not always hopeful," she said in a small, sad voice. She was tired of denying it, pushing that part of herself down -- the wicked part she refused to acknowledge, but that always lurked in her mind. She needed him to know that she was imperfect. "Sometimes, I feel it inside of me. A darkness that longs to be set free. And I feel I could do anything -- just for a taste of it."

Her gaze sought his, looking for disappointment or even disgust that the perfect Persephone was flawed. But it was not disapproval she saw in his gaze. Instead, she saw heat flare and burn in his eyes and she felt the answering heat, deep in her core, rise to meet him. He still held her hand to his face and her fingers longed to stroke his firm jaw.

"Well my wife," he said finally, "the King of Darkness can

help you with that." And he turned her palm towards his face and bit down into the center. She gave a gasp of pleasure as he licked the pulse beating swiftly at her wrist. She would never know who moved first, but suddenly he was on top of her and the blanket was thrown from her body. She lay naked under his fully clothed form and she wanted to cry with the pleasure of it as the silky cloth of his tunic rubbed against her. She could barely think over the heartbeat in her head and she knew she was drunk on arousal, and that if he stopped, she would scream. Shameful, her mind cried at her, but oh it felt too good to care. If it was the curse that drove them, she just did not give a damn right now. She rubbed herself against him, pressing herself greedily into him as his teeth tugged at her lower lip. She groaned against his mouth as he thrust his tongue roughly into hers and felt one hand travel to her breast. His mouth left hers and she tried to pull him back, but he resolutely proceeded down her neck, past her shoulders, until he paused right above her pink budded nipple, and thought fled when he bent his head. She arched off the bed as she felt his hot tongue lapping at her, but he pushed her back down as her head thrashed madly on the pillow. Tangling her hands in his hair, she watched his dark head through narrowed eyes and the sight was unbearably erotic.

He lifted his head and smiled at her and then his lips took hers again, his long fingers lifting her jaw to allow him better access. He supped from her like she was the finest ambrosia, and when she gave a tentative touch of her tongue, his body jerked over hers. She stiffened, embarrassed she had done something wrong and she tried to turn her face away, but his hand prevented her movement. He whispered in her ear as he bit down gently on the small lobe, "Do that again." So, she did, and this time as he tightened over her, she felt the long, thick length of him pressed against her thighs. It seemed he did like it very much indeed. His hand travelled from her breast, to caress her stomach, and then finally to that aching spot between her legs, where he paused. She almost snarled in frustration.

"Does it ache here, Persephone? Do you want me to make it better?" She felt sweat beading her face and she nodded desperately. "Tell me," he murmured.

"Please," her voice came out a whimper.

She felt him smile against her lips. "Since you were polite my wife."

And then he touched her, and the world vanished for a moment as she felt a white-hot energy begin at that small center of herself. For a moment, pure bliss seemed to fill her, but the black tentacles of fear began to surface and wrap around her, making that white-hot pleasure fade. She felt panic press into her mind as his fingers travelled lower to the place that she ached. Wife. Wedding. No, her mind cried, no she could not bear it again.

She grabbed his wrist. "No," her voice wavered as she pressed her legs tightly together.

He did not seem to comprehend her at first, his hand poised over her exposed lady parts. "No?" he repeated, as though the word confused him.

Her face flamed, he must think her mad. Madder than even he was. He must think her a wanton! Because that is what she thought of herself. She was broken and no matter how hard she tried she could not seem to right herself.

"Do you want me to stop Persephone?" he asked. She nodded and bit her lip that was swollen from his kisses. Kisses she had begged for, Gods -- that she had longed for. He watched her for a moment and then lowered his hand to touch her. The touch was brief but when he withdrew his hand it glistened with a golden iridescence. "And yet you are wet with need for me. So, can you explain then why you want to stop? Do not tell me that you did not enjoy it. I have the proof on my hands." He brought his fingers into his mouth tasting her honeyed nectar. A gentle curve appeared at the corner of his lips.

She blushed furiously at the obvious sight of her arousal and she turned her head from the view. "I--I do not like it. I do not wish to be touched by anyone. You or anyone else. I am sorry, I should not have touched you."

He stood up and she wanted to cry with exasperation and unfulfilled desire as he pulled the blanket back over her body. "Anyone else?" he queried staring at her intently for a moment. "Oh, Persephone, you little liar," he said quietly. "You long to be touched so badly you almost orgasmed with one touch. Sometime soon you will have to trust me with the necessity for the truth. Time is running out for both of us."

He bent and extinguished the candles next to her bed. "Goodnight, sweet wife. If you leave this room again, I will not be responsible for the things that I may do to you."

And then she was alone in the darkness, aching fiercely between her legs and wishing to the Gods she had let him finish what they had started.

Hades quietly slipped from Persephone's room. He had stood watching her for several moments from the shadows as she had shifted her legs uncomfortably. Her hand had travelled several times close to the delicious apex of her thighs, but each time she jerked it back almost angrily. Would this goddess not even allow herself pleasure in the privacy of her room? He had watched like a voyeur, his cock aching furiously, and when he could withstand no more, he turned and left. She had been undeniably and feverishly aroused, as much as he had been. And yet, still she had stopped him. His chest pulsed at him with rage and wept hot blood at his infecundity. How much more of this could they both endure?

He made his way outside, into the quiet darkness, and he closed his eyes for a moment. The sounds of the river echoed loudly through the Underworld. Persephone had been different tonight, her usual fire abated after the torment of today. He would rather she berate and chastise him than to see her spirit diminish. She feared the darkness and Hades could not allow for sorrow to touch his wife. He walked to the edge of the river, and bending down, lifted his hands above the rapidly churning water. A golden light bubbled up from the murky depths. It took great concentration to force the pulsating orb from its comfortable home, but it finally gave way with a last tug of resistance and Hades could almost hear its reluctant sigh. He levitated the orb of light out of the tides and then bent close to it, feeling its warm light throb against him. Leaning down again, he whispered to the river, telling the Styx he was looking for someone, that he needed her to bring a special friend to him. The water splashed back and forth, greeting him joyously, and it bubbled wildly for a moment when finally, a little fawn stepped out of the waves, jumping with long, wobbly legs to reach the shore. Its rump was covered with fine, lovely white dots and its large brown eyes stared up at Hades adoringly. For a moment, it bowed its head towards him and then it jumped towards his chest. He gave a contented sound as Hades caught him and began to dry him vigorously with his cape.

"Hello, little friend," he greeted. He leaned towards the river and whispered, "Thank you, Styx." A gentle splash of the river acknowledged his gratitude and the water jumped to caress him softly. Turning back to the fawn he murmured quietly, "Come, I think there is someone who would like to see you." And then Hades carried both the orb and the little fawn into the castle.

CHAPTER
IX
THE GIFT

PERSEPHONE WAS RIDING a large white stag through the forest. She could feel the adrenaline rushing through the creature and she knew instinctively it ran from something, that some horrifying terror gave chase behind them and if she turned around, if she dared to look, she would look into the eyes of death. The deer leapt over the treacherous terrain and she feared she would lose her balance and that her body would be crushed beneath his furious hooves. But they could not stop, the unknown terror drove both of them. Stopping would mean certain death. Faster and faster they travelled, the branches pulling at her hair and skin causing deep scratches and welts to form. Her thighs clenched tightly against the stag's heaving sides and her heart stuttered as it made its way down to a river, the decline dangerously steep. And then it happened. The stag stumbled and she felt herself flying as a sickening snap filled the silence as she soared overhead. When she landed, she heard the crunch of her own neck and the pain took her breath, but oh, she would not die. She would never be allowed that release, but she could watch the things she loved torn away from her, over and over again until there was no part of herself left. She knew before she raised her eyes what she would see, but even so, she gave a cry of despair as she looked at the stag, blood dripping slowly from its soft black nose and mouth, matting the thick white fur of his chest. Its lifeless eyes stared back at her and then strong rough hands went around her throat.

Persephone awoke mid scream, her loose hair wild about her face. She rubbed her arms and laid there for a moment as her pulse raced madly. It had felt so real, she could still feel the sorrow at the death of the beautiful stag. How many nights must she pay penance? She crawled out of bed knowing she would not fall asleep again, and as she stepped down, a sheer pink gown flowed to her feet. It was a beautiful dress, outlining the shape of her breasts and clinging tightly to her curves, but the strange thing was that she did not remember changing into it. When she had fallen asleep, she had still been naked under the covers, after Hades had... after they had touched each other. She closed her eyes tightly remembering the sweet pleasure -- she had wanted him beyond reason, beyond sanity. Her heart gave a painful twist at the memory.

She remembered the look in his black eyes, the touch of his lips against her breast and it had felt sinfully good. Even now she longed to pull that lovely gown from her body and imagine his strong hands touching her in every intimate place. She longed for his touch. Persephone actually clung to the chair nearest to her to prevent her wayward feet from stepping towards the door. Oh Gods, but this was intolerable. The curse, it must be growing stronger!

She needed to take her mind from him. She stood suddenly and traced the carvings that were etched into the quartz of the fireplace, her fingers running over the delicate images. Did Hades support Eros because he too was often represented as a monster? Why was he exiled to this world? From a purely unbiased standpoint, he was a beautiful God, and she could only imagine how Aphrodite would like to get her gorgeous claws into him. He would be no outcast at the orgies that filled the halls of Olympus. But maybe he had already lain with the Goddesses on the mountain, she considered reasonably. The thought of the Aphrodite's lovely pink lips on Hades' perfectly proportioned ones twisted her belly with an ugly sensation that felt strongly like jealousy, but that surely could not be.

Why on Gaia would she be jealous of Hades' conquests? She was merely grateful to him, that was all. Never mind that he had trapped her down here, she still had behaved extremely foolishly to allow herself to be at the mercy of a demon like Eurynomos. Like it or not, she could only feel a true gratitude to him that he had saved her at great risk to himself. But the attraction was simply due to the curse. It was certainly not due to the way his black eyes flashed, or his sensuously curved mouth, and most assuredly it had nothing to do with the exquisite shape of his muscular arms and body.

She eyed the bottle of wine that Jocasta must have left for her near the chaise, and she walked over and poured herself a large glass. She drank deeply from it. Perhaps with enough wine she could forget the memory of Hades bowed at her breast and the delicious tingle she had felt at the touch of his tongue. Perhaps with enough wine, she could forget the agony of having her body torn apart by Eurynomos. By the time she poured herself a second glass, she felt a lovely hazy feeling and she carried the glass back over to inspect the engravings.

With a rather loud hiccup, she eyed Psyche's sisters with a critical eye. Hades was right, they did look rather malicious, perhaps Psyche had been a fool not to see it. She considered her husband. She could not deny the moments of kindness she had seen in him, from the children at the festival to the many people in his kingdom, even to Cerberus. She had to admit he was not the ogre that she wished him to be, at least not completely. And if she was feeling these wretched urges, how much worse would it be for him, who had been pierced by that damned golden arrow.

As her fingers traced the tears on Psyche's face, she wondered if she was making excuses for him. She was a prisoner here and she was lonely. And she was no stranger to the mistakes that could be made due to loneliness. If Hades could not address this curse on his own, well they simply must consult someone who could. Perhaps her mother would be able to shed light on the matter, and she missed her mother dearly. If she could only see her, she was sure her mother might know a way to fix things. She would broach the subject again when she saw him next, that is, if she could bear to look at him in the eyes ever again.

With another hiccup she sank to the floor and leaned her head back against the wall, feeling a particularly erotic scene of Eros and Psyche press against her back. At least they had enjoyed themselves for a time, she reasoned, even though it had ended so badly. Maybe the interim made the ending more palatable. Her eyes felt heavy but she refused to let them close. If she did, the nightmares would return and she could not bear the thought of seeing the dead staring eyes. She lay like that for some time, and though her eyes continually drifted down, she jerked herself awake each time, denying herself the sleep her body so desperately needed. The glass tipped precariously in her hand, so she took another sip as the red liquid sloshed over the edge. She felt herself drifting off again and her eyes closed for several moments, but this time when she forced them open, she saw two very long, very muscular legs standing in front of her.

"Why are you sleeping on the floor?" his deep voice inquired.

She forced her bleary eyes to open wider and felt annoyed that she had to lean so far back to look up at him. Must he be so tall, she thought irritability. His dark hair fell over his forehead masking his expression, but his lips, well, those looked soft and sensual in his dark face. No matter how ferocious he may be, his lips could never be anything but enticing.

She considered him, staring at his lovely mouth and it took several seconds to realize he had asked her a question. She tried to force her mind to work. What exactly had he asked her? Something about the floor perhaps.

"The floor is quite comfortable," she replied vaguely.

"With Psyche's exquisitely molded breasts pressed against your head? I find that hard to believe."

She pushed her head more firmly against the wall, schooling her face into a serene expression as a particularly sharp portion of Eros' anatomy pressed painfully against her skull.

"I am quite at my leisure," she lied. "Besides, I could not sleep."

"Ah, a guilty conscience disturbing your slumber?" he questioned.

Her heart sped at his question. He could not know how closely he had aimed at the truth.

"No more guilty than yours, dear husband," she countered

sweetly, the end of the sentence punctuated with a particularly loud hiccup. Oh dear, what unfortunate timing, she thought.

"But mine is particularly guilty. How interesting to think that Persephone could have as many dark deeds at her feet as the King of the Underworld." He eyed the glass she held loosely in her hand. "How much wine have you had?"

"Not nearly enough," she replied reasonably. "It is perfectly lovely stuff. I must remember to thank Jocasta for leaving it." She took another sip to emphasize her point.

He leaned down and she sucked in her breath as his long fingers wrapped around her hand, remembering the feel of them wrapped around her breasts. He quickly released her and raised the glass to his mouth swallowing the rest of the liquid. She watched attentively as he lowered the goblet, his lips stained an enticing red. When his tongue licked at the drops, she scowled at him. He had no right to be so appealing, she thought unreasonably.

"How rude!" she exclaimed aloud.

Fortunately, he misinterpreted her meaning. "You will thank me tomorrow. I had not thought to find my very proper wife inebriated at this late hour."

"I am no such thing!" And if her voice slurred slightly it was no business of his. "Why did you come here?" she demanded. "To bother me some more?"

"Ah, what a charming mood you are in. I came to check on you, and I actually have something to show you."

"What?" she asked suspiciously.

"Hmm, I think the suspense will do you good. First we must address my intoxicated wife." He grabbed for her suddenly and before she could protest, swung her into his arms.

"We will do no such thing!" She kicked at him, her small foot connecting with his stomach, but he did not even seem to notice. "You could at least pretend it hurt!" she fumed.

He glanced down at her and seemed genuinely confused. "What?"

"Oh, never mind!" She squirmed as he reached the bed, her face blushing as she recalled what had happened there only hours ago. "The wife wishes to be left alone!"

He placed one knee on the bed to drop her gently on the mattress and she shrunk back when he settled next to her. As he leaned towards her, she breathed in his scent. The slight smell of frankincense teased her nostrils, and he smelled warm and sensual and… she opened her eyes, realizing she had closed them again. His face was close to hers and a smile played about his lips. They stared at each other for several endless moments and she sucked in a gasp as he leaned forward to trace the dark circles under her eyes with a soft caress.

"You are not sleeping, Persephone. Is it the terror of today or is it something else that haunts you?" he asked.

She hesitated a moment and she was so tempted to bare her soul to him, to trust him with her darkest secrets, but fear made her silent. She replied lightly, "Who would not be haunted in the land of the dead? Do you not feel haunted, husband?"

"It would be foolish to allow the dead to haunt you," he replied.

Even in her hazy brain she realized that he had not truly answered her question. She narrowed her eyes and he shook his head, obviously sensing she was about to argue. How odd that he knew her that well.

"But I do not wish to discuss the dead with you, my sweet. Let us leave them buried tonight. I merely wish to help you sleep."

She blinked at the endearment. "And how do you intend to do that?" she asked in a wary voice crossing her arms tightly over her chest.

He followed the movement and laughed. "What a delightfully suspicious mind you have. I will not touch you, I merely wish to lay with you and tell you a story."

"A story!" she exclaimed with genuine surprise. "Where did you learn it from?"

He had laid back fully now, his long legs stretched out, and he placed one arm behind his neck as he glanced down at her with a grin. She felt a flutter in her stomach.

"I was a child once, too, you know," he explained.

She pictured him then, a small pale boy with soft black curls around his face. He had probably been a little imp. Had he known then he was fated to rule the land of death? She discreetly scooted as far to the edge of the bed as possible and then she too stretched out her legs. They were considerably shorter than her husbands. "And who taught these stories to you?"

A shadow passed his face before he replied softly, "My mother."

She studied him closely. It was subtle but she saw the sudden tension in his muscles. She longed to run a hand against his rigid arm, but she knew it was the wine's persuasion, so she kept her hand tightly against her side. He expected her to interrogate him, but she found that for the moment, she was merely content to hear his voice.

"Well, mothers do tell the best stories." She settled her head back with a sigh of pleasure and closed her eyes. "I am prepared to be beguiled by your tale."

"Very well," his deep voice muttered, and she felt a chill go down her spine at the richness of it.

Long... long ago. A mother held her infant to her breast. The new life beat against her heart but something troubled her. She clung to her child as she brushed the hair across his face and she said with a cry. You were born this day - to die. She lifted the baby up towards the light, with sorrow with woe, with terrible plight. She looked at the bundle with fear undisguised - I am sorry my love, but today you must die.

Forgive me my choice, the good mother said. My actions my deeds are ones that I dread. My hand it was forced, a choice I cannot defy. Forgive me my son. I must say goodbye.

You will be wrapped in darkness, you will be wrapped in sin. You will be all alone. You will be trapped from within. But I will always be near you. I hope you can try, to forgive me this evil, of which I comply.

Now hush my sweet child. I hope and I pray. That you will escape. That you will find a way. Until that time comes, please know that I - am setting you free by watching you die.

When he looked over, her eyes had closed and she lay with one small hand tucked under her chin, dark hair curled gently around her face. He lifted his hand and let the silky locks travel through his fingers. Her other hand was stretched towards him almost as though she were reaching for him. She would hate that, he thought with a smile. Her rosebud lips were slightly open, and she looked so innocent he felt his heart twist painfully. Keeping a wide space between them he laid back his head and closed his eyes. It eased the ache in his chest to be near here, even briefly, and he would get up soon and find Charon. He needed to make plans. There were too many unanswered questions and he was letting his obsession with his wife push other matters from his mind. He meant to rest only for a moment, but for the first time in a very long time, Hades drifted into a peaceful, dreamless sleep as his reluctant wife lay curled next to him.

When Persephone awoke, she sighed with pleasure. She felt like she was swathed in a warm cocoon and she snuggled closer into the warmth. It had been a lovely rest she thought happily, and for once no nightmares had haunted her. She kept her eyes closed and then rolled over, opening her eyelids slowly to stare into the dark, enigmatic eyes of her husband. Contentment filled her briefly as she took in his face until her mind processed the situation and then she flushed furiously. His arms were wrapped around her and their noses were almost touching. Why would he be in bed with her! Gasping, she glanced down and was relieved to see that she still wore her nightgown. She recalled her wine-soaked conversation and realized with dismay that he must have spent the entire night with her. His lip curved as if reading her mind.

"Yes, dear wife, you did indeed sleep with the King of Hell," he said as he glanced down, his gaze pausing for a moment at her breasts and then back up to her eyes. "You seemed to have survived the night." He reached out a hand towards her and she gave a squeak of dismay and rolled from the bed to land with a loud, indignant thud. She righted herself quickly, and shot him a glance as she stood to her full height. To his credit he only had a half smile on his face.

"Are you all right?" he asked solicitously.

She cleared her throat and majestically said, "Yes. You may leave now. I wish to get ready for the day."

"You do love to dismiss me," he murmured. His lazy gaze perused her and she forced her hands to remain at her sides when she wanted to push at the heavy hair falling over her shoulders. He rose slowly from the bed and for a moment she was hopeful he would leave so that she could have some time to collect herself, but then he crossed the bed. It was not fair, she thought as she watched him prowl closer to her, that he could look so tantalizing in the morning.

"Do you have a headache?" he asked, his eyes narrowed on her. She realized she had been staring at him like some moonstruck nymph. With dismay she realized she suddenly felt nervous, but instead of delivering a cutting response, she could only shake her head furiously. He eyed her suspiciously and then replied, "Good, because I have a present for you."

He lifted his hands and a sphere of white pulsating light appeared between his palms. It vibrated faintly as he held it between his hands, and Persephone gasped with pleasure. She had never seen anything like this before, not even on Olympus. She stepped closer to the sphere and was immediately infused by its warm glow. She felt something spring into her chest, something she recognized as hope. It had been so long since she had felt its gentle touch. "It is beautiful!" she whispered, touching the edges of the globe. It gave a soft hum of pleasure as though it enjoyed the contact with her as much as she did.

"This is a Helios' orb. It is what we use to light the Meadows and Elysium. This is for your room, so you can tell when the sun rises and sets on Earth. Most importantly, you will be able to grow flowers with it. This is your sunlight." The orb floated into the air and illuminated the bedroom. Hades waved his hand at the constellations on the ceiling and they morphed into a beautiful blue sky. "At night when the sun sets, you will see stars again."

"Oh, thank you," she said quietly, blinking back the sudden tears in her eyes. "I could not ask for a better gift."

He raised his hand. "There is one more gift, Persephone, and I somehow think you will like this one even better."

He motioned toward the door and as she followed his gaze, she could not stop the strangled cry that left her throat. The little fawn was standing in the doorway, its lithe body held up by thin, knobby legs and it had small white dots that formed a heart on its back. She ran towards it, tears leaking from her eyes as she cried, "Olive!" When she reached the deer, they bounded towards each other simultaneously and the deer fell to the ground guarded tightly in Persephone's arms. She pressed her forehead to the fawn's and whispered, "I have missed you so much, my dearest friend." She pressed a kiss to the soft spot between Olive's brown eyes and closed her own, her heart aching with happiness. "I will never leave you again, I promise you. I am so sorry." She felt Hades standing behind her, and she whispered in a tight voice. "How did you know?"

"I found him when he first entered this world; he was lost. I could feel his attachment to you, and I felt your soul calling for his. I knew he was important to you."

She felt a tear roll down her cheek and she buried her face against Olive's soft fur. "I never got to place the coins over his mouth so that the boat could bring him here."

"He told me there was an accident, his neck was broken," Hades responded.

Persephone sobbed, "My sweet friend, you were brave. I ran to find coins, and when I came back, his body was gone. I never forgave myself."

She hugged the fawn and it gave her face a gentle lick. "Thank you," she turned around to look at Hades. "I love him more than anything. I can never repay you for this."

Hades bent down beside her and he gently stroked the fawn. Persephone watched in surprise as Olive closed his eyes happily. He had always been skittish around others, but he trustingly rubbed his head against Hades' gentle hand. Had Hades befriended the little fawn, she wondered? Before she could ask him he stood.

"You are welcome. You do not have to be lonely here," he seemed to whisper the words into her ear, and she shivered at his nearness. He stepped back from her and she grasped his cape between her fingers, halting him.

"Where are you going?" she asked.

He stared down at her and then smiled, "Wheat from the chaff my love," he replied, "wheat from the chaff."

CHAPTER
X
CONTENT

PERSEPHONE SPENT THE next few days decorating the room with Olive as her constant companion. Sometimes Cerberus would paw himself into the room and make her small group a trio. At first Persephone had watched with trepidation as the dog's heads had sniffed and smelled the small fawn, and she stood close lest she need to defend Olive. After several seconds of inhaling the fawn's scent, however, all three heads seemed to deem him as harmless and now, for several hours every day, they curled next to each other on the bed, the four heads snuggled closely together. Persephone had watched with delight as they had chased one another around her room earlier today, Olive's long legs bounding gracefully as the dog panted and nipped playfully at him. With only Olive and Cerberus as company, she was free to transform her room as she saw fit. Pink peonies crawled up and around the canopy bed and patches of soft, green moss now carpeted the floor. A roped swing hung from a willow tree in the corner of the room, while her fireplace was adorned with garlands of flowers. Much to the distress of Jocasta, the pond in the back was filled with blossoming lily pads and even a few frogs could be seen in the depths, but Persephone assured her that this was how she had always bathed at home. The bedroom had been transformed into a garden and for the first time in a long while, Persephone felt content. She would read books on the swing as Olive laid on her lap and a very small Cerberus would curl up at her feet. The room had blossomed, and so had she. Tiny white flowers trailed wherever she walked and even a few could now be found in the hallway that led from her room. As long as she took care to bring the orb with her every day, the flora need not be confined for just her enjoyment.

When the orb dimmed and the stars appeared on her ceiling, she knew it was the night on the earth. She would light a fire, and after placing candles around the room, she reclined on the mossy floor, staring up at the ceiling as the constellations danced across the sky. She was wonderfully peaceful, but she could not help but to wonder what her husband was doing? She had not seen Hades in days. If she did not know better, she would have thought she had imagined the passion brewing between them a few days ago, but she knew her imagination could not be that creative. Was he avoiding her? Perhaps he sought solace in the arms of another and she closed her eyes tightly against the thought, surprised at the pain that image conjured. What did he do in his spare time, she wondered? Certainly, he was not merely working this entire time. She had not ventured far from her room since her encounter with the demon, but it was time that she visited her husband at his work.

She put on a long black robe and made her way down to the

throne room. Olive followed behind her as a trail of flowers blossomed in their wake. She approached the large black doors and hesitated, remembering the horror she had seen behind them once before. But there was no room for cowardice, and she needed to find Hades and see if he had made any progress with the curse. And to make sure he was okay, her mind insisted to her annoyance. She pressed her ear to the cold wood and heard only silence. This time she would be bold and would not cower like a frightened child. Grabbing the iron handles decisively in her hands she threw the doors open and stepped inside. She gasped as a blinding light filled the room and shielded her eyes. As she peered closer into the center of the room, she realized two golden figures stood before her, the taller figure embracing the smaller one. She started moving forward only to see them fade quickly away, taking the brilliant light with them -- only the sound of her breathing filled the room.

She blinked and stared at the spot where they had been, but they did not appear again. The room was empty. "That was very curious," she said slowly to the baby deer. "But in any case, what is not curious here? We may as well enjoy ourselves since we seem to be alone now."

And she swooped Olive into her arms and together they danced. She performed many of the intricate steps she had seen on Mount Olympus as a little girl, eventually transitioning to the country steps of the people who lived near their temple who had never suspected a Goddess had watched them night after night dancing in tune. She finally ended with the dance of the dead that she had learned with Hades after the parade. She was breathless by the time they finished, and with a laugh she leaned against the ebony throne at the front of the hall, letting the fawn slip gently from her arms.

She sucked in her breath the moment the rock touched her skin and stepped back. Two large throne chairs sat side by side, but she knew Hades had always sat alone at the Throne of the Dead. When she had touched the chair, she had felt such strong emotions: remorse, uncertainty, sorrow. He was always so stoic, but were these the feelings he pushed down so deep inside himself that even he did not recognize them? How many souls had stood at the feet of a God who was forced to deal out their judgment? How old had Hades been when he first was given this wretched task? Walking up to the chair, the goddess sat down rubbing a slim hand over the dark stone, letting the sensations fill her. The sense of isolation and forsakenness increased, and her soul gave a small cry of distress at the magnitude of the overwhelming loneliness emanating there.

"You are so alone," she whispered.

CHAPTER
XI
UNWELCOME GUEST

HADES TIED THE sash around his chest tightly to secure the thick robe as he readied himself for the day. It was becoming more and more difficult to hide the blood that seemed to flow continuously from the gaping wound in his chest, but it was imperative that he hide his injury from prying eyes. Even the smallest whisper of a curse could threaten the entire infrastructure of the Underworld, and by association, the world above them. If the dead knew that he was ill the repercussions would reach even Olympus and the pandemonium would destroy everything in its path. It was only a thin line that separated the dead from the world they had previously come from, and that thin line was maintained by him. It was his burden to bear, and he had learned to relish the relentless work of it. Eyeing himself one last time in the mirror to ensure his chest was covered, he left his room.

It had been several days since he had allowed himself to

even look upon his wife, and his wound wept angrily at the loss. He knew she was afraid of her desire, and until he could figure out why, it seemed a safer option for both of them just to simply avoid each other. But every night when he lay in bed aching fiercely with need, he cursed himself most violently.

He pushed open the throne doors deep in thought, and when he looked up he saw her. She sat on the throne chair next to his own, and for the first time this beautiful Goddess of the Forest looked like the Queen of the Dead. A sheer black gown clung to her curves, and were it not for the apt placement of golden leaves, her delicious body would have been entirely revealed by the fabric. A long golden necklace hung from her delicate neck and a matching belt was secured at her narrow waist. Her hair was loose, and the royal crown sparkled on her head. A small uncertain smile lit her face and he forced himself to take a breath. He noticed a small velvet bed placed at the bottom of her chair where Olive was dozing. He approached the throne and took her small hand in his own and the pulse jumped in her pale throat. "My Queen, to what do I owe this pleasure?" he asked.

"I thought I would join you today," she replied in a cheerful tone. "Perhaps this will provide me with a more accurate perspective than standing by the door did."

Hades smiled and reluctantly released her hand taking the seat next to hers. "This is the first time in years someone has made it to this room before me," he quipped.

"That is a feat indeed then. Since you have been so busy these last several days maybe I could be of assistance?" Her voice hitched at the question when he knew she was trying to sound matter of fact.

Did she know the appealing expression that was on her face, he wondered? He should send her away but the temptation to stay close to her was too much to resist. Nodding his head, he picked up the itinerary for the day that lay next to his chair.

"Your assistance would be appreciated." He indicated the parchment. "This list is made by the Judges; Minos, Rhadamanthus, and Aeacus – They sort and judge the souls first and I am given the final say over a select few, if for instance, their placement is unclear, or perhaps if they are very wicked."

"Or very good?" Persephone asked.

"Yes, or if they were very good. The rest I greet and welcome to the Underworld." Hades handed her the parchment and she began reading it. "I always make it a point to meet with the children first and then the elderly followed by the humans who fall in between the extremes of age. Lastly, I meet with the wicked."

Suddenly a bustle of activity came from the door and the Judges entered first, three ancient beings who seated themselves on an ivory chaise. Aeacus sat in the center with a black scepter in his hand while the brothers, Minos and Rhadamanthus seated themselves on either side of him. Several servants then rushed into the room, some carrying parchments, others lining up against the wall, and one carried a crown in his hands. The door closed loudly behind them and Hades glanced at Persephone to see her watching the bustling servants with a distracted air. The servant with the crown approached the throne, bowing before them and after a slight nod from Hades, placed the golden laurel crown on his head and a golden signet ring on his finger. He glanced at his wife and saw she was pulling nervously at her gown and he placed his hand suddenly over hers to still her.

Her pulse beat rapidly against his fingers like the gentle beating of a bird's wing. His sweet Persephone was nervous, and he wondered why she had placed herself in a position where she knew she would feel uncomfortable. It could not be due to concern for him, could it? The thought was too tantalizing, and he would not allow himself to believe such wishful thinking. But the fact remained that she was anxious.

"Do not be nervous, Persephone," he whispered in her ear and her eyes fluttered for a moment. "Only those with impure souls should fear death. For the others, it is merely the second part of their journey."

She swallowed and nodded her head. Placing his hand on the arm rest of the throne, he waited to see if she would place hers over his, the appropriate protocol for a queen as she sat at the right hand of the king, but he would not force her. She hesitated, staring at his hand and then slowly, like a lamb sniffing a wolf, placed her slender one over his own. He wanted to groan with the pleasure of her touch. It was only with great force of will that he directed himself back to his duty.

With a final glance at Persephone, he lifted his left hand and said, "Let them in."

Persephone's hand tightened as the door opened again and a mass of children entered. Hades thumb lazily stroked her wrist and it somehow comforted her as she took in the tear streaked faces of the little ones. Some were babies not even a day old who were carried by mothers with haunted faces, others were older children, alone and terrified as sobs wracked their small frames. She felt tears well in her eyes at the sight of their sorrow and confusion. It was almost unbearable to witness their fear, and for a moment she had to avert

her eyes from them.

Hades spoke then, welcoming them to their new home. He explained that they would be going to the Meadows, where it was always sunny, a place where they would never experience pain or loss again, and that they would not be alone there. With a flick of his hand figures suddenly stepped from the shadows and Persephone felt a moment of alarm as she saw the dark figures race towards the children. As the shadows reached the group, they suddenly materialized and the children were embraced by those they had known in life. Grandparents lifted them high and mothers and fathers hugged their children fiercely. Suddenly the room was filled with laughter and joy until the figures began to fade in shadow once more, this time taking the children with them. The room echoed with silence and only one figure now remained, a small girl with large blue eyes. The little child, who chewed on her thumb, trembled with the sorrow and sadness of Algea.

Persephone glanced at Hades worriedly and he resumed the gently stroking of her wrist. "Little one, do you know no one here?" he asked her in a kind voice.

She shook her head with a small hiccup. Persephone could bear it no longer. She stepped down from the throne and approached the little girl taking her small, cold body in her arms as she wiped the tears from her face. She turned around to see that one of the Judges had approached Hades and they were talking in quiet tones. Turning back to the child, she smiled at her.

"Do not worry, this will be sorted out." Persephone gave a gentle wave of her fingers and a wreath of daisies appeared. She placed the garland on the child's head, eliciting a smile from her.

It was strange, but somehow she knew her name though it

had not been mentioned. "Kynthía, would you like to meet Olive?" At the sound of his name the fawn dutifully trotted over and they played with the deer together while Persephone watched Hades from the corner of her eye. He nodded towards the door and it opened allowing a young woman to step through before it closed again.

She approached the throne nervously and bowed.

"Rise Ianthe," Hades said, and the woman quickly scrambled to her feet. "You did not survive childbirth." His question was a statement as he stared at the woman.

A tear fell to the woman's cheek. "Yes, your highness, my baby lived, but after he was born, I kept bleeding and bleeding. I heard my baby's cries, but I could not go to him and the blood pooled around me until, finally, all I knew was darkness."

The sorrow in her voice made Persephone's heart contract. Why was he asking these questions of the poor woman? She tightened her arms around the child and gave him an imploring look. He spared her a brief glance and shook his head slightly.

"And you know no one else here?" he continued. She shook her head. "Come closer." A look of terror crossed the woman's face, but she stepped towards him obediently and when she was close enough, Hades raised a hand to press against the woman's forehead. He withdrew it suddenly. "I see the love you feel for the child you left behind and the yearning to love that you still have." He stood suddenly and motioned for Persephone to bring the child to him. Persephone stood and carried the little girl in her arms and watched as the young mother stared at her with tears in her eyes. "Would you care for this child?" Hades asked.

"Oh yes," Ianthe whispered, "oh yes, I would do that." The young woman lifted her arms and Persephone placed the little girl gently into them, watching with delight as Kynthía wrapped her small arms around Ianthe. "Thank you, thank you so very much," she cried as she laid her head against the soft hair of the child. Persephone felt her eyes grow damp as they too began to fade into the shadows. Hades stepped towards her and took her hand to guide her back up to the throne once more.

"That was lovely," Persephone whispered.

"Some do deserve a happy ending," Hades murmured.

There was a slight pause as the judges adjusted their lists and Persephone leaned towards him. "Hades," she began hesitantly, "something odd happened when I talked to that little girl. I knew her name, without being told, I knew things about her. It was.. unusual." She meant to say more when she saw an odd expression cross his face, he looked almost.. pleased. "What?" she asked with some concern, but before he could respond the doors opened again.

"Ah, the elderly," Hades whispered to her as groups of grey headed adults entered the room, greeting each other jovially. "They look back on life's mistakes with humor and tell exciting tales. Most of them had learned patience and wisdom by their age and accept the next chapter of their lives with grace."

Each approached the throne, some more wizened than others, but Hades laughed aloud at each of their jokes and looked enthralled by some of the heroic tales they boasted. He introduced them all to Persephone and they looked at her with beaming, rheumy eyes. One particularly ancient man smiled at her with a toothless grin. "How did you meet your lovely bride then, your Majesty?"

Hades eyed her mischievously. "I saw her in a field of lavender and you could say, I swept her off her feet."

Persephone gave him a serene smile. "Yes, you could say we

met at target practice."

As each bowed away from the throne, they too faded into darkness until the throne room was once again quiet. Persephone moved to pick up her list when the door suddenly burst open and a young man strode through, a very alive human man, holding a small harp in his hand. He looked frightened but determined as he approached the throne and Persephone gasped as she glanced at Hades. A harried servant followed in his wake, bumbling explanations to Hades, but he raised his hand to indicate silence.

"Would you like to provide an explanation?" Hades asked in a low voice.

The man raised his head looking into Hades' eyes. "I am Orpheus, and I am looking for my wife, Eurydice," he paused. "I will not leave without her."

"Many men would like their wives back," Hades hissed. "How did you get past Charon and Cerberus?"

Persephone had to admire the young man's courage because he kept his gaze steady on the angry God. She could see the sweat beginning to bead on the man's forehead. "I lulled them to sleep with my Lyre," he replied defiantly.

"And perhaps aided by the Sun God," Hades replied in a cold voice. "No mortal could have survived the descent into the Underworld. Still, you are either a brave or foolish man and I do not often have much use for either."

"I am a man in love," Orpheus replied angrily, his gaze touching Persephone's briefly before returning to Hades. "Surely you can understand that."

She felt Hades' eyes on her and kept her face averted from her husband's. Love forced by a curse, she thought sadly. What a love this mortal man must have to brave the wrath of a God and the terror of the Underworld. She could attest to those horrors first hand. She glanced at Hades under her lashes and saw the stubborn set of his jaw.

"Tell us about your wife," Persephone said in a soft voice.

The human man looked at the Goddess and bowed before her. "May I sing it instead, my Queen?" When Persephone nodded her head, Orpheus pulled out his lyre and sang about Eurydice. He sang about her death, about his heartbreak, and he sang for every soul who could never be with the person they loved. Time in the Underworld stood still and Persephone felt a tear fall down her cheek .

She leaned her head towards her husband and grasped his hand tightly, even as she kept eyes fixed on Orpheus. "Hades, please let them be together," she whispered, "let them have their happiness. Surely, just once in eternity you can make an exception?"

He did not respond and when she finally dared to look at him, she saw he was studying Orpheus thoughtfully. "You may take Eurydice back," he said. The audience in the room gasped and two of the Judges stood with outraged expression on their faces, but Hades once again silenced the crowd with a wave of his hand. "But, under one condition. You must climb out of the Underworld and trust your wife is following behind you. If you look back for her before you reach the top – Eurydice will return to this world, and you will not meet her again, not even in death. Have faith she is following behind you, Orpheus."

Orepheus had fallen to his knees, and when he glanced up tears stained his cheeks. "Thank you, mighty God," the young man said in a trembling voice, "I will not look back."

Hades stared at him and Persephone felt a chill of uncertainty at the shadows in his eyes. "Make sure that you do not. If you trust her, all will be well. Otherwise, you will live with the ghost of regret."

Orpheus was ushered out and Hades stood. "I think this is enough for one day."

He put his hand out and they left the throne room together, Olive trotting contentedly behind. They walked out into a secluded courtyard she had never seen before. It was filled with flowers made of emerald and ruby and a fountain tiled with lapis lazuli sat in the center of the hidden jeweled oasis. Persephone watched with a light heart as Olive walked to the fountain, drinking the clear water. Persephone turned eagerly to her husband with a smile on her face.

"When will we know when Orpheus and his wife reach the top?"

Hades looked down at her with his dark, enigmatic gaze, finally turning away and she watched as he bent down to stroke Olive.

"He will make it to the top," he said with his back to her, "But before he gets there, he will lose faith, look back, and lose her forever. I saw the doubt in his heart. His weakness will cost him what he loves most."

"But you must warn him," she cried.

She grabbed his arm angrily and turned him around to face her and she could feel the strength in his body as he allowed her to move him. Weakness, the word repeated in her mind, she understood it all too well, she thought bitterly.

"Please do not let them be separated. You have the power to stop this! He loves her. Do not let this happen!"

"This loss will inspire something greater," he replied, tucking a strand of hair behind her ear. "It is meant to be. It is fated. He was always meant to lose her."

"It is cruel!" she said jerking away from him. "You are cruel. You gave him hope when you knew that he would never see her again. It would have been better to have sent him away!"

"He was given what he asked for, it is his own weakness that will betray him. And you asked for me to give him what he wanted, did you not? He could have waited for her, lived out his years until death united them once more, but he was not satisfied with that. Whenever possible I do not interfere with the free will of humans, Persephone."

"But you did not mind interfering with mine!" she cried angrily. "Why do you choose not to help them?"

"You forget," he replied calmly, "it was not I who interfered with your free will. In any case, Orpheus will inspire love in hundreds of generations. Is that not enough compensation?"

"I hate this idea of love," she said pacing. "It is cold, painful and punishing. Why even give him the hope? Why pretend? It was needlessly cruel!"

Why indeed, Hades wondered. The truth was, the music of Orpheus had bewitched him. And the sweet pleading words of his wife. He simply could not resist her with the music of the lyre in his ear. He regretted what he had seen in Orpheus' heart, but he could not change it anymore than he could change his own. He understood Orpheus too well, the consuming infatuation, the doubt -- he bore those same detestable traits in every infinitesimal fragment of his wretched soul.

He reached for Persephone and pulled her into him, ignoring as she stiffened in his arms. "Forget Orpheus, he had his time with his wife." He tilted her head back and traced her plump lips with his finger, even as her eyes flashed at him. "I think I deserve some time with my own." He lowered his head and caught her full lower lip between his teeth and bit down hard enough so that she gave a delicious shiver. He rubbed his lips over her own and for a moment she was soft and pliant in his arms. He felt her lips begin to part when she hurriedly shoved him away.

"How dare you," she choked.

Hades dropped his hands and felt impatience and anger pull at his heart, his wound pulsing angrily.

"Something holds your heart back from me," he said, "It is always at the forefront of your mind, but you push it away, hiding it deep inside – a wound that no one else can see." She stepped further back from him and it enraged him that she should fear him. The small tentacles of madness slipped into his mind, and try as he might, he could not seem to push them away. He wanted to make her as miserable as she was making him. He stepped closer to her and twisted his hand with a quiet laugh. "But I can see it, Persephone, even if you will not share with me." With a wave of his hand he drew out her memories and they danced before both of their minds as he caught glimpses of her past, foggy and distorted visions that were fading in and out - flashes of her with a tall, shadowy figure, embracing, kissing, touching. He jerked himself from her mind, his heart beating wildly.

"You…you are in love with someone else," he murmured.

She staggered away from him, almost falling as she looked at him in shock, her cheeks flaming. "No. No, I am not."

Hades breath came in short spurts, it explained everything! Her hesitation to lay with him, her revulsion at his touch. What hope was there of winning her heart now? Jealousy curled like an angry snake around his heart and he felt rage begin to join that ugly emotion. She was his, damn it, and he would not share her with anyone.

"You are a liar, Persephone," he hissed at her. "I saw your embrace. Who is the man? Who is your Orpheus? No wonder you were so sensitive to his plight. Tell me his name and I will summon a misfortune so great he will wish he had never been born. If I cannot have you, neither will he!"

Persephone looked at him with cold dislike. "You are disgusting, you are just the same as all the others! I am nothing more than an object for you to claim. And you wonder why I do not like to be touched? I have seen the weakness of your sex -- enough to revolt me! There is no other man, there is no man at all for me."

Hades sneered at her, stepping closer, too incensed to hear her words. "How you protect your lover. Do not lie to me - I have seen it. You ran to him and kissed him in the forest. You laid with him! I can see his revolting hands running up your thighs. No wonder you dislike lovers separated."

"How dare you!" she yelled, visibly shaking. "Stay out of my mind! Is it not enough you hold my body here, now you want my memories as well? Stay out of my head! You are not welcome there."

"You act as though I have you locked up in Tartarus."

"A kingdom with you is still a prison!" she shouted, "You hold me here against my will and then insult me. You accuse me of things you do not understand, and of which you have no right to know."

He stared at her and then laughed, pulling at his hair. "You think you are in a prison. Have you any idea the torment that consumes me day after day, the poison that seeps through my body with the need for you? My body is a cell that I cannot escape, my mind is an enemy that never gives me rest, and you are my captor, Persephone. You who delight in my captivity."

She stared at him like she was seeing him for the first time, her solemn green eyes looking into his and he felt himself falling into her. He wanted to fall to his knees before her, to bury his face into her soft flesh and let her take away his pain. She raised a hand towards him but he jumped back like Medusa was touching him. It was weakness -- this feeling.

A voice whispered into the back of his mind, "She makes you so...weak". This sick desire to touch her he could not allow himself.

"No," he said in a low voice. "No, I do not want your pity, you fear me. But the truth is your fear is nothing compared to the fear I have of losing myself in the madness of wanting you. Do you think I want to feel this way?I will never be free from this torment."

He turned suddenly on his heel and forced himself not to run from her. His chest was aching and his mind felt fragmented. He had, of course, touched the souls of mad people before and it was eerily similar to the fracture he felt in his own head. A breaking point was coming -- the curse was growing stronger. There was one person he needed to see, one who may hold answers, and he only hoped it was not too late.

Persephone stared after his disappearing form, anger and sadness welling up inside her. How could she long to both comfort him and thrash him at the same time? And underneath everything else that was going on burned the hot flare of desire, an insidious burn that was blooming despite her best efforts to quench it. She wanted to weep in frustration for herself and for him.

But how right he was. She kept secret demons locked away in the darkest corners of her mind. If only she had said how she felt and told him the truth. Why could she not admit that she was lonely? Was it not the very thing that drove her from her mother's temple? She wanted to run after him and tell him that they were in this together and that they would figure something out. He was no more to blame for this predicament than she was. How much she wanted to say but was too cowardly to be as open and honest with her feelings as he just was. She had hidden truths in the dark for far too long, allowing those truths to fester and poison her heart. What was her other choice? To marry Ares? She could never do that!

"I do not hate you, Hades," she whispered, "but I can never love you."

Hades paced in his study and then spoke aloud, "Charon bring Venus to me."

He hated to allow any of the Olympians to enter his kingdom; the games they played held no appeal to him, the stakes were always things that he would never risk. Nothing held meaning for them except to gain power. Venus was perhaps the most dangerous of them all -- with the pretence of love she offered to mortals and Gods alike. He did not trust Venus anymore than he trusted Zeus. They all had their own agenda, but he no longer had a choice. It was one of her arrows that had begun this madness and she may have an idea of how to undo what had been done to him. She may help him -- for a price of course. If she did not, if she was unwilling to offer assistance, he feared what would happen to his kingdom.

Bending over the desk he looked down at the golden arrow, brushing a hand through his hair. The wound in his chest throbbed with a force that would have brought a village to their knees.

"She loves another," he whispered.

The pain could be endured, he had felt pain before, though even having his body torn apart by the demon paled in comparison to this hurt. However, if he lost his mind... well the thought was frightening. Images of his father played in his thoughts and he felt the familiar terror begin to clog his throat. He had learned long ago to suppress those memories, to control his reactions to fear. But he seemed to be losing his grip on his restraint. What scared him most of all was the blinding realization that losing Persephone would be worse than losing himself.

He kept replaying the foggy memory, slowing it down to watch her. The look on her face as she ran to her lover. It had been love in her eyes. How long had he waited to see even a glimpse of it when she looked at him. He looked at his own eyes in the reflection of the arrow. All that glanced back was a hardened and bitter king that no one could ever love.

There was a knock on the door. It was Charon, "My King, Venus wishes to speak with you."

Setting the golden object on a shelf, he let out a breath, "Let her in," he replied, letting the familiar coldness settle over him. Never let them see your weakness, a long ago voice whispered sweetly in his mind.

Venus sauntered into the room. She was so mesmerizing it was almost painful to look at her. Her pale skin emitted a white glow and long silvery hair fell to her feet and topped her head like a halo. Guileless blue eyes stared up at him and it was like looking into a fathomless sea. Perfect, plump pink lips seemed to beg for attention and as she stepped closer the scent of gardenias filled the air. She was beauty itself and Hades fought the need to gag at the cloying flowery smell. He had never liked gardenias. Her nipples were erect under her diaphanous gown and if he looked close enough he could make out the outline of her pink areolas. They regarded one another and then she moved closer to him so that her breasts brushed against his arm as she pressed a kiss against his cheek. He could not be sure if it was the memory from many years ago of those sweet lips wrapped around the cock of Zeus, or the fact that she was every bit as vicious as his brother, but he fought the urge to wipe his face.

"Pluto," she whispered in a throaty voice. "Or do they still call you Aidoneus? I much prefer that name."

"I no longer answer to that name," Hades replied coldly.

She licked her lips. "Very well, Hades, How can I help your majesty? It is such a rare occasion that you seek the presence of the other Gods," she finished with an obsequious smile.

"You know why I sought you, Aphrodite," he said in a low voice. "It was your arrow that pierced me. Tell me how to break this spell."

A look of delight crossed her face and her cheeks flushed even as her eyes dilated. Was she close to orgasm he wondered in revulsion.

"Oh you know the answer to that Aidoneus," she replied drawing out the "s." She stepped closer to him again and ran a finger down his wound towards his groin. He grabbed her hand with just enough pressure to halt her movement and she smiled at him, arousal darkening her eyes as the smell of flowers intensified. He let go of her quickly and a look of anger flickered in her face.

"The love of your queen will break the spell."

He stepped away from her with disgust and rubbed his hand

against his chest, smearing it with blood. "This," he said, showing her his hand, "this is the love of my queen. She does not, cannot love me. There must be another way. Do you know who directed this arrow at me?"

"Your enemies are too many to name, Hades, it could have been any who sought to destroy you and your little wife. You could pierce her heart," Venus continued with a smile. He turned angrily and he felt her step with him, like a malicious shadow whispering in his ear. "Think how lovely it would feel, to have her hot blood all over your hands. Does she not deserve it? Is it not her turn to bleed? It would feel so good to have her beg you to fuck her, just think of you sliding into her warm, tight--"

He twisted towards her and grabbed her roughly, halting her words, his cock aching at the images she was weaving. "Stop it! Find another way to break this spell. You must know!"

Another smile lit her face and he noticed for the first time that she had particularly sharp teeth, like a snake he thought. "But Hades," she whispered, "Persephone does love you." He glared down at her small form and then blinked as Persephone stood before him suddenly. Her green eyes stared at him with unmistakable desire even as she shoved her hand beneath his robes and he groaned as she began to stroke the head of his cock. Her other hand pulled the dress from her shoulders exposing her small perfect breasts. She pulled at one breast with the same motion that she tugged at his cock and he closed his eyes as sensation began to pull at him. He had wanted this for so long, his lust filled mind thought as the scent of flowers filled the air around him. Gardenias. Not the smell of the meadows, the fresh, pure scent of morning. Not Perspehone. He pushed her away from him suddenly and she stumbled to the floor pushing her long blonde hair from her face as she looked up at him with a smile.

"You are growing weaker, King, to be so easily fooled." She spread her legs apart and put her hand between them. "I have laid with both your brothers, I have always wondered what you would be like. Your cock is considerably impressive even among God's standards and there is no reason that Persephone would have to know." She lifted her wet hand to her mouth and licked it, closing her eyes with pleasure. "And I am delicious."

"I desire you even less than my wife does me," he replied coldly.

"Oh Hades, then you must want me very much," she groaned with a little shiver of delight. "She has longed for you for so many years. To love her. To fuck her. Oh, all manner of delightful thoughts," Aphrodite said closing her eyes. "Even I may blush."

Real anger pushed at him, she was simply trying to torment him. Persephone had not even known who he was before he had met her at the fields. He wanted to rip Aphrodite limb from beautiful limb. She knew how much he wanted his wife, how he longed for her to love him.

"Stop playing games with me," he said in a dangerous voice.

"Or what, Hades? What will you do to a God?" The question hung in the air between them. She was ancient enough to know and he could see the knowledge in her face as fear flickered in her gaze. She looked at him for a moment and for once there was no trace of malice. "I do not play games. You should be happy Aidoneus - you have what you desire."

"Not like this. I did not want it like this."

She stood slowly, her large breasts swaying as she smiled again. "It does not matter how we get what we want -- as long as we get it."

He made a noise of disgust. "Of course you think that. You fit in well amongst the Gods, each intent on their own pleasures, a coven of madness."

She fell to her knees before him and tried to pull at his robes again to get a glance. "Speaking of insane," she said casually as she brushed his shaft, "did you forget what is approaching rapidly?"

He grabbed her wrists with one hand and pulled his robes tightly shut with the other. "I do not know what you are talking about," he said through gritted teeth. "And if you try to touch my cock one more time I will cut your hand off."

She pouted up at him, "It would just grow back. Hmm, though, think what we could do with an extra hand," she said, her face alight with interest. "The possibilities are endless. And besides I just want a look. It is so big." She sighed at the look he gave her and then stood up, pressing her erect nipples against his flesh. He tried to push back but she pulled him closer, a surprising amount of strength in her thin wrist. She bent over and whispered in his ear, "Here is my advice then. Pluto, your planet, squares Venus in the sky soon. How well will you be able to hide your infatuation then? You better protect your little lamb, so she does not get eaten by the wolf."

Once again she turned and his wife was before him. She let her gown drop to the floor and this time her fingers curled into herself and the sight of her sweet body was almost more than he could endure, and he pushed her against the desk, pressing his face into her neck.

"Persephone, I love you," he murmured. He heard a quiet laugh and drew back to see the pale eyes of Venus staring into his own.

She stood adjusting her gown and laughed. "Lovesick Pluto. You are pathetic." Venus exited through the doors with a giggle, "Goodbye Aidoneus, protect your lamb. She is so very sweet and you are so very ravenous." With a flick of her fingers she was gone.

Hades stood trembling. How could he be fooled twice by such a cheap trick. The sight of his Persephone naked and willing was enough to cloud his judgement. He brought his shaky hands to his face and felt the sweat dripping off his hair. Pulling a scroll from the cabinet he looked at the transit Venus had warned of. She was correct, it was coming, and soon. Astrologically, Venus squaring Pluto was not a good day. At best, it brought out possessiveness, jealousy, violent behavior in your love life, and it was squaring him. It had happened before of course, but never when he had been cursed. Never when lust and love waged war in his mind until there was nothing left of himself. All his insecurities and wrath would be directed at the one person he did not want to fight. He would get a good taste of the darker side of his soul and he feared what would be revealed. He didn't think he would like the revelation.

He slammed his hand down on the desk, "Merda."

CHAPTER
XII
THE PAST

L IGHT GLIMMERED THROUGH the trees kissing Persephone's soft skin with its rays. She pranced down to the
river and kissed the waters with her fingertips, "Tell me you
love me," she whispered to the shimmering stream, "Tell me."

A hand pushed through the water grabbing her arm and trying to pull her through the glassy water. "Under the Stars," the river
hissed like a snake. The first word reverberated, "Under, under, under…" and then the arm began to pull her down, down, down into
hell.

Olive woke her, licking the tears from her face. She grabbed
the fawn tightly in her arms, crying desperately, "Oh my beauty, my
precious friend. What would I do without you?" Lifting the deer into
the air she cried, "Let us stay here today. We will invite Cerberus
and feast on fruits and a bit of meat for him and we need not see
Hades today…" She bit off her words as she remembered the look

of desolation on his handsome face the previous night. How was he feeling today, she wondered? It was selfish and cowardly to avoid him and their problem would not be solved by her hiding. Besides, had she not done that enough in her life? Her almost entire existence had been spent hiding from the world and that had not worked out too well, had it? She gave Olive a gentle kiss on the nose and then set him beside her.

"On second thought, I will not have him thinking I'm recreant." Jocasta was likely busy and she could manage well on her own. She moved to the mirror and began piling her hair up on her head and kohl rimming her eyes, the little deer watching her. "Olive, find me a dress. One that says I will not bend even if the wind blows!" Morning glories in the room climbed up and she bent her head to greet them and they tilted towards her gently, touching her face with silken softness. Olive's tiny feet tap danced across the stone floor dragging a dark blue toga that sparkled with starlight constellations as if Nyx herself had woven it. Knowing Hades, perhaps she had, Persephone thought wryly.

Her face lit up, "It is perfect!" she exclaimed. "Thank you, Olive." She took the dress gently from Olive's mouth and placed it over her head. "You are right of course, Olive," she said as she quickly began to pin diamond stars in her hair, "I better hurry, I refuse to let him be first to the throne room." She lifted her skirt and ran eagerly to the throne, the small, sweet purple flowers of lobelia trailing behind her. She gave a self-satisfied smile when she saw that the room was empty, she had beaten him again! She was enjoying her small victory, however petty it might be. Hearing footsteps and the shuffling of guards, she knew her husband must be approaching and she wiped the smile from her face, quickly grabbing a nearby

scroll to hide behind. She listened intently as he entered, keeping her eyes fixed before her.

She heard him approach her and she jumped as he took the scroll from her hands turned it around and had a momentary glimpse of his broad chest before he handed it back to her. "You will find it easier to read when not upside down, wife." She blushed and raised her chin as she threw the scroll back onto the table. She gave up the pretense of disinterest and studied his face which was paler than usual, and dark circles stood out in stark contrast under his eyes.

"You look wretched," she said cooly.

"Ah, and a good morning to you too, my beautiful wife." With an exaggerated bow, he took her hand and at the last minute turned it so he was pressing his cool lips against her palm. She felt her pulse quicken and she knew he could feel it against his fingers as he raised his eyes to look into hers. "I hope it is acceptable if I kiss your hand - since my kisses are so offensive to you."

Persephone coldly withdrew her hand and looked back down at the itinerary of the morning, seeing nothing, but making sure at least this time it was facing the right direction. "And will you be reading my mind or just the prisoner's minds today my king?" she asked sweetly.

As before, a servant brought his crown which he placed on his head, followed by the signet ring on his finger. Still not breaking his gaze, he replied, "Well, since I hold you here as a prisoner, I guess I shall be reading all your minds today, my queen." The judges had entered the room and he took a seat on the throne, putting his hand out as he waited for her to rest hers against his palm, "Come now my wife. Is my touch so disturbing to you?"

She reluctantly placed her hand on top of his and he glanced at her, "Your hands are cold."

"As cold as your kingdom, my husband."

His expression was stone as he replied, "But not as cold as your heart, my love."

The doors opened, and the new arrivals poured in, but he found for once he was too weary and in no mood to greet the new subjects. He rested his head in his hand for a moment trying to summon the strength to speak when Persephone spoke up suddenly, graciously welcoming the dead to their new home. Had she picked up on his weariness? It was a struggle sitting next to her as she smiled at the newcomers. She smelled so fresh, like the earth, like a newly grown garden and her every move made him ache with lust and an unwanted sweeter emotion that was too painful to acknowledge. "Futuo," he thought. "I cannot focus today."

Hades could hear the sounds of iron dragging against the ground and knew what was coming next and he sat up suddenly. He did not know if he wanted his wife to see this. With her sweet and noble sensibilities she would not like the retribution he dealt out. He remembered how she reacted when he had ripped the man's heart out and he had done far worse than that before and would still.

"The wicked are coming," he murmured quietly. "Would you prefer to leave?"

She regarded him but he could read nothing in her expression. "I will leave when you leave," she finally said.

"Very well then. I will handle these visitors," he said firmly. "Who better to judge the wicked, afterall." Before she could reply he clapped his hands and the gates opened once more. Hades' demeanor changed and all appearance of fatigue vanished from his face as an icy cold gleam came in his eyes. He placed a hand over his wife's hand and looked to the Judges, nodding. A quiet foreboding hush settled over the room and he felt Persephone's hand tighten over his. The sound of heavy chains against the floor grew louder until finally a man was brought in in shackles by two guards and thrown roughly to the ground.

Hades stared at him in silence for many moments and then finally said in a silky voice, "State your name to the room."

"I am King Tantalus," the man replied, his voice booming with a false bravado.

Hades voice was cold "You are not a King here. Tantalus, kneel before me."

Tantalus was brought before the throne and shoved onto his knees as Hades stepped closer to probe his memories. Tantalus was a selfish and boastful king whose only aim in life was to impress the Olympians, and Zeus had foolishly granted him attendance at Mount Olympus, a rare privilege to a mortal. Hades could see that Tantalus had dined with the Gods and stolen from them, taken the ambrosia back to his Kingdom. But he was worse than a thief. He watched as Tantalus had murdered his own son, Pelops. He had then served his body to Zeus as a surprise at a banquet. The Gods unknowingly feasted on the king's son's flesh. He saw Demeter, her face ravaged by grief as she dined at the table, and afterwards how she had cried in horror at the knowledge of what (who) they had unknowingly eaten. And Tantalus enjoyed every bite of meat. Hades forced himself not to glance towards Persephone. He did not need to see anymore.

"Sycophant," he said in a low voice, "Cannibal. Filicide. You murdered your own child. You filleted the skin off his bones and had your chef harvest his meat and organs to impress Zeus at his dinner table."

"My son should be honored to be in the presence of the Gods," he screamed, spittle flying from his mouth. "Demeter herself feasted on his flesh!" He heard Persephone gasp in horror behind him and he twisted his hand lifting the prisoner up into the air until his feet dangled off the ground.

"You disgust me!" Hades yelled, remembering the look of pleasure on his face as he had partaken of his son's flesh. And the memories blurred as he saw the gleam of pleasure in his own father's bulging eyes as blood dripped from his mouth. He pushed the visions away as he glanced at Persephone behind him and saw the streak of tears on her face. He lowered his hand and forced his thoughts to quiet.

When Tantalus fell to the ground with a bone crunching thud, he said calmly, "Pathetic excuse of a father, to feast off the flesh of your boy. You are no better than Cronos." Hades stopped, and a sinister smile spread across his face, "And you will join him." He lifted his hand and the king wasted away before their eyes, and he let out a gasp of pain, shrieking mindlessly for food and water.

Hades saw Persephone sink back in her chair, clearly frightened by the scene playing out before her. The evil king's memories were too abhorrent and Hades felt the need to punish him quickly and decisively. Retribution for the sins of corrupt sadistic fathers. Hades stepped nearer to the prone figure at his feet and bent to his ear to whisper, "This is my punishment for you, the curse of insatiable thirst and hunger. Never again shall food or water touch your lips. Forever will you be surrounded by food and drink - almost able to grasp it - but never able to reach it."

The king began to sob as the words echoed in his ears and

he licked his dry lips. His bony hands reached to Hades robes as he pulled at them helplessly. "You cannot do this to me, I am a King! I am a King, like you!" he cried.

Hades loomed over the man and replied with a sneer, "And I am a God." He ripped his robes from the already skeletal hands of the prisoner and looked to the guards, "Remove this king." Tantalus shrieked in fear as the guard's drug him by his arms through the door.

After the King, another man came, and then another and another. Persephone had felt pain in her heart when her mother's name had been mentioned by the depraved and monstrously evil king. How Demeter must have suffered to know that she had fallen prey to King Tantalus' savage trickery and she found that she could not be sorry for his punishment. There was an eloquence in the fate that her husband had dealt to him. She watched in silence as again and again Hades was faced with accounts of horrific crimes and he showed mercy to none. Each one was sentenced to a lifetime of pain in Tartarus. When the last man was dragged through the gates, Hades let out a quiet, almost imperceptible, sigh. Persephone glanced at him surreptitiously and noticed that the shadows in his face had increased and his eyes held a bleakness that frightened her. Would he not even show himself mercy? His handsome profile was set in a ruthless expression and she wondered just what had happened last night after he had left her. He looked like the cold and remote God he was, but somehow she was aware that underneath his stern demeanor, weariness eroded him. He would never allow himself the luxury of rest, yet somehow Persephone knew that all she had to do was show the slightest indication of fatigue and he would pause the proceedings. She stifled a delicate yawn behind her hand and felt his eyes on her. He turned to the Judges. "Enough... enough for to-day," he said. As the judges and servants filed from the room, Hades slumped into his chair and rubbed his chest, deep in thought. She wondered if she should just leave him there, thinking that he might get some rest in his throne room. She began to rise when he placed his hand over hers. He seemed unaware that his hand smeared her own with his blood.

"Will you dine with me?" he asked quietly, his gaze still staring straight ahead. She paused only for a moment, and then nodded her head. Of course, he knew her answer even though he was not looking in her direction. He stood, keeping Persephone's hand in his and they left the throne room. He led her up a private staircase, opening a discrete door at the top that led into an intimate, warmly lit dining area. They were high in the castle and large windows dominated each wall showing exquisite views of the Underworld. She wondered just how many rooms this palace held as he pulled back a chair for her. He took his own chair and they sat in silence as the food was served. She shifted uncomfortably in her chair. Despite their often heated arguments, she realized that they rarely had moments of silence between them. A dark lock of hair fell against his forehead and he looked like a lost, lonely boy. What a ridiculous thought, she chided herself. Still, a little conversation may help his dark mood.

"What are the rivers below?" she asked him.

Hades turned towards her and his eyes were almost feverish in the glow of the candlelight. When he spoke, however, his voice was cool and clear. "Acheron is the 'River of Pain,' and the other is the Lethe, which is the 'River of Forgetfulness.' Sometimes the souls drink from the Lethe to forget the hardships they faced above ground."

"They lose their memories?" she asked in surprise. "But what a sad choice to make."

"Is there not a single thing that you would like to forget?" he queried.

She did not answer, instead picking through the assortment of fruits and honeycomb on the table thoughtfully as she considered his words. "Have you ever wanted to drink from the Lethe?"

He tore his eyes from her face and looked out the window - his dark hair obscuring his expression, "I woke up next to the Lethe once -- I do not remember why." She waited for him to continue but his voice simply drifted off, his face still averted from hers as he stared towards the churning river below.

"Is something wrong?" she asked in a soft voice.

He was silent and she wondered if he had not even heard her. He turned towards her suddenly, though his eyes did not meet hers. "King Tantalus..." He paused. "You see, my father, Cronus..." he stopped again. Persephone grasped his hand and was surprised to feel it tremble slightly beneath her own.

"Tell me," she urged.

He raised his eyes to her face and she saw the fire smoldering in them. "That man was so much like my father, hungry for power, lascivious, and paranoid. My father, Cronus, feared one of his sons would steal his throne. I was his firstborn. He swallowed me - trapping me inside him. For years I lived in a dungeon, chained to the walls, alone. Demons in my father's body would tear at my skin and beat me. They shattered all hope out of me. It was an endless death repeated over and over and it was my father who rejoiced in my torment. To betray your child in such a way; it is a crime for which there is no punishment that is fierce enough."

She stroked her hand gently over his and he grasped hers tightly. "I never want to be like him," he said, the words pouring quickly almost frantically from his lips, "I see too much of my father in Zeus, who swallowed Athena and her brother, fearing they would dethrone him. Her brother is still trapped in Zeus' gullet, and it is repulsive. Everytime I see my brother I want to rip his insides open and free the prisoner inside him. I never want to be like that! I said I would never be like that. But then..," he paused.

"But then?" she whispered.

"I see how I have trapped you here, holding you as my prisoner and I realize I am no better than my father. I was born from incest and rape. I could hear my mother's screams from inside my prison when Poseidon and Zeus were conceived. She was terrified of Cronus but completely under his control. He would beat her, rape her-- he cared for no one but himself and he delighted in her pain. And I was powerless to help her."

Persephone brought her hand to his face, brushing his matted hair from his forehead. He leaned into her cool hand, closing his eyes briefly and she could feel the feverish heat of his skin against her palm.

"It was not your fault, Hades. I am sure your mother understood that. You were but a child and your father was a monster, a God that no one dared to cross. Try not to think of these things," she said, "What good will it do?"

His eyes blazed open at her words and she felt fear creep up her spine at the expression in them. "I cannot forget it. The sons are never free from the sins of the father. His blood runs through my veins. That same seed of madness in him was planted in my mother

-- and I grew from that seed, like the sickening perverted fruit from an aberrant tree. You have seen it, Persephone. You saw it on Olympus. The God's, they take what they want - not caring who they hurt. Just as I have done. Their subjects are playthings for their amusement. Zeus changes lovers as often as a man changes his clothes. He rapes and he torments and he will never be checked."

"You are not your father, Hades," she said in a quiet voice.

He smiled at her mirthlessly. "You do not know that, Persephone. You fear me. I have seen how you look at me; I see how you look at me now."

"Well," she said lightly, "do not let it go to your head. I am afraid of everything." He gave her a look and she was pleased to see that a small smile touched his lips. "What of your mother, Hades?" she asked softly. She wished she had not said the words when she saw the pain in his eyes.

"Rhea," he breathed. "My name was 'Aidoneus' then. During those grueling ten years of the Titan Wars, I was given a 'God killing' sword by the Cyclops, along with a helmet of invisibility. A twin sword was gifted to Zeus. The Cyclops had chosen us to be the only two God's that could call upon the two deadly blades. We were given these with the knowledge that they were to be kept safe and secret. These are the only two weapons that can destroy a God." He took a sip of his wine and his hands trembled. "After the Olympians defeated the Titans and the war was over – Cronus was thrown into Tartarus. I saw my opportunity to destroy the man who had tormented me and my brother. I snuck down to Tartarus and drew out the sword - I fought Cronus with all my might, lifting the weapon to deliver the fatal blow, but when I lowered it to strike him, my mother threw herself in front of the blade." Persephone gasped in horror but Hades did not seem to notice, locked in painful memories long repressed.

"I carried her body outside the gates of Tartarus," he continued. "I asked her why - why did she do it? She told me she did not want to see me become a murderer like my father. It was too late for that. She laid in my arms, dying. Her blood seeped into the ground, and a pomegranate tree blossomed over us, red like her blood. Zeus and Poseidon found us. We helplessly watched her eternal existence fade away into the ether. To be immortal and experience this helplessness was insufferable - it was an emotion none of us had ever felt before, so... powerless. They were furious at what I had done. My punishment was to rule over the dead, never see the sunlight or walk amongst the living -- for eternity. They held me down and forced me to eat the fruit of the tree that had grown from our mother's blood. They chanted a curse towards the heavens, 'Aidoneus, you shall be known henceforth as Hades, the 'Unseen'. Never to be spoken of above ground, to be written out of history and so feared on earth that men dare not utter your name. Destroyer of life, you have become king of death.' My fate was sealed, and I was once again, a prisoner. I, their wicked brother, must judge the wicked men and to remember every day my place in this wretched world. They slipped the rubied signet ring on my finger and concocted a story about us drawing lots to divide up the kingdoms – Never could anyone ever know that there is a weapon that can destroy a God."

Persephone felt herself flush with anger at the injustice of his brothers. Instead of comforting their brother, they did their best to push him over the edge of reason, blaming him for their mother's death. Instead of compassion, all they offered was more pain. Before she could think better of it, she rose from her chair and knelt before

him, taking his face into her hands, turning him gently towards her.

"You... you punish yourself... They had no right to deal such a punishment to you. They, who practice cruelty like it is a skill to be honed. Your mother had a choice, Hades. Just as we all do. You are still punishing yourself and she would not want that. She gave her life so that you could be free from the chains of your father. With his blood on your hands you would be tied to him for eternity. You sit on your throne dealing out judgement but it is really yourself you are sentencing day after day. Stop following protocol and start breaking the rules. Do not let your brothers dictate the course of your life."

He shook his head. "My damnation stains me, Persephone, with you...with all of you. A crimson stain, a cursed badge I forever have to wear. My history is written in your world - it will always paint me as a monster until I become the very thing I have been pictured to be."

She gave a grumble of protest at the stubborn set of his jaw and then she did the only thing she could think to do to break him from his painful confessions. She brushed her lips quickly over his. It was only the slightest touch and she pulled back before he could even react. She stood up and then turned around to look at him shyly, but her voice was pragmatic.

"I think you should show me the different realms tomorrow. Take a break from your duties." She paused and re-phrased her sentence. "Or, perhaps have a different kind of workday by showing your queen around the Underworld. We can start with the Asphodel and then head to Elysium."

"Adopting me to your menergie of injured creatures? I am not one of your helpless animals," he countered.

"I do not think anyone would call you helpless," she replied lightly. "Prove you are not a lone wolf by accompanying me tomorrow."

"I could warn you about the dangers of letting a wolf loose with sheep," he replied with shadowed eyes.

"Will you come?" she insisted again, ignoring how her pulse quickened at his warning.

"How could I resist the temptation?" he murmured, and she could not tell if he was being derisive or earnest, and which was worse.

She held out her hand, "You need to rest." He placed his large hand in hers and stood, towering over her and yet she felt strangely protective of this enigmatic, powerful God. She pulled at him insistently and to her surprise he complied, following her lead.

They walked in silence, hand in hand, back to her room. Step by step, dark hunger seized his mind. He should stop and insist that he return to his own rooms. This was madness, barely controlled desire...lust; he tried to push the sensations away, but sweat began to pool on his forehead and he felt the maddening pulse of arousal at the touch of her small hand in his. He had to leave, but when she opened the door to her room and willingly allowed him to enter, the temptation was too overwhelming to resist.

She turned back smiling at him, "What do you think?" she asked with an earnest expression on her beautiful face. She had no idea the derangement that was closing in on him. His wife would not look at him with such trust if she knew the raging erection he concealed beneath his robes.

A wolf with a lamb, he thought with disgust, remembering Aphrodite's warning. And how he wanted to devour her. He forced himself to look around her room and saw the beautiful garden she had created and it seemed a stark contrast to his tormented, twisted and depraved thoughts.

He pulled his hand gently from hers on the pretense of inspecting her creations. He needed distance between them, so he moved to the fireplace scrutinizing the vibrant pink and violet flowers that wrapped around the hearth. "Persephone, these are lovely." He turned to see his wife had lit a few candles, proud to show off her work.

She beamed at him and grabbing a handful of cherry blossoms, she came closer to him once more and said with a laugh, "Yes, it is so much better."

He stared at the curve of her lips and then turned away from her, "I should leave."

"Oh no, wait," she exclaimed, "I made something for you."

"What?" he asked harshly, wincing inwardly at the rude tone. He watched as she took a bowl from near her bed and threw the cherry blossoms into the mixture as she ground them carefully and a soothing aroma filled the air.

"For your wound," she replied. "I know I cannot heal it, but it may help a little." She was pushing him towards the chaise and like a helpless fool he let her steer him when he should be fleeing from her.

"You really cannot help yourself, can you?" he asked as she settled him carefully against the cushions. Cerberus appeared suddenly in the doorway and jumped onto the chaise, curling against his side with a contented sigh. "You would try to help a hydra if you could."

She gave the dog a pet on the closest head. "Oh surely you

are not comparing yourself to a hydra, your majesty." She had pulled his robes from his chest, and he knew he should stop her. Her touch was only making him ache more fiercely, causing the wound in his chest to trickle blood. But it felt so good to feel her cool fingers on his body. It was a testament to her innocence that she did not notice the portion of the robes over his groin, and then he frowned. But she was not innocent, he remembered as he recalled the lover in her memories. His attention reverted back to her as she gave a small gasp and her eyes widened in shock at the state of the wound. It was a raw, bloody mess, and instead of healing had only grown in size since the arrow had pierced his chest.

"It is horrible, isn't it? Perhaps you would prefer the hydra?" he inquired politely.

He watched as she tried to school her expression into calm once more as she replied, "Oh, I do not know, the hydra may give me less trouble." She stepped away and went to the pool of water in her room and brought a bowl back when she began to gently clean his chest, his stomach, his arms. Did he imagine it or did her fingers linger over his skin? He closed his eyes and let the sublime sensation of her cool, small hands wash over him. He felt feverish and chilled at the same time and her touch seemed to both soothe and torment him. The sweet scent of crushed petals filled the air as she applied the paste over his gaping flesh, and though the pain did not abate, the sensation was still amazing.

He glanced over her bent head and his eyes drifted to the bed. A lock of long, dark hair tickled his stomach and he had to suck in his breath to keep from inhaling her scent. Lust was crawling into his brain like an insidious worm, whispering to him to "take her," to wipe the other man from her mind until only he was in her thoughts;

He wanted to consume her as she consumed him. He wanted her to burn with want, to know the pain that pulled at him until he was senseless with need, no better than a rutting animal. Memories and dreams flashed through his mind, hers mingled with his own until they blurred seamlessly and he did not know the difference between fantasy and truth. The image of his cock deep in her body, parting the soft, pink folds, her mouth taking him deep, his tongue shoved deep in her wet, dripping body. All of the images began to whirl together until he grasped his head, smearing blood with his sweat. "Stop," he whispered.

She glanced up at him, her eyes luminous and trusting in the candlelight. "I am sorry, did I hurt you? I am almost finished." She dipped a clean eucalyptus leaf into the bowl. "May I continue?" she asked.

He paused, knowing he should stop her and run from the room like the coward he was, but instead he nodded his head. Or perhaps he was a coward to stay, to let her stroke her hands over his injury while his cock pulsed like a heartbeat in his groin. He was slowly losing his mind. He pressed one hand against the wall and it brushed the soft, pink peonies that had spread across it. Soft and pink, like when she had touched herself. His fragmented mind tried to grasp the memory but it slipped away from him, blurring into the others. But that had not been her, had it? He crushed one of the soft petals in his hands and he closed his eyes against the dizziness.

The flower lay broken in his hand. He destroyed everything he touched, she would leave him, he thought with panic. Force her to eat the seeds. Trick her into staying in this hell. She will leave you -- the way everyone has. Fuck her, until your seed runs downs her legs, fuck her so deeply that a part of you will grow in her womb and she will be tied to you for eternity. It would be so easy, so easy to push your cock into her warm, wet welcoming entrance and she would be helpless to resist. He shook his head against the thought, never. Never. She looked at him with a curious expression on her face and he wondered vaguely if he had said it aloud. He wanted to tell her to run from him, warn her, but he could not find his voice. Her face was swimming before him as blackness began to dance in front of his vision and he pushed away from her trying to stand up. He felt her hands grabbing for him as he felt himself falling to the ground and then… blissful blackness.

Persephone shook him frantically as Cerberus sniffed at his face with a quiet whine. "Hades, Hades."

She stared down at his pale face and panic filled her. With the shadows under his eyes and the dark crescent of his eyelashes against his snow-white skin, he looked dead. Far away from the world and from her. But he was a God and Gods could not die. Who knew what this curse could do. A trickle of blood escaped from beneath the careful bandage she had constructed over his chest. It moved slowly down his chest, stark crimson against the paleness of his skin. A God could not die, she repeated to herself like a mantra. But then what was wrong with him? She ran to the pool again and gathered water. She dipped a cloth into the water and began to press it against his flushed skin and her heart was beating like a drum.

"Please wake up," she whispered. Please."

She bent and pressed her lips to his and lay against him, the moments passing as he lay still beneath her, his heartbeat the only sign of life. Would the light never be allowed to touch him, this isolated King of Darkness? How long he had suffered believing he was a murderer when he held morals so strong. Her heart broke for

215

him, for the things he had seen, and the deeds he had been forced to perform. The smallest change in the rhythm of his heartbeat alerted her and she pulled back to see his eyelashes flutter, her own pulse beginning to accelerate with relief. Cerberus moved closer, the three heads licking his face with renewed vigor. Hades gave him a gentle push and sat up while Persephone moved back on her heels.

"What happened?" he asked.

"You fell, collapsed actually," she said trying to sound matter of fact, when all she wanted to do was throw herself into his arms with relief. He stared at her and then lifted a hand to her face and she was surprised when she felt the dampness against her cheeks.

"Were those for me?" he asked, an expression crossing his face that she could not fathom.

She wiped impatiently at her face. "I was worried when you fell, almost crushing poor Cerberus." She indicated the dog who was quite intact and happily wagging his tail. Hades gave him a skeptical look. His dark eyes looked feverish still, and she moved closer to him. "What is wrong?" she repeated for the second time that night.

He raised his eyes slowly to look into her own. "It is worse at night," he said, gesturing towards his wound. "When you touch me… and when you do not touch me. It is getting harder."

She looked away from him and bit her lip. "I am sorry. Is there anything I can do to help? I can leave, you can spend the night here so you can rest."

He laughed mirthlessly, running his hand through his hair, smearing the blood on his face. "It does not matter where I am, Persephone. You haunt me. I do not rest, even when I sleep -- I see you. The thought of you… there is no escape for me. It was… overwhelming. It is overwhelming now." Something flared behind his eyes and she felt fear pricken her skin.

"Would it not be easier if I left here? Left your palace?" she asked in a small voice. "Maybe seeing me makes it--"

His hand shot out and grasped hers painfully and his face was twisted in rage. "If you think to leave me I will find you and I promise you, you will not like the consequences."

She jerked her hand angrily but he did not let her go, his breathing rapid and his glazed eyes blazing into hers. She gave another tug and this time he released her. "Do not threaten me! I am not your enemy, Hades."

"Sometimes I wonder," he said, keeping his burning eyes focused on her face.

She began to rise when his hand caught her wrist. "Please do not go," he said quietly. "I am sorry. Stay with me. Just lie with me. Help me keep the demons at rest, I am tired of fighting them."

She was not sure how long they stayed that way, his hand a shackle around her wrist as she stared down at him, on her knees. Was it an imprisonment though? She could break the easy grasp he had around her. But maybe she did not want to, maybe she wanted to offer him what small comfort she could.

"All right," she whispered.

Without further discussion he pulled her to him and she toppled to the floor. He rose above her staring down at her and she caught her breath, but then he carefully turned her on her side as he curled his larger body around hers. They lay on the plush rug before the fire and she could feel something wet soaking into her gown, blood or sweat, probably both, and lower down her body, his large erection pressing into her back. A shiver went down her spine, whether of longing or fear she did not know. Her emotions were too confused and too disordered; she could not begin to analyze them. She felt his hand travel down her arm and graze her breast and she gave a small jump.

"Tell me you love me," his dark voice breathed into her ear. She tensed, wondering if she had heard him correctly.

"What?" she asked, her voice a mere thread.

"Tell me, Persephone, that you love me."

She caught her breath and felt tears fill her eyes. She could not love, she was incapable of it. "It would be a lie," she whispered.

"Then lie to me. Tell me the sweetest lie your lips can conjure. You can live with a lie and I cannot live without it. Lie to me and it will be better than any truth." She said nothing as she felt his hand on her face, tracing the tears. "Please," he said, biting the lobe of her ear. His hand moved to her breast and he touched it gently, tracing her nipple through the soft material. And she wanted him to stop, was desperate for him to stop, afraid of the sensations that were rising in her.

"I love you." The moment the words left her lips she wished she could take them back. They felt wrong on her tongue, a mockery of the declaration, and she had felt him catch his breath, but in pain or pleasure she did not know. She tried to turn to look at him but he forced her back down as he pressed kisses to the side of her face and she wondered at the dampness on his skin. "I am sorry," she said.

She felt him pause above her and closed her eyes tightly as tears threatened to fall again. She looked up at him finally, and his dark gaze shone oddly in the firelight.

"Oh, Persephone," he whispered, "if only you could lie with your eyes." He stood then and she heard him leave the room. And as she remembered the dampness on his face and the sheen in his eyes, she realized that it had been tears that had shone in their depths.

CHAPTER
XIII
ELYSIUM

THE HANDMAIDENS WORKED furiously that morning preparing their mistress for her journey to Elysium. Her body was scrubbed so thoroughly that her skin was pink and raw by the time she emerged from the bath, her hair brushed with such vigor she was surprised to see any remained on her head, and even her poor toes were subject to their meticulous ministrations. They dressed her in a sheer, cream colored toga that plunged down the front, a golden chained belt was fastened around her waist, and gleaming bands were placed on her upper arms. Her hair was kept loose about her face and her lips were darkened with the crushed petals of her roses. Persephone had watched carefully, making sure they did not take too many petals to cause harm to the plant. They were giddy with excitement at her visit to Elysium and they were full of both questions and advice as they nestled flowers in her curled tresses. Persephone let their chatter flow around her and she hoped it would settle the sick feeling in her stomach. Jocasta had tutted when she had not touched her breakfast again, but everytime she thought of last night she felt sick. Why had she said those words to him? Why had he asked her to?

Her gaze narrowed as she studied the gown. "Is this toga not too transparent? You can almost see my hand through it!" Persephone exclaimed.

Jocasta laughed, "Well that is the point my dear. Your husband should enjoy more than just the view. But desire starts first with a glance." The women snorted with suppressed laughter, both grabbing a dry brush to stroke against her skin. "We are hoping that tonight will be the night when the magic happens."

She was tugged back and forth as they rubbed her down with oils, and when she began to feel dizzy, Persephone pulled the brushes gently from their hands and set them on the dresser. "Magic? Will someone be performing tricks tonight?"

They looked up at her with surprise and laughed again. "Your husband will be when he beds you!" The younger servants howled with laughter and Jocasta shooed them away.

Persephone felt her face burn. "That is impertinent!" Once the two younger women were out of hearing distance, Persephone leaned closer to the older woman and whispered, "And besides, how do you know we have not already?"

"It is not impertinent to assume that two people who love each other will spend the night together. Especially when they are a husband and wife," Jocasta said, patting Persephone's cheek. "And how do I know you have not shared a bed yet? Well, I have not seen a man after his wedding night still watching his wife like a hungry wolf, and you look at him like you have not had a good meal in…

well ever! "

Persephone's blush turned deeper. "Do people talk about us?"

"My dear," Jocasta said in a motherly tone, "you are the beautiful, new Queen of the Underworld who does not share the rooms of her new, very handsome husband. Of course they talk about you."

She stood, still embarrassed that the servants gossiped that she was not sleeping in her husband's room. She paused before the mirror trying to pull at the low neckline of her gown and then gave up the fight. She replayed Jocasta's words in her mind. Two people in love? There was that word again, could she not escape it? "You think I am in love?" Persephone asked in what she hoped was a steady voice.

The older lady bent to fasten the sandals around her ankles. "Sometimes love roars like a lion, but sometimes love...it is a whisper, a whisper in a world of roars. Love is whispering to you dear." She rose and looked Persephone in her eyes, her eyes sad as she surveyed her. "I hope you will listen to the whisper."

Her nieces returned and Jocasta said in a louder voice, "Well, I think you are ready, your majesty!" Then all three were pulling her through the halls to the stables, pushing her to the doors, chortling as Jocasta leaned forward and whispered, "Let the magic happen." And gave her one final push through the stable doors.

Hades was bridling one of the horses as she stumbled like an oaf through the doorway, catching herself quickly before she landed on the ground. He looked up just as she caught her balance, eyebrows drawn over his dark eyes. "Are you unwell?"

The infernal blush returned and she eyed the doorway, but the women had vanished leaving her alone with her husband. She pushed her hair from her face and tried to look queen-like as she replied, "I am quite well. The maidens were a bit over exuberant this morning." Hades laughed softly, turning his attention back to the bridle. Well, he would at least not mention last night it seemed. She moved closer to him, eyeing the horse.

"Who is this?" Persephone asked, anxious to change the subject.

"This is Aethon," he replied, running his long fingers through the thick black mane. "I have been told she is swifter than an arrow, which perhaps seemed appropriate given the circumstances." Before she could respond he extended his hand to her. "Come and meet her." She placed her hand in his without thinking and caught her breath as he brushed his thumb against her palm before lifting her hand to the horse's soft, black nose. Aethon gave a delicate sniff of approval, and Hades brushed Persephone's hand against the horse's elegant neck. "She is beautiful isn't she?" he asked softly behind her. Persephone could only nod, her mouth suddenly dry at his nearness. His warmth seemed to soak into her and she wanted to lean into him, let the heat of his body take away the chill that she always seemed to carry with her, that seemed to be so much a part of her.

Persephone cleared her throat. "Which horse will I be riding?"

"Aethon," his voice was a dark whisper behind her.

"And you?" she asked.

"Aethon," he replied again. Persephone turned to look at him and he let their hands drop, but did not step away from her.

She looked up into his shadowed, inscrutable face and knew she should argue and demand her own mount. It was clear by now that any physical contact between them was dangerous, but all she

223

said was, "Oh."

A smile played about his lips. "Shall we go?" She nodded and Hades grabbed her waist, his large hands spanning her rib cage. In the sheer gown she could feel his fingertips pressed against her cool skin and she closed her eyes, savoring the sensation, very glad he could not see her face. He lifted her onto the raven-black steed, and if he let their bodies linger together longer than necessary, she would not be the one to mention it. Once mounted, she leaned forward and brushed her hands again over the horse's ebony coat. She suddenly felt Hades hard body behind her and then he pulled her tightly against him and murmured, "Aethon, take us to the Meadows."

The horse took off, her hooves pounding furiously beneath them and Persephone let out a gasp of laughter as the wind pulled at her hair and gown. It felt like she was flying, flying higher and higher and leaving the world far behind them. Hades pressed Persephone closer to his body and she let him, let the movements of the horse press them tightly against each other, until the three of them moved as one. Aethon sped through the landscapes of the Underworld like a whirlwind, until finally the River Styx appeared ahead. The wind tore at her and Persephone felt a thrill of uncertainty as the horse turned towards the water. She caught her breath almost letting out a scream of warning, but then Aethon began running on the water, her hooves sending glittering sparkles in the air around them.

Persephone let out a gasp of delight and turned her face towards Hades, almost brushing her lips against his ear so he could hear her against the rushing wind. "How can the water sparkle without the light of the sun?" she asked breathlessly.

"Those are souls lighting the waters. Souls glisten. Like

stars."

Persephone stared into the sparkling waters below. Like stars. "Under the stars," she whispered and she began to turn her face towards him when this time she did let out a small scream as the horse dove into the river. The waves pulsed around their faces as they descended down into the starlit waters and her breath caught in her throat. She was reminded of her descent into the Underworld, but how different this was as lights of brilliant colors shot all around them. Souls. Pure white light dancing across eternity, more beautiful than any night sky. Suddenly the heavens seemed suspended in time as the world turned topsy turvy, so that they were hanging from the darkness itself, and she felt the blood rush to her head as Aethon galloped in the upside down universe. And all the time his strong arm was kept so tightly around her. Had not he always kept her still when the world moved in chaos around them? She closed her eyes tightly, afraid that they would fall into nothingness, but she knew that Hades would never allow it.

She realized they had stopped moving when she heard his voice in her ear, "Open your eyes, Persephone." As she let her eyelids slowly lift, she let out a quiet sound. They had crossed time itself to enter another universe. They stood in clear endless water that sparkled from the bright sun hanging high in the azure sky. "Can you swim?"

"Of course," she said, piqued, and then she had only a moment to process his smile as he took her hand and pulled her from Aethon's saddle and they tumbled into the soft, warm water beneath them.

Persephone watched as Hades swam towards her in the clear water, his dark hair billowing around his face and she felt her heart give a curious squeeze at the smile on his lips. She floated in the water, her dress and long hair encircling her, and she let him reach her when she shoved her hands causing a small wave to crash against him. She gave a laugh, bubbles coming from her lips at the expression on his face and then she began making long strides in the water. She felt a hand on her ankle as he pulled her back to him and she gave a noiseless little scream. He pulled her against him giving her a stern expression as she gave him her most innocent look. Clearly not convinced, he took her hand and they swam together, his long legs propelling them faster than hers could alone. When they reached the surface Persephone emerged from the water to feel the sunlight warm on her face and she kept her eyes closed against the heavenly sensation. When she glanced over, Hades was watching her, rivulets of water travelling down his face. He looked so darkly sensual she found it hard to catch her breath or look away. She swallowed as one droplet of water disappeared slowly down his neck. Persephone opened her mouth, anxious to break the quiet moment, when a large wave splashed over her head. Strong hands grasped her as she sputtered to the surface again laughing.

"Yours was much larger," she said, trying to school her features into a ferocious expression.

"It is not revenge if you do not pay it back ten fold, my sweet," he said in a courteous voice, his face close to hers.

She held up her hands. "Truce?" she asked.

"Now where is the fun in that?" With that cryptic statement he took her hand and they waded from the waters, petals falling onto the surface like gentle raindrops. Aethon was already waiting at the shore. Persephone turned in a circle surveying the land around them.

"This is beautiful," she breathed.

The Meadows consisted of lush green grass as far as the eye could see and ivory flowers danced in the fields and she felt an irresistible urge to join them. Giving Hades a mischievous look, she set off and she felt him on her heels, the sunlight illuminating their skin. She heard other living things in the tall grass and made out rabbit and deer and creatures of the forest following behind them; her heart felt light. She was amongst those beings who made her the happiest, the free spirits of the wild. Hades ran ahead of her and she barrelled into him and his strong arms kept them upright. She looked up, her breath coming in short gasps and mingled with laughter.

"Must we stop?" she asked.

"This is only the Meadows, do you not want to see Elysium?"

She bent and scooped up a rabbit that was settled at her feet. "Oh, can we stay here just a bit longer?" She rubbed the soft fur against her cheek and then lifted him to Hades' face and to her surprise he bent and rubbed one soft ear between his fingers.

"Bring your friend and I will show you the lake," he said.

They walked through the fields and came to a large lake bordered by olive trees and pink wildflowers. Hades led her towards the shore and there they sat playing with the animals that had followed them, and to her delight even a badger came eventually, its striped little face peeking curiously at her.

Finally Hades asked again, "Are you ready for Elysium?"

"It cannot be better than this," she said, reluctantly setting down the skunk that had settled into her lap.

He smiled, "It is." Hades whistled and Aethon appeared again. He jumped onto the tall back of the horse and she stood up as he raced towards her, grabbing her in steady arms as he placed her in front of him.

"To Elysium, Aethon." The horse bounded towards the forest beyond the meadows, booming hooves echoing through the woods as she swerved in and out of trees. As the horse flew over the ground, the landscape began to change again. The blue skies turned purple and pink and a vast ocean replaced the endless fields of the meadows. Craggy mountains appeared in the distance and waterfalls fell from the sky, pouring their sapphire waters into the ocean below. It was Elysium, it was heaven. Never in her life had she seen anything so beautiful and she found for once that words failed her. Hades steered the horse to a precipice on the edge of white cliffs which stretched around the sea. The grass was green and lush, the terrain mountainous with cypress trees decorating the landscape. Roses draped over the jagged rocks and melted down into the ocean. He helped her off the horse and she looked out at the eternal pink skies.

"Hades, your kingdom is greater than Zeus'. Never in my life have I seen anything like this. Nothing on Earth can compare. Not my mother's temple, not Posedian's sea, not Mount Olympus."

"That is praise indeed," he replied, taking her hand again to lead her down a long white staircase carved from the mountain. At the bottom lay a blue lagoon surrounded by lush grass and red roses that grew along the shoreline. Persephone grabbed Hades' hand and ran towards the water, forgetting her shyness in the excitement and for a while they were consumed with who could produce the largest wave. Persephone's shrieks of outraged laughter echoed off the mountain as a particularly enormous one sent her under water.

She waded towards him. "You win!" she cried laughing still. She paused as she heard his low laughter, realizing she had never heard the sound from him. He had laughed previously of course, but always with irony or dark humor. She had never heard him laugh with happiness. She walked closer, mesmerized by the sound. "I like your laugh," she said softly. She was close to him now and only several inches separated them from touching. She was surprised at the look of uncertainty that crossed his face. Was the Prince of Darkness feeling shy, she thought with astonishment. Taking pity on him, she grasped his hand again and pulled him towards the shore. "I am hungry! Let us find some food."

They sat on a swing in the inlet, picked grapes from the vines and watched the sunset, shades of orange and yellow playing across the sky. A pale icy moon rose over the horizon and she watched in wonder as the sky turned a brilliant shade of shifting green.

"What is that?" she whispered in awe.

"That is the Aurora Borealis," Hades replied, one of his hands wrapped around the rope holding the swing as he glanced upward. She watched the phenomenon, mesmerized as it lit up the night sky.

"I have never seen one of these," Persephone said, turning her face to look at him.

"The first of many things I hope to share with you," his low voice said. The colors bounced off of his pale skin and in the changing shades his expression was impossible to read. She gave a small shiver and he stood suddenly, his back to her. "I will make a fire to dry us." Persephone walked to a nearby cove that held many fruit trees and gathered a variety of each, arranging a platter for them. They sat by the crackling fire and she raised her hands to the enticing warmth.

She stared at the flames, deep in thought, as she realized that

this was the first time, perhaps since childhood, that she had felt truly free. Free to run with no walls holding her inside. She had been held so long within the confines of her mother's temple and then behind the gates of the Underworld that she had forgotten what it meant to have no restrictions. She looked up at the stars. "Thank you for one of the best days of my life," she said.

His heart ached at the sight of her, her face alight with the colors in the sky. She smelled of honeysuckle and dewdrop and he almost thanked the God above that had cursed him with the arrow that had forced his hand. He did not respond to her simple statement, he found he could not find his voice, but instead he picked up the small hand close to his own and pressed it to his mouth. He pretended to look up, to watch the sky, but really he watched her, wanting to absorb every emotion that passed on her face, however briefly, to carry the memory of her with him -- forever. He kept her hand in his and to his surprise she did not pull away.

"Why did you not marry Apollo or Hermes?" he asked suddenly, the question one that had long nagged at him. "They have their faults, but they both could have protected you from Ares seeking your hand."

She picked up a mango and bit into it thoughtfully as she considered his question, the juice running down her full lips, and he wanted to groan. He forced his eyes back up to the sky, "There were many reasons I refused them," she said finally. "I did not love them. I did not respect them. I did not desire them. Marriage to them would be like all the others on Olympus, superficial and unfaithful. They had no affection for me; I had no affection for them. Besides," she continued, "I like being alone. Like Athena."

He glanced at her then, relieved she had finished her fruit.

"No you do not, Persephone," he said. "Your soul starves for love."

"How do you know what my soul 'starves for'?" she demanded.

"Souls are my specialty," he said, the tinge of mockery back in his voice. "Were those the only reasons you refused them?"

He saw her tense and he could not bear that distrust enter between them here, so he reached for her, pulling her into his arms and whispered into her hair, "No more questions, Persephone, just sit with me and watch the sky. For tonight that is the only thing I will ask."

For a moment she was stiff in his arms, but then he felt as her body began to become pliant against his. He could feel her heartbeat against his chest and it seemed to beat to the rhythm of his own. Or was it his heartbeat that acquiesced to hers? Was such a thing possible?

A star shot across the sky and Persephone tilted her head back to look at him, her lips brushing against his jaw. Did she know or was it merely an accident of proximity? "Make a wish," she said against his ear.

Hades brushed a lock of her hair from her face, watching her expression. "If I could have one wish it would be to have a family. "Her eyes shot quickly to his face and then glanced away and he felt her muscles tighten beneath him. When she said nothing he finally asked softly, "Do you not want children one day?"

She kept her face averted from his as she replied, "No," in a quiet voice. "And you are not supposed to say your wish, you know. It may not come true."

Hades laughed, "Superstition failed to impress me long ago." He hesitated and then continued. "It is unusual that a fertility goddess would not desire children."

She did turn then, her hair whipping across his face as she re-garded him with narrowed eyes, "Strange that a God of Death would want to bring life into the world."

Hades smiled, though it did not reach his eyes. "I was not al-ways a God of Death, Persephone. Though my time here has taught me how closely death and life are intertwined. From death comes rebirth; from endings – new beginnings."

Unabashedly he stated, "If I could, I would trade all the rich-es in my kingdom for something more priceless - a family that loved me."

"I thought I wanted children too... once," she admitted.

"Ah, once… but not anymore? That is a shame Persephone, you would be a magnificent mother." He could imagine her with a sweet babe against her body and the thought was so enticing that Hades could not bear to look at her. He set her away from him and stood, walking closer to the fire. It was not difficult to guess what had changed her mind. Her hope for a future died the day she mar-ried him. Who would want to raise a family in the Underworld, who would want to share a family with him?

He felt her step closer to him, her heat mixing with his. "It is not what you are thinking," she said softly. "I just cannot… I do not …" her voice paused and then she continued. "It has nothing to do with you. I think that you would make a devoted father."

He turned around, "Then what did change your mind if it was not me?"

Her green eyes stared up into his own, uncertainty mingled with a deeper expression in their depths. "I do not know."

"You lie either to me or to yourself. You can trust me, Persephone. Tell me what happened," he said, his voice a mere whisper. For a moment, pain flashed in her eyes and she opened her mouth -- the words almost spilling from her lips before she stepped away from him.

"I do not know," she said again. "But I decided I did not want children before I came here, so you cannot lay that particular decision at your feet. You are not responsible."

He reached for her hand and brushed his thumb against her palm. "Someday, Persephone, you will trust me." He pulled her towards him. "Come, little flower. There is something I want to show you."

Persephone felt her throat tighten as she realized Hades was leading them towards the darkened caverns they had passed earlier in the day. Their footsteps were soft on the ground as she peered reluctantly into the darkened entrance. It looked black and forbidding and she pulled back as they neared the gaping mouth. The last time she had entered a cave she had left with a great deal of her flesh missing.

Hades looked down at her. "Afraid? This time you enter the darkness with me, I will not allow any harm to come to you."

"I know," she said, surprising both of them. She let him pull her forward and they entered the blackness together. In the distance, golden light danced in the inky blackness and she was relieved to see that they were travelling towards it. Thousands of tiny golden threads hung from the ceiling and glittered throughout the cavern and they weaved through the small threads, bathed in their light. As the wisps of gold touched her cool skin, she felt warmth soak into her flesh and a million thoughts echoed in her mind. Sorrow and joy; pain and pleasure, emotions swirling so swiftly she felt dizzy from their potency. "What is this?" Persephone whispered, reaching up to touch one of the thin beams of light as they waved gently in the wind, like thin spider webs blowing in the summer breeze.

Hades lifted his hand to one of the threads, letting it run gently over his fingers. "These are the golden threads of fate. Each string is a person, the glow is their life. When a person's time ends, the light extinguishes, and the thread is cut."

"It is the Cave of Fate," Persephone whispered, a shiver running through her as the delicate threads brushed against her. The cave opened up into a small room that was covered in dark stone. It was cold and barren and Persephone longed to run back into the free open spaces of Elysium. There was something lonely about this cavern of souls and a chill seemed to have settled into her own. He pulled her reluctant hand and they walked towards a gleaming thread that swayed gently. Persephone looked at its glimmering light and a peculiar sensation travelled through her as she moved closer. The sway of the thread seemed to follow the cadence of her heart and she wanted to both caress it and turn her back on the slim brillant fiber. "What is this?" she asked.

He brushed the silken web almost reverently and she felt the contact within herself, within her spirit. She had felt that touch before, but the memory fluttered from her mind, leaving only shadows in its place.

"Persephone, this is your thread of life."

Shock filtered through her mind and a sliver of fear travelled down her spine, causing her to step back as she stared at the thin thread held so softly in his hand. "But I am immortal, how can I have a thread?" she questioned.

Golden light reflected in his dark eyes. "We all are spun of

golden thread," he said, "Gods are not immune to death. One day, we too, will pass."

Persephone looked down at the fibers he held in his long, pale hands and frowned as she saw a mark on its golden length. She hesitated and then placed her hand over it, withdrawing her fingers from the thread quickly when it vibrated at her touch. She indicated the dark indention with her head.

"What is this?" she asked.

He ran his hand over the mark and she shivered at the touch. "That is the scar on your soul." He raised his dark eyes to her face. "You hide it away so no one can see it, but that does not erase it. It stands out all the brighter because of your desire to suppress it. You alone know why that injury is there and what caused it."

"It scarred my soul?" she asked, tears swimming in her eyes as she shook her head.

He lifted his hand and brushed a tear away as it fell down her cheek. "Tell me, Persephone. What happened? You do not have to bear it alone. Let me share your burden."

She grasped his hand tightly as tears began to stream down her face. "Hades, I…" Her voice was cut off abruptly as laughter reverberated through the cave. Persephone turned quickly but Hades had pulled her behind him.

"Stay behind me, Persephone," he said in a low voice.

Three women stepped from the darkness, their eye sockets empty and gaping as they sniffed the air. Each held a portion of a golden thread between their gnarled hands, stroking it like a lover's touch. A milk white eye was held in the hands of the creature in the middle and she placed it in the blackened socket with a sickening squelch, its dull pupil staring ahead unseeingly. Persephone watched in horror as a golden scissors was raised to the gleaming thread and she wanted to cry out in warning, but it was too late... the thread had been cut and Persephone's eyes filled with tears as it turned a dull grey. A life that had been stolen. As if sensing her distress the pupil turned to Persephone and a finger beckoned to her. She felt Hades hands grasping for her but she was out of his reach as she stepped towards the Fates.

"Little Flower," three voices echoed in different cadences, "you want to leave this place, but you cannot. In the end, you will want to stay - but you will not. Think quick, or the King's castle will tumble down - it started with an arrow; it will end with an arrow."

The voice of the crone in the middle echoed in the cave, "The man who kissed you in the woods is coming. You will see him again, little girl."

Persephone's heart began to beat uncontrollably at her words. "No," she whispered. She felt rough arms grab her, Hades had pushed her behind him again. A gnarled hand reached toward the ceiling, grasping another glittering thread between the claw like fingers, as a loud slice rent the air again and a second thread swayed to the ground, grey, dull and lifeless. They came closer to Persephone's thread, and Hades took a menacing step forward. The three heads simultaneously turned towards him, eagerly sniffing the air. "The answers you seek are in the Lethe and wound tight in golden threads. It destroyed you once and could destroy you even now." The milk white eye turned towards her again. "She will bring about your ruin. She will destroy you."

Persephone's legs trembled beneath her and she felt Hades' arm tighten. She tugged on Hades robes and tried to pull him further away from the frightening creatures. "Do not listen to them," she begged. "Please, let us go away from here."

Hades raised his hand, the wind helping to rush them from the temple as the Fates began to laugh, their voices rising to deafening tones and Persephone covered her ears as they began to scream. "Which one did you trust? Which one do you trust? The man who kissed you in the woods is coming. He is coming; He is coming in you. The king will be mad; the king will go mad. The king will be mad."

Persephone bent her head to his chest, the wind tearing at their clothes as they rushed through the tunnels. He will come. She could feel the bile rising in her throat.

"No," she whispered.

She pressed her face closer into his robes, letting her tears soak into them and she felt his hand brush her hair. They stopped suddenly and Persephone raised her head, seeing with surprise that they stood in her bedroom. Her legs trembled beneath her as Hades stepped away and he lifted his hand to steady her.

"How did we get back?" she asked, looking around blinking, her voice muffled by tears.

"As the King of the Underworld, I am entitled to use hidden tunnels." Hades brushed her cheek. "Persephone, do not listen to the Fates, they twist their words to confuse and dismay. Their true meaning is nearly impossible to decipher."

"But they knew…" she whispered painfully.

"They knew of the man in the woods," he finished for her. "What are you afraid of, Persephone?" She felt herself begin to tremble and Hades shook his head. "That is enough for today, I think. Jocasta?" She stepped in from the doorway and Persephone could feel her concerned eyes fixed on her face. "Take care of my wife. See that she rests."

He turned away from her and Persephone grabbed his hand. "Where are you going?"

"The darkness calls, my love," he said with a small smile. He lifted her hand to his mouth and then he was gone.

CHAPTER
XIV
THE LETHE

HADES MADE HIS way to the Stables, his hands trembling beneath his robes. Anger was warring with confusion, the emotions causing blood to flow in eddies down his chest as he quickly saddled Orphnaeus. The Fates talked in riddles, but their prophecies were rarely wrong. The man from the forest was coming and Hades had not imagined Persephone's horror. Did she fear Hades' reaction to the appearance of her lover, or was there a more sinister reason for the haunted look in her eyes? They had promised that he would find his answers in the Lethe and it was time he returned to the River of Forgetfulness. The connection between his forgotten memories and Persephone was unclear, but he had no choice -- he must retrieve them. The day he had woken up by the river's shore he had held a cup in his hand, which he had pitched into the river, his mind disoriented and throbbing. He had avoided the Lethe since that day, wondering what had caused him to seek the amnestic waters. What could possibly have been so agonizing that he could not bear for it to even reside in the darkest recesses of his mind? He rode through the darkness like a man deranged, Orphnaeus flying over the rough terrain. If he wanted to retrieve his memories, he would have to locate the original cup he drank from. The river held hundreds of thousands of cups abandoned by those souls desperate to purge their mind. He slowed as he neared the shoreline, his chest damp with blood and sweat as he scanned the waters below. Seconds, minutes, hours passed as he sat, keeping silent vigil. And then he saw it -- a ruby red flicker that danced under the waves then disappeared far below.

"Mine," he growled.

He flung himself from the horse and dove into the icy waters, causing his breath to shoot out in a quick gasp as the chill began to spread through his body. Tentacles of other memories that had been sacrificed to the river began to wrap around him: a young girl hanging from her neck, her tongue bulging from her mouth as her body swayed in the breeze; a father kneeling at the cold, blue body of his child that stared ahead with wide glassy eyes; a husband's hands wrapped tightly around his wife's bruised neck as she lay motionless beneath him. He felt himself sinking under the weight of grief and regret, while all the time the icy water dug into him, pushing him deeper and deeper. As he was pulled further into the murky waters, he felt his resolve waiver, wondering why he had leapt into the Lethe, feeling content to give into the icy blackness. A gleaming ruby cup swept past his fingertips, and he fell as the current pulled it from his loose grasp. Perserphone. He pushed forward, clamping the cup tightly in his hands even as icy arms tried to pull him deeper. With a wave of his hands, a brilliant purple light pushed them back

and Hades shot to the surface, gasping for breath as his head rose above the water. He pulled himself from the river, breathing heavily as he lay on his back letting the cold waves pulse around him. He may have lost consciousness briefly for his eyes shot open as he felt Orphnaeus' cold nose pressed against his face. He lifted his hand to stroke his muzzle.

"I am okay, Orphnaeus, but you are right, we should go." Using the horse to brace himself, he stood and allowed himself a moment to lean against the solid warm strength. "Come, let us go to Acheron." He pulled himself into the saddle and leaned heavily forward as they rode to the opposite river-- Acheron, 'The River of Pain,' the river that would return his memories. He dropped from the saddle, staggering slightly, then strode to the water, the cool depths coming close to his feet. He was careful not to let the icy hot waves brush his skin, for the waters of the Acheron brought with it insurmountable pain. Bending to fill his cup, he stepped from the pools, walking to a nearby cave. He sank against the wall, letting his long legs stretch before him as he stared down at the cup in his hands, seeing his distorted reflection stare back at him. What dark memories would return to him when he allowed the water to touch his lips? She will destroy you. It mattered not, he was ruined anyway. But Persephone still had a chance.

"Acheron," he whispered, "bring back my memories no matter how painful." And he drank deeply from the cup. As the water touched his lips his muscles began to clench and he felt his stomach twist against the putrid taste. He almost dropped the goblet as a rigor went up his arms, but he forced it back to his mouth, pouring the entire contents down his throat. He pushed his head tightly against the wall as a wave of agonizing pain moved over him and he bit his lip to suppress screams. Tasting blood in his mouth, he finally had no choice but to give in to the ripping pain coursing through his body. He felt his insides were being ripped out and he wished for death as his agonized howls echoed through the cavern, but no one could hear him. A surge of pain filled his body, and he begged to put him out of his misery as his muscles spasmed and his body convulsed. He thought that perhaps this would be the worst part, but then the memories started flooding back.

He was at the River Styx watching Persephone in the forests above, her dark hair spread across the green earth as she cuddled a small deer to her chest, smiling happily. Watching her had become his ritual, and for those few moments, he felt happy, he could separate himself from the death and despair that filled his existence. The first time he had seen her he had sought the calmness of the River after visualizing the brutality of a father against his young children. He had felt broken by the wickedness of the man he had sentenced to Tartarus, tainted by the sharing of his vicious memories.

Styx had shown Persephone to him, her beauty and kindness acting like a balm to his torn, wretched soul. He was not sure when he began to love her, but he only knew that he did, fully and reverently. Everyday he sat by the river, he wrote briefly of what thoughts had passed through his mind during the day.

Persephone, I wonder at the cruelty of the world. Sometimes I lose hope that there is any goodness left in mortals and Gods alike, but then I see the innocence of a child or the love of a mother. I see you and I remember that there are those who still hold kindness in their hearts.

He realized one day as he sat, that he had written several pages, just streams of his consciousness, but he decided that he would send them to her. He left the message unsigned and placed a black rose with golden tips over the letter, wrapping it with a golden thread. He bent to the Styx, asking if the river would deliver it to the stream Persephone visited every day. When he returned later that day to the River, he watched in surprise as a letter floated towards him with a red rose placed on top. Persephone had written him a response.

Dear unknown one,

I thank you for your letter. I too wonder at the savagery that exists in the world. You say I am kind, but it seems sometimes the only peace I find is in the meadows and the forest and I wonder if I am a coward not to do more to help the world. My impact in this life has not been perhaps what it could be. Tell me more of yourself and perhaps I may offer you advice, though my experience is limited, unless you seek assistance in horticulture. In that, if you will excuse my immodesty, I do excel. I will offer you this last thought -- do not despair of the world entirely. Today I saw three fox cubs in a den and life cannot be too bad if they exist in it. Do not give up hope for a better world.

Persephone

One letter turned into two, and two letters turned into four. They wrote for weeks, and as those weeks turned into months, Hades began to feel that he could not live without her writing. She told him about Olive, how she had longed to know her father, her hopes, and fears.

 I sometimes feel that I am living a half-life, safely hidden from those who wish me harm, but is that how one is meant to live? I long to roam, to be free to see every tree, swim in every river and get to know every badger. Yes, badgers! I wonder how long I will sacrifice my freedom for my safety? I feel like a bird who has never been allowed to fly. And is it worth the cost? I think of how my father loved my mother, despite the risk to himself. Love is worth the danger, I think. Think of Eros and his lover, I believe that someday they will find their way back to one another. Their story is sad, but underneath it all, is hope. Hope that they will somehow move past all the obstacles that keep them apart. Hope. What this word has come to mean to me. Hope that tomorrow I will find the life I dream of. How dreary my thoughts are, I find they turn darker as the sun drops from the sky. Olive is currently laying his head in my lap and the first stars are just beginning to appear on the horizon. I wish you could meet him, he is the dearest creature. Please write again soon, your letters have become the most important part of my day. I hope that you will not always be unknown to me.

Yours,

Persephone

He remembered the day she told him she loved him and he confessed how he loved her. He wanted to spend his life with her, make her his Queen, and he her King. If she waited by the stream he would send a message telling her when they may meet in person. He would meet her at the surface, revealing his true identity and if she was willing, he would ask for her to become his bride. I will kiss you under the stars. He folded it carefully sending it down the river to his beloved.

Persephone's letter returned within moments, her usual elegant hand haphazard in her haste.

I do not care who you are my prince. If you are mortal or God it matters not. I will love you forever. Just come for me, make me yours.

For the first time in his life he found a reason to love immortality. He placed her letter in a drawer with the others. A lifetime with her would be a life worth living. He decorated a lavish room for her and spent days chiseling the fireplace with engravings of Eros and Psyche for her arrival.

Memories, they were painful to watch. He watched how happy he was, how hopeful, how stupid. It hurt. He watched their story again not knowing how it would unfold and was helpless to look away.

It was sunset when Hades travelled to the stream with a rose. Flower petals danced on the summer breeze as he looked for Persephone, but he was alone in the forest. He strood along the shore, and then a small huddled bundle drew his eye. A sickening feeling twisted in his stomach as he approached and saw Olive's small, broken body, his sad brown eyes blank as they stared into nothingness. He laid a hand over the deer's eyes closing them and looked around carefully to see what had harmed the little deer when he saw the crushed black rose petals scattered on the ground. He followed the petals, his heart in his throat, fear for Persephone making his feet fast. Then he saw shreds of paper thrown onto the grass. Turning the fragments of the letter, he recognized the writing as his own, under the stars. He saw a separate letter sealed, and when he opened it, Persephone's writing filled the page.

Never write to me again. You are a monster that no woman could ever love. I curse the day I met you. Everything you touch brings death and destruction and I hate you, hate all that you are.

The words danced before his eyes. It could not be real, but it was her hand. She had written those words to him and he felt his heart shrivel in his chest. He crushed the letter in his hand, bending over the body of the fawn, trying to choke back a cry of despair but the pain escaped his lips as a savage bellow. It sounded like the wild scream of a dying animal, and that is what it was, the last soulless cry of a broken creature. He yelled out her name, but his voice merely echoed, lonely and alone through the trees.

"Persephone," he moaned.

He pulled himself from the ground, keeping the deer's body tucked close to his own. How he made his way back down the River Styx he would never know, but he only began to stir as he recognized the sound of the water next to him. He laid the deer's body next to the river, gently brushing its head and then approached the gates to the Underworld, whispering, "Elysium." Locking the door to his room, he poured a glass of wine with unsteady hands. He gulped down the first glass and then poured another. A bowl of water stood next to his bed and he walked over to it, waving his hand over the surface, "Persephone," he spoke her name like a prayer.

She appeared in the water, lying on her bed, her mother grabbing handfuls of letters from a small chest on her desk and throwing them into the fire. Persephone raised her face and it was tear streaked and ravaged by grief.

"Oh Mother, I have been so stupid. He is a monster, he has no soul."

Hades pushed the bowl from the table, shattering it against the wall. Blood dripped down his hand and he grabbed his glass, kicking open his door and almost running down the halls. He did not stop until he reached the River Lethe, drenched in sweat, his breath coming in short, heavy gasps and he fell to his knees, letting the water soak into him.

"How could I think a flower would love a thorn?" he said hollowly." How could I think she would ever love me?" He flung his hands into the icy depths. "I wish I had never seen her, I wish I had never loved her." His heart contracted and he felt an actual twist in his chest. "I will carry this as a scar." He growled.

All you touch brings death and destruction, the words echoed in his mind over and over. He saw the light fade from his mother's eyes, the madness in his father's, the disgust on Persephone's beautiful face. A monster.

Looking up into the heavens that he could never touch, he threw back his head and shouted, "Are you happy! Are we even? You have taken everything from me. I will never love another and my hope of happiness is lost." He grabbed at his chest, wishing he could rip his heart out of it, wishing he could die. "How can I rule this kingdom? How can I rule these lands? I do not want to be here!" His curses fell empty into the Underworld. He screamed like an animal as his tears fell into the Lethe, "I hate her… I love her." He bent down to the river staring into the water, his reflection looking back at him and knew his decision had been made. "I will forget her, I will forget this. I want to be free of this pain."

He plunged the goblet into the water, filling it to the brim "Lethe, erase the memories of her and what happened between us." He brought the cup to his lips and then paused. The wind blew through his dark hair as he sat staring over the darkened land that stretched for eternity. An eternity of never knowing her, never remembering how sweet her words had once been or how he had loved her. And how she too had once loved him. He would always be alone, but could he not leave a trace of her memory, a touch of light in his eternal blackness? "When I remember this, let me know that I loved her, gently, but that I knew I could never touch her. That is what I ask of you, Lethe. That she remain a distant, calm memory in the back of my mind. A lightness to touch the darkness in the longest nights. A quiet love. One that I never pursued."

He drank deeply from the goblet and began to double in pain, screams of agony being torn from his lips. The moments passed as the cries began to quiet and silence filled the night once more. Hades sat up slowly raising a hand to his dishevelled hair. His head was aching fiercely and his unsettled thoughts disturbed him. He glanced down at the cup lying on the shore and then over to the River. He had drank from the River of Forgetfulness. He wondered what could possibly have driven him to seek the oblivion of the waters, searching his mind for any hint of what could have led him to this point, but found merely… blankness. He picked up the rubied goblet and then threw it angrily into the dark waters next to him. Standing, he began to make his way back to his palace.

Hades woke from the memory like awakening from a night-

mare. He had the answers now. He was the reason her eyes turned hollow and fearful, why there was a mark on her soul. She had known him the whole time, known him and hated him. Persephone had played a game with him, or worse - her words were empty. After telling him she would love him no matter who he was, she fled the minute she guessed his identity. How well she acted her part, he had believed every lie she told him. His heart quivered in his chest and the blood dripped hot against his cold skin; he wished he would bleed out, that his life force would drain into the river, so he could let the peaceful blackness claim him. But he was not to be allowed that sweet release. He would never be free from the torment of her hatred. He brushed his hand across his face, the tears smearing with his blood as he stood and emerged from the cave, wishing he had never sought the truth.

CHAPTER
XV
VISIONS

PERSEPHONE LAY ON her bed staring up at the starry ceiling. Under the stars, the words seemed to echo in her head and stirred both helpless longing and revulsion. Longing for what she once believed in and disgust for what she had found. She thought of Hades' eyes as the sun had shone in their black depths, the smile on his lips as they had played in the water. The day had held an almost dream like quality and for that span of time she had felt… happiness.

But the sun had set and the old fears had emerged from the shadows, reaching for her, consuming her. He is coming. A cold sweat began to trickle between her breasts and she pushed herself impatiently from the bed, her dark hair tumbling across her eyes as she pushed it impatiently from her face. She began to pace, and Olive cast his large concerned brown eyes towards her. When would she finally take control of her life? She was so tired of being scared;

she had come so close to telling Hades what had happened in her life -- when the Fates had appeared. The Fates who had promised that she would bring about Hades' destruction. Those words had driven ice into her soul. She had seen with her own eyes how the blood still poured from the gaping wound in his chest, and how he was tormented endlessly because she could not love him. Both caused by a cursed golden arrow with her name on it! But the dark, horrible truth was that she could not love anyone. She was hollow inside and she had nothing to give anyone but a heart that had turned to stone. It was her dark and terrible secret -- that she was shadowed and empty. Evil had touched her and had stolen her light, even her soul bore the scar of darkness. And now, evil was coming for her.

Olive touched his damp nose to her hand as she resumed her relentless pacing and she sat back on the bed, pulling the deer's warm body to her chest.

"Olive, I am so tired," she whispered. "I have nothing left to give anymore." The fawn lifted his face to hers, pressing his soft pink tongue against her cheek." Thank you, Olive, my dear one." She laid her head next to his, and she felt the quick flutter of his heart. Strange that one's heart continued to beat even in death, the rhythm of life pulsing through his small body. Hades would know why, she could ask him when she saw him again. "Hades," she uttered on a silent breath.

She let her eyes begin to drift when a sudden chill pushed against her. Her eyes flashed open and a darkness seemed to dart from her vision. Grasping Olive tightly, she turned her eyes slowly to face the moving shadow and a dark vision rose before her, tall, menacing, and full of malice. Her voice caught in her throat as the smoky image begin to drift towards her. Without thought she leapt

from the bed, Olive clasped tightly as she let out a scream of terror, racing from her rooms towards her husband.

She reached his doors, flinging them open as she pushed herself inside, closing them quickly behind her. She pressed her body tightly against the golden frame, Olive cradled securely in her arms, and her small noise of distress drew Hades' eyes. He was standing before the fire adjusting the belt on his robe, his hair damp and slicked back from his high forehead. He had clearly just come from the bath and she flushed, remembering the hard, muscular strength of his body. She straightened as he approached her with narrowed eyes, and she drank in his dark face. But his gaze held no trace of the warmth she had seen in Elysium -- he looked cold and untouchable. She will destroy you. He drew closer to her but stayed out of arm's reach, when she wanted so much to hide in the warmth of his embrace. Was he afraid of her now, she wondered.

"What is wrong?" His voice was so remote that she shivered at the loneliness of it. She felt for the handle behind her, wondering if she should retreat, but the angry shadow from her room was too near, and she felt fear curl inside her, driving the words from her mouth.

"There is a man in my room," she cried.

"Stay here," he said. He grabbed her arms briefly, setting her away from the doorway, and let go quickly as if she burned him… or disgusted him. In a second he had slipped into the blackness of the corridor and she was alone. Persephone walked to the fire and sat in the chair Hades had probably recently vacated. She could smell his faint scent in the room, dark, earthy, masculine, and something else that was purely -- him. The blue flames danced merrily in the hearth, but the warmth did not penetrate her and she shivered in the chair as the minutes passed.

Had Hades sought answers from the Lethe as the Fates had told him? Did he find what he had been looking for? The Fates had warned of the danger of seeking the River and there was a blankness in his eyes she had not seen before. He had looked at her before with anger, with despair, with passion, but never with the emptiness she saw now. Persephone jumped when his voice was suddenly close to her ear and Olive leapt from her lap.

"There is no one in your room," he said.

She leaned her head back to look at him, her gaze searching his. "He was there! It was a dark shadow, looking at me. Watching me." His expression remained unchanged, saying nothing, and a horrible thought occurred to her. "Do you believe me?"

Hades did not answer her but returned to the door, where a servant had appeared. "Bring Charon and several guards. Search the castle for a man. Check on Cerberus." He closed the door again and went to the table pouring a glass of wine. "Here, drink this, it will warm you."

She took the wine from him, letting her fingers brush over his. His face tightened but he stepped away from her, sitting at the chair farthest away from her.

"Do you believe me?" she asked again, her voice strained.

"Do I have a reason not to?" he asked rather bleakly.

The question hung in the air between them and her heart gave a peculiar twist at the implacable expression on his face. It was like looking at the cool, handsome face of a stranger.

"I have no reason to lie to you," she answered, her voice so soft she wondered if he heard her.

"Tell me again what you saw."

"I told you! It was a shadow and it was watching me. He moved towards my bed and I could feel his... anger. I see things down here!" she cried, leaning towards him, imploring him to believe her. "This place is playing tricks on me. And a few nights ago, I saw two golden figures in the throne room and now this. Am I going mad?" she asked desperately.

He continued to watch her, his face partially hidden by shadows, half light, half dark. "I want to see what you saw," he replied finally. "May I touch you?"

Her brow furrowed at his question. Yesterday his touch seemed to follow her like the rays of the sun that had caressed her skin, but now he required her permission? What had happened at the Lethe she anxiously wondered.

"You may," she said in what she hoped was a steady voice. He stood, then came closer to her. His hands drew her up slowly, his touch impersonal, his fingers cool as they moved against her skin. He placed his fingertips over her temples as she had seen him do to so many of the prisoners who had knelt before him in the throne room. For a moment, panic settled over he as she realized that he would be able to delve into any of her memories. She was helpless against his dark power, but then, thoughts, ideas, and dreams raced across her mind until she saw again the terrifying, shadowy figure that hovered over her. Suddenly, the dark figure vanished from her mind and was replaced by the golden figures that were entwined in the throne room, their sweet embrace causing her breath to catch. That vision, too, passed from her memory and she was once again staring into the dark eyes of her husband. He dropped his hands from her face, but he was so close that she could feel his breath on her cheek.

"Did you see him? What is he?" For a moment she thought he may close that small space between them, but then he merely moved away from her, pouring himself a glass of wine.

"You cloak the truth well. You are very good at clouding your thoughts. You have taught yourself to push memories away and it is difficult to see anything beyond shadowed movements, impressions." He took a deep sip of the wine and then turned towards her again. "May I take these memories from you, so that I may study them?"

"You want to take my memories?" This time it was her who took a step away from him.

"Only these two. I want to see what you saw, see it through your eyes. I assure you, I will leave the rest of your memories intact, and I will return them to you in their original state when I am finished."

She eyed him, trying to read anything in his expression. He had proved time and time again that he would do anything to keep her safe, to keep the demons at bay from her. She did trust him, she realized in surprise, she trusted him with whatever small piece that remained intact of her tattered soul. Taking a step closer, she gave a slight nod, not able to give voice to the emotions that had risen in her chest.

He took her arm again and drew her to the bed. "Sit," he said softly. She complied, stretching out against the satin sheets, but her body was tense as he slid onto the bed, rising over her. "Relax," his voice prodded softly. "It will be over in a moment." She had closed her eyes, but they shot open when she felt his fingers flex against her face and her hands tightened on the smooth covers, letting their cool softness bunch in her fingers. "Relax," he repeated again, and then his head lowered and she gave a small groan as his lips moved against hers. She ran her hands through his dark hair, pulling him closer, and his tongue brushed at the seam of her lips as she opened her mouth beneath his, welcoming the intrusion.

At the touch of his tongue against hers she felt memories begin to shift again in her mind; she was a child in the forest, her mother laughing as they splashed through a river, then older as she stood at a banquet in the lavish halls of Olympus feeling hungry eyes on her, then crying in her bed in the quiet night of her mother's temple, aching with fear and loneliness. She was helpless as the thoughts swirled in her mind. And then -- the shadowed man hovered to the forefront of her vision while the golden figures hung suspended in time. He sucked and pulled at her lips and she felt panic consume her as the memories began to dim, become vague, and his lips seemed to draw away the figures until nothing remained of them except the awareness of loss. She felt a tear slide down her cheek as his head began to draw back. His lips were next to her ear. "Do you still hate me? Do you still curse the day you met me?" She stiffened beneath him, the words had been so soft she did not know if they were real or imagined, echoes of memories in her mind. Then he rolled off of her and sat on the edge of the bed, his eyes closed -- deep in thought.

"The dark figure could be anyone. I see no features," he stated calmly. He twisted his fingers in intricate patterns, rewinding the vision over and over, trying to get any clue of what the vision was. "The room was too dark, but you are right, it is full of malice towards you, it wishes you harm." There was a knock on the door. "Enter," Hades said. It was the guards. The search so far had yielded nothing and Cerberus had seen no one enter or leave the Underworld. He instructed them to continue their search and to station more guards outside of the palace. Hades walked back to her, "You are safe now, no one is down here. Whoever or whatever it was has vanished."

"I am not safe," she replied quietly, sitting on the edge of his bed.

"Someone is coming." He is coming. She began to stand, panic racing through her when Hades gave a gentle push against her shoulders and she fell back onto the bed. He placed a blanket over her and then sat close to her feet.

"Time is broken down here -- with Cronos locked in Tartarus. He is the keeper of time and there are moments when you can see glimpses of the past and the future -- things that have happened and things that have yet to occur. It is possible that the figure was a premonition of things to come. There is nothing we can do tonight."

She shivered at his words, at the memory of his horrible father who had committed such atrocities against his own son. He spoke cooly, but she knew that the hurt and rage simmered near the surface. His hand was so close to her own, but his remoteness kept her from grasping it. His posture was stiff and he looked ready to flee, when she longed for him to stay with her, to warm the coldness from her and keep the fear at bay.

"What else can you see?"

Hades gaze moved into the blue embers of the fire. "Sometimes you can see fragments of time - things that might have been, but did not come to pass. Endless futures that will never come to be. Time and fate are woven intimately together and one may alter the other. It is almost like watching another version of your life play out. Some better and some far worse. It can play tricks with your mind and can even drive you mad. Time is cruel -- like my father. It withers mortals and sucks the life out of them." His face hardened as he stared into the flames, "Time… haunts all of us."

"But why would this dark figure feel such anger towards me?"

Hades' eyes moved towards her then, "In two days, Venus squares my planet, in the sky. The symptoms of the curse will heighten. My jealousy, insecurity, anger, and frustration will all be directed towards the one thing that consumes me... you."

"What I saw, could not have been you," she cried, sitting up. "It was mocking and filled with hate. You have never tried to scare or harm me!"

"In two days, I will no longer be me," he cautioned her.

"Who will you be then?" she asked, her voice a whisper of sound.

He smiled and it came nowhere near his eyes. "I will be the monster you have always feared."

She raised a hand to her throat. "What can be done?"

"I do not know. If I send you away - I will come and find you. Down here, no one can keep you safe." He paused, his eyes moving from hers. "I might have to imprison myself in Tartarus."

"No!" she exclaimed, this time giving into the impulse to grasp his hand tightly in hers. "You cannot do that. You would be tortured, think of all the evil men you have sent to spend eternity there. If you lock yourself in with them it is as good as asking for them to destroy you! There has to be another way."

"I do not know if there is," he said. "Tartarus seems appropriate. It is where the monsters go, after all, and if it can hold my father, it can hold me." He removed his hand from hers and opened a drawer from the table near his bed, pulling out an object wrapped in a black silk cloth. He pulled back the thin material to reveal a jewel encrusted dagger, the light of the fire reflecting off its steely, ebony surface as he lifted it towards her.

"This is for you," he said with intent.

She instantly recoiled at it, the thought of touching that cool, deadly blade causing her stomach to twist. "I do not want that," she said, trying to scoot away from him.

He grasped her hand in his and easily pried her fingers open, forcing the hilt of the cold steel into her hands. The dagger was entwined between their fingers, the iridescent blue stones sparkled against the black blade as she felt a hot burn begin to scorch her fingertips through the sheath; Hades let go of her quickly.

"A fierce soul carved this dagger from the rock in the Acheron and dipped the blade in its waters. Its cut is painful enough to stop even the most powerful Gods in their tracks. This will not kill me, only maim me. One slash will give you a good head start. This is yours."

Green eyes rose to black. "You want me to use this on you?" Her voice was tight and almost unrecognizable to her own ears.

"I want you to protect yourself," he demanded.

"And you think that I would have no issue to hurt you?" she asked pointedly.

An emotion flickered in his eyes but was gone before she could assess it. "I think you will do what you must to survive," he replied.

Persephone held the dagger loosely in her hand, feeling the coldness of the steel on her palm. She closed her eyes against his words, wondering if he really believed her to be that selfish and why his words hurt her so much.

"I am tired," she whispered.

"You should sleep," his deep voice said.

"Alone?" she asked.

"I think that is best."

She opened her eyes. "I do not want to be alone tonight."

"I will watch over you, nothing will harm you tonight. Sleep, Persephone."

She watched him walk away from her as he went back to the fire, sitting in one of the shadowed chairs. The darkness swallowed him and she felt the gap widen between them as he disappeared from her view. Tears began to fill her eyes and she could not stop them as they trickled down her face. How had they become so close only to have such a cold distance between them again? He seemed revolted by her now, ever since the Fates had warned him against her. Tell him the truth, her mind whispered, tell him. She longed to set the words free from her lips, but too long had they been held prisoner in her heart, and her mouth was kept frozen against the truth. She brushed her face against the pillow, wiping away the traces of moisture on her face and she closed her eyes, willing herself to sleep, wondering why it felt like her soul was breaking. As she felt herself begin to drift, she reached for him in the shadows.

"Do not go to Tartarus," she pleaded into the darkness.

Hades stood over her, watching the gentle fall and rise of her chest. Her lashes were dark crescents on her cheeks and she was so beautiful he felt the pain of it in his chest. His love burned for her, as it had always burned for her, long before the cursed arrow had pierced his chest.

266

He moved to the daybed in front of the fire, opening his palm to reveal Persephone's thread of life. The golden light flickered across his face as he studied it, running his fingers back and forth over the mark. "I am sorry, Persephone," he whispered, "for daring to love you, for letting my darkness touch your light." He clenched his fist around her thread lowering his head as his heart contracted. "What a vile world it is to have loved and have lost you twice."

CHAPTER
XVI
RESENTMENT

ERSEPHONE DREAMED OF the Meadows that night. She was running through the fields, the wind in her hair. She looked out over the lakes and saw storm clouds gathering ominously, turning the brilliant blue sky black, and hiding the moon as thunder rumbled across the ground. Rain poured down, turning into thin golden threads that wove a web around her arms and neck, imprisoning her in the raging squall. She heard a scream echo in the distance and quickly turned her head, but before she could move, the Fates appeared before her echoing, "The man from the woods, he is coming. The King will go mad."

She turned around, revolted by their sunken faces, and she realized she was in a cave. The darkness made it difficult to see, but she knew that he was there and she began to run, searching, searching, knowing that someone important was near. The one who called to her soul, the one who completed her. He was hunched over in pain, clutching the gaping wound in his chest, and she could see the beat of his crimson heart as he gasped for air, blood dripping from his mouth. His eyes turned towards her and they gleamed red in the darkness. He growled, as mist began to shroud him from her view, "Little girl. You have a scar on your soul. I see you." She reached towards him, but the wind had begun to carry her away as she screamed his name, screamed the truth at the red eyes in the mist.

She jerked awake and jumped from the bed, her heart beating wildly in her chest. The flames had reduced to coals in the hearth, and she looked for Hades in the darkness.

"Nightmares?" a low voice asked. Hades was standing at the foot of the bed watching her.

She put her hand to her head, "They are getting worse."

"They tend to do that down here. Come," he reached his hand towards her, "I wish to talk to you." She immediately placed her hand into his, smiling up at him as he led her to the dimming fire. He indicated the chair, then took a seat beside her, pulling the signet ring off his finger. Grasping her hand again he placed it onto her finger. "This ring will give you access to all the realms of the Underworld. Today, you will deal with the punishments of the men who will be sent to Tartarus." She looked down at the ring, with shock and he gently turned her face towards him. "Listen to me, Persephone, this is important. You must remove the ring when you leave the throne room. It is not permitted past the gates of the Underworld."

"Why are you giving this to me?" she asked, her voice trembling, as she began to slide the ring from her finger. "I do not want this, I do not want to sentence men to Tartarus. Where are you going?"

He steadied her and forced it back onto her slim finger, stilling her small hands in his own. "You are ready, Persephone, you must be. The time is coming when I may no longer be able to care for this Kingdom or care for you. What is happening is beyond me. Someone must protect the dead. As my wife, as my Queen, this falls to you. My riches, my power, my kingdom. Everything I have will be yours. Do not turn your back on them, Persephone."

"But surely there is someone who is better suited than I? I cannot do this Hades. I have done little more than grow flowers my whole life. I am worthless--"

His hands tightened over hers. "Do not say such words," he answered harshly. "You are pure and strong and worth everything. I would trust no one as I would trust you with this Kingdom."

"But Charon or even your brothers…?"

"There is no one else. No one else I trust to take care of my people."

"I cannot rule this land, Hades," she cried frantically, "I cannot. I do not want this responsibility!"

"Want it or not, the burden will fall on your shoulders. There is no one else, Persephone, there is…only you." He moved his hand along her finger holding the very tip of it between his. "You are sweet and you are kind and though you may not realize it yet, you are strong."

She pulled her hand away from his, the weight of the ring feeling like an unwanted burden. He was wrong, her mind cried out, this illness must have clouded his judgment.

"I am not strong," she said, her voice rising with hysteria. "I am the weakest of the Gods on Olympus. I could never be as powerful as Athena, or Poseidon, or...or you. I..I am anything but strong. I am a coward! You subject this world to the judgement of a coward!"

Placing a hand on her shoulder he gave a gentle nudge. "You knew the name of Kynthía. And you knew other things about her beyond her name, did you not? Why do you think that is? Already you have begun to be able to touch souls, to probe their depths. Whether you know it or not, whether you accept it or not, you are already the Queen of the Underworld. Your sorrow, your resilience, your compassion for even the most vile... these make you stronger than you know. You are not afraid to feel, Persephone, and that makes you braver than the hardiest of soldiers." He paused, staring into space, and he blinked suddenly looking into her eyes. "And your ability, to...to let go when the time comes. These are the traits that make you strong. I would not want a cyclops or a war God sitting on my throne. I want you. The little goddess who cares for her little creatures. The one who weeps over the loss of every soul, however small or inconsequential to the rest of the world. Zeus will take over this kingdom the second an opportunity arises. If that happens, he will have unfathomable power over not just the living, but the dead. I cannot allow that. You cannot allow that. He will come down here demanding sacrifices and unending praise - never feeling the need to show his face while expecting blind obedience from his subjects who worship at the feet of their invisible cruel God. He will treat my subjects as he treats his own - disposable. But, they will hurt eternally at his hand and they will never have the release of death. I love my people. I do not want them to suffer below as they have above. Be a formidable queen - for me."

He wore high collared robes but she could see the tiny dark veins crawling further up his neck, rising like deadly serpents against his pale skin.

"Hades," she whispered, reaching towards him. "How can I help you?"

He was just beyond her reach and he gave her a smile, so sweet it made her heart ache. Was this the smile he had before he had been tormented by his father, forced to kill his mother? Was this the man hidden behind the cold facade?

"You cannot help me, Persephone, I am far beyond that now," he answered. "It is the ending I have always been destined for. You hold no blame in this."

She shook her head, stepping closer to him, panic racing through her veins at his meek acceptance of ... what? Not death, but something far worse. He would be locked in eternal madness, his beautiful mind untouchable, where she could never reach him. He deserved so much more from this life than he had received, so much more than she had been willing to give him. If only she had not misplaced her trust, if only she had not allowed herself to be shattered. She grasped his arm in her frantic grip, but he turned her gently towards the dressing room.

"You must change, my Queen, your subjects await you. The time for resolution is past. This game is played out."

She moved behind a dressing screen and began changing into a gown, her entire body trembling. Her hands shook as she tried to reach for the back of her dress, but she felt his hands there and he was fastening the clasps she could not reach. Always there when she needed him.

"Where are you going?" she asked again, fear making her voice low.

"I will prepare for tomorrow, prepare for the end -- so I do as little harm as possible to this realm -- and to you." His strong hands pushed down on her shoulders and he leaned towards her. "You can do this. You are stronger than you realize."

She turned to face him and she could not help the sheen of tears in her eyes. "Your wound…it looks very bad. Is there nothing we can do?"

He placed her hand over his heart and said with a weak laugh, "You could try loving me. That might help."

She could feel the rhythm of the heartbeat beneath her palm and it felt slow and sluggish, and fear prickled in her own heart, causing it to accelerate in her chest. It felt like the heartbeat of a dying man. As his shadowed eyes watched her, she saw the fragility that lurked in their depths.

Her mind rejected the knowledge of his weakness, but the reality made her knees tremble beneath her heavy gown. "I am sorry, Hades," she whispered. "I am so sorry."

"No," he said fiercely, fire reappearing in the blackness of his gaze. "Never, never be sorry, Persephone. Never let guilt control you, for only the most despicable of men would use that to sway a heart. For those moments… for some of those brief moments, I knew what I wanted in life. I knew everything I've ever wanted could be found in you. All that I could ever ask for is reflected in everything you are. I will never be sorry. I hope that I will remember, somewhere in my mind, that even for the briefest second in time, you were mine and I was yours. I can ask for nothing more; I have received much more than I ever expected to find."

"Hades," she whispered and if she did not know it had died long ago, she would swear her heart was breaking. She pressed her lips against his and he groaned helplessly, pressing his mouth

against hers. Then he let out a painful gasp against her lips and he pushed her away, falling to his knees as blood began to drip from his mouth, falling in long pools to the ground.

"Hades!" she cried, dropping to the ground beside him, her tears falling to join the blood flowing at their feet.

He gently pushed her away, struggling to catch his breath, as he wiped the blood from his lips. "I need to rest. You know your task for today, Queen Persephone."

She pulled at his hand. "Do not be stubborn! Let me help you. You do not have to deal with this alone. I should stay with you!"

Suddenly his eyes shifted and as his black gaze narrowed, anger and lust shone in their depths. His hand shot out, his fingers snaking painfully around her wrist as Persephone gave a small cry of distress. "I am always alone, little girl. I am the Necromancer, I am the King of Death -- and no one touches me," he whispered. "The line between love and hate is thin and soon it will be crossed. If you do not like love, how will you like hate? It is coming for you, Persephone." He hissed out her name and the lines on his neck stood out darker against his skin, pulsating with his words. "What will happen when love turns to resentment, my Queen?" Suddenly his expression cleared and as he let go of her wrist, she realized for the first time he looked afraid. "Go, Persephone," he said softly. "Go and do not return to this room." He grasped the dagger that still lay on the bed and tucked it into her hands, closing her fingers over it. "Be a formidable queen -- for me."

CHAPTER XVII
FORMIDABLE QUEEN

PERSEPHONE FLED FROM the room and she wiped impatiently at the tears on her face that would not stop flowing. The madness was closing in on him, the curse was drawing to its inevitable conclusion and she could not bear it. His mind was growing darker and his body weaker and soon there would be nothing left of the strong King who had once ruled this Underworld. Dear Gods, she had played her part in destroying him, and now he would not let her help him. He would lock himself in Tartarus, living out whatever remained of his eternal life with those wretched evil souls that he had sentenced there.

"He cannot be around Cronos in this condition," she whispered to herself. "He cannot be around the monsters he has punished. I will help him if he will not do it himself." The words were a vow on her lips as she made her way to the throne room.

The room was full as she pushed open the doors and all eyes

turned to her. She almost stepped back, hating being the center of attention, but then she remembered his words. Be a formidable Queen.

She would, she would do it for him. She would do it for the innocent souls who resided in this Kingdom. She raised her head, taking her time to walk across the marbled floor before she took a seat on the ebony throne. Her heart contracted at the sight of Hades' empty chair, but she kept her face expressionless. One of the judges approached her and she looked up recognizing that it was Aeacus. He was frowning.

He knelt to the ground. "My Queen, here is the schedule for today." He handed her the scroll, and she pulled it open, her brow furrowing.

"This list holds only one name, Aeacus. Where are the other names?"

Aeacus looked up to her, his ancient eyes looking into her own. "Your husband came in early and judged all the souls. However, he felt that this last soul required your expertise and he left his judgement to you."

Persephone leaned back against the cold stone of her throne and breathed deeply, trying to calm her racing heart. Hades trusted her to decide eternity for this soul. She would not disappoint him. "Let him in."

The guards brought in a man and threw him to the ground. Persephone looked down at him, taking in his disheveled blond hair and sweet blue eyes.

"Tell me your name."

The man bowed his head, avoiding her gaze, "Goddess, my name is Theo."

"And what is your crime, Theo?"

The judges interrupted, "My queen, this man's crime…"

Lifting a hand, she interjected, "I would like to hear what Theo has to say."

Theo looked up at her then, his eyes clear and true. "My queen, I died fighting a man who attacked my wife. My crime is that I snuck to Hypnos' cave in the Underworld – to steal poppies and make a draught to put you and your husband to sleep so I could return to my body above."

The judges once again interrupted, "He tried to cheat death, your highness! Hades will not tolerate such behavior. It is a certain sentence to Tartarus."

Persephone sat higher on her throne and turned to glance down upon the judges. "But I am not my husband and he is not here."

Theo had piqued her interest about the sleeping draught. This could be what she needed to help Hades. She stepped down from her throne and stood by the young man bowed at her feet. Her intuition told her he was an honest man, a husband who loved his wife. A man who had only tried to avenge her. She bent to Theo, pressing her fingers to his temples as Hades did and as she moved forward, she whispered in his ear,

"Where does Hypnos reside?"

He looked up at her in surprise, but kept his voice very low as he replied, "He lives in a cave by the River Lethe. A cavern surrounded by poppies."

"Thank you," she whispered. Persephone stood and moved back towards her throne, "Tell me, why you would risk your soul's eternal fate to cheat death?" she asked in a loud voice.

Theo calm eyes filled with despair, "My queen, a man forced

himself on my wife, I came home catching him in the act. We scuffled and we both died in the fight. Now my wife is alone in the world. There is no one to comfort her after that bastard's assault on her."

"I see." Persephone calmly looked back towards the judges. "Where is this man now?"

The judges convened for a moment and then Minos, or maybe it was Rhadamanthus, pointed at their list, "Rastus is to be judged tomorrow, my Queen."

She looked back down at Theo, seeing the streaks of sorrow on his face. "Bring him in now."

"But your majesty--" the judges exclaimed

"Now," she said in a cool voice.

After several moments Rastus was dragged into the throne room. The tall doors slammed behind him and Persephone observed the young man. He was tall and muscular, rather attractive actually, but his eyes were mean and sly. Persephone stood by the throne, the light glittering off her diamond toga.

"Is it true you forced yourself on this man's wife?"

Rastus looked at her with a grin, "No, your majesty. Does it look like I would have to force anyone? She begged me for it."

Theo's scream of rage echoed from across the room. "Liar! I saw it with my own eyes."

Persephone put her hand up to silence Theo, then she stepped closer to Rastus. "I will ask you again. Did you rape his wife?"

Rastus looked her up and down, his gaze lingering on her breasts and his voice sneered in distaste. "I'm not afraid of Hades's pathetic flower queen. Let the King judge me, I answer to no bitch." With that, he spat at her feet.

She looked down at the young man and moved slowly towards him. "Oh, but you should be afraid Rastus. I am the Queen of the Underworld and I deal in death." She weaved her hands and heavy black vines chained him down to the floor, wrapping tightly around his limbs, and twisting around his neck until he began to make gurgling noises, his eyes bulging in fear as he clawed desperately at the vines. A small vine grew and slithered up his face. It went into his ear and pushed its way deep into his brain and Rastus screamed in agony.

The Queen knelt down to him as an ebony flower blossomed from one of the vines and as it opened a drop of ruby blood dripped from it's center. She whispered to the blossom, "Did you rape her?"

The plant probed his mind, contracting and constricting until the vines around his neck made him choke out the truth, "Yes," he screamed.

She looked at the Judges, standing calmly. "Castrate him. Send him to Tartarus. Take Theo back to earth and put his soul back into his body."

The Judges looked at one another, shock on their faces. "But my lady---"

"You have questioned me for a second time, you will not get a third time." She knew they did not approve, that they did not accept her, and she did not give a damn. She looked back at them, her hair falling over her face. "I have made my decision. I did not ask for your opinion. Now follow your orders." They straightened hastily and Persephone almost laughed as they stumbled over each other, shouting orders to remove Rastus from the throne room.

She paused for the briefest moment, and her heart skipped a beat as she felt a presence, a soft touch against her soul. She had felt it before, she realized with wonder, when she had touched the golden flower in the meadow and again in the Cave of Souls. It was achingly familiar, sweet and perfect as it moved against her.

"Hades," she whispered softly. It was as if her husband had been watching her from afar, wrapping her in his arms, offering her the comfort she desperately sought but could never ask for. The minute she sensed it and tried to grasp it, the feeling vanished and she was left alone once again. She blinked, bringing the dark throne room into focus.

Persephone moved towards Theo, bending down to take his hands, bringing him to his feet, "I hope you live a long happy life with your wife. We will meet again one day. Until that time, enjoy every blissful second above ground."

"My queen," he breathed, "how can I ever repay you?"

"You already have," she whispered. "Live well, Theo."

CHAPTER
XVIII
POPPIES

PERSEPHONE HEADED QUICKLY to the stables looking for Aethon, her footsteps quiet on the marble floors. Theo had given her a way to aid her husband and she would pursue it regardless of the costs. She rode bareback to the Lethe and the horse's hooves rumbled beneath her, the fabric of her skirts slicing the wind as it flew behind her.

"Faster Aethon," she urged, as she bent low over the mare. "Take me to Hypnos, take me to the Cave of the Poppies -- for Hades! Fly for Hades!" Aethon let out a huff of air and she knew the horse understood.

It was a matter of life and death; the death of Hades' sanity if she could not find the means to help him. She rode past the calm river, past the strange glittering gems reflected in its blue depths. She rode until her legs ached, she rode until Aethon's sides were heaving. Then she saw it. Clenching her legs against the horse she jumped lithely from its back. It was as Theo described; bright red flowers grew from the entrance of the dark cavern and she hesitated only a moment before she made her way into its dark and shadowy depths.

She walked carefully into the cave. It was so dark she could not even see her feet to watch her step and she felt herself falter, unsure of the way. She bent, trying to catch her breath, hyperventilating as demons and men flashed through her mind and she let out a cry of rage. How long had the darkness scared her? What had Hades said? What is the light without the dark? Darkness was merely part of the light, it was nothing to be afraid of. Men and demons did not define it. Without the night there were no stars. The dark held a beauty all its own and she let the shadows move over her, relishing their gentle embrace. She raised her head, taking another step forward and then another, when a slow soothing voice echoed in the blackness.

"Neither light nor wind makes its way here, and yet the King's sun enters." It was Hypnos, the God of Sleep. She could make out a figure, blacker than the darkness of the cave as he made his way towards her. A long thin veil covered him completely and when he reached her, bony fingers grasped her hand, raising it to his covered mouth to kiss it softly. "You do not visit my kingdom often, Persephone, your nightmares keep you awake. They keep you from me."

"I have not come to talk about my dreams, Hypnos," Persephone said slowly, as Hypnos began to circle her.

He turned from her then, templing his skeletal finger tips together and his dreamlike voice turned almost childlike. "In dreams we find our deepest desires, our secret fears. To know the dream of another is to know their soul. I collect them, I keep them. In dreams we can truly live. I know you dream of another's kiss." He began to move back towards her, his dark veil blowing gently at his feet. "I see you in your husband's dreams. They are filled with you, my child. His visions of you are very... engrossing."

"It is because of my husband that I am here," Persephone said, her voice growing sluggish. She pushed her hair from her face, forcing her mind to focus. She would not allow him to draw her down a rabbit hole, she was done playing games. "I need the flowers from around your home. Tell me your price." -

"Why not just grow them yourself?" he asked, his soft voice moving gently in the darkness.

"I need your poppies, strong ones, to put the King to sleep. I need a spell cast on the flowers." She stifled a yawn behind her hand, her eyelids drooping briefly.

Behind the veil, Hypnos smiled and Persephone shivered. "Oh, I cannot deny that the thought of having the King of the Underworld in my kingdom for an extended amount of time does not please me. I can give you the strongest flowers I have," he said, "I know why you need them. I have seen it in both your nightmares." He was silent then whispered in a melody, "I see everything in your dreams."

She forced her slumberous eyes up to his veiled face, pushing back the anxiety his words conjured. There was no time for fear anymore. "I know what haunts my dreams. Take me to the poppies."

"As you wish, my Queen." Suddenly he grabbed her arm and led her further back into the cave. It was blacker than night and the air was stifling as they moved swiftly through the shadows. In the blackness she could make out the vague form of a man sleeping on a bed of ebony marble and she jumped in surprise. Hypnos put a finger to his lips. "Shhhhh. Do not wake him." Further he led her back into the darkness, until finally he stopped and she felt him suck in a deep breath. A sweet, nutty smell filled the cavern and Persephone almost stumbled against the lethargy that had stolen over her. "Kneel, my queen." She hesitated then unsteadily fell to the ground as she felt his hand move over hers, brushing her fingers against soft, satiny leaves. "These are the stoutest, these that grow in the darkest of places," he whispered in a gentle hush. She began to gather the flowers as quickly as possible, blind in the blackness, frantic as she felt sleep pulling at her eyelids, languor wrapping around her mind. The flowers beneath her were soft against her skin and she felt her body relax into them as her eyelids began to droop.

"I should let you rest," the enchanting voice said from behind the veil. "Your dreams are particularly violent and I relish the break from the tedium of the mundane. But your husband will find you and your plan will be for naught. I for one prefer not to be ruled by a mad King." She felt bony fingers wrap around her arm and looked down, seeing the skeletal hands pulling at her flesh.

"Why did I come here?" she whispered, her mind struggling to remember even as her eyes closed. Those hands grasped her more tightly, lifting her paralyzed body from the floor and she drifted as her body moved gently in his arms. She blinked as cold air suddenly filled her lungs and she realized she could see the night sky. Hades, her mind whispered. She must hurry. He bent to lay her gently at the foot of the cave and she stood slowly, turning to face Hypnos. He was holding the brilliant poppies, wrapped tightly in red silk and they regarded each other over the offered bouquet, his skeletal hands wrapped tightly around the stems. Why did taking the flowers from this strange God seem like a betrayal to her husband? He trusted her to protect his Kingdom, but he would not trust her to protect him.

A smile curved the thin slash of mouth she could see just beyond the veil. "Are you sure you wish to travel down this path, young one? Hades is strong, my child. You must make a stout drink if you want him to fall asleep. You will need to keep flowers by his bedside once he is slumbering. Lift his head and make him drink more elixir regularly to keep the spell going. Do not let him wake up." He grabbed her by the arm then, so tightly she knew she would have bruises. "Do not play games with your husband unless you are certain you will win. He is a formidable foe who will sacrifice himself to watch his enemies burn. Tread carefully lest you find yourself on the wrong side of his wrath."

She nodded her head and she felt Aethon approach behind her. She already knew that if her plan worked, if she was able to save Hades, he may never forgive her. For the price of his life, it was a sacrifice she was willing to make -- the final gift to a man who would save everyone but himself. She grasped Atheon's mane gently, pulling herself up on her broad back.

"I have set a course and I will follow it to the end, come what may. The poppies," she demanded, extending her hand towards him.

"Oh, how you have changed, gentle one," he said softly, his head tilted up towards her as he brushed his hand over the poppies, "Strange is it not, that you would risk everything to protect a man you do not love?" The wind rippled through the fabric of his gown as dark eyes burned at her from behind the cloth. She said nothing and he motioned his hands towards the heavens, "The man from the forest. He is coming for you."

She circled around him on Aethon and Hypnos handed her the bouquet, her cool fingers brushing against his bony ones. "I will be ready when he comes."

"Caution, my queen. He is growing darker."

Persephone urged Aethon forward, glancing back at Hypnos's black figure hovering in the distance. He was coming. She forced herself to look ahead. It was time to close this chapter; her past was coming for her and when it arrived she would be there to meet it. The scent of the poppies weighed both her and Aethon down, the mares hooves stumbling as they flew over the shore next to the Lethe. What had Hades discovered in the depths of those blue waters? The poppies in her hands gleamed in the darkness. "He only needs to be asleep for a couple of hours before the Pluto-Venus transit ends," she whispered. Aethon began to slow as the stables came in to view and she quickly dismounted, leading Aethon to her stall and escaping quietly back up to her room. She threw her cape on her bed and turned the lock in her door. It would keep out the servants, and Hades would not seek her again. Time was ticking now and every second mattered. Olive trotted over to her from the bed and Persephone stroked his soft ear as she began to lay out the poppies. She walked to her bed and searched carefully, giving a little shout of satisfaction as she plucked a black hair from one of the pillows.

"He thinks he will lock himself in Tartarus, Olive. He thinks that I would meekly accept his demise as I would the setting of the sun. I will not! I will protect him if he will not protect himself. He deserves someone to protect him." To love him, she thought. Olive's nose nudged against her leg. "Exactly, Olive. Now we get to work."

She spent the rest of the afternoon mixing the potion. It was a complex spell and Persephone wrote it out several times, ensuring she could follow the steps precisely. Too weak an elixir and he would wake up too soon... too strong an elixir and he would never

wake up at all. She counted the steps in her head as she went: a forward stir five times, six counter stirs, four leaves of the poppy, a hair of the drinker, ten forward stirs, twenty counter stirs, four leaves of the poppy. The hours passed as she hovered over the boiling pot, stepping away from it when the fumes overpowered her, and by the time she finished, her hair curled around her face in damp strands. The drought was a perfect red and now she just needed to make him drink it. He had forbidden her from entering his rooms again but he needed to be near his bed when the spell took effect. She must simply disobey him. Setting the elixir and the remainder of the poppies out of sight, she called Jocasta to her room. The maid started at the sight of Persephone's hair but did not utter a word as the Queen instructed her to set up dinner for her husband and herself in his bedroom. Jocasta's beatific smile made Persephone's breath hitch, the servant obviously thought things were going well between them. She could not know of course that Persephone planned to slip a potent sleeping draught into the king's wine to keep her husband from going insane. After helping to arrange the dinner, Jocasta returned and assisted Persephone as she placed a red gown over her head. The center was diaphanous gold and thin strips of red cloth covered her breasts and arms, billowing around her legs. As Jocasta left the room, Persephone hurried to pick up the vial of potion and tucked it into the folds of her dress, then went in search of her husband.

She saw that the golden doors of his room stood open and Hades leaned against the doorway talking in low tones to Charon. "Escort them to Elysium," his voice drifted across the hall to her. As always, Charon's face was hidden from view, but her husband's face was lit by sconces in the hallway. He was wraith-like in his dark robes, his pale skin almost white against the blackness of the high collar. Persephone took a step closer and his black eyes shifted to hers. "That is all I think, Charon." The River Guide left and Hades merely continued to watch her, his back against the door.

"I thought I told you not to come back," he said quietly.

"And you thought I would listen? I do not think you could ever call me a dutiful wife."

"No indeed," he murmured, "I would not. Why are you here Persephone?"

She began to edge closer to him, her eyes fixed on his. "I wanted to see you, one last time, before things... change. It is safe tonight. You said the planets would not shift until tomorrow. Let me stay." Her voice was soft, conjuring in the darkly lit hall. She watched as his eyes followed the outline of her breasts in her gown and she could see the internal struggle in his mind as he fought with what he wanted and what he thought was right. Please Hades, her mind whispered.

He looked up then, searching her eyes. "This is the last time, Persephone. Do you have your knife?" She nodded her head. "Fine. Come into my crypt." He did not move from the doorway and she brushed past him as she entered.

Surveying the room she saw that Jocasta had indeed set a scene for seduction. The table was laid with decadent foods, their intoxicating aromas filling the room. Roses and candlelight had transformed the chamber into a romantic garden and the soft light played across his dark face, and she felt it again, the twinge in her chest. If only tonight were as simple as a wife loving her husband. Her hands shook as she took the goblets and filled them with wine and then tipped the elixir into her husband's glass. She turned quickly and was relieved to see he still stood near the doorway, watching her.

With a smile she brought his goblet to him and took a tentative sip of her own.

"I thought there was some mistake, when Jocasta told me that my wife had requested us to dine together, since our interactions usually involved you running away." Involved, her mind repeated the word, digesting it, rejecting it. Past tense, like their time had already come and gone, that this brief interlude was already over. The thought was like a dagger in her heart and the surprise of her emotions made her breathless. Persephone stepped closer and pressed her fingers against his lips, shaking her head. She did not want to hear bitter words tonight, too much time had already been spent in anger.

"Please," she whispered, "not tonight. I do not want to fight tonight. I just want to be with you. Okay?"

He stared down at her. "Okay," he said softly, his lips moving against her fingers. "No fighting tonight." She reluctantly let her fingertips drop, enjoying the smooth touch of his lips against them. "You look lovely," he muttered, his eyes travelling down her length again. "I am a lucky man to spend the evening with such a Goddess." Hades went to his dresser and ruffled through it, finally pulling out a necklace. "This goes with your gown." He held it against the light and tiny red stones glittered in the golden chain.

"It is beautiful," she said, fingering it gently. Are they rubies?"

"They are pomegranate seeds," he replied. "From the first tree of the Underworld." He lifted his eyes to hers and wordless understanding passed between them. She knew how much that necklace must have meant to him, set with the seeds of the tree that grew from his mother's blood. He walked up behind her and fastened the chain around her neck and she felt his breath against her hair. His body tightened suddenly and he moved swiftly to the opposite end of the table. "Charon told me you did well today. In the throne room," he said quickly, his breaths coming in short gasps.

"Thank you." She felt warmth fill her at his praise. "I did what I thought was right, what my heart told me was the truth. The Judges did not approve of my decisions, I am afraid."

He smiled. "They seldom approved of mine when I first started. They will learn to respect you as you deserve. You are their Queen." He gestured for her to sit and once she did he approached the table, moving slowly towards his chair as he placed his goblet before him. She knew she was looking too much at his cup and she forced her eyes down to her plate, raising them again when he sat.

"Why did you choose Theo and Rastus for me?"

His eyes lingered lovingly on her breasts and then rose to her eyes.

"Ah, but I did not choose Rastus for you to judge. You chose him yourself."

She gave him a ferocious look. "Certainly you would have known I would judge Rastus after hearing the crime he committed!

"Perhaps," he replied. "I make it a habit not to know too many things. We do not even know ourselves completely."

"You did not answer my question," she said.

He lifted the goblet and her heart stuttered, but he paused at her words. "I was tired, and he was the last prisoner of the day. I knew he would be good practice for you."

"I could have judged more prisoners," she said, frowning at him. "There was no need to tire yourself."

"Next time, I promise, you will have the whole list." His

eyes were luminous in the light as he watched her. "Why did you let Theo go?

"He loved his wife -- enough to die for her, enough to live for her. He deserved a second chance."

Hades looked at the necklace beating to the rhythm of her heart and only nodded. Eager to get him to drink, Persephone lifted her glass in the air and said, "To my first day dealing judgment." They toasted and sipped from their cups and Hades watched her as he drank, his eyes never leaving her face.

"Have you decided on what you will do tomorrow?" she asked.

"Charon and I discussed that. In the morning I will be locked in Tartarus. The doors shall remain closed until this transit in the sky passes. What he finds once he retrieves me will determine what happens from there."

She stiffened in her chair. "And you made this decision with the help of your old friend rather than your wife?

"Persephone," he murmured, "I thought you did not want to fight tonight? There is no other choice, you know that."

She tried to smile at him, but found her lips could not seem to make the movement. "You are right, I am sorry. Is the wine not to your liking? I can bring you another glass."

He shook his head. "Tomorrow I will need the full power of my mind, whatever remains of it. Wine dulls the senses and arouses those I do not need aroused."

She blushed at his words even as she bit back a sigh of frustration. Looking up she saw his eyes moving over her and she suddenly knew how to get him to drink his wine. She stood, keeping her goblet in her hand as she approached him. He looked up at her

294

warily as she crawled into his lap, his body strong and hot beneath hers, and a gasp escaped his lips.

"You are right," she whispered. "Tomorrow everything will change. Tonight belongs to you and I." She swallowed the remainder of her wine and his eyes followed a ruby drop as it ran down her mouth and disappeared between her breasts. She picked up his goblet and pushed it against his lips and he let her tilt the liquid into his mouth.

"What are you doing, Persephone?" he asked, his voice edged with pain.

"I do not want to be alone tonight," she whispered. "Stay with me."

Her hand raised again to bring the cup up when his hand grasped her wrist. "Your heart is racing. I know this is not what you want."

She nuzzled her face in his neck, breathing him in and she felt something awaken deep in her body. "Do not presume to know too much," she whispered in his ear. "Remember?" She bit down on his ear lobe as he had done to hers and she felt him shudder beneath her. "Relax." This time he let her bring the cup to his lips and he drained the remaining liquid from it and she set the empty goblet on the table.

"Persephone," he said, drawing his face back to look at her. "Orpheaus passed some time ago. Today I collected his soul and reunited him with Eurydice."

She stared down at him in shock. Why was he telling her this now? He had travelled to the surface to collect a mortal soul. Why? Was Orpheaus not sentenced to wander, just like her father? "But you said… you said he would be cursed to roam the Earth alone. Why did you change your mind?"

"Because it is what you wanted," he said, purple ringing his eyes as his gaze met hers, "because I love you." Before she could respond he brought her head down to his and covered her mouth with his, swallowing her gasp of sorrow. He sipped at her, like he was drinking nectar from her lips, like she was the last promise of hope to a dying man. His mouth moved to her neck, his teeth dragging along her soft flesh and she groaned in pleasure. Lifting his hands he tore the material from her breasts and sat back staring as her nipples hardened in the cool air. She lifted her hands to cover them but he caught her wrists.

"Perfect," he breathed. And when he closed his mouth over one taut peak, she did nothing to stop him. As his mouth moved to her other breast she felt his hand move against her thigh and touch the wetness between her legs. Gods, she waited for the fear to come, but all she felt was pleasure. He loved her and she...she needed to stop him. She was a liar, manipulating his weakness to get what she wanted. She felt his hands draw up her back, unfastening the small buttons Jocasta had helped her close just hours ago. Surely the potion would take effect soon, how far would she have to take this? He would never forgive her once he learned the reason why she had pursued him. She began to pull away, feeling ashamed that she had taken advantage of his sickness. His hands were hot on her skin as he pulled down the gown, when they suddenly paused against her back. She looked down at his face and she saw the dawn of awareness in his unfocused eyes.

"What was in the wine?" he asked. He stood up suddenly and Persephone fell to the ground, watching aghast as Hades stumbled like a drunken man to the window. She leapt towards him, grasping his arm tightly as he began to fall and half pulled him to the bed. "What did you put in the wine, Persephone?" he demanded again, his words slurring.

"I am sorry," she whispered, "but you need to sleep." She gave a sudden cry of pain as she felt his disordered attempt to probe her mind. But she knew, despite his stupor, he had found the memory of her in Hypnos' cave.

"You lied to me? You drugged me and seduced me and use my feelings for you..." He did not finish his sentence, trying to push himself from the bed, but she forced him gently back down, his powerful body helpless against the lethargy.

"You were going to lock yourself in Tartarus," she replied fervently. "I could not allow you to sacrifice yourself."

His head shook on the pillow, his dark hair falling against his face as he groaned. "This will not work, Persephone. Why did you do it?" He reached down to touch his wound and his glazed eyes laughed mirthlessly at the blood staining his fingers. "Why?" he whispered again. "My wound still bleeds. I know it was not love."

"You will be safe," she said softly.

"No, Persephone," he whispered, the bleakness in his voice causing a shiver to run down her spine. "All you have guaranteed is the destruction of me and possibly yourself. There is no honor in what is to come. This will not hold me."

"You will be safe," she said again, the tremble in her voice making it a question. She bit her lip as she hurried from the room, returning with a bouquet of poppies. His eyes were closed and she hoped he had fallen asleep but his hand shot out and grasped her wrist, his fingers slack against her skin.

"Get those cursed flowers away from me," he growled at her. His hand dropped from her suddenly and she grasped his arm, tucking it carefully against his side.

She brushed his dark hair from his face and he pressed his feverish head against her palm. "Rest, my King, rest." She ran her fingers over his lips and then poured another vial into his mouth watching as a drop of the elixir fell from his lips down onto his pale skin, like blood in the snow. "Forgive me," she whispered. "Forgive me for everything." His lips were red from the poppies and she leaned down pressing her mouth against his, tasting the bitter potion against her tongue. "Is it you I distrust, or is it myself? If I were to tell you the truth... If you were not cursed, would you really love me? Could you love me? Could anyone love someone as foolish as I?" She stared down at his dark beautiful face. "You see, it is I who am cursed. I who am not able to love." She bent again kissing his forehead and then slipped from the room praying that she had done the right thing.

CHAPTER
XIX
THE TRANSIT AND THE TRUTH

THE TRANSIT HAD finally arrived and Persephone lay in bed, shivering beneath the blankets. She had lain awake all night remembering the look of betrayal in Hades' eyes. Would he forgive her? Would the potion be enough to keep him safe? Hypnos had seemed gleeful at the thought of the King slumbering and Hades would be locked deeply in his kingdom. She did not trust the God of Sleep anymore than she did Zeus, but there simply had been no other choice. Tartarus was not an option. She pulled herself reluctantly from the bed. Shadows stood out darkly beneath her eyes and she turned impatiently from the mirror, dressing hurriedly. There was much to be done and she had to check on Hades before beginning her day. Leaving Olive tucked in her bed she made her way down the hallway, her footsteps soft on the stone floors. Persephone cracked open the door to her husband's room and she saw his shadowed body thrashing against the sheet.

She moved deeper into the room, disturbed at the violent movements he made in the bed. Surely the poppies were strong enough that he should have been in a deep slumber? His head tossed from one side of the pillow to the other, his black hair matted against his head. She bent down to wipe the sweat from his brow and pulled her hand back quickly with a gasp. His skin burned as if he was on fire. The sheet was thrown to the ground, and his robes were loose, revealing the veins running up his neck and lower jawline that were purple, tinged with black along the edges. She watched his chest rise and fall quickly with gasping breaths as if he were a mortal with a fever. She had seen that rapid breathing before, always followed with the inevitable conclusion of death. Was it the curse he was fighting or the stupor of the poppies? What if she had made the draught wrong and poisoned him? She bit her lip anxiously and with a wave of her hand she pulled out a compress from the air composed of lavender and feverfew, gently patting his forehead. His eyes fluttered and she noticed the color looked different, darker than his usual tone. Taking a candle she bent down, pulling the eyelid apart, to inspect his eye. Red and black veins made their way into the center, obscuring the color of his dark iris and she leaned closer. Suddenly his eye flashed purple and looked straight at her before rolling back into his head. She jumped back almost screaming. He had known she was there, she thought, her heart beating wildly in her chest. How was he even partially consciousness? She hurriedly uncorked a vial of elixir she had brought with her and poured more draught down his throat. At this rate she would run out of the potion before evening. The curse appeared to be advancing rapidly. How was he strong enough to fight against Hypnos' most powerful poppies? She may need to return to Hypnos, but she was afraid if she entered his somniferous cave again she would not leave a second time. She would join that hidden figure that slept deeply in its depths. She watched him for several minutes and breathed a sigh of relief as his body quieted. Reluctantly she turned to leave, knowing that she must complete his tasks to alleviate as many questions about his absence as possible.

The list in the throne room was long and Persephone fought down a wave of impatience. She would need to check on Hades periodically to ensure he was dosed with appropriate elixir, but how could she do that if she was locked in this room all day? One of the Judges approached her with a frown on his ancient face and she could not be bothered to make the effort to figure out which one it was.

"Where is Hades?" he queried.

"The King wished me to continue greeting the souls today. He has other tasks to attend to. Do you take issue with his judgement?" The Judge opened his mouth and Persephone continued quietly, "Pray be seated. I have no wish to delay the proceedings with needless questions." His ancient face took on a deep expression of disapproval and he turned on his heel making his way back to his compatriots, their incensed whispers reaching her ears but she simply did not care. She raised her voice, twisting the ring on her finger. "Bring in the children."

The hours passed as she gently ushered the souls into their next life, taking the time to comfort those who needed comfort, to sort out the souls who needed special consideration -- but all the time in the back of her mind -- was Hades. Was he sleeping still, locked in the deep embrace of Hypnos' willing arms? She will destroy you. But surely the poppies would offer him far better protection than being locked in Tartarus.

Part of her had known that if he had entered into that black Kingdom, he would never emerge again. She forced her mind away from her hopefully slumbering husband, seeing that they were half-way down the list and she prepared herself for the next wave of souls.

When she finally left the throne room, her head was pounding. She hurried through the palace and when she reached the doors to Hades' room, she paused, her pulse racing as she saw the door was ajar. Had someone entered his room? Stepping closer slowly she heard the quiet voice of a woman and she rushed through the doors and then her heart truly stopped. Hades was alone in the room just where she had left him, but he was awake and staring down at his bed. He was scratching at his heart and his clothing was torn, his hair in wild disarray. Deep bloody gashes were clawed over his chest as if he was slowly trying to reach inside his body to rip out his heart and he stood unnaturally still. Movement drew her eye and she realized that she was wrong, he was not alone in this room. There were shadows moving in his bed, writhing in the sheets and she heard a deep groan of pleasure, realizing with a gasp what those shadows were doing. The door closed behind her and the lock clicked loudly in the quiet. Her husband was watching a shadowed couple having sex on his bed, her husband that she had tricked. Her husband who had warned her of his impending madness -- and she was locked in a room with him.

He looked over at her finally and his eyes glowed in the darkness. This was not her husband she thought as she stared at his red gleaming eyes. There was no trace of recognition in his eyes and she felt a tremble travel through her. She did not know this God.

"How easily the lamb walks into the wolf's den," he whispered, finally, his voice vibrating with anger. She turned to grasp the handle to the door, but he lifted a hand and pulled her body across the room towards him. She let out a frantic cry, grasping desperately for the door but the force was too strong and she stumbled towards him. He grasped her painfully and pushed her down into a chair. He stared down at her and then bent to rub his hands through her hair, pulling the strands tightly against her scalp. His breathing was heavy against her face, "Oh, I know you. My little beguiler, my wife 'in name only'." His fingers pressed against her jaw.

"You are hurting me!" she cried.

"We would not want that, now would we?" He reached down to his chest and rubbed the blood against her lips and she shuddered as it smeared across her face. "I would not want you to have to bleed, like how you bled when your lover fucked you. When he took what belonged to me."

"Stop! Stop it!" she said, rage rising in her own mind. She tasted the metallic taste of his blood and she tried to grasp his hand but he grabbed her wrists tightly and she felt the press of his fingertips against her bones. "How did you…"

"How did I what? Wake up?" His laugh was low and deep. "Hypnos says hello. He woke me after I nearly strangled the life out of him." He pressed his face closer to hers. "You should have made the draught stronger if you wished to lock away a King."

"Hades," she said softly, "let me get Charon, maybe he can help us."

The look he gave her was so filled with scorn it made her gasp. "You think to imprison me. You think I would let you ever

have such power over me again. You had one chance and you failed. And when I awoke I could see so much clearer. I can see you so much better now wife."

She could hear the sounds of the entwined shadows breathing heavily, the sounds of their bodies joining as the larger shadow thrust over and over, and her face burned as the woman let out a deep moan of ecstasy. She pushed against him, trying to avert her gaze from the bed but he shoved her back down, grasping her head between his hands.

"You are such a coward," he hissed at her. "You are as afraid to look at sex as you are to have it." He turned her head forcing her to stare at the bed. Her eyes widened as she saw the long dark hair of the woman spread against the pillow and recognized the strong profile of the man. It was an apparition of them! Hades sneered in her ear, "Visions of what might have been. I told you, time is broken here. Does it make you sick to think in another life you fucked me?"

"I do not want to watch!" she cried. "This is disgusting!"

"I disgust you," he spat at her.

"I did not say that, I said--," but he had moved away from her, watching intently as the shadowed Persephone mounted her husband.

She closed her eyes, ashamed and aroused at the sight of her fictional being pleasuring Hades. The scent of the poppies made the air heavy and she felt her eyes drift. She had to get out of this room, for her sake and for his. He was enraged by her, consumed by her and it was unsafe for them both.

Hades had warned her, but she had ignored him and now his worst fear had come to pass. There was no trace of her husband in this man's eyes, only madness lurked in their depths. Her eyes had

305

closed again and this time when they opened she saw Hades lean body standing before her, his heavy erection evident beneath his robes. He pulled her up, pressing her tightly against him.

"Do you know what I want to do to you - to my 'wife in name only'? I want to water you with my mouth, plant my seed in your garden and watch it grow. I want to fuck you so hard this curse pours out of me and into you. Until you are the one begging for me on your knees like a pathetic bitch."

"Stop it!" she cried, standing unsteadily from the chair. "Do not speak to me like that. This is not you, Hades. Do not do this." Her voice was slurred and she tried to move away from him but her limbs were heavy as she fell against him and his fingers dug into her flesh.

He laughed into her ear. "Or what, you will drug me?" He bent low jeering in her face. "You have drugged me with flowers, and you have drugged me with love. What will happen when you fall asleep my enticing wife?" He forced her face up and pressed his lips against hers, kissing her roughly and she made a sound of pain against his mouth and she felt him swallow it greedily. It was too familiar, this forceful embrace, and she kicked at him but it only incensed him more. She heard her clothes rip as his hands began to tear at her and he gave a punishing bite against her lower lip, pulling so hard she feared it may burst between his teeth. Then he threw her down onto the bed as she tried to cover her exposed breasts.

"You still try to hide yourself from me. I am very sick of your maidenly modesty." He began to unfasten his toga. "I do not need to watch a vision when I can have you here and now. Spread your legs like you did for your lover and let us continue where we left off."

She sprung up from the bed and slapped him hard across the face, drawing blood from his lip but he did not even pause. As he came nearer to her she drew back her fist and punched him as hard as she could while delivering a swift kick to his groin. He fell to his knees and she hoped he would stay there.

"Hades, stop," she said again. "Stop this, this is not you!"

He stood up from the floor and slowly put a hand to his face, blood dripping from his nose. He looked down at his fingers then drew them into his mouth, his tongue licking the blood from his skin, smiling at her. Wind whipped through the room and his eyes glowed red as the symbol of Pluto appeared on his forehead, glowing white against his pale skin. "If a lamb strikes a wolf she better kill him." His voice was low and demonic, echoing against the walls as he stepped closer and closer to her. "You and I have crossed the threshold. You make me weak and I detest weakness. I detest you. I cannot have something around that makes me so... infirm. You are the source of all my suffering and if I do not destroy you, you will certainly destroy me."

The Fates' voices echoed in her mind as he wrapped his fingers around her neck and they tightened briefly, her breath catching before he lifted his hand. She was slammed onto the bed and she gave a helpless cry as she was unable to shift against an invisible, immovable force. He stood over her, menacing and evil and so much like the figure from her nightmares. She felt herself spiraling, dreams converging with reality until she wanted to scream out in anguish. But the nightmare from her dreams was not him, just as this man who stood over her was not her husband. The wind rippled through her hair and clothes and she saw the fire flare in his eyes and it seemed to crackle in the air. Flames began spreading up the curtains of the canopy and the heat was painfully close to her flesh. Tears filled her eyes as the fear and anger slipped away and she saw the fire reflected in the darkness of his eyes. She had brought this powerful God to his knees, this good man who loved children, who mourned his mother and was gentle with animals. What had he become because of her? She pulled wildly at the invisible chains restricting her, and he watched out of hooded eyes. She gave up with a vicious curse, the chains immovable against her, and she looked into the mad King's eyes.

"Hades, do not make me hate you."

He climbed onto the bed towering over her and grasped her legs in his hands spreading them apart, "You have always hated me. Now I will make you love me."

She moved her fingers and reached into the belt of her dress, feeling the cool handle of the blade he had given her last night. Opening her palm, a small plant grew from the center, black berries hanging from the green leaves, the belladonna concealing the Acheron dagger that she clasped tightly in her hand. She saw his eyes flash to the plant and she knew that he had seen the dagger hidden inside the delicate leaves.

"You fucking bitch," he growled. He made to reach for the dagger when she shot vine after vine from her fingertips, the strongest, thickest vines she could grow. He tore one branch off and another took its place, then another as if it were the Hydra, and she felt his hold on her loosen. She sat up from the bed and hurled her body towards him and together they toppled on the bed as he struggled to remove the dagger from her hand. Suddenly he gasped and grabbed his side, looking down to see a twisting vine pushing the dagger through his flesh, breaking the skin. He looked at her hand and saw that it now held only the plant, the blade missing from beneath its leaves.

He laughed. "Clever girl. I will make a queen of you yet." She stared at him, horrified at the smile on his face, aghast at the blade that was held against his pale skin by thickened green vines. Suddenly a strong voice invaded her mind. "You don't have the courage wife."

"Forgive me, Hades," she whispered, and she twisted her hand and the vine pushed the dagger deep inside him -- up to the hilt. His back arched and twisted as he let out a scream.

His eyes opened suddenly, pain and panic glazing his vision, and in his black gaze she saw her husband staring back at her. He was fighting against the demon inside of him, struggling to rise to the surface, but the red was already reclaiming his eyes.

"Persephone…run." He raised his hands and blasted the doors open, and she hesitated, but his eyes were already fully red and she jumped from the bed, running away from him. Do not look back. She heard his voice in her mind and she did not know if it was real or just another memory, echoes of dreams that would always haunt her. She swept past her room and did not stop running, out, out, out of the gates of Hell.

She rushed from the castle and shook her head, clearing the tears from her eyes as she paused before the gates of the Underworld. They were inexplicably open. Every step she took from him was a painful pull against her heart and her stubborn feet paused before the threshold. Persephone. She shivered at the longing of the whisper in the wind. Gold glittered in the breeze and she remembered the stream of gold she had watched from her window at her mother's temple. If she left him would he die?

"Hades," she whispered, closing her eyes, the wind pulling at her hair, pulling her back towards him. Low dark laughter bellowed behind, cursing her name as she forced herself past the gates. She reached the cliff that Orpheus had climbed and began to make her way to the top. Up the rugged rocks she sped, as fast as she could and she could hear movement behind but she dared not look back. "Do not look back." Orpheus had not heeded his warning -- but she would! The sky grew closer and closer as she climbed up the treacherous mountain towards the light. She reached the very precipice and then froze. The landscape was blanketed in thick snow, the trees barren and the flowers dead beneath the heavy white blanket. She took a step out of the cavernous darkness towards her freedom in the sun. A hand reached out and grabbed her pulling her back into darkness.

Hades pulled her tightly to his chest, cradling her in his arms as blood seeped into her gown. "Forgive me!" he cried.

She jerked away from his grip, fear and shock making her step back from him. "Let go of me!" She stumbled away from him and her arm was flung out of the cave, the signet ring on her finger glaring brilliantly in the rays of sunlight.

He grasped her arm quickly and pulled her back into the shadows and she looked up at him with wide, horrified eyes. "I am sorry, I forgot that I was still wearing your ring!" she gasped in fear. He looked down at her and she saw the love reflected in his gaze.

He grabbed her hand, gently pulling the ring off her finger, placing it back onto his own. "Say nothing, Persephone. They are coming." She mouthed no, trying to grasp the ring from him but he kept his hands in hers as a painful sound filled the air and the sky turned an eerie shade of green and gold. Persephone pressed her

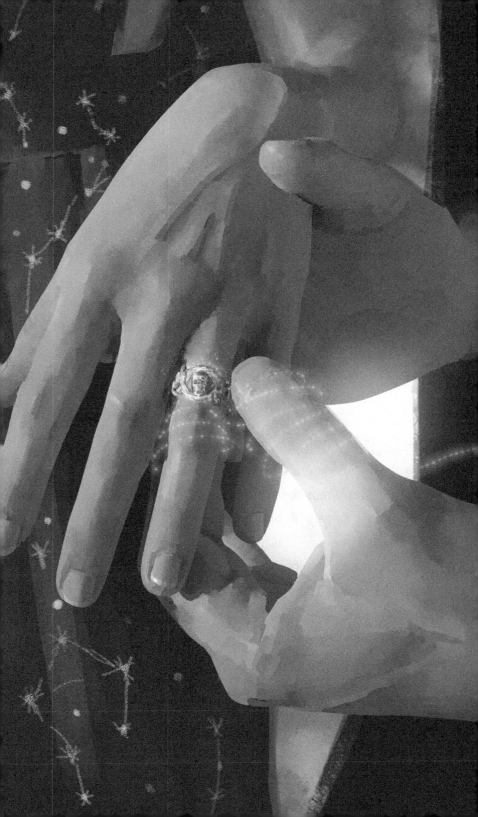

body against Hades as shivers began to wrack her. His hands ran through her hair and she felt his fingers trace the bruises on her lips. "Forgive me," he whispered again.

Their bodies were separated as six armed guards thudded down from the skies and Persephone fell to the ground as Hades was shoved against the wall. She looked around and she closed her eyes tightly. They were Ares' soldiers. The Earth shuddered again and one last figure flew down from the sky and thudded to the ground. She knew who would stand before her and when she opened her eyes she saw he was there. Ares had found them.

His blond hair escaped his metal helmet and his blue eyes were gleeful in his beautiful face. He circled Persephone on the ground and then turned to Hades; his face twisted as he looked at the God of Death.

"What do we have here? A lover's tiff? My father explained the rules to you, Hades. Your seal is never permitted above ground. Take him!"

The guards grabbed Hades' hands, pinning them behind his back and Ares wrapped his fingers tightly around Persephone's arm. She pushed against him but he slapped her so hard that her head hit the wall and her vision blurred. She heard Hades snarl but then Ares pulled her roughly to her feet.

"I could take you to Mount Olympus," he said with a smile, "and deal your judgement there. But I think it fitting to return the little couple to their land of bliss, so I can rip the flesh from your bones in your own Kingdom." He approached Hades and kicked him with the sharp edge of his boot. "Get up, King," he sneered. "Your subjects await."

The guards hauled Hades to his feet and Ares kept his hand

painfully tight around Persephone as they descended down the steep cliff she had just climbed. She prayed that the gates would be closed but they remained opened and they entered the Underworld as easily as she had left it. She glanced quickly at Hades but his head was bowed, his dark hair obscuring his face. Why had he not closed the gates? She bit back a frustrated fearful cry as they entered the palace, wanting to shout a warning to any of the subjects who remained in the castle. The guards footsteps echoed loudly in the hall, which was mercifully empty. No sign of any life was present in the darkened palace. When they burst into the throne room, the guards threw Hades roughly to the ground and he lay on his side, his face pale as he looked up at Ares. The effects of the drugs, the curse and the transit had weakened him and Persephone cursed herself. Ares pushed her to the ground, dismissing her as inconsequential and then he slowly approached Hades. Taking his sword he cut the back of Hades' toga, ripping it from his body. He walked around Hades sizing him up, his eyes gleaming as he noticed the arrow wound and claw marks. Blood dripped down Hades' arm and the black veins now ran completely up his neck spreading to his lower face.

"What are we hiding?" he laughed. "You are wounded -- and badly." Hades said nothing, watching Ares passively. "Chain him!" Ares cried, flinging his hair back. The guards rushed forward and Persephone stood too, attempting to race towards Hades, but Ares grabbed her and pulled her tightly against his body, pressing his erection against her back. "I will deal with you later."

Ares pushed her away again as he unstrapped a golden whip from his belt. "This came wrapped around you when Cronus vomited you up." He ran his fingers over the tawny thong, smiling wickedly, his teeth gleaming in the shadows. "I am going to enjoy beating the man who steals from me."

"Let Persephone leave the room," Hades yelled, "She should not have to watch."

Ares pulled her again from the ground, eyeing the ripped front of her gown, "She is not going anywhere," he snarled. "I think she should watch as I tear the flesh from your bones. This traitor is what you prefer to me? You let him fuck you, I can see it on your face. You are a whore."

She pushed away, turning to look at her husband. "Hades," she whispered, reaching her hand towards him.

Ares gave a swift angry inhale, then lifted the whip cracking it hard on Hades' back. Hades pushed his face into the stone, taking the first blow in stride. Ares snapped his fingers dousing the strap in fire and raised it again, crashing it as hard as he could on the God's back. Hades let out an anguished but reluctant scream that sounded more like a mortal man than a God, and Ares relished in it.

The scream broke Persephone's heart and she cried out as the blood spurted from his back, arcing across the room to splatter against the wall. The old scars were pulled open and she remembered how Eurynomos had carved out his flesh. No one had ever protected him and she would not let this honorable man fall at Ares' knees, -- not for her.

She rushed forward and forced herself to grab Ares' arm before it could descend again, "Stop this!" she cried. "This was not his fault. He broke no rules! It was me. I was the one wearing the ring when I went above ground. Punish me, not him!" She turned to her husband who lay passive on the floor and she screamed at him, "Hades, stop punishing yourself and start breaking the rules! You do not deserve this!"

Ares sneered at her. "How touching, the little wife protecting her husband." He lifted his arm higher this time and the whip began to descend but she lifted her palms and vines wrapped around the whip, halting its descent.-

She stepped closer to Ares and forced him to look at her. "Your anger is with me," she said quietly. "I am the one you want to punish. Is it not my blood you want flowing at your feet? I betrayed you, did I not? Leave him alone." Her voice was persuasive and she poured every ounce of magic she had into it. "Punish me."

She could see the blood lust and hatred in Ares' sky blue eyes and he stepped closer to her. "What will you give me if I do?"

Hades struggled against the chains and finally she could see anger on his face. "Persephone, stop!" he cried desperately.

"Anything," she said, "Everything. Just leave him alone."

Ares dropped the whip and turned Persephone around, ripping the back of her dress. Two men grabbed her arms dragging her to a rock, chaining her hands to the stone. Hades looked over to his wife and saw fear flash in her eyes, but underneath was something he had not dared to dream.

"Hades...I..." she said with longing.

Just as Ares lifted the whip, Hades tilted his wrist waving his fingers. Time slowed down almost to a stop. Persephone felt a lightness fill her and she watched in shock as they both flew out of their bodies and were standing in the center of the throne room, bathed in gold. She glanced at Ares and the whip moving slowly through the air towards their bodies, still tied to the stones. She saw the chained Hades on the stone with the bleeding, raw back, and then looked at the golden, smiling Hades who stood before her. Her hands were spun from millions of golden threads and their bodies glittered in gold as she lifted a shining hand, touching his face. He looked pure and clean and a smile curved his mouth that reached his dark eyes. He was beautiful and looked like everything she had ever wanted wrapped in one perfectly flawed package.

"What is this?" her voice sounded distant and seemed to echo loudly in the room while being only a whisper in her mind. "How is this possible? Are we dead?"

He shook his head. "These are our spirits, Persephone. Our bodies lay still on the rocks, but I released our souls to allow them to commune. Your spirit has something it wishes to tell mine." He looked at her smiling, his voice reverberating against her. He lifted his hand to her face and leaned close to her, seeing the confusion on her face. "You are bearing your soul to me," he said with a beautiful smile.

Everything around them moved in slow motion except them, and the fear and the pain disappeared until there was only him. Only her. Only Hades and Persephone covered in gold. He took her hand and placed it against his chest that was covered in smooth, healthy flesh. His wound had vanished and she rubbed her fingers in wonder against his warm skin.

"Why did you take my punishment, Persephone?" he gently asked.

"I… I do not know," she said helplessly.

"Do you not?" he again queried.

"I could not let him hurt you. I could not bear it! I am sorry Hades, so sorry for bringing you to this point." A golden tear travelled down her face and he bent to kiss it away. She watched in shock as he pressed his palm against hers and their threads began to intertwine, weaving seamlessly until she felt him inside of her, until she was part of him, their consciousness so close she could not seperate where she ended and he began. Echos of his thoughts began to play in her mind. It was as if he knew his penalty would bring her barriers down and she felt every moment that had led to this, a carefully plotted game of chess that had led her to her soul's desire. In this glittering form, as their threads bled into each other, she knew the truth; she had found her soul's mate.

Hades leaned forward to kiss her, his lips soft against hers. As a warmth filled her from the inside, she suddenly remembered the golden figures that she had seen, embracing in this room -- exactly where they stood now. She felt his love and she kissed him back, pouring everything she had never said into the touch of her lips. Her heart began to pound and she looked down to see it was illuminated in her golden chest, a crimson glow with a small thread of darkness in its beating center. Hades lifted his hand to place it over the wound and she grabbed it, suddenly frightened.

"This is where my darkness seeps in. I have tried so hard to hide it, even from myself."

He whispered, "I do not fear the dark. Share your darkness with me as I have shared mine with you." He took his hand and placed it over the wound in her chest.

The mark began to flutter and vibrate and shone with a brilliant light as memories flooded his mind's eye. He looked into her past and saw Persephone make her way to the river to wait for his letter, instructing what time they would meet. She was smiling, Olive trotting next to her and she bent down to rub his soft fur as they walked to her destiny. What if he was displeased when he actually met her? What if he changed his mind? She forced her feet forward, anxious to meet this man who occupied her thoughts and dreams, desperate to meet the man she loved. When she arrived, a man with tawny hair was standing by the water holding the letter, and he rose.

The man, no a God she realized with a shock, turned from the shadows holding the letter. It was Ares and his face was beautiful in the dappled sunlight.

"I could not wait for you any longer," he said, his pure voice strong in the twilight night. The wind touched the golden strands of his hair and she felt it pulling her back towards the temple.

She smiled uncertainty, hovering at the edge of the water. "It is you? You have been the one writing me?"

"It is, my beloved. I will kiss you under the stars," Ares said with a smile as he opened up his arms wide. Persephone ran into them and kissed him in the forest, under the darkening sky, pressing her lips against his over and over. "I love you!" she cried. "I have waited for you for so long," she whispered, pressing her head against his chest.

They stood under the trees kissing one another and any misgivings she had at the discovery of his identity she pushed away. If he was not who she had imagined as her lover, his letters showed his true nature. His compassion, his cleverness, his wisdom were all there, displayed into every word of his writing -- and she knew him. She loved him. He was as much a part of her as her own heart. She drew back as she felt his tongue touch the seam of her lips and his hand fondled her breast. "Would you like to meet my mother?" she naively asked.

Ares started laughing. "I do not think Demeter needs to be present for this, unless she wants to join in the fun." Her brows furrowed, confused by his words, when he lifted his hands to her neck and wrapped his long fingers against it, squeezing tightly.

318

She pulled desperately at his hands even as her vision became blurred from fear. "Stop," she choked out.

"You do not like hands around your throat, my beloved?" His face was leering at her, his beautiful blue eyes narrowed and fanatical as a shadow passed over the setting sun. Olive began butting Ares with his head and Persephone gave a moanful cry and reached for her little friend. Ares picked up the little fawn and grasped his thin brown neck and a sickening crunch filled her ears. She screamed and fell to her knees, staring in horror at Olive's empty eyes.

Ares covered her mouth with his hand as she struggled to break free. She began to claw at him when Ares pushed her roughly to the ground, throwing Olive's body near the river like he was refuse, like he had not been her dearest friend.

"If you keep screaming, I will break your neck like that fawn," he promised, smiling down at her. She pushed at him but the God of War was strong and he held her arms down. "I will enjoy taking what should have been mine long ago."

Hades watched as he pulled up her skirts running his hand up her pale thighs, as the other hand covered her full mouth. She bit his hand hard, drawing blood, and he slapped her face and she hovered on the edge of consciousness. He began to beat her in earnest, punching and kicking her, hitting her breasts and the delicate point between her legs, until Persephone curled into a ball, tears streaming down her swollen face. Olive's lifeless eyes stared into hers.

"Why must you make me hurt you, Persephone?" he asked, his voice calm as he finally drew away from her, licking her blood from his knuckles.

"Let me help my fawn," she pleaded.

He handed her a scroll telling her if she wanted to help Olive to write another letter. "Tell me I am a monster that no woman could ever love. Tell me you curse the day you met me. Tell me everything I touch brings death and destruction. Tell me you hate me!"

"I do not understand!" she cried, earning another slap to her bruised face.

"Write it," he breathed into her mouth as he bit her lip so hard that blood filled both of their mouths. He laughed and sat behind her with his hands around her neck, kissing her as she wrote the letter. With the last word written, he turned her around to face him and she sobbed, her tears smearing the words, and she lifted her hand, asking him for coins to place over the dead fawn's mouth.

"Shh, my lovely." He said crushing a black rose between his hand, spreading the petals against the ground. "Do not to make a sound." The sun shone behind him and he looked like a giant black demon above her.

He pushed her back to the ground, tearing at her clothes and she pushed and kicked at him but he was too strong. He lifted her skirts and forced himself inside her, tearing at her protective barrier and she felt the hot blood running down her thighs as she cried out at the burning pain. He thrust into her over and over again ripping the soft tissue. He bit her breasts and pressed his mouth against hers, drinking in her screams, sweeter than ambrosia on his lips as he swelled inside of her, licking the tears on her cheeks.

"This is love," he told her. "This is our wedding night, let me kiss you under the stars my love. Let me fuck you under the stars." And he began to laugh as his hot seed filled her, mingling with the virginal blood on the ground as he spasmed over and over.

She lay in the dirt, her body and spirit broken. She looked

into Olive's dead brown eyes.

"I wish I would die," she cried.

He turned her face towards his, squeezing her face brutally until she gave a small moan of pain, and he smiled. "Oh you will, Persephone," he replied, "but not yet." He reached down, squeezing the soft mound between her legs and she whimpered. "I will return for you, this is far from over."

He left her in the forest, bloody and battered, blood staining her white cotton dress. She lay there in the darkness until finally she began to cry, calling out her mother's name. Demeter found her lying in the dirt and she did not need to tell her mother what had happened when she had met her lover in the forest. Persephone could see the rage and disbelief in her mother's eyes as she took in the blood staining her pale thighs, the bruises covering her flesh, the bite marks on her breasts.

"Please," Persephone whispered, closing her swollen eyes against the horror on her mother's face.

"Who was he?" Demeter asked, her voice shaking with barely suppressed rage.

"Mother," Persephone's voice was a plea.

"Tell me and I will ask no more questions, I promise. All I ask is his name.

"Ares," she said, her voice so light she wondered if Demeter would hear her. "I am such a fool. Because of me, Olive is dead."

"No," her mother whispered fiercely. "Your only crime is that you trusted a monster. You are innocent my love." Snow rained down on the summer wind as her mother wrapped her gently in her arms. "Come my child, we will return for Olive after I see to you." Unable to stand, Demeter carried her broken child back to the temple and Persephone felt her mother's tears falling against her face. Her heart twisted strangely in her chest and then was silent as she remembered Olive's blank eyes and she felt something inside of her die. Hope. Love. Faith. She would never trust again! Persephone let her eyes close as Demeter's temple came into view.

Hades had seen enough and he lowered his hand from her chest. Aphrodite had told the truth. Persephone had loved him all this time, she just did not realize it.

Their spirits ricocheted back into their bodies as the whip flew through the air, crackling with blazing fire as it descended towards her. Hades pushed himself from the rock, grasping the flame laced thong in his fingers before it could crash down on Persephone's back. The leather wrapped around his wrist and fingers, his flesh sizzling as the whip marked him. Ares stared at him in shock before Hades pulled the whip from his hands, flaying it against the floor with a loud thunderous crack against the marble. The God of War stared down at the scorched floor in horror before raising his eyes to the gleaming purple gaze fixed on him.

"You will never touch her again." Hades growled, his purple eyes blazing into the azure eyes of Ares. "You will never speak her name."

The King of Death began to smile and he was bathed in a violet light as he lifted his burnt, slashed hand into the air and pulled from the shadows a blue-flamed sword held tight within his bloody grasp.

Ares gave a cry of disbelief, then lifted a blade from his armor and the guards surrounded him, lifting their spears and shields high, shielding the God from Hades' view. With a twist of Hades' hand, Persephone was lifted off the ground and pushed out of the room, away from the deadly weapon. For the briefest second their eyes met until every entry into the room slammed shut with a deafening boom. The locks turned in synchronicity with a click, click, click until each golden door was barred and Hades began to laugh, a deadly and menacing sound. His face twisted in macabre delight, as he pointed the flaming blade at the soldiers.

"Fools!" he hissed. "You dare enter my domain, I am the master of death, wielder of spirits! I collect souls and watch them burn. All I see before me are terrified, mewling, dead men. Your souls... are... mine."

The guards viciously began their attack and Hades swung the blue flamed weapon at his adversaries, slicing their souls in half. He picked up the whip, cracking it around another guard bringing him close and ripped the life straight from his chest, throwing his dead lifeless body to the ground. With a flick of the wrist he snapped another man's neck. The guards were attacking in droves, seeming to multiply and he was throwing one body after another to the floor. He pushed through the men and looked for Ares but could not find him. Hades finished them off one by one until they were annihilated. He searched through the pile of bodies tossing them about the room, but Ares had vanished. "The coward ran away and left his men to die," Hades snarled.

Fists pounded on the door echoing through the burnt tomb and he waved his hand to unlock the hatch. Persephone stood staring at him from across the room. One heartbeat passed, then two heartbeats. She stood still, looking at the guards littered on the ground, the blood smeared across the marble, a grisly mural of death. Hades dipped the silver blade back into the shadows and he wondered if she would run again. He could have hidden their bodies, denied who

he was, but he did not want to lie to her. There had been enough deception and she deserved the truth from him no matter how frightening. So he stood there, amongst the dead, blood pooling at his feet, waiting to see what she would do. He heard her breath hitch and then they were running to each other and she fell into his arms as they tumbled to the ground. For the first time since he could remember, he was happy.

CHAPTER
XX
SCARS

E TOOK HIS wife's hand and pulled her to her feet. "Come," he said softly. They walked to the stables and he quickly readied Orphnaeus knowing his wife preferred to ride bareback. He lifted her onto Aethon then jumped onto his mount. "Follow me," he said, his pale face ghostly in the shadows, blood staining his skin like war paint. Orphnaeus raced from the stables and Aethon needed no command to follow. They galloped, side by side, and Persephone realized he was taking her a way they had never travelled before. He brushed her arm, drawing her attention to the murky river adjacent to them and the horses began to slow.

Lifting his hand to the air, the waters parted and Persephone watched in wonder at the shadowed creatures who pushed against the pulsing wall of water. "Let's fly," he said and then they both surged forward, Persephone urging Aethon through the passage, the water thundering around them. She could hear cries of sorrow and turned to see faces looking at her from behind the wall of tears, pressing their pale hands against their watery prison. Spray from the pressure of the lake cried down as the horses raced through the passage and she forced her eyes away, turning towards Hades as he galloped ahead. She could see his bloodied back as his torn robes flew behind him. In the distance stood large golden doors and without pausing Hades lifted his hands and they opened slowly. Behind her she could hear the waves crashing down, thundering deafeningly as the water began to re-cover the path.

The horses ran through the gates which slammed loudly behind them as the last strand of Aethon's tail crossed the threshold, and she looked in wonder when she realized they were once more in the soft green lands of Elysium. The horses cantered up a small hill and then slowed as they reached a temple high on a cliff overlooking the sea. Persephone looked at it in surprise, it must belong to a minor God, but what was it doing down here? It was a temple that she would have loved to have had, if she had not become Hades' Queen. Hades grabbed her around the waist, lifting her off the horse and her body slid against his as he brought her to the ground slowly. He leaned in close to her, holding her tightly against him and she wondered if he would lower his lips those last few inches to hers. The night was still and the silence was only broken by the gentle sounds of the forest and the crashing of the sea. She began to lift her face towards his, closing her eyes as she soaked in the peaceful tranquility of Elysium.

"Shall we go inside?" he whispered.

She jumped, blushing as he stepped away from her but he kept her hand firmly in his. Hades guided her inside the temple; it was a modest setting compared to the palace. There was an intimate seating area, a scullery, and two large bedrooms, decorated in soft, pale tones. Outside was a pool tiled in blue aventurine, and beautifully carved marble statues were artistically placed around the temple. Hades lit a fire in the main room fireplace, and rich golden flames rose in the hearth. He then went to one of the bedrooms, bringing out a white plush robe in one hand.

"That is my room, usually. Once again," he said quietly. "your room is across from mine. If you wish to switch, you have only to let me know, you may have whatever room you wish." He pressed the robe into her hand and she took it, biting her lip, wondering why she felt disappointed that they would not be sharing a room. She gave him a small smile.

"Thank you, I am sure that will be perfect," she said. He nodded and turned back to the fire as she stepped into her room, closing the door softly. An elegant rattan bed with clean, white linens rested against the wall and she sat down staring out of the large open windows that looked out at the ocean. She closed her eyes, breathing in the cool, calming scent of the sea, forcing Ares evil face from her mind. What had he thought of her confession? Was he disgusted? She began to pull off her tattered gown, unable to stand the memory of Ares' disgusting touch, and then she secured the soft robe tightly around her narrow waist. Pulling her dark hair loose around her face, she studied herself in the mirror. She looked... different. She realized that she looked every bit an empress and gave a little gasp as she studied her reflection. Somewhere in the interim between being a captive at her mother's temple and a prisoner at her husband's palace, she had gained something, some extra quality that she had always lacked. What was that expression in her gaze, she wondered?

She surveyed her luminous green eyes and looked to the stranger in the mirror for answers, but she only gave her an enigmatic smile. Her heart raced in her chest and she rubbed at it.

Suddenly longing to speak to Hades, she stepped from her room and saw that he had changed into a white robe, as well. His dark face was accentuated by the crisp whiteness of the cloth. Her eyes travelled over him and she noticed the soft black hair that curled around his neck. He looked strong and beautiful and she felt herself reaching towards him, longing to run her hands against his skin. She jerked her willful hand back and rushed into her room quietly, pressing her hand against her rapid heartbeat. He may not want her to touch him now, she reminded herself. Her fingers trembled as she brushed the blood-red gemstones across her throat. He knew about her past now but he had not turned away from her. She would not hide from him even if he was disgusted; he had not abandoned her. With a resolute nod of her head, she pushed open the door and forced herself to move towards him. He glanced up as he saw her approach, and a smile lit his face. She blinked at the twin dimples that creased his cheeks, then reluctantly forced her eyes away from him. With the crackling fire the room looked warm and inviting. This temple was lovely and she had once dreamed of living in just such a place. A peaceful oasis where she could retreat to at the end of the day, and just -- be.

"Whose home is this?" she asked.

He moved in front of her and she had no choice but to raise her gaze to his -- and flames flickered in their black depths. "It is mine," he replied watching her.

"Yours?" she asked with surprise. He pressed a glass of wine into her hands and she accepted it gratefully, her mouth suddenly parched. "But I thought you lived in the Underworld?"

"I live there, but this is my home. I come here when the darkness becomes overwhelming. It is where I can find peace. My hidden palace. I must spend most of my time in the Underworld, but there is no rule I must spend all of my time there."

"It is beautiful," she replied, running her hands over the stone walls. "Who built it? I never imagined to see a temple like this here." She glanced up when he did not reply and saw with surprise that he looked embarrassed.

"I did," he said finally.

"You? Truly!" She stepped closer, fascinated by the slight flush on his face. "With magic?"

He shook his head. "No. With my hands."

"What!" she cried, her voice loud with surprise as she gaped at him. "All of it?"

"All of it."

"The walls?" He nodded. "The roof?" Another nod. "The bed in my room?"

"I weaved it," he said.

"Did anyone help you?"

"No," he replied.

She looked at the beautifully crafted table. "Did you carve this?"

"Yes."

She pointed to a marble figure near the doorway. "This statue? Did you sculpt it?"

He laughed, "Yes."

"Well," she said gently. "It is so lovely. You are a talented craftsman. If you were a mortal I can see how you would have earned your keep." She fingered the intricate engravings against the hearth. "It must have taken you a long time."

"It did, but patience and I are old friends. I started to build it when I first began to judge souls. To understand a small part of what it meant to be human I came here to live as mortals do. Now I come for the pleasure of a simple life." He took her hand in his and pulled her towards him. "Come sit with me." He drew her down onto the soft daybed by the fire.

He sat close to her and she felt his strong thigh as it brushed against hers and she gave a shiver at his nearness. She could feel those sensations again, rising low in her body, travelling to her heart and she resisted the urge to touch her chest, knowing his eyes were on her. His hand lay on his knee and the flesh was raw and raised from Ares' whip. She picked up his hand, rubbing her fingers over the burn.

"Does it hurt?" she asked in a hushed voice, lifting her eyes to his.

"Only a little." She closed her eyes and raised his hand, brushing her mouth over the burn, letting her lips linger against his hand. "Persephone," he said softly.

"Will you teach me sometime? To heal like you healed me. I would like to be helpful. I could heal your back."

"You already are helpful, but I will teach you. I will teach you anything you want to know." She pressed his hand against her face, hiding her eyes from his view and he felt dampness against his skin. "Persephone," he said again, turning her to face him. Her eyes were downcast, but he saw the tears that fell from them, tracing down her cheeks. "Why did you not tell me what happened? Any secret you would have shared would be safe in my keeping.

"I know," she whispered. "I did trust you, I do. I wanted to tell you so many times, but I was … ashamed. Mother and I decided that no one had the right to know. Look how Athena punished Medusa after Poseidon attacked her. I remained silent for so long that the lie became easier than the truth. I thought if I never spoke of it again, I could forget." Her voice hitched. "But I remembered it all the clearer and it was always at the forefront of my mind, until I let it become the part of my life that defined me. And I regret it. I regret it so much, Hades. I carried this secret, fearing the day I would marry, and my husband would discover the truth and that he would be disgusted by me. Ares showed me that day what love was between Gods. I trusted him, trusted what he had told me. I was a fool. I never want to feel that pain again. I never want to love, to feel that loss. Love is a selfish thing that breaks you and I never want to love... again." She lifted her eyes then and deep wracking sobs shook her body. He pulled her into his lap, letting her tears fall against his chest, stroking her hair away from her face.

They were similar, in ways she did not even realize. He pulled her tighter against him as he rubbed a hand down her silken hair and pressed a kiss against her forehead as she began to hiccup against him.

"He is a monster for what he did to you, to make a mockery of love and marriage. He wanted to scar you forever. Do not let him. He does not define any part of you." The reality of how her attack was largely his fault dawned on him, and he wanted to scream in rage for not protecting her. His cowardly need to hide who he was from her had provided a perfect opportunity for Ares to take advantage of her trusting nature.

"Gods, how could I have been so foolish?" he said aloud.

"I am broken," she whispered under her breath, raising her face to his.

He stared into her luminous eyes. "We are broken, but our shattered fragments fit together making us complete. What happened that night has nothing to do with what is between you and I, Persephone."

She raised her eyes to his, tears making the green look like crystal. "But when you look at me, all you will see is him. You will remember…," she said with sadness.

He pulled her tighter against him. "Never," he whispered fervently against her. "When I look at you all I see is -- you, the sweet Goddess of the Forest, a ferocious and just queen. I want every part of you. The light and the dark. Your past and your future. Everything you are. You have committed no sin, Persephone. It is time to forgive yourself. You did nothing more and nothing less than love someone. His actions were monstrous, an immoral crime against a pure soul." He wrapped his fingers around her jaw, turning her face towards him. "You judge yourself so harshly. Give yourself permission to absolve your heart of this guilt. "

"But I trusted him, it was my fault…"

"No," he said softly. "It was not your fault." Hades hesitated. He was not ready to tell her it was him she had been writing to. He wanted to know more but his intuition told him to wait. Why and how had Ares known how to act? He hoped that she would forgive him when he revealed the truth. He knew he would never forgive himself for his cowardly anonymity.

She pressed her face against his chest. "This is why I cannot love you. My happiness was stolen from me. I fell in love with a lie - and... I… I miss the lie. I miss who I was before, though I was so foolish," she said bitterly. "The minute I give my heart to you, and you get what you want, you will hurt me and you will leave. I cannot survive that betrayal again, I cannot lose the small part of myself that remains." She lay silent against him but he could feel the dampness of her tears soaking into his robe.

"Persephone," he whispered, stroking the strands of hair away from her wet face. "No one knows better than I that there is no hope for a future when you live in the past. I can feel the loneliness beating in you, I felt it the first time I ever saw you. Your heart is broken but it is full of love, it only needs to heal. Let me help you. Let me share your burden." He lifted her into his arms and the doors to the temple swung open as he approached them. The cool night air pushed against them as they stepped outside and he felt Persephone shiver in his arms.

"Where--?" she asked.

"Trust me," he said softly, his voice rich magic against her ears. He could hear the sea as he brought them towards the shore. The water covered his ankles and he strode out deeper into the depths, holding her carefully in his arms. "Let me close this wound. Let me take the pain from you." She stared up at him, her eyes wide and frightened, but she nodded her head slowly. He sat her gently down into the water and they stood facing one another.

"Take off your robe."

She pulled it tighter around her body and he could see her struggle against her intrinsic need to cover herself. He waited patiently and watched as her fingers began to loosen on the fabric and the robe slowly fell to the water, exposing her gleaming flesh to the soft touch of the moonlight. He brought her long hair forward, letting it cover her breasts and the junction between her legs.

"I am going to touch you now," he whispered. She trembled as he placed his hand to her heart. He began to chant an ancient language and the words merged with the sounds of the tide as he dipped her gently back into the waters of the sea. Her heart beat in rhythm to the churning ocean and as he prayed over her and he could feel the wound closing, the blackness beginning to fade away. Suddenly she gave a mournful cry that echoed loudly in the night and he could feel the delicate flesh of her heart reopen, the muscle tearing in her chest. Her frenzied thoughts pressed into his mind and he could see her holding a newborn babe in her arms, her tears falling against his cold, still flesh. He pulled her from the water and wrapped his arms around her shivering form. The final secret she had held from him was revealed.

"Gods! Persephone, you lost a child?" He felt his tears mingle with the salt water in her hair and he pressed his face against her head. He wanted to scream in the darkness at the God who had altered the course of her life. He wanted to unleash his fury, but she did not need his anger; she needed gentleness and understanding to heal. Her mouth opened and he could see her struggle to form words, but only sobs came from her lips. Brushing his mouth against her, he pressed two fingers to her head, quieting her sounds of distress. He began to move carefully through her fragmented thoughts and he was once again in the forest with her, her belly was large and swollen with child as she fell to the ground in pain. He watched as she gave birth, alone, in the silent woods. He watched as she clung to the lifeless child, bending over his tiny blue body as she tried again and again to breathe life into the small, silent chest. A hooded figure emerged from the darkened trees, lifting the child from her arms. Persephone fought desperately, but she was too weak to reclaim her son, and in the end could only watch helplessly as the cloaked figure disappeared with the small bundle into the forest. She stumbled after the figure, her dress bloodied with the evidence of her delivery and --- she vanished from his view. He felt someone pull tightly at him, bringing him from the memory and he looked down to see Persephone grasping him tightly with white knuckled hands. Her fingernails dug into his arms and blood fell from his skin to swirl into the water below.

Grief and horror were reflected in her eyes and she tried to pull away from him but he kept his hands around her, dipping her back into the waters, repressing the rage he felt into the recesses of his mind. He continued chanting the ancient dialect then whispered words she finally understood.

"Let me carry this sadness. Let this be my burden to bear. Let me fight this battle for you."

She struggled against his hands. "No," she cried in a strangled voice. "Do not. It is not yours to bear."

"Let me," he said softly. "Let me take your pain. I am already made of scars."

He began to pull the darkness from her, a shadow of self-loathing rising from her chest, and he grasped the shade of blackness, pressing it against his lips as he began to swallow it. An overwhelming pain filled his heart and he felt regret and sorrow move through him as he stumbled against their heavy weight. He righted himself and when he looked down, Persephone's clear eyes were staring up at him.

"Why?" she asked with anguish..

He pulled her from the depths of the sea and picked her up in his arms. As he walked back to the temple, he finally looked down at her. "Your pain was already a part of me. You never have to bear the sorrows of life alone, Persephone."

She raised a hand up towards him but her eyes were already beginning to drift shut. By the time he entered her room, she was asleep in his arms and he tucked her into bed beneath the soft, warm blankets. And for the first night in a long time, she slept without nightmares.

CHAPTER
XXI
THE GUEST

B Y THE TIME Persephone awoke it was dusk. He knew now. He knew everything about her, the darkest moments of her life. She had loved her child, wanted it even though he had been the result of Ares' barbaric savagery. When she had felt it begin to move inside her, she had been horrified and nauseated that she bore the fruits of that vile union. As he had grown though, she began to long for him, a little person she could care for, that she could love. Her mother would have been disgusted by the small creature who had taken root in her womb, so she had kept him a secret, even from Demeter. She knew that many women would not want the evidence of molestation and she understood their perspective, but she could not fault the tiny spirit that moved within her own soul. He had felt so much a part of her, and Gods help her, she had loved him.

The child had grown at a rapid pace within her womb, and

instead of the many months of gestation that mortal women experienced, only a few moons had passed when she began to fill the first pains of his arrival. The cramps began to increase and she hurried to the forest to welcome him, making sure she was far from the river where he had been conceived. She had wanted to bring him into the beautiful world she loved, and she lay on the ground pushing for what had seemed like hours. When he finally emerged she wondered why he did not cry, why his sweet flesh was dusky. She breathed into him over and over, finally sobbing over his still, perfect body. Until he too had been ripped from her arms; she could not even keep his body for a proper burial. She had searched for that hooded creature who had spirited away her son, but he had vanished like smoke into the forest. The memories drifted over her and she lay in bed, keeping her eyes closed when she heard the quiet sound of laughter. The window was open and she could make out voices now. Her husband's deep voice and another one, a male she did not recognize. She forced herself from the covers and dressed quickly in a simple robe, letting her hair flow freely down her back.

She pushed open the door to her bedroom, and when she entered the common room, Hades stood there alone. He turned towards her and took her hand, bringing it to his lips. The brush of his mouth against her skin made her shiver and she bit her lip as his dark eyes moved over her.

"Did you sleep well?" he asked.

"Yes, thank you," she replied in what she hoped was a steady voice. Her stomach gave a loud growl and she blushed, pressing her hand against it tightly. "A little hungry, I guess."

Hades laughed. "I am not surprised, it has been some time since we have eaten a proper meal. We will dine soon. A visitor will be joining us tonight. He is in the courtyard, perhaps you could go introduce yourself? I will be out shortly."

"A visitor? Who is he?" She was not in any particular mood to welcome guests, she thought glumly.

"You have never met him before," he replied softly.

"Should I not change? I am only in robes."

"I do not think he will mind, he is just anxious to meet your acquaintance." He stroked one finger against her palm. "Trust me, you will want to meet him." He steered her towards the doors and then she was in the courtyard and a young man stood with his back towards her, facing the calm blue waters of the sea. Strands of his dark hair blew in the warm breeze and she wondered again who he was. For some reason the sight of his tall form surveying the sunset made her heart accelerate, which was absurd. She did not know this man. In Elysium it was most likely he was a famous poet or philosopher. Her footsteps were soft on the ground and she was very close to him by the time he noticed he was no longer alone. When he turned towards her, a stricken look crossed his face and then he gave her a courtly bow, his dark hair covering his expression.

"Queen Persephone," he murmured, his voice pleasant and soothing. "I have waited so long to meet you." When he raised his gaze to hers, his deep green eyes looked longingly at her. Everything about him was achingly familiar, like a long forgotten dream.

"Who are you?" she said, taking a step away from him. Her hands trembled as she noticed the determined set of his jaw, his high cheekbones. It was the same bone structure she saw everyday when she looked into the mirror.

He stepped closer to her. "Persephone, do you not know me?"

She began to shake her head and then stopped as she stared into his green eyes. Her green eyes. "You remind me of someone, but that cannot be. He was cursed by Zeus, kept from his family for eternity. What is your name?" she demanded.

His gaze lowered again and when he raised his eyes, tears sparkled in their emerald depths. "My name is Iasion, Persephone. I am your father."

Her head became curiously light and she felt herself slipping into blackness when strong arms wrapped around her and she was looking up into the face of her father, the beloved face she had never been allowed to know. Suddenly she pushed herself up and threw herself at him, so that they both fell to the ground and she was crying against his chest. "Father," she sobbed. "I have loved you since I grew in my mother's womb. I have missed you with every sunset and sunrise."

"My daughter," he cried, wrapping his arms fiercely around her, and she felt his tears fall against her cheeks. "Forgive me." He whispered the words over and over again, until finally they both fell silent, content to simply hold one another. They sat like that, wrapped tightly in each other's arms, until Persephone pulled back from him slightly, looking up at him shyly.

"But.. I thought you were cursed by Zeus. That is what my mother told me. How did you come to be here?"

"Come, my daughter," he said, standing, extending his hand to hers. They walked to a nearby chaise and sat, Iasion never taking his eyes from her face. "You look so much like your mother."

Persephone laughed. "She says I look like you."

"Does she?" he whispered. "I was cursed, Persephone. I remember laying with your mother and then suddenly I knew nothing.

I walked for eternity it seemed; I was a faceless wraith -- untouch-able, unlovable, and unseeable. I truly do not know how long those moments lasted. It could have been hours, it may have been a thou-sand years. I existed in that state until one day Hades found me. He restored my voice and my mind and brought me here. He changed the terms of my sentence and I have lived in Elysium since then. And though I was free from my chains, I could not seek you from this realm. After a short period of time, Olive came to live with me as well."

"Olive?" she repeated, processing his words slowly.

How had Hades known about her father? She had never told him, and Iasion had resided here long before she had been brought to the Underworld. Was it possible he had come here for another reason entirely unconnected to her? But that was too much of a co-incidence. Perhaps Zeus had told him, but then her mother had as-sured her that Zeus had not told another living soul of what he had done. And how had Olive come to be involved? Her father and her sweet Olive brought to live eternity in the most coveted realm in the Underworld, by a man who did not know he would someday be her husband.

"But father," she began, "I do not understand--"

Her words were cut short by Hades' appearance. Steaming platters of fish were carried in his hands, and they were covered with sweet smelling herbs that tantalized her senses. "Hungry?" Hades asked with a smile.

"Famished," she replied. She stood to help him lay out the platters and she leaned against him briefly, pressing a quick kiss to his cheek. Her questions would keep until later. For now she simply wanted to relish that her father sat next to her, and after all this time they were together. "Thank you," she said, her voice breaking over the words.

His eyes moved over her. "I would give you anything," he replied softly. Her father cleared his throat and suddenly Hades expression lightened. "I will be back with some wine."

When he returned, Hades raised a toast to them and they sat in the gathering darkness, celebrating the reunion. Her father was a skilled storyteller and the hours passed quickly as the wine flowed freely. Persephone could not keep her gaze from moving to her husband, the moonlight caressing the shadows of his dark face. The goblet of wine was held loosely in his long fingers, his black hair tumbled across his face as he laughed while Iasion recounted a tale of his youth. Hades' eyes connected with hers as he brought the glass to his lips and watched her over the rim.

Iasion looked at her and then stood suddenly and said, "I think I will depart for home now. I thank you, King, for allowing me to dine with you tonight. I thank you for so much." He bowed towards Hades, and Persephone jumped to her feet and threw her arms around her father's neck.

"I will see you soon," she said with a smile.

"Yes, as soon as you desire, my child. Whenever you have a need -- I will be there." He bent down to kiss her forehead and with a last embrace, he began to make his way from the temple. Persephone watched until his figure disappeared in the distance and then she turned to her husband, stumbling slightly. She had had too much wine, but she felt pleasantly warm. He lay still on the ground looking up at her and she tumbled down next to him, lifting his hand to her face.

"How can I repay you?" she asked. "For Olive. For my father."

He took her hand and brought it to his lips. "You owe me nothing, Persephone."

"Why did you bring my father here?" she asked, watching him as carefully as her bleary eyes would allow her. "As far as I know, in his short life he did not do anything to change the world drastically."

Did she imagine it or had his eyes flitted away from hers. "He helped to make you, did he not?" He lifted his face to hers again. "I found your father one day, his soul aimlessly roaming. I knew he was a good man, that his punishment had been false."

"So it was just coincidence then, that he came to be here?" Her question ended on a hiccup.

"Do you believe in chance, Persephone?"

"I do not know what I believe anymore." A soft breeze blew around them and Persephone closed her eyes, letting the small currents drift around her. "I smell roses," she said with enthusiasm.

"There is a rose garden near here. Roses are my favorite flower, save one."

"You are my favorite flower," she said sleepily, and then covered her mouth with her hand. "Did I say that out loud?"

He laughed. "I am afraid so. Let us go inside. "Come, little flower. I think it is time for you to visit Hypnos."

Persephone had fallen asleep as soon her head touched the pillow. Hades turned from the room; they had both drank far too much and when she finally came to him he did not want any artifice between them, whether it be wine or the final secret he withheld from her. He needed to tell her, she deserved the full truth from him.

He returned to his room, changing quickly out of his robes and when he turned to the mirror he inhaled swiftly. His chest was smooth and pale, with only a small scar over his heart. He was healed, which meant-- Persephone loved him! He had to tell her that he was the man from the forest, that he was the one who had written her the letters. He would figure out later how Ares had intercepted him and why.

She needed the truth if there was any chance that she could forgive him for inadvertently leading that monster -- Ares -- to her; forever changing the course of her life. He quickly slipped back into her room. The moonlight was shining gently on her face, her small hand tucked against her chin. Tomorrow, he thought. Tomorrow he would finally tell her the truth.

CHAPTER
XXII
OMISSION

A STREAM OF SUNLIGHT woke Persephone from her slumber and she stretched contentedly on her bed, throwing off the covers quickly. Humming to herself, she dressed in a plain cotton tunic and hurried outside to enjoy the first rays of sunlight. The sea thundered against the shore and the brilliant pink sky reflected in the aquamarine waters of the pool and glittered against the turquoise blue stone. Persephone felt happy to be alive. There was a petal floating on the surface of the water and she picked it up absently, turning it over in her hand. Maybe she could ask Hades to bring Olive here, she would like to let him play in the sunny endless fields. Her father would love to see him again, she was sure. Her father! After all this time, she had finally come to know him and her heart soared.

She wondered again how he had come to be here. A smile lit her face as she remembered how her father and Hades had traded stories. Could life really be this wonderful, she pondered, that they all could have a happy ending? Her heart gave a pang as she wondered what Demeter would think when she learned her true love resided here. She rubbed her fingers absently against the smooth petal and glanced down as it's perfumed scent filled the air. The petal was a black rose and the bouquet was hauntingly familiar. A memory began to unfold like black, twisting tentacles in her mind, wrapping around her heart. How many times had she smelled that particular sweetness? She turned the petal over slowly; gold marked it's edges. This was the same rose that had been tied to the letters she had fetched from the river, the letters her lover had sent. The roses Ares had scattered to the ground before he had raped her. Her breath was coming in short gasps. She had confessed her father's name in those letters, and Olive's, as well. She began to stumble down the hill in the direction that Hades had indicated the garden was, and a cry of denial fell from her lips. Rows of black roses grew, all covered with golden tips, their scent cloying in her nostrils. She ran her fingers blindly over them, not noticing when a thorn dug deep into her palm causing blood to trickle down her wrist. Had Ares shared what was inscribed to him? Was he simply part of this twisted game? The garden began to blur, and Persephone felt faint as she pieced together a sick picture of what all of this meant.

A hand grabbed the petal from her fingers. "I can explain." His voice was low and urgent.

She whirled away from him. "You lied to me!" Her entire body shook and she fisted her hands to keep from attacking him, this stranger who stood before her. "I told you everything, you made me share everything with you. And I find these!" She gesticulated wildly to the roses. "Who are you? Did you help Ares orchestrate all of this? Laugh while he made a fool of me? While he hurt me?"

"No!" He tried to grasp her hand but she pulled herself away from him.

"Do not touch me!" she screamed.

He held up his hands and he took a step back, eyeing her like she was a wild animal. His face was stony as he looked at her, his careful mask back in place. "I will not touch you, I promise. But let me show you the part I played in this. I would never have willingly allowed Ares to do any harm to you, surely you know that?"

"And yet he did," she said coldly. Fury was uncurling inside her, a blind rage that she had never felt before and she was shaking from the strength of it. "Show me then. Let us have done with this farce."

He turned on his heel and she wondered if he had the courage to turn his back to her. If she had the blade of the Acheron she would be tempted to plunge it into him, to betray him as she thought he had betrayed her. She forced herself to follow him and he made his way through the house into his bedroom. He took a golden box from a table near his bed and handed it to her.

Her hands shook as she opened the lid and froze when saw the letters inside. Her letters. Her handwriting. She picked up the one on top and the words danced across her eyes. Here were her memories from long ago, from another life -- when she was a different person. How sweet were the words she had written. How stupid she had been. Her hand trembled as she threw the letter back in the box. It felt like poison against her skin.

"So?" she asked, her voice trembling. "I do not understand. How did you get these! Did you steal them from Ares?"

Hades moved the box away from her, closing the lid reverently. "I did not steal these from anyone," he said quietly, his eyes lowered. "Ares was never the one writing to you."

He lifted his burning black gaze to hers and she knew then. The knowledge rushed through her and she felt herself breaking; the final cut that would destroy her and it had been Hades who had delivered it. She backed up, the wall the only force that kept her from falling to the ground and she reached behind her, pressing her shaking hands against the sturdy, cold stone.

"You?" Her voice was a ragged whisper. "It was you?"

"Persephone, please," he began and his emotions slipped through his careful mask, anguish reflected in his face as he stepped closer to her, but she was too far gone to care.

She held up her hand. If he touched her, if she felt him against her flesh she would shatter into a million pieces, so broken that she would never be put together again. She could feel her palm pulse with power, the need to punish him growing inside of her. Her fingers closed against her palm, digging her fingernails into the wound the thorn had made.

"Stay the hell away from me. How could you?" Her voice was unrecognizable to her own ears and her throat was raw from the suppressed screams of denial. "You kept such a secret from me all this time. Where were you on that day? A part of me died and you did nothing! You led me to a demon and let him destroy me. Made me think I had loved a rapist and a murderer!" Blackness closed around her vision as her chest moved rapidly and she tried to slow her breathing, but the air seemed too heavy.

Hades growled suddenly and grasped her arm, pulling her from the room, through the hallway and back outside again. "You need air," he said. He sat her on a chaise, releasing her immediately, and then leaned against a nearby cypress tree. She shivered against the warmth of the sun, sucking in deep gulps of air.

"I had sent a letter telling you I would arrive after sunset. Ares must have waited at the riverbank and intercepted it. How he knew to look for it I do not know. He waited for you, pretending to be the one writing you. By the time I arrived, I only saw Olive and my shredded letter. I thought you hated me."

"And why did you not tell me the moment you saw me again? You kept me ignorant of the truth," Persephone cried.

"I drank the water Lethe after I returned. I forgot that you had ever loved me, that we had ever written to each other. It was a weakness, I know, but I was half-mad by the time I returned to the Underworld. It was not until the Fates intervened that I realized there may be a connection between my forgotten memories in the Lethe -- and you."

"And your memories returned -- when?" she demanded, her voice a hiss.

"After the Fates I sought my memories. I thought you knew and were lying to me."

"So wonderful to hear that your first thought was that I was a liar," she said. "Why did he attack me?"

"I do not know. Either his hate for me or his lust for you -- possibly both. Perhaps it was merely that he did not want to see me happy with someone that he wanted. That question remains un-answered," Hades said.

"Why did you not tell me?" she questioned despondently, her rage beginning to burn out so that only desolation remained in its fiery absence; a cold emptiness that was covering her soul. "As soon as you knew, why did you not confront me?"

"I told you," he said in a tired voice, "at first I thought you were lying to me."

"And when you found out the truth? What reason was there for your lie then?" she asked.

"I was selfish," he said softly. "I was a coward and afraid you would hate me when you discovered the truth, when you found out that it was I who unknowingly must have led him to you; that I had loved you long before the curse."

Her eyes drifted to his chest and she gasped when saw the small white scar that stood out over his heart. But that meant… she sat stiffly on the chaise, her eyes fixated on his smooth skin. That small scar betrayed her and she almost fell from the divan, catching herself before she stumbled to the ground. His eyes were following her movements, but he remained still as she stood.

"I want to be alone," Persephone demanded.

"Persephone, do not run away from this." He moved then, blocking her path. "Everything I said in those letters is what I am, who I am. Every word was the truth. My love for you was written in those letters."

"Run away?" she repeated, her voice hollow. "It is too late to run away from the damage already done. My connection with you altered the course of my life. You should have told me who you were from the beginning. You should have warned me."

"Would you have given me a chance if I had told you who I was, the King of Death? You hated me so much when I brought you down to the Underworld. Do not hate me now for loving me," he beseeched.

"Through your omission you assured that our love was damned from the start. You made us fated to be apart. If you had

354

trusted me…" her voice broke and she turned away from him, staring sightlessly at the crashing waves below them.

She felt his hand move against her hair, and with her back to him, she closed her eyes at his touch. He said, "Someone interfered with our love. You are right to blame me. I was so blinded by my feelings for you that I was unable to see the danger."

"And how long will they continue to meddle? How long will they let us have happiness?" she asked.

"You are right," he said, dropping his hand to her arm and turning her gently towards him. "The choice is yours, Persephone. I release you from your oath, from your vows. The curse is broken. You are no longer a prisoner. You can go freely. You have fulfilled your part of the bargain and I will fulfill mine. You are free to choose."

"Free," she said bitterly. "I am never free. Ares will wait for me and I will have no choice but to hide again in mother's temple. And what of my life here? Olive and my father? You kept me here and now I am hopelessly entangled. I am half in and half out of both worlds now. I do not fit in anywhere. I will not be completely happy with either choice. You have ruined me." She pushed his hands from her again, spinning away as tears began to fall from her eyes. "I need to be alone. Do not follow me!" She flew from the courtyard as she let her feet carry her away from him, and she felt her heart breaking.

She ran through the dazzling landscapes of Elysium -- seeing nothing. The story of Eros and Psyche played inside her mind, how they had been destined to love and to lose. They were kept apart from each other through their mutual distrust. Their love had not been strong enough to survive their own self-doubt. How familiar her story was to theirs. Her feet caught on the earth below her and she tumbled, sprawling against the soft ground. As she lay alone and broken she gave in to her weakness and sobbed, letting the earth absorb her tears. When she was finally exhausted she sat up, wiping her face, and she saw that a white flowered tree of sorrow had sprouted from her tears. She touched it gently and suddenly realized who she wanted to speak to. She was still the Queen of this world and she knew she could find him with simply a command of her mind. "Where is Iasion?" she whispered. She saw his hut in her mind and she pushed herself from the ground, running to find her father.

It took her only minutes to locate his house, nestled in a quiet valley. He was sitting near the window with a scroll in one hand, and he stood when he saw her. He appeared at the doorway but his smile quickly faded when he saw her face. She flung herself into his arms trying to explain her dilemna, but her words only came out garbled.

"Come inside, child," he said gently. He took her arm and set her in the chair he had recently vacated, pouring her tea from a pot that was steaming on a nearby table. The scent of ginger filled the air as he passed her a cup. She took a deep steadying gulp of the hot drink. He sat across from her, bringing his chair near her, patiently waiting for her to finish her tea. "What is wrong?" he finally asked when her sobs had subsided and her cup was empty.

"Hades and I... well you could say we quarrelled, but I think that is too tame a word."

"I see," he said, a small smile on his lips. "What could you have fought about? He loves you, you know."

She tried to smile, but her face merely crumpled into tears

and her father wrapped his hand around hers. "Father, there is so much you do not know. I -- I am afraid it is too late for us."

"No," her father said intensely, his hand tightening over hers. "It is not, Persephone. I was separated from your mother, my death creating a permanent divide between us that I can never breach. Do not allow a misunderstanding to keep you from the one you love."

"Father," she whispered. "I am so sorry..."

He shook his head. "That is long past my love, you have nothing to be sorry about. Tell me. Tell me your tale from the beginning and we will see if we can make sense of it all."

She moved to sit before him, laying her head against his knees as she started from the beginning. The first time she had seen the letter travel down the river towards her. Her father listened, weeping when she wept, smiling when she smiled. When she repeated Ares' savagery in the forest she felt his body shake with rage, but his hand remained a gentle touch against her face. The sun began to set when she had finished, ending with Hades' final revelation. The room fell silent, her voice hoarse from speaking for so long.

"How he loves you, my dear," he said softly.

"If it is love, how can it be so hurtful, so flawed?" she whispered.

"Oh, my dear Persephone. Love is nothing, if not flawed. Tell me, when your mother speaks of me does she regret our relationship?"

She sat up, leaning back on her heels to look at him in surprise. "Of course not. You are and were the love of her life."

He nodded. "I was, and she is and was, mine. I was murdered before we fully got to know each other. We were parted quickly and I died for daring to love her. But, I would do it again. I would relive it all again. Even my death." He took her hand in his. "Life is unpredictable, it is flawed, it is messy and sometimes… sometimes it ends badly. But I can tell you from experience - it is better to have loved than to live with the memory of regret. Your mother loved a mortal, knowing he would grow old and die, always knowing she was meant to lose me. She does not regret it. And now we have you."

"Your love was selfless. Hades… and I… there is so much mistrust between us. Not only his, but mine. We are both guilty."

"A choice lies before you, Persephone. You can forgive, or you can move on with your life, away from here. Darkness lies between you, but between the strands of black, there is a destiny which calls for you." He rested his face on his hand and watched the darkening sky. "You are afraid. You found out that the depth of your feelings for him run much deeper than you realized. It terrifies you to love someone so much, that one person could hold so much power over you. But Persephone, you must allow yourself to live. The deeper emotions in life are never safe to feel, but they are worth the price. They are the reason we breathe, why we dream of tomorrow."

She stared up at him in shock, that he had dared to speak the words that she had pushed to the deepest recesses of her mind. Her anger, her rage, it all stemmed from fear. Fear that she would never be enough for him. He stood and pulled her gently to her feet.

"Do not live in the shadows, Persephone. You are a Goddess, eternity stands before you and that is a very long time to live with regret. Forgive him. Forgive yourself."

"I am afraid," she said in a small voice, her hand tightening almost painfully over his.

"I know," he replied. "But all the things in life worth having inspire a little fear. Let yourself step from the shadows. Nothing but the truth lies between the two of you now, see what you can make of it. Now go my dearest. You have spent enough time with a surly old man."

"You are not old," she said with a watery laugh.

"I am older than you," he smiled down at her.

She embraced him fiercely as they stood in the doorway, and their heartbeats pressed against each other as the last rays of sunlight touched their skin. She turned away from him, stepping into darkness.

It was nightfall and Hades paced the room. "This is intolerable!" he growled suddenly. He exited the temple and grabbed a torch from a sconce on the outerwall of the dwelling. Heading to the stables, he mounted Orphnaeus and urged him forward into the black night. He should not have let her wander by herself. He believed Elysium was safe, but how far Ares' reach was able to extend now, was unclear. She had been reckless when she left. What if she had fallen and was injured and alone? He cursed himself as he sped through the forest and he was so absorbed in thought that he almost missed the small, pale figure in the forest. The horse reared as he pulled up abruptly and Persephone looked up at him as she was sitting on the darkened floor. Her arms were wrapped around her knees and shadows covered her face, shielding her expression.

"Where have you been?" he asked, relief making his voice rough.

"I went to see my father," she said.

"I see." He waited for more but she said nothing. "And why are you sitting here?"

"I was thinking," she replied calmly, "on what he said,"

"And what did your father say?" he inquired coolly.

"That I am in love with you -- and it frightens me."

He was shocked into silence.

Persephone continued, "And so I have been sitting here thinking. Do I love you? Or do I hate you? Or maybe I hate to love you."

"And what did you decide?" he asked finally.

"I think," she said softly. "That I love that I love you. That I have loved you for so long that you became as much a part of me as myself. Maybe the best part of me. And that scares me, that I have given you so much power over me, that you could destroy me so easily. But when I looked inside of myself, I found that the hatred I felt was never for you. It was for myself. And I have forgiven that poor lost girl. I decided I was worth a little absolution."

"Are you sure?" he said in a strangled whisper.

"Search my mind." she answered.

"I-- what?" he asked, not sure if he had heard her correctly.

She stood up then, stepping close to his horse. "Search my mind," she said again. "I want you to."

He dismounted, extinguishing the light, plunging them into darkness. Only the faint light of the moon illuminated them. He moved to close that short space between them.

"Are you sure, Persephone?" he asked again.

"Yes," she answered, and she moved his shaking hand to her temple, and closing her eyes -- opened herself to him. He was moving through her thoughts then, watching as she read his first letter, feeling her love grow until it overwhelmed everything else. She loved him with a fury that rivaled his love for hers, and it was in spite of the darkness, despite the scars that marked him from the inside out.

I will love you forever, her voice whispered in his mind.

"Forever," she whispered, pressing her lips against his.

Persephone felt him freeze, but there was nothing to stop her this time. No more fear, no more hesitation. She wrapped her arms around his neck and brought him closer to her.

"Do not be afraid," she whispered against his ear, as he trembled at her touch. She bent suddenly and pressed her mouth over that small scar that lay directly over his heart. "Love me back."

And suddenly he came to life, bringing her face to his, slanting his mouth against hers, kissing her, devouring her. She would have been afraid, except she wanted this darkness, she ached for the dark magic of his love to consume her.

"Look at me," he said fiercely, and she lifted her dazed eyes to him. "I love you. Say it back, say it again."

"I love you," she whispered.

And then with a groan he lowered his mouth to hers again and all thoughts were pushed from her mind. His mouth trailed over her neck and she felt his teeth move against her rapid pulse. Her white gown blew against them, enveloping them both in a pale, white, gossamer light. She pressed herself closer into him, as close as she could get, relishing the strength of his body against hers. And then his mouth was on her breasts, sucking her through the thin material of her gown and she gasped in pleasure, pushing his dark head closer.

"It's not enough," he whispered against her, "it will never be enough." He moved his mouth to her other breast and she felt her legs give out beneath her and he followed her to the ground. He was a shadow in the black night moving over her, pushing her legs apart.

She felt the cool night air against her thighs and saw his dark head close to her legs, her gown lifted high. She tried to pull him up, back towards her mouth, but then his head lowered and she felt his tongue move inside of her and she could only helplessly writhe against him, holding his head as his fingers pressed against her thighs. His used his mouth ruthlessly and when he moved to that tiny bud at the apex of her womanhood, she gave a scream into the night. The world tumbled away from her until she was moving in a beautiful blackness filled with stars as she convulsed against his mouth.

She came down from the high and she thought he would rise over her, join his body to hers, but then his fingers moved inside her and the slow build began again and she could feel her dampness soaking into him. He moved up, his mouth against her ear.

"I have never tasted anything as sweet as you. Do you know you weep gold, my goddess? That it flows from you like ambrosia that was made just for me to drink."

She shuddered against him, almost climaxing at his words. Then his mouth clamped over her breast as his fingers worked their magic inside her, and she trembled against him, feeling herself go over that dark edge again. She spiraled over and over as he pleasured her. As she felt herself begin to emerge from that secret carnal place, she wrapped her arms around his neck and he smoothed her damp hair back from her tear streaked face, pulling his face back to look at her.

"Did I hurt you?" he whispered.

She shook her head. "More," she said, " I want more. I want everything." She sat up and pulled her gown from her body, her pale flesh glowing in the dim moonlight, and then she was tugging on his clothing and he was helping her. She had a moment to appreciate the long, thick rigid length of him, and then he was pushing himself inside her. When he finally filled her, the blackness overtook them both and they seemed to become one with the night as endless waves of ecstasy moved over them.

When he collapsed over her, she could only move her hand against his nape, stroking him gently. He was still buried deep inside her.

"Does it always feel like that for you?" she whispered in an awed tone.

He raised his head, pressing his head against hers. "Only with you," he replied, brushing his lips over her face. "Always with you."

"Always?" she asked.

His smile was wicked. She gave a small gasp as she felt his cock harden inside her and he began to move again. "Let me show you."

CHAPTER XXIII
THE GAME

THEY WOKE IN each other's arms, her beautiful back pressed against the front of his body, and against all odds, he felt himself harden again. The morning light flickered through the trees to make patterns on their bare skin and Hades brought his mouth to Persephone's neck, tickling and kissing her with his lips.

She turned over with a smile and they lay nose to nose. "Good morning," she greeted him contentedly.

"Good morning," he said, smiling as he saw the delicious blush that moved up her face.

"You are a skilled lover," she said suddenly.

He laughed. "Thank you. I was using every skill I had learned over the centuries. I have had the advantage of time, you know." He lifted her hand, letting his fingers travel lazily over the delicate bones of her wrist. He shook his head, reading her thoughts, as he brushed the dark strands of hair from her face. "There is nothing common about you, Persephone, including this. I have never felt these feelings before, or tasted something so... enticing. The light of the universe spills from you, my little flower." He did smile this time as he watched her whole body turn red.

"Well, how many Goddesses have you known?" she questioned.

"I have known many," he said. He saw the insecurity flash in her eyes. "Persephone," he began gently. "You forget I once lived amongst the Olympians. After the war, the Gods would celebrate with orgies; their bodies so entwined you could not tell where one ended and the other began. I saw many things there. But I have never seen what pours from you."

"And were you...one of the entangled bodies?"

"I was not," he confirmed.

"And my ... my mother?" she asked.

Hades gently took her hand. "After the wars your mother was absent from the temple, spending her time with Iasion." The relief on her face was instantaneous. "Her commitment to him drove Zeus mad. He lusted over her until his desire became a sickness. He let everyone believe that he had caught her, used her, and discarded her."

"I wish," she said wistfully, "I wish that my mother could see my father again."

"You know that is not possible, Persephone," he said in a soft voice.

"I cannot bring her into Elysium. As the Queen of the Underworld, you are the only other besides me who is permitted to travel between worlds. Even as a Goddess, your mother is not able to come into the Kingdom of the Dead. My palace is the last stopping point. Only the most ancient, powerful of Gods may enter and they can only stay a short period of time."

She tangled her hand with his. "I know, but it is so unfair that Zeus took everything away from them."

"Not everything," he replied, kissing her nose. "No more sadness now, my love. I think we should return to the house before your father finds us."

He helped her to dress and it took twice as long as usual, as he explored each curve and hollow before he covered it. By the time they made it back the temple she was breathless and flushed. She went into her room and she saw he had come in with her and she held out her hands, shoving him out.

"Enough," she cried. "I can hardly walk and I need to get dressed and ready for the day!"

He laughed as she closed the door against him, and she leaned against the frame and could not help the wide smile that spread across her face. She loved him, she wanted to cry it out, screaming it aloud until even cursed Zeus himself heard her.

"I love him." She whispered it to herself, tasting the words on her lips. She decided she liked it very much, indeed.

She dressed quickly, choosing a pink gown that was as light and airy as her joyous mood. By the time she went out to the court-yard, Hades stood with two longbows in his hand. He smiled appreciatively, watching her move closer to him.

"Do you know how to shoot?" he asked her.

Persephone made a derisive noise, placing both hands on her hips. "I can outshoot you."

A grin spread across his face. "Ah, my confident wife. Want to bet on that?"

Taking an arrow from the quiver, she eyed him. "Let us make a bet. If I win, we come back to Elysium and have an official honeymoon -- a whole week. You will have to let Charon take over. Or perhaps, Cerberus."

"Oh that is tempting. If I win, however, you judge the souls tomorrow. All of them."

She looked at him aghast. "That is a horrible bet! Choose something else!"

"It is what I want. Not all of us only think of going to bed, Persephone." He gave her an angelic look and this time she actually snorted. "Now, how bad do you want that honeymoon?" He queried. "I very much want to get out of work." His long fingers released the string of the bow and the arrow thudded hard into the bullseye.

"Hmm, decent," she murmured, stifling a yawn beneath her delicate hand. "You are shattering my perception of you, I thought you lived to work." Persephone pulled the bow close to her chest, then let loose the arrow and it made a small zing as it flew straight through Hades' shaft, slicing his wooden arrow in two.

"I have married Eros!" he cried with mock surprise. "Beginner's luck."

"It is not luck! My mother taught me, and father taught her," she said indignantly.

Twisting the string of his bow, he picked up another arrow. "I have a feeling your mother taught your father. Next time, remind me to ask for a lesson." He grinned at her. "Best of three?"

His arrow flew from the bow hitting the center of the target again, splintering her arrow.

Persephone concentrated her aim, then shot. She let go with deadly precision, once again, cutting his arrow in two. "You are almost as good as I am," she said, her smile sycophantic. She sobered as she saw the casual way he held the bow in his hand. This God had fought in the most vicious wars this world had known. "Did you fight with a bow in the Titanomachy?"

"No, I was a close-range combatant." The quiver held only two arrows, he looked to her. "You shoot first this time."

She drew the arrow out, taking her time to arrange her bow, but when she released it she could tell she had overcompensated and gave a sigh of disappointment as the arrow narrowly missed the bullseye. "Looks like you will have tomorrow off duty, husband."

"How lucky for me," he murmured. "I am quite fatigued." Hades placed the last arrow lazily in his bow and carelessly drew back, the arrow not even making it to the target. "Oh dear," he said with mock distress, "I missed."

"You threw the game!" she hissed with indignation.

"Did I?" He asked, a slow smile pulling his lips as he stepped towards her. "I think you overestimate my skill." His hand slowly began to push the gown from her shoulders.

"What are you doing!"

"The God of the Dead always pays his debts." And with that, he bent his head to hers.

They fell asleep, exhausted and sated, their sweat slick bodies clinging to each other. Hours had passed, when suddenly she was jolted from sleep, the room now covered in darkness. A rustling noise had awoken her and she glanced at Hades; he was in the throes of a bad dream. He was breathing rapidly and his body thrashed beneath the covers, sweat drenching his skin. "No," he cried, his hand was clutching the sheet so tightly she saw his knuckles whiten. Were these the same nightmares that had haunted him when she had made him drink the elixir of poppies?

"Mother!" His voice was an agonized cry.

"Hades," she whispered urgently. "Wake up!" She shook his shoulder, but he remained tightly trapped in his nightmare. Closing her eyes, she opened her mind to his, willing him to listen. Wake up, she pleaded, her words a cry in her head.

His dark eyes flashed open and he jerked out of bed, gasping for breath. She wrapped her arms around him, pulling him close to her and he laid his head against her heart.

"What did you dream of?" she inquired softly.

For a moment all he did was breathe against her and then he finally replied, "I watched myself kill my mother again. I see her face over and over... as I plunge my blade into her and I watch her die. It plays out endlessly in my dreams -- my eternal nightmare. " He pulled himself away from her, burying his face in his hands and she felt the shiver that ran over his broad back. "I am a murderer, a failed assassin who sent the one he loved best to her grave." He looked at her suddenly, his hands moving to grasp hers. "I fear that I love you so much. I am cursed to lose those whom I love. I could not bear if I--"

"Hades," she intervened, moving closer to him. "Nothing is going to happen to me. You are innocent," she said, brushing her lips against his. "Your mother loved you. She drove that blade into her chest, not you."

He dropped his head, pressing his forehead to hers. "Persephone," he whispered, "I wonder if I am selfish to keep you here, in this darkness. I have seen where the shadows lead. My brothers' have a blood price that is yet to be paid. Zeus will rewrite history and he will sacrifice as many innocents as necessary to come out the victor. He will not tolerate my happiness and you make me... very happy. Sooner or later, he will make his move against me. I do not want this vendetta to touch you."

She jerked up, pressing her fingers against his jaw, bringing his face to hers. "I am not leaving you. I will not leave you. We have not been through all of this only to be separated now. Whatever you face -- I will face it with you."

"I do not deserve you, my fierce Queen. You deserve a prince with a light beauty to match yours. I am afraid you only ended up with a shadowed phantom."

"But I am made of shadows, dark prince, and it is you who lights my soul," she said softly. "I will not leave you."

"But--"

"Hush," she said firmly. "Let us go back to sleep, I will protect you from any bad dreams."

She cradled him in her arms like she would a wee babe, and to her surprise his breathing eventually slowed and she knew he slept. The hours passed, but her eyes did not close. She watched and guarded in the blackness, making sure that nothing came to touch him.

CHAPTER
XXIV
JUSTICE FOR THE DEAD

SUNLIGHT WAS STREAMING through the room and Persephone woke, reaching towards Hades, but the bed was empty next to her. She sat up and saw that a gown was spread across her dresser, and she dressed herself as hurriedly as possible, leaving the stays loose at her back. As she moved through the house, it was still and empty and she felt a pang as she realized this small reprieve was over. The doors were open and she paused as she saw Hades, his back silhouetted against the brilliant dawn. She took in the orange-pink sky, the pound of the waves against the shore, and the sweet scent of nature, locking it all into her mind. A chill of foreboding told her to keep this memory close, and she shivered in the warm morning air. The Fates had said that she would want to stay, but that she would not. But, wasn't that her choice to make? She wanted to stay.

Hades turned towards her suddenly and his face was composed, no trace remained of the nightmares that had haunted him. "You look lovely this morning," his voice was caressing as he took her hand. "We must go I am afraid. I sent the horses back earlier so we will take the river."

"Can I not say goodbye to my father?" she asked.

He shook his head. "We will return here soon. I wrote him, letting him know we had to depart. I have left my responsibilities for too long. I suppose I allowed myself to be most pleasantly distracted," he finished with a smile.

"I suppose you did," she replied. "And I wish I could say that I was sorry, but I am not. Promise me we will come back here?"

"I promise. Come, my Queen." He led her down to the seashore, and further from the temple there was a dock where an elegant boat waited. He helped his wife down into the craft and jumped in after her. Lifting a large oar, he began to push the small craft through the sparkling waters.

"Could you not use magic to take us there?" she inquired.

"Ah yes, but I enjoy the simple life here, remember wife?" he answered.

She laughed, letting her fingers dangle in the warm waves, the sunshine dancing across her face. A cave appeared near the shoreline and Persephone was not surprised to see him heading towards it. It seemed her destiny to end up in the dreaded, dark caverns, and she kept silent as they drew nearer. She held her breath, preparing herself for the suffocating blackness, but as they entered, she looked up in awe. The caverns sparkled with thousands of pale blue lights that shimmered and lit their way down through the narrow passage.

"It is magical!" Persephone exclaimed.

"They are glow worms. Beautiful little creatures, are they not?"

She glanced at her husband, as he looked up fondly at the glowing lights. "Yes, beautiful."

"We are almost there," he continued, smiling down at her.

Dread pitted her stomach at the thought of returning, but she forced a smile on her lips. Things would be different now at the palace, she assured herself. The curse was over and she would not let memories of that time corrupt their future. The shore appeared and Hades docked the boat in a little cove, securing the craft with surprising efficiency. She began to stand, but he moved swiftly, taking the seat next to her own. His large body was pressed against hers and he leaned back, bringing her to lay over him, so that they looked up at the mysterious blue lights.

"Just a little while longer," he murmured against her neck. "Let us just pretend we are two young lovers looking up at the night sky. No responsibilities except to ourselves."

The blue light flickered over his face, lovingly shaping his high cheekbones, straight nose, and perfect, full lips. How I love him, she thought, and she felt the ridiculous prickle of tears against her eyes. Why did this sense of doom always seem to hover at the edge of her life?

"Are we not young lovers?" she retorted with a glare, hoping that he would not notice her sudden melancholy.

"You are young," he replied, laughing. She felt dampness on her cheeks and she lifted a hand to her face, but he reached for it too, wiping small white, crystals from her skin. His gaze narrowed as they melted on his fingertips.

"Snow," he muttered. "Something is wrong." He pulled her to her feet, wrapping his cape around her, his long fingers securing it around her neck. "Come. We will go the rest of the way on foot." As they hurried out of the cave, Persephone saw that chunks of ice were pushing into its entrance and the river was beginning to freeze over. They stepped from the cave and she gasped. It was a blizzard outside and the wind whipped wildly around them stealing the breath from her chest. Hades strode to the main docks of the river and she saw the Judges were waiting.

They gave a gasp of relief as they saw him, their long robes flying behind them as they hurried to the King. "My lord," Minos cried. "The upper world is covered in ice and the death toll is mounting. We are behind schedule with sorting. A tragedy seems to have befallen the world above and the souls are demanding retribution for their unjust deaths. I fear we have a rebellion on our hands. The rivers are frozen and Charon can barely ferry the souls across." His eyes drifted to Persephone and his face twisted with animosity, the hostility so ripe in his gaze that Persephone gave a small gasp. "I fear you have been preoccupied, my King. Never before have I seen such anarchy in these halls. I cannot help but to attribute it to certain changes that have recently occurred here."

Hades grasped Persephone's hand tightly in his hand, taking a step closer to the Judge. "You think to blame my wife?" he questioned with anger, his voice a lethal whisper in the wind. "I left for several days, as I have done in the past, and return to find chaos in my Kingdom. If you cannot manage to maintain stability in my absence I wonder if I need you at all? And if you look, or speak to your Queen in such a way again, you will do so without your eyes and your tongue in the future. Now leave me!" Minos' face had turned pale and he turned and rushed out hurriedly, the others falling into step behind him. "I will take you to your rooms," he said, pulling her quickly beside him. "You will stay there until I sort this out."

"What?" she cried, pulling against his grasp. "No, I should come with you! I should help you sort them. If there is a riot, you will need my help."

"I forbid it," he hissed out between his teeth. They crossed the threshold into the palace and Hades bellowed, "Phoebe!" The handmaiden appeared, running hurriedly down the halls. "Take your Queen to her room," he ordered.

Persephone grasped his arm tightly, angry at his dismal. "I am the Queen!" she seethed, looking up into his face, the veil of coldness firmly back in place. "I will not be pushed away. There are two thrones and I am supposed to sit on one of them. My place is at your side."

"Today it is not," he replied coldly. "These souls are angry and I do not yet know what is happening or what the Judges have said to them. If they have tried to place blame with you, the sight of your face could incite dissension. Stay here where you are safe and let me deal with this today."

He gave Phoebe a nod and turned his back on her, his footsteps soundless as he moved down the marbled halls. The sounds of muffled, raised voices increased as he approached the throne room. Hades pushed open the doors and paused as he took in the crowded room, hundreds of angry faces turned towards him. He allowed none of his shock to show, keeping his face a blank mask and their voices quieted as he strode towards his throne. Sullen, furious eyes followed him as he crossed the large room. He sat slowly, eyeing the dead when the doors opened suddenly and Persephone stepped into the hall.

The cries of the mob were deafening as they hissed at her. A chant was rising and Hades realized in horror what they were saying.

"Murderess." A rock was hurled through the crowd, hitting her face, and she gave a small cry of pain.

Hades took a moment to locate the man who had thrown the stone before fury caused his vision to blur, and he lifted his hands, throwing the bodies away from her, the floor quivering with the force of his rage. He rose from the throne, his hands lifted as purple fire arced between his fingers.

"Touch her again and I will rip your souls apart until you are little more than cinder on this floor." His voice was a deadly whisper as he walked towards Persephone. He raised his hand against her cheek, his fingers brushing away any trace of pain from her skin.

"Her mother murdered us because she is here!" An anonymous voice called out from the crowd. "She as good as killed us. And here she sits on the throne while we starved and froze to death! She should burn!" The crowd began to become louder and Hades could feel them pressing closer, their faces filled with loathing. Persephone tried to step closer to the crowd and he could see she meant to comfort them. Hades knew that they would as soon rip her body to pieces as listen to her words. He pulled her behind him.

"You think to dictate to me," he said in a low voice. "I welcome you into my Kingdom as guests and it makes you greedy and gluttonous and demanding. Your Queen is blameless. I am the reason for your deaths. I took Demeter's daughter against her will. Demeter grieves for her child - neither of them are responsible."

"She is the one who brought this upon us!"

"Throw her in Tartarus. Send us back above!"

The mob's chants rose to a thunderous roar, the hundreds of cries and curses merging together until the last ounce of Hades' patience drained away. Tilting his head back, he let the words tumble from his lips, "Mors omnibus." The whispered phrase echoed loudly through the hall, ending with a hiss as the room was plunged into darkness.

Persephone reached for Hades but she was rooted in place. She felt a soft touch against her face as an insidious silence trickled through the room, a heaviness that covered the air. Suddenly the room was immersed in a brilliant purple light, the violet hues seeming to emanate from Hades' skin as he levitated from the ground. The flesh around his eyes was black and his irises glowed crimson, veins etched onto his flesh. He opened his mouth and the voice of death poured from his lips. "Mors tua, vita mea. Do you forget to whom you speak? I am death. I am King of the Damned, the Infernal; I have been known by many names. You can die once or you can die a thousand deaths. Your souls will empower mine." His feet returned to the ground and he took a step closer to the crowd, smiling, his canines sharp and extended. A hiss filled the room and he lifted his hand, as a doorway opened in the floor. The door flung back and tormented cries of misery echoed from the gaping blackness. With a wave of his hand, the man who had thrown the stone was lifted from the ground and thrown into the pit of darkness. Flames burst from the depths as his body disappeared over the edge and a cry of agony was quickly cut off as the door slammed shut again. He turned back to the crowd.

"Who wants to join him? Who dares to whisper treason against their Queen? It is your choice, eternal fire or the meadows? Loyalty or treachery? I would like nothing better than to watch you

all burn." His eyes flared purple when an archway opened through the wall, filled with the beautiful, bright light of Asphodel. The crowd pleaded suddenly, the mortals falling to their knees begging for mercy. Hades motioned his hand and they flooded through the gates to the meadows, pushing each other in their desperation to escape the King of Death. "Welcome to the Underworld," he mocked. The door thundered shut as the last soul stepped through.

Persephone moved forward, but she was suddenly pushed against the wall, staring into the eyes of a demon. "You disobeyed me," he rasped, his blood red eyes boring into her own. Instead of being afraid, she pressed her face against his chest.

"I am sorry," she cried. "I thought I could help. Is what they said true? Did my mother do this?" When she looked up again, the red was fading from his eyes, revealing his dark gaze.

"I believe she has inadvertently started an endless winter -- due to her grief of losing you. But they did not blame Demeter, they blamed you. Someone is working against you. They would have ripped you to pieces if given half the chance," he declared heatedly.

"I thought I could reason with them," she said quietly.

"Have you never before seen an angry mob?" He cried in exasperation, shaking her slightly. "They cannot be reasoned with! They demand blood and the only thing more powerful than their rage -- is fear. They see you as a killer and only your fall from grace will satisfy them. They wanted to see you brought to your knees and expected me to deal you your punishment."

"But--but I am their queen, I should not cower from them! It is my responsibility to see to the safety of this Kingdom. To help you."

"I know my sweet wife. But... sometimes a more subtle and

lethal attack is needed. I fear another wave will be coming tomorrow. Unless we can find a way to stop this everlasting winter."

"What can we do? I am worried about my mother."

"As am I," he murmured. "Without knowing where Ares is, I am not sure that it is safe for you to go above ground. It may not be safe for you to travel to her temple, in any case, with mobs of mortals all directing their anger towards you."

She watched his pensive face. "What are you thinking?"

"Write to your mother. Let her know how you are. Zeus will not be happy losing so many souls to me. It may force his hand. In the meantime, do not wander the palace. I must see how badly the rivers are frozen, perhaps I can unfreeze them enough that Charon may be able to pass. Stay in your room, Persephone. I mean it. I will find you when I am finished. There is nothing more you can do tonight."

A protest rose on her lips but she bit it back when she saw the look in his eyes. She remembered his confession, that he was afraid she would be destroyed as his mother had been. Perhaps this once, she could do as she was bid. He had been right, she should never have come into the throne room. He walked her back to her chambers, silent as they made their way down the hall. When they reached her room he pushed the door open.

"Stay here, Persephone," he repeated again and she was reminded of her first night here. How much had changed since then. She would give anything to protect the man who stood in front of her, this dark God who was hers. With a kiss he was gone and she was once again alone in the darkness.

After a happy reunion with Olive, Persephone spent a restless evening in her room. Events were unfolding quickly and she felt as if they were stumbling helplessly forward, yet unable to stay ahead of the hands of fate. She wrote a long letter to her mother and Charon came to collect it, but it felt like too little, too late. When she inquired about Hades, Charon's hooded face turned to her silently, and then he slipped from the room wordlessly like the quiet wraith that he was. She gave a frustrated sigh, barely resisting the urge to throw her shoe at him. She longed to check on Cerberus, but it was likely her little friend was quite busy ensuring that the masses of souls who had arrived stayed put. And more would be coming, there was no doubt of that. The winter above was fierce and relentless, sweeping across the land like a dark shadow of death. Even the Underworld felt the bite of the numbing cold. Where was her mother now, she wondered? Guilt tugged at her; had there been anything she could have done to reassure her? First she had been unable to contact her mother, but after discovering her love for Hades... could she have contacted her mother then? Would it have protected or endangered Demeter to place her between herself and Ares? She had allowed herself to become distracted, and because of that distraction, death and disease ran rampant in the world above. Perhaps she was responsible for this. She sat suddenly, overwhelmed by guilt, leaning against the bed as she pushed her face against Olive. So many deaths lay at her feet; how could she go on when such a heavy burden weighed down on her? Hades found her there many hours later, and she gave a start as she felt his hands on her back.

"What are you doing, Persephone?" he inquired softly.

She turned to look up at him, his face unreadable in the darkness. "I must have fallen asleep," she replied vaguely. "Were you able to ferry the souls tonight?"

He nodded, sinking to the ground next to her. "I was able to melt the ice enough that we were able to bring them through. But it will be frozen again by morning. You wrote to your mother?"

"Yes, I gave the letter to Charon," she responded.

"Good," he mumbled in a tired voice as he reached behind him to rub Olive's soft fur. The deer pressed his nose into his hand. Persephone moved to kneel in front of him, letting her eyes drift over him. His eyes were closed and the delicate flesh beneath was shadowed, lines of strain evident on his face.

She brushed a dark strand of hair from his forehead. "You should eat," she said softly. "Do you want me to bring you something?"

"I am hungry," his voice was a rumble against her as he pressed his face suddenly against her neck.

"What would you like?" she asked breathlessly.

"You," he growled. He pushed her back and moved between her legs.

CHAPTER XXV
THE ARCHER

HADES WOKE, pulling himself carefully from Persephone's arms. He looked down at her; Olive's small brown form was curled tightly against her legs and Persephone's dark hair covered her like a blanket, the pale flesh of her breasts visible between the strands. She was... beautiful, she was everything he had ever wanted, and he would give anything to crawl back into bed and curl against her warm, lush body and pretend that the world outside did not exist. However, there were things he had to settle and already he might be too late to undo what had been done. Would he lose her as the Fates had warned? His heart twisted painfully at the thought and he rubbed his hand over the small scar on his chest -- so many questions that needed answers.

He dressed quickly, and from his dresser he removed the

letter that Charon had secretly delivered to him yesterday, the one that Persephone had written to her mother. It was time to talk to Demeter. He moved quickly through the empty palace, stopping in his study to take a golden helmet from a shelf near his desk, then he hurried into the stables. After saddling Orphnaeus, he placed the helmet over his head and a curious swooping moved over his body and he could see that his form had vanished. The helmet of invisibility; it had been in his possession since before the wars, but he used it rarely now. There was a time when this helmet had consumed him, the desire to vanish from existence overriding every other need. But there was a price to pay for invisibility. After his mother died, when he had first been sentenced to live in this dark world, he had wanted to disappear. He had worn the helmet day after day, and he felt himself become more and more insubstantial, almost weightless. He became addicted to the anonymity and though he knew he was becoming weaker, he kept the helmet on, travelling deeper and deeper into the Underworld. He became a part of the shadows and it was then that he had first met Eurynomos. He had paid a price and learned that the helmet should be worn only when necessary, but now -- he needed it. He had no time to spare for the interference of mortals or Gods.

With a wave of his hands, the gates of the Underworld opened and Hades leaned forward to whisper, "Fly Orphnaeus." The horse gave a huff, small flames licking from his nostrils as they galloped up to Earth, up the mountain that lead above the Gates of Hell. The gates thundered shut behind him and he raced through the snow-covered landscape, the frozen terrain unrecognizable. The river where he had first seen Persephone was iced over and the trees of the forest were barren and stark. He soon reached Demeter's small temple. It looked abandoned, covered by deep drifts of snow, but he knew he would find her inside. He dismounted from Orphanaeus and rubbed his hand against the steed's soft ears. "Stay put old friend, I will return soon," he muttered. His footsteps were soft in the snow and he pushed open the gates of the temple, leaves blowing across the abandoned halls. He took the helmet from his head, his black hair tumbling from it slowly. The quiet was deafening inside, like an empty tomb. He moved quickly through the rooms, knowing where he would find Demeter.

She lay upon Persephone's bed and she turned her face when he entered, her glazed, dark eyes focusing on him. Her hair was in wild disarray and it looked to be some time since she had last bathed, as dark smudges lay across her face. "Hades, but I thought--" her voice cut off, a mere croak, as if she was unused to speaking. "Persephone?" she asked, sitting up quickly.

He held up a hand as realization dawned on him, her thoughts and guilt speaking loudly in his mind. "I think you have something to tell me, Demeter," his voice a powerful sound in the room. She made a small whimper of distress as he pushed into her memories, though his touch was gentle. He watched the day Demeter discovered her daughter was to marry Ares, how she had gone to Zeus demanding the engagement be stopped. He saw her desperation as she fled from the throne room of Zeus, furtively disappearing into the dark halls of Olympus as she sought an audience with Aphrodite. Venus gave her a look as Demeter pushed into the darkened room where she was pleasuring Hermes, and the God gave an agonized cry as she let his cock slip out of her.

"Why do you seek me, Goddess?" Aphrodite murmured, sauntering towards her, smelling of sex and gardenia. "Did you wish to join us?"

"No." Demeter replied in a flinty voice. "I have need of you, may I speak with you privately?"

A lovely smiled suffused Aphrodite's face, and grasping Demeter's hand, they left the unfortunate Hermes and made their way into a secluded corner of the palace. Demeter told Venus the entire tale, and when she had finished, she pulled back to look at her. "Can you help me?" Demeter asked, her low voice vibrating with emotion.

"There is someone she loves," Venus whispered slowly. "Persephone thought the love had died, yet it burns secretly and brightly within her." She told Demeter of the love in Hades' heart, and though it was shrouded in shadow, it grew strong and true within his soul. "He was the one who wrote her the letters. Someone interfered with the delivery of those letters, and their destiny."

"Ares," Demeter hissed, too loudly.

"Perhaps," Aprhodite replied in a cool tone. "She will be safe in the caves of the Underworld. No one can protect hrt here, but she would be protected in Hades' realm. He is the last choice that remains to you. You must either give her up to the God of War, or abandon her to an unknown fate in the darkness with the God of Death -- who loves her."

"There is no choice," Demeter cried, "Ares must not be allowed to touch her again. I must tell her, so she will not be afraid. She will not understand."

Venus shook her head, her golden curls dancing, and raised a finger to her lips. "You cannot tell her. Neither of them can know that it was you who shot the arrow. You cannot tell Persephone that Hades, not Ares wrote those letters. She will not believe you. Great harm may be done if you attempt to interfere once the curse takes hold. It must play out of its own accord."

Demeter flinched. "Is there not another way? I could tell Hades--"

"Hades does not remember that he wrote the letters. He drank from the River Lethe and those memories belong to the river now. You cannot rely on him to help you, his love is buried almost as deep as hers, though the flame still burns. He would likely not even grant you an audience. He despises Olympians."

"But I could lose her!" Demeter lamented.

Aphrodite grasped Demeter's arms, her delicate fingers painful on her flesh. "You will lose her, Demeter, in every way, if you allow Ares to wed her. Ares does not love her, he only wants to own her, then destroy her. The choice is yours, but I will help you, if you allow it."

"And if the curse fails?" Demeter whispered. "What then?"

Aphrodite ran her fingers over Demeter's face, tracing her full lips almost lovingly. "Then he will go mad and your daughter will be locked in the Underworld with him. The choice is yours," she repeated again. "Who do you trust more? Ares or Hades?"

Demeter hardened her face. "How do we do this?"

The Goddess of Love smiled and Demeter shivered. "Come, Goddess." Hades watched as Aphrodite took Demeter's hand and pulled them both through a window from the highest tower of Zeus' temple. Demeter gave a cry of shock, but instead of falling, they climbed high above the palace, the wind lifting them beyond the clouds, and high above the sun, until they hovered in the darkness of the universe. "Lure her out of the temple, Demeter."

Demeter put out her hands, and in her mind, she planted a

golden flower in a lavender meadow, casting a powerful spell over the petals. The golden pollen would draw her out into the open. Aphrodite outstretched her arms and a golden arrow and bow appeared. With her fingers, she fused Persephone's name on the arrow and Demeter could hear the sizzling of metal.

"Even the God of Death cannot ignore a love arrow," Aphrodite said. "He will have no choice but to seek her out, to claim her."

Thunder rumbled beneath their feet as Venus opened her luscious pink lips, cursed words falling from them.

I, Call upon Venus and the Universe
To Bring an irreversible Curse upon the King of the Dead
With Whoever's name is inscribed on this arrow
Let the king scour the earth to find her
Let no man, beast or God stand in his way until her heart is his.

Until she loves him, he will feel torment, desire, lust.
Until She loves him he will bleed out tears.
Until She loves him every inhale will be poison to his lungs
Every exhale, terror of losing her.

A curse on you, Hades!
A curse through your veins that will poison your mind!
A curse on your sanity
A curse on your immortal soul
Until you posses her heart
Your free will be damned
Without her love…you will go…mad!

They could hear the rumble of Ares' war cry, his voice echoing in the infinity of the universe, and they knew he was coming for Persephone. "Hurry," Aphrodite cried, thrusting the arrow and bow into her hands. "Hades must find her before Ares." Venus pushed Demeter forward. "Do not miss."

Demeter drew back on the bow, the arrow still hot in her hands from Aphrodite's curse. She shook the tears from her eyes and then hardened her heart. "I will not."

He watched the arrow fly from the bow as it fell towards Earth, towards him. He had seen enough.

Lowering his hand, Demeter once again sat up from the bed. "I had no choice," she whispered. "I could not let him touch her."

"You play the distraught mother well, Demeter," Hades said in a cool voice. "You are an even better shot than your daughter." He pulled down his robes, showing her the small, white scar.

Her eyes moved over his chest, her pale face becoming somehow paler still. "I am sorry for your suffering, Hades. It was not -- not, my intention. I only thought of Persephone and I knew that you loved her, and could protect her in a way I no longer could. I did not protect her enough to keep that animal's filthy hands from her. He stole her innocence in my forest!" She screamed the words, her pain so powerful the ground trembled beneath his feet. She must have felt it for she took a calming breath and continued in a quiet voice. "I would do anything to protect my child, even if that means giving her up. I know you are a good man, Hades. No one need tell me that you were trapped into your fate. When you disappeared to become ruler of the Underworld, I knew that you would take any kingdom dealt you and raise it from the ashes to create an indomitable fortress. What better-guarded place from Ares and Zeus than your kingdom?

That degenerate snake was sending the Stymphalian birds to carry her away. They were destroying crops and killing villagers, so Zeus promised her to his son. Pledged her to that… rapist!" She spit the word. "I could no longer convince Zeus to put off another marriage. Aphrodite came to me and told me of your feelings for my daughter. I was desperate to do anything to protect Persephone. Together, we devised a plan that would give us both what we wanted."

Hades' gaze moved to Demeter's eyes. "Give you both?" he repeated.

The scent of gardenias filled the air and Aphrodite walked through the door, her long blond hair trailing around her. She was holding a golden arrow and she held it out to him. Only a single letter was inscribed on it, 'A'. She moved closer to him, brushing her lips against each of his cheeks, before pulling back with a beaming smile.

"I told you she loved you," purred Aphrodite.

"You said many things that night," he replied stonily. "Whose life do you intend to ruin now?" he asked, indicating the arrow.

Aphrodite's wide blue eyes widened in excitement and her smile grew positively beatific. "In my entire existence, there is one man I have never been able to hit with a love arrow. Only one man who can dodge my bow, the only man I have ever loved." She pouted suddenly. "It has been quite distressing as you can imagine."

"Touching," he drawled. "And why am I being regaled with this story?"

"Ares. And you will help me," she said, simply. "I love him, but his hatred for you makes him infatuated with having your wife. And pretty though she is, she cannot hope to compete with me. No offense." It was unclear if she was apologizing to Hades or Demeter.

"But," she continued, with an airy wave of her hand, "if you plunge this arrow into his heart, it will eliminate both our problems."

Hades gave a snort of disgust. "I have seen how your love arrows work, Aphrodite. You could as soon drive him mad as to love you. The world should not be afflicted with a love-sick Ares. Besides, Persephone is safely within the Underworld. I have no need to assist in your love affairs. I owe you nothing."

Her smile caused a shiver to travel down him. She moved closer to him and pressed her lips against his ear. "Oh, but Aidoneus, you never found Ares, did you? Where do you think he went?"

A quick intake of breath passed Hades' lips and Demeter gasped, "Aphrodite, what have you done?"

"I told you, Hades," she replied, her face devoid of all deception, "it doesn't matter how we get what we want, as long as we get it."

Hades mind flashed to the memory of the dark figure from Persephone's vision. He had assumed he was seeing himself -- but it hadn't been. It was Ares. Ares had been watching her, lying in wait for the perfect opportunity to take her and he had provided it. She was alone in the Underworld with not even Cerberus to protect her. He spun out of the room and he heard Demeter calling his name, but he did not turn around. He ran to his horse and charged through the snow like a demon, tearing over the Earth as he raced back to the Underworld. He waved his hands, opening the gates, jumping off of Orphaneus even as the horse still galloped. Hades bounded towards the castle, running through the halls. He pushed into her room, crying her name, and then stopped. There was crimson staining the sheets, pools of it dripping to the floor. A message on the wall was written in blood, her blood: "Her life or yours." A small noise drew his attention and he saw the tiny fawn huddled, shivering in a corner. With gentle hands he lifted Olive.

"It is alright little one. He cannot harm you anymore. I will find her." He set the deer on the chaise before the fire, and then with icy determination in his veins, made his way back to Orphaneus. "Up again, Orphaneus."

By the time he returned to Demeter's temple, Aphrodite was waiting on the bed with Demeter.

"Where is she!" he bellowed. He grasped her from the bed, shaking her so hard he heard her neck snap, but she merely pushed it firmly back in place with an annoyed look.

Aphrodite flicked her wrist, lifting a golden arrow between her and the King. "You know how to find him. He has brought her to his temple. I need you to plunge this into Ares' heart at close range. He is impossible to hit from a distance. You must be sure to pierce his heart with it."

Hades roughly pushed her from him and she tumbled to the ground. "I will kill your lover and rip his soul into shards," he growled, his eyes flaming purple. "And then I will come for you."

Venus crawled onto her knees before him, no trace of sensuality in her face. There were tears in her eyes as she clawed desperately at his robes.

"Please," she cried. "Please, I love him. Help me," she begged. "Help me. You know how weak love can make you," she whispered, "you know better than anyone. I am tormented by the thought of him."

"Your lover is a rapist! A murderer who delights in tormenting the innocent," he spat. "This is who inspires love in you? I should do the world a favor and rid it of both of you."

She stood up unsteadily from the ground, leaning against the wall, darkness flickering in her eyes. "You know the burden of destroying a soul. I have seen you hesitate before taking a life. It is what makes you strong... and weak. What will Zeus do to you if you kill his son? You think he will let you keep your wife?" She bent over and whispered in his ear, so Demeter could not hear. "Besides, he has his father's sword. The golden blade."

Hades turned pale. "That is impossible!" he whispered. "He cannot pull that sword, only the sons of Cronus... how?"

Aphrodite shook her head, shrugging. "I do not know. Perhaps Zeus lent it to him. Maybe Ares is tired of you stealing his soldiers, or maybe Zeus wants to grow his kingdom by eliminating death. Either way; they are tired of you. He now has the golden sword and the wife of the man he hates - that is indeed a dangerous combination."

Demeter had remained silent until now, but she rose from the bed quivering with rage as she approached Aphrodite. "How dare you use my daughter," she cried furiously. "When you visited me, driving words of despair and loneliness into my mind, was it to guilt me so that I would be filled with regret? You told me that Hades had gone mad, that he had trapped Persephone, that she was little more than a prisoner! You lied to me so that I would be so overcome with remorse that I drove a perpetual winter through all the land; so that Hades would have to leave Persephone to seek me, leaving her alone to be abducted by your depraved and vicious lover?"

Aphrodite threw up her hands, watching Demeter out of wary blue eyes. "Oh please, Demeter, you wanted her down there. Do not blame me that you have frozen the earth with your regret and loneliness. Easily led minds get what they deserve," she replied with a smirk. "Zeus now demands Hades send his precious daughter back -- so everyone wins except the God of the Dead. You played Hades just as much as I did."

The words were like a knife in his heart. "You want me to risk my life and kingdom and think I will send my wife back? Was it you, Venus, who whispered Persephone's names to the dying mortals, placing blame at her feet?" Her eyes gave him the answer he needed, and he leaned down to pick up his helmet, then walked out of the temple and looking towards the snow-covered cliffs that Ares' temple resided on.

Venus followed him, her laughter drifting on the wind. "You hold no cards in this game, Aidoneus. You will fight for her because she is the only thing in this entire Universe to ever truly love you. Your father did not love you; your mother did not love you; your brothers do not love you. You cannot live without knowing she is alive. Love makes even the strongest God weak. You will die for her if necessary, but more importantly, you will let her separate from you so that she may survive. And is that not the ultimate sacrifice?"

He turned around to face her, his expression cold and unreadable. "What do you know of sacrifice? You know nothing but the pleasure between your own legs. Hermes!" he bellowed suddenly.

With the call of his name Hermes appeared with a flash on the winds, jumping out of a swirling current to bow before him. "Hades," he murmured. He eyed Aphrodite's breasts and then forced his gaze back to the dark God. "You bellowed for me?"

"Hermes, I want you to bear witness. If something should happen to me, my kingdom and all of the realms will be passed on to my wife. Everything goes to her and her alone. No Olympian shall ever have my kingdom. Do you understand?"

Hermes gave a slight nod of the head, unsurprised by Hades' bequest. "Everything goes to your wife. Got it." He snapped his fingers and then opened his hands, a contract held between them. The letters shined on the golden parchment. Hermes produced a quill and Hades signed the form quickly. She will destroy you the Fates had warned. He found he no longer cared. For a moment, just for the briefest moment, they had been happy. It was enough. It was more than he deserved, and he was ready to die if necessary. If he was killed by the God's Sword, his soul would also be destroyed and there would be no life after death. But there were worse things than dying; he had seen them, he had lived them.

"Shall I stay?" Hermes inquired, carefully tucking the parchment into his robes. "I can lead you up Ares' mountain."

Hades nodded, unsurprised that Hermes knew his business. He turned back to face Aphrodite. He took the arrow from Aphrodite's small hand, holding it between his own. "A?" He looked up at Venus. "For Ares or Aphrodite?"

Venus placed her hands over the "A" inscribed on the cool metal. "For us both," she replied softly.

"You expect me to pierce a War God's heart with an arrow at close range, while he is swinging at me with a 'God Killing' sword? You do realize there is every chance I will not succeed and we will both lose. I with my life and you, your love."

Aphrodite did not flinch. "You will not fail. You were a warrior in the Titan Wars." She lifted her hand clenching her fist. "Harness that power again."

"You speak of war as if you understand it," he replied with a sneer. "Surviving is mostly luck."

"What is love if not war?" Aphrodite asked, her voice so soft Hades was not sure if the words were spoken or whispered in his mind.

He felt a hand on his back and he turned to look into Demeter's face, so much like Persephone's, her large eyes sorrowful as she stared into his. "Hades, you do not have to do this. Take her away and then run back to the Underworld. Lock the gates. You do not have to fight. You owe these manipulating monsters nothing, you owe me nothing. You have sacrificed too much already. She will not survive losing you." Her lips trembled as she looked up at him.

Once again the Fates echoed in his mind: You will want to stay but you will not. Zeus demanded her return. He took Demeter's hand in his.

"Even with a decision to run Demeter, I may not survive. This will not end with my death or my survival. What will happen when Zeus' men bring her back to you? Can you protect her from him, forever hidden in your temple? Will she be forced to be with him? Marry him? If she is to be taken from me, I want her to be safe. Venus is right. His heart needs to be turned away from her. There is one thing you can do for me."

"Name it," Demeter replied.

"See to my horse, make sure he does not freeze to death in this fucking winter." Hades motioned to Hermes. "Take me to Ares. Let us end this."

CHAPTER XXVI
THE BATTLE

THE TWO MEN stepped out into the snow, the blizzard seemed to have abated temporarily. Hermes put his hand on Hades' shoulder.

"I wanted to marry her, you know," he said with a wry grin.

Hades did not remove his gaze from the mountain tops, "I know."

"Set her free, Hades, your union will only bring the both of you pain. There is too much between you to ever be happy. She belongs in Olympus with the rest of her kind. And you belong--"

"I think I have had enough advice for today, young messenger," Hades replied with a snarl. "Take us to his temple."

As they shot through the sky, hurtling towards the mountain above, Hades heard a whisper in his mind -- You will not be alone.

They reached the edge of Ares' domain and Hermes turned to

him, giving him a swift bow. His eyes were fathomless as he looked up at Hades and there may have been regret in their blue depths. "Here is where I leave you, Dispater. I wish you luck. You do not deserve the hand you have been dealt, but the cards are yours all the same." He vanished as suddenly as he had appeared and Hades stood alone on the precipice. The stench of death was unmistakable. The mountains were made from the bodies of dead men, their corpses lining the ground, wrapping around the trees. Rain began to fall, as lightning crackled through the sky and the rivers ran swift, their waters swirling with blood. Soldiers lined the rugged mountaintops as Hades ascended the mountain, their swords drawn but no one touched him. He knew why they waited. Their God dictated their orders and Ares would want to watch. He finally reached the peak and there Ares stood on the furthest ledge, holding the glowing golden blade of the "God Killer" against Persephone's throat, the crimson jewels of the pomegranate necklace shining around her neck. Hades stepped forward, his eyes moving over her battered form.

"Ares," he called in a calm voice, "let her go."

The grip Ares had in her hair tightened and the blade edged closer to her flesh. With his opposite hand, he dug his fingers into her neck, and a small rivulet of blood ran down her throat. Hades wanted to cry out but any reaction would merely fuel Ares' bloodlust. Persephone must know it too, for she did not make a sound as he moved the blade to graze over her throat, merely keeping her eyes fixed on his. She was brave -- his wife.

"And why would I do that?" Ares contemptuously asked.

"I do not want to kill you," Hades said.

Ares laughed, the sound tainted with madness. "Do you not see what I hold in my hand? I will not die today."

Hades kept his gaze focused on the small drop of blood that travelled down Persephone's chest. Hades said, "Zeus has ordered Persephone to be given back to her mother. I am complying with that. This fight is only between the two of us. Our marriage will be dissolved." He could see the stricken expression on her face even at a distance and he knew Ares saw it too. "Let me say goodbye to her. Whether I live or die, this is the last time I will see her."

Ares smiled. "Oh no, that is too easy, corpse whisperer. Swear an oath on your precious Styx that you will fight me and I will let you say goodbye. You can die by my blade or die from breaking your oath. Either way, I do not care as long as I can be there to listen to your last breath."

Hades bent, placing his helmet on the ground. He lifted his hand in the air and again the blue flamed sword he had wielded in the Underworld appeared. He grasped it, using the edge to slice his palm and he raised his right hand, a silver goblet appearing in his outstretched palm. "By my blood I swear, on my mother's grave and on the River Styx. If you let me say goodbye, I will fight you." He drank deeply from the cup as the blood trickled down his arm seeping into the ground.

Ares' laughter filled the air as he pushed Persephone towards Hades. "Here," he called, "take the little bitch. I am not sure I want your seconds anyway."

Persephone fell down the hill roughly, but Hades caught her before she could land at his feet. He picked her up against him and she clung to him desperately, her eyes welling with tears. He brushed his fingers against a bruise swelling on her cheek.

"Why did you do that?" she whispered frantically. "You cannot fight him. You heard what he said, he has the God Killing sword.

He will kill you." She pulled at him, her hands urgent. "We can hide in the Underworld, we can leave. He cannot fight both of us."

Ares was calling out orders behind them and Hades watched as the troops lifted their bows and Ares was shifting his feet restlessly as he readied for battle. "Oh, Persephone," he whispered. "How I have loved you. Remember that." He bent forward, pressing his lips against hers briefly, and then he placed the helmet of invisibility on her head and pushed her away. "Run," he said softly to the empty space beside him.

A scream of denial filled the air, shaking the mountain. The sky rained arrows and Hades twisted his hand. A legion of troops collapsed on the ground, falling like puppets over the hillside. He pulled the blue-flamed sword again from the air, and Hades flew up the mountain, using the wind as his shield to repel any arrow that came towards him. He climbed up the bodies of the dead soldiers, relentlessly cutting down any man that came into his path, his eyes fixed on the mad God who stood laughing as his own soldiers fell on the mountainside. When Hades reached the top, he leapt into the air, arcing his blade towards Ares, even as the War God lifted his own; as the swords struck, a flash of yellow-green light illuminated the heavens and the Earth reverberated with the force. The two Gods weaved in and out of the shadows, each swing causing the ground to tremble beneath their feet. Lightning twisted around them as Hades jumped and Ares quickly shielded himself with the body of a decaying soldier. For a moment, Hades' blade stuck in the ribs of the corpse, but then he used the body to knock Ares to the ground, the momentum freeing his sword so that the was able to slice Ares arm with the edge. Quickly he removed the arrow from his robes attempting to stab Ares in the heart, but his armor was too Impenetrable.

Ares laughed up at him. "You are trying to put a love spell on me? If you wanted to fuck me, Hades, all you had to do was ask."

Hades realized he would have to rip the armor off if he wanted to penetrate the War God's body. He was pulled back suddenly. Soldiers were jumping down from the cliffs surrounding them, hundreds making their way towards them, some of them dying from the fall. Hades twisted his hand and the crunch of a hundred necks breaking simultaneously filled the night air. "You needlessly sacrifice your soldiers," Hades roared. "This fight is between you and I. No one else."

Ares stood then, brushing the decaying entrails of the corpse carelessly from his body. "It matters not how many die before I kill you. All that matters is that you die."

Persephone watched from the ground. She had realized she was invisible when she looked down and she could no longer see her hands. It was confirmed when the soldiers ran past her without even a glance. Briefly fingering the golden chain around her neck, she stood and silently began to move closer to Hades. Lifting her hands into the air, she wove thick, poisonous vines up and around Ares' legs, the thorns digging painfully into his skin.

He chopped them away with his sword and snarled at Hades, "Between you and I? Your bitch is interfering." Hades punched him hard in the face and Ares fell back, slicing at Hades stomach as he collapsed to the ground. The sword just cut the edge of his skin, but the pain was like nothing he had ever felt, the burning and ripping of flesh so powerful that his sight was temporarily obscured. Suddenly he felt claws tearing at his back; the birds of Stymphalian flew down from the skies gashing his arms and face with their metal beaks

and claws, tearing relentlessly at this skin. He pushed them away with a bolt of light, wiping the blood from his eyes.They began to pour from the skies in thousands and Hades turned to look at them when a giant burst of ice and snow hit the creatures. Hades looked briefly towards the meadows below and saw Demeter. He knew who the voice had been that whispered to him as he ascended the mountain. He watched as she froze the troops on the mountains and blasted the birds back with a second, arctic wind. The snow drifted down to Earth covering the land and the temperatures dropped to a deadly degree. Thorny vines were twisting over the mountain and covering everything in their path. Climbing roses pulled the troops to the ground, blanketing them until they suffocated beneath their weight. The vines leapt into the air, dragging the birds to the ground. Tiny spores opened at the end of each vine putting them into a deep slumber. He knew it was Persephone. He had been right, even a Stymphalian she would not kill.

More vines burst from the ground, stronger and thicker than before as they wrapped around Ares, and he realized Demeter and Persephone were working together, the creeping plants frozen solid as they erupted from the soil. Hades leapt forward, ripping the breastplate from Ares' chest, tearing apart the metal, but a shoulder shield was still covering his heart. Hades grabbed at his arm and tore the armor off of it, breaking nerve, sinew and bone as he ripped it from the War God. Ares let out an agonized scream and stabbed Hades in the leg with his blade. Hades swung the arrow but Ares knocked it from his hand and it tumbled down the mountain.

"One of us dies tonight," Ares cried, spittle dribbling from his lips. He yanked his arm and snapped the bone back in place. "No more games."

They ran towards each other, clashing swords again. Yellow met blue and an explosion from the blades flung both weapons out of their hands, driving the swords over the mountain side. The Gods circled each other.

"I am going to enjoy killing you," Ares taunted. "Perhaps I will fuck Persephone one last time. See if you taught her anything worthwhile."

Hades flung himself towards him, plummeting him with his fists. "You fucking rapist," he spat, knocking him to the ground. He beat him over and over and watched with pleasure as his perfect nose shattered beneath his fists, blood splattering Ares' beautiful face, and still it was not enough. He would not be satisfied until he felt his brain in his hands. Ares grabbed his fists suddenly and sparks began to wrap around his hands, traveling up Hades' arms.

Hades drew back slowly, his eyes narrowed as he looked at his nephew. "Careful," Hades whispered, "your Zeus is starting to show." With a mighty blast, Hades blew them both to the ground. Both of them landed hard on the snow covered ground below and Hades realized too late that Ares lay right next to the silver blade. He gave another war cry, lifting it off the ground as he stood with unsteady legs. Ares stumbled towards the God of Death with a gleam of madness in his bulging eyes, the sword dragging against the snow covered ground.

"How ironic that you will die by the blade that you killed Rhea with."

Hades crawled back towards the edge of the cliff. "You know many secrets, Ares," Hades said in a quiet voice.

Ares laughed gleefully. "Do you want to know a secret? After I kill you, I will obliterate her. First I will fuck her and then I will destroy her. Maybe I will do the same with Demeter too, just for good measure." He snickered again. "You think this ends here?" A voice penetrated Hades mind, I will take everything from you.

Hades placed his hands against the rocks at his back, preparing to bring down the mountain over both of them as Ares lifted the sword high above his head, strange lights of madness dancing in his eyes. Something sped past him, a small golden light and Hades watched in shock as a golden arrow flew into the War God's heart, plunging deep in his chest. Ares eyes widened in disbelief, looking down at his chest as he fell to his knees, dropping his weapon. Hades flew to his side and pushed the arrow deeper, making sure to pierce his heart. As he did so, both men cried out in concert and Hades clutched at his heart in pain. He stumbled slightly and saw the small golden tip protruding from Ares' back. Perhaps Hades had pushed it too far, he thought with satisfaction. He began to move away when Ares' hand snatched out, grasping him.

"Hades," he whispered, his blue eyes hazed with pain. Hades shook him off impatiently. They both turned at a small sound, invisible footsteps in the deep snow.

Persephone removed the helmet, her long, dark hair tumbling over her shoulders. She held a beautiful mahogany bow embellished with exotic red flowers; the flowers of the pomegranate tree. The golden chain at her neck had the jewels torn out of it and he knew what she had done. Her lips were stained with the seeds of the pomegranate. Ares watched her with stunned eyes, his hand grasping the arrow as blood pooled around his fingers.

"It began with an arrow and it ends with an arrow." Her voice was strange in the frozen air, and the wind crackled around her as she stepped forward, her emerald eyes glowing in the darkness.

"Persephone," Hades whispered.

The wind moved lovingly over her and she looked like a huntress, like a ferocious, conquering Queen with the Gods of War and Death bowed at her feet.

"I told you, I will not be separated from you," she said softly. She lifted the bow and raised her face to the heavens -- to Mount Olympus, to Zeus. Her voice echoed eerily in the snow filled meadow.

"This bow shows the world that I am part of the Underworld." Lightning flashed across the sky, the Earth trembling as it arced above them. "I am the Queen of Shades, the Queen of Death, and I rule the Kingdom of the Damned." She turned back to Hades, her voice quiet once more and he knew he did not imagine the red flame in her gaze. "This bow shows I am part of you."

Demeter had reached the valley where they stood and she gasped as she saw the bow held in her daughter's hands. "Oh, Persephone," she cried, "what have you done?"

Persephone took a step towards her mother, the red gleam fading from her eyes as she dropped her bow. Hades wrapped his arms around her and they both vanished from view.

CHAPTER
XXVII
PARTED

THEY KNELT IN the water of the Styx and Hades pulled her towards him, the gentle waves pulsing around them. "Persephone," he cried. "I told you, do not eat the seeds of the pomegranate. Those seeds are cursed, there is no way to reverse this. It cannot be undone. You are a prisoner here. You belong to this dark world now."

She pulled back, her green eyes flashing. "I do not want to undo it. You think that I would let them take me from you? You are mine and I am yours. Zeus would remove me from this Kingdom and I would be unable to protect it, and I promised you I would. I am bound now -- irrevocably; bound to the Underworld, and to you. Whatever perils you face, I face them with you, whatever sorrows you have are mine too." She pressed her lips against his. "You sing the song of my soul; you have seen my darkness and I have seen

yours. I am as much a part of the shadows as I am of the light."

He cradled her against his chest, letting the water wash away the blood, cleansing them of the putrid stench of death. "How many seeds did you eat?" he asked in a rough voice.

"Six. All six seeds on the necklace and I would have eaten more if I could have."

"Six," he echoed in horror. "You will not be allowed on Earth for six months of the year. You are entombed here. A prisoner."

"Hades," she said with a smile, "this is my home. Wherever you are is my home. Come, let us go to your room."

She helped him as he limped from the river, down the quiet hallways of his palace. He collapsed on the rug near the fire, as Olive nudged the door open. For a quiet moment, they sat before the hot flames, a small, broken family. Hades watched his wife carefully, seeing the red lights that danced occasionally within the emerald depths, like fire spreading over a forest.

"Persephone, the Olympians-- they will still be coming for you." He shivered and she frowned as she looked up at him.

"What is wrong?"

"Ares scratched me." He touched the small wound at her neck, closing the skin the rest of the way with the healing warmth of his fingertips. "You do not seem to be suffering any ill effects."

"Mine was barely a scratch." She began pulling at his wet robes. "Take them off! Let me see."

He laughed unsteadily. "You always seem to be undressing me these days."

"Hmph," she murmured, bending over to inspect the long gashes over his thigh and abdomen. "They look like they are festering already. I need to clean them. Can you tolerate the pain?" She

asked, raising her eyes to his. He nodded and she grabbed a poker from the hearth, holding it over the flame. She raised her hand over the glowing rod and whispered, "Tui gratia Iovis gratia sit cures." He stiffened at her words, and she moved to stand over him, her eyes crimson in the shadows as she lowered the poker. His flesh sizzled as she cauterized the wound and Hades breathed in sharply, sweat covering his body, but he did not utter a word of protest. She eyed him and he nodded; she placed the rod into the flame again and came back, repeating the incantation as she held it over the gaping flesh of his stomach.

"Where did you learn that spell?" he breathed, as his flesh sizzled once more when she lowered the poker.

She hesitated only briefly, then lifted her hand with a small smile, an aloe plant held in her palm. "One cannot ingest the seeds of the tree of the Underworld without being imparted some dark knowledge." She carefully broke a leaf from the plant, rubbing the soothing, cool juices against his burnt, pink flesh.

His brows drew together, but he was silent as he reached for her. "Your turn," he whispered. Hades leaned forward kissing her, taking his time to remove her wet, bloodied clothing. After he washed every part of her skin, he pulled her against him and they lay before the fire, waiting. The time for goodbye was coming soon. Hades could hear the footsteps echoing down the halls and when the knock came on the door he was already standing. Persephone grasped for him, but he took her hand gently into his, pulling her to her feet.

"Come, my love. There is no preventing what is to come."

"I do not want to go!" she cried, dragging her feet. "Do not let them take me."

"I know." He quickly wrapped a robe over himself then pulled one of her own dressing gowns from his closet. "But this is only temporary, you ensured that you will come back to me." He brushed his hands over her face, then taking her hand, opened the door. Charon stood before them and he silently lead them towards the throne room.

The doors were open and Hermes stood with his back to them, his caduceus held firmly in one hand. He turned suddenly, and his eyes moved over Persephone as he bowed to them both. "I am sorry, Hades," his voice was soft, appealing, as he continued, "but I must take her back. Zeus is -- enraged. He seems to have weakened with the fall of Ares." Hermes twisted his staff thoughtfully between his hands. "He lays in his chambers, ill, but his fury is strong. He says you kidnapped Persephone. You brought your seal above ground. You climbed up one of the peaks of Olympus and almost killed his son. No no, you have broken too many rules, Hades. You flaunted the laws of Olympus and for that you must be punished. Persephone must be returned to her mother."

"My brother heard the Queen's words," Hades replied coolly. "Persephone partook of the pomegranate. Six seeds were ingested and by Zeus' own curse she must remain within my world for sixth months. No matter how many tantrums he throws within his bed chambers, it does not negate this truth."

Hermes' blue eyes flashed and he stepped closer to them. "You both play a dangerous game, Dispater."

"This is no game," Hades said softly.

Hermes gaze flickered over Persephone again. "Did you ingest these seeds of your own free will, Persephone?"

Flames flared in her eyes and Hermes took a wary step back, and Hades could not help his smile. "They do not call me Persephone here, messenger." Her voice was low and she advanced closer to the God. "I freely ingested the fruit of the Underworld, but my husband already told you this."

"I see," he replied slowly, he cocked his head to one side, studying her face. "I had heard you were changed, Queen, but I did not know how much. Nevertheless, six months from this day I will bring you back to your husband. Tonight, I am afraid you must leave with me."

"One more night," Persephone demanded, her voice cold.

Hermes looked at them exasperated. "I cannot. Zeus will tear out my heart. You must come with me."

"You are lucky I do not tear it out and eat it," Persephone hissed. She pointed to the door. "Leave, messenger, so that I may say goodbye to my husband."

As soon as the door closed on Hermes' rigid back, Persephone collapsed against Hades, tears pouring from her eyes. He held her shivering form tightly against him, stroking back her hair. "Do not cry, sweet one, we will see each other again. Six months is not long and Olive and I will be waiting for you." He brushed his lips over her face, her eyelids, her nose.

"Olive!" she cried. "My father, I cannot--" her voice cracked and Hades pulled her closer.

"Hush, I will take care of them in your absence. They will, like I, wait for you to return. Such a short time means nothing for those who love."

"The Fates were right," she whispered. "I wasted so much time, hating you, fighting you."

"No, no Persephone," he whispered fiercely. "No time was wasted between us, I would do nothing to change how I feel for you in this moment. Nothing," he breathed against her lips.

A knock on the door echoed in the chambers. He kissed the tears away from her face. "Do not let them see your sorrow, my Persephone. They do not deserve those parts of you. Are you ready?" He looked down at her, her face pale, and she bit her trembling lip, but nodded. "Enter," Hades called.

By the time Hermes returned, her cold mask was back in place and Hades struggled to ensure his own was, as well. They stopped by his chambers, bringing Olive with them, and Persephone held the deer tightly against her chest. Hades held Persephone's hand, and they walked from the castle down the long path toward the entrance of the Underworld, Hermes walking behind them. Her eyes kept filling with tears which she wiped away on Olive's fur, and she pressed her hand tightly against his.

"Be a formidable Queen," he whispered, and she shot him a half-smile that broke his heart. As they approached midway to the gate, he lifted his left hand and a blinding blue light came through the gates as an eclipsed crescent moon formed over the exit.

A choked cry escaped her lips, "I do not like goodbyes."

The large gates echoed in the vast cavern as they unlocked. "Go wander, Hermes," Hades hissed at the messenger, and with a small salute the God moved passed the gates and they were alone.

They turned to face each other, Olive pressed tightly between their bodies. "How will I live without you?" she whispered.

"You will never be without me. Even if my soul was ripped from me, I would find my way back to you." Something flickered in his dark eyes. "No matter what is to come, I will always find you."

He twisted his fingers and murmured, "Olympus." The light of the crescent moon burned black. "You know," he continued, "I never thought I would find you. That I could find a reflection of my own soul, all the parts of me that were good; I find them in you. You are--everything, Persephone."

As they came to the gate, she pressed her face against Olive, planting a soft kiss between his eyes before setting him on the ground. Hades gently took her hand and led her to the opposite side but did not cross the threshold. The gates closed and locked and Persephone gave a small cry, reaching her hands through the bars. He grasped her hands.

"It feels like a prison," she cried.

"For me or you?" he whispered.

"For us both."

"Do not forget my love, that a part of you still belongs to the world above," he said, stroking her fingers. "Selfish as I am, I cannot deny this. You are half lightness, half darkness. Part rebirth, and part death. They need you -- as I do. And when the first snowflakes fall across the meadows, I will come for you. Do not doubt it."

"I may belong to both worlds, but my soul is yours, as is my heart."

"As is mine, to you," he replied.

"Do not forget me," she whispered.

He wiped the tears from her eyes, "Never."

Hermes appeared behind her. "Come, Queen," he said quietly. "It is time to leave."She did not turn, letting her eyes drift over Hades. With one last look, she moved from the gates. Hermes moved closer to her, about to take her hand when she shook her head. "I have no need of your touch, Hermes."

Hermes gave a gentle nod of the head. "As you wish, your majesty." A beacon of light shone down on them and they began to move upwards, ascending into the shining whiteness. Persephone turned her back to Hermes and kept her eyes locked on her husband. They moved further away and Hades stood still at the gates, watching until she disappeared into the light and was gone.

He did not move from the gates, but stood staring into the darkness, his hands wrapped tightly around the iron bars. A prison. Olive's soft head pressed against his leg and he bent to pick up the deer. He began to retrace his steps to the palace, not even aware of the direction he headed. He stopped at Persephone's door, noticing that the room was still in disarray, the message of blood still covering the wall. Had such a short time passed that no one had touched it? It would have to be cleaned when the servants came to the palace. He moved to his rooms, settling the deer on his bed, then wandered aimlessly around his lonely, empty palace. His feet took him to the room made of ruby. It held all the weapons of the Underworld, including the pitchfork, gifted by the cyclops. Hades held up his hand, and the blue sword appeared. With a wave of his hand he unlocked a secret chamber within the wall and stashed the sword away. He held up his hand again and Persephone's mahogany bow materialized in his grasp, while his helmet appeared in his other. He sat the helmet against the floor then brought the bow closer to his face. His touch was loving as he inspected the beauty of the bow, the delicate engravings of pomegranates carved into the weapon. With this she had given her freedom, sacrificed her fate to protect him, to protect this beautiful, dark world. He reverently hung it onto the wall.

Suddenly, he felt a dark presence; a malevolent shadow that was watching him. He turned slowly; the room was empty but he felt

the insidious, malignant wraith. Hades. His name echoed through the chambers, like a cursed whisper, like a warning.

He peered once more into the darkened corners but he stood alone in the shadows. He moved quickly, locking the compartment his sword was hidden in. Turn around, the voice whispered.

"Who is there?" Hades demanded. "Show yourself!"

Did you think it would be that easy?

Suddenly, he fell to the ground, writhing in pain as he grasped the wound over his stomach. The sensation was shocking and he gasped, crying out as a burning agony moved through his body, travelling from the wound to his head, and he began to convulse, his limbs seizing. His anguished cries turned to laughter and his coherent mind was reminded of Ares as he had stood on the cliff, but that thought was ripped from his head and he lay blank and empty in the hall of ruby. He stood abruptly, a smile on his face as he grabbed the helmet of invisibility and exited the room.

CHAPTER
XXVIII
VILLIAN

PERSEPHONE LAY ON her bed, her mother reclining next to her. The snow and ice had vanished and already the pink and white buds of spring were covering the barren trees of the temple. The rivers ran freely once more, bubbling merrily in the meadows, and birds' songs echoed across the forests. Persephone had never felt more miserable.

Demeter picked up her daughter's hand, her eyes moving sadly over her daughter's face. "Can you forgive me, Persephone?" she asked quietly. "It was never my intention for you to lose in all of this." She had told her everything that had happened, that she had sought out Aphrodite, enlisted her help; that it had been her who had shot Hades.

Persephone threw herself into her mother's arms. "Of course," she cried. "Everything you did, you did to protect me. I cannot say the same of Aphrodite." She finished, drawing back to look at Demeter. "Did she get what she wanted?" she asked bitterly. "Did Ares fall in love with her?"

"That part of the story is still unwritten. I do not know what happened after you and Hades vanished. I took your bow, which somehow has disappeared as well, and when I returned to the temple, it was empty. Since then, I have been righting the wrongs that I brought to the land." Demeter's eyes lowered. "That is a burden I will always have to bear."

"Mother," she said softly, "we have all been a part of this sick game, though we knew it not."

"Are you alright, Persephone? Truly alright?"

"I miss him," she said, "I feel like half of me is missing, that I am incomplete in every way. I love him. No matter where I go, I am always leaving someone I love behind," she whispered.

"Oh daughter, forgive me for the part I played in this." Her hands tightened over Persephone's and then she stood. "You should rest now if you can." She bent, kissing her daughter's forehead. "Goodnight, my love, I will see you in the morning."

Persephone turned on her side, staring at the half-moon through the window. "Alone again," she whispered.

Persephone.

She sat up suddenly, peering through the moonlit shadows. "Hades?" she breathed. "Are you there?"

He was standing over her, the helmet of invisibility held at his side. She jumped from the bed with a shout of joy, wrapping her arms around him. "What are you doing here?" she cried in a hushed whisper.

His dark eyes moved over her. "Breaking the rules. I needed to see you."

She pulled him close, pressing her face against his chest. "Would you love me even if I was wicked, Persephone? I am the villain in this story."

She moved back to look at him. "I love every part you," she replied with a confused smile. "And you are not the villain. That role belongs to another."

"How sweet your words are," he whispered. He raised a finger to his lips, and took her hand leading her from her room, moving through the quiet halls to the just blossoming garden outside.

"Let me have you, one last time until you are back with me. I have to taste you one more time. Will you let me?" His eyes burned at her and when he began to pull her dress from her slim arms she did not stop him.

He pressed his lips against her neck and he lifted her gown higher, pushing her up against a tree, and she wrapped her long legs around his waist. He pushed himself into her tight entrance and she gave a small gasp of pain, but his lips were there to swallow it and then she was throwing her head back as he began to move. A strange lassitude was stealing over her and she wondered if this was merely a dream. He whispered words to her, dark words she did not comprehend and then he leaned forward murmuring in her ear. "My power will grow inside you." And he reached between her legs as she shattered into oblivion. "When the first snow moves over the meadows," he promised. Darkness consumed her and she felt herself falling as strong arms wrapped around her.

CHAPTER
XXIX
PAWN IN THE GAME

PERSEPHONE WOKE FROM a nightmare; the first she had had since Hades had cleansed her in the sea. She was alone in the shadows, but something was watching her. It felt like that shadowed wraith from the Underworld, but worse -- far more deadly, far more malevolent. It whispered horrible truths to her and she shivered, crying out in the darkness. She woke with a small scream as something moved against her.

The game is just beginning, Queen, I am coming for him.

She pushed herself from the bed, running to the window gulping in the fresh morning air. It was just a dream, she assured herself, just a dream. It was only natural on her first night back on Earth. She turned suddenly and gasped. A single black rose had been placed on the ground by her bed.

She bent, lifting the rose to her face. The scent was bitter-sweet. Hades had been there. And he had taken her in the garden; she felt the evidence between her legs. Why could she barely remember it? Why had he left her without saying goodbye?

"Six months," she whispered to herself. "I will ask him in six months."

Hades sat on his throne, silent and still as he stared ahead of him. He stood suddenly, walking down a long hall that led to a pool of still water. At the edge lay a grave, a pomegranate tree bowed over a lonely tomb. Stone steps descended into the glassy mere and Hades walked down the stairs, into the cool waters of the lake. He moved through the water, towards the mountain that bordered one side and there located the stairs that led into a cavern within the stone. The heat was oppressive, and he could feel it pulsing through the massive iron doors that were carved into the rock. He lifted his hands, and the golden blade appeared; he studied the engravings on the sword and smiled. "The game has just begun."

END